W9-CAP-463

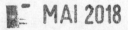

THE DUTCH WIFE

THE DUTCH WIFE

ELLEN KEITH

PATRICK CREAN EDITIONS
An imprint of HarperCollins*Publishers*Ltd

Published by Patrick Crean Editions, an imprint of HarperCollins Publishers Ltd

First edition

HarperCollins books may be purchased for educational, business,
or sales promotional use through our Special Markets Department.

HarperCollins Publishers Ltd
2 Bloor Street East, 20th Floor
Toronto, Ontario, Canada
M4W 1A8

www.harpercollins.ca

Library and Archives Canada Cataloguing in Publication
information is available upon request.

Canadian edition: ISBN 978-1-44345-425-4
International edition: ISBN 978-1-44345-654-8

Printed and bound in the United States
LSC/H 9 8 7 6 5 4 3 2 1

To my grandmother Harmien Deys,
who lived and lost during the war
and left everything behind in pursuit of love.
(Your G-rated edition is on its way!)

It is in fact far easier to act under conditions of tyranny than to think.
HANNAH ARENDT

The Dutch Wife

CHAPTER ONE

THE INFANT IN THE BABY CARRIAGE OPENED HER eyes and saw that I was not her mother. Her face grew red, wrinkling up like a walnut. I forced myself to swallow and glanced ahead, where three German soldiers patrolled the gated entrance to the Vondelpark. Beside me, Theo's voice dropped to a hush. "You go on alone; it's less suspicious. Just act calm." He pressed his lips to my hair before ducking off into the nearest shop.

I leaned down to coo at the child. "Shh, quiet now. Everything is all right." But my pulse betrayed me. My knuckles blanched around the handle of the carriage, and I adjusted the blanket to conceal the telltale seam beneath her, the hidden compartment that would give us away. Forged ration coupons and foxhole radios Theo and I had built, secreted away in cigar boxes. Not to mention a pistol.

Through the fog, swastikas flying from a nearby building caught the morning sun, and the soldiers smoked as they checked the identification of passersby. A few metres back, Theo pretended to be absorbed in a rack of newspapers. He nodded in encouragement. The little one stared up at me as I carried on, but when the wheel of the carriage stuttered over a loose cobblestone, she started to cry. Loud, grating wails. I debated turning around, but the damn *moffen* had already noticed. The soldier who looked my age, or no more than twenty-four, stepped forward. "And where are you rushing off to?" He hitched the rifle strap up over his shoulder. "You're the first pretty pair of legs to come by all morning."

The nape of my neck tingled. The baby's cries escalated while the soldier held out a hand for my I.D. papers, and his gaze dropped to my chest as I drew them from the pocket of my peacoat. I tried not to cringe, hoping Theo was too far away to notice.

The other soldier approached, his brow like a pan greased for baking. He peered into the carriage. "What a racket. Does it need to be rocked?"

I checked the padding, the blanket, but nothing had shifted. "She's just hungry." My words were too sharp, and as I tried to calm her, I wondered if he recognized the inexperience in my actions. Sweat dampened the folds of my blouse while I waited for them to demand I pick her up. The men looked me up and down unabashedly.

The one studying my identification squinted at me. "Marijke de Graaf. Just how old is this photograph?" He held it up for his companion to examine. My curly hair was longer in the photo, my face a little fuller.

"Four months."

The child, finally quiet, sucked her thumb, her cheeks scarlet with tears. After an unbearable pause, the soldier handed back my papers. "Well, it sure doesn't do you justice." He winked and waved me on my way.

My mouth was dry, my arms tense as I continued on into the park, humming a nervous, shapeless tune. I found a bench near the tea house, where more uniforms were scattered between the suits and dresses at the tables: soldiers eating pastries, looking out over the water at the ducks and squirrels as though our city had always been theirs.

Within a few minutes, Theo found me. He bent down to check on the child before giving me a kiss. "They took their time with your papers, didn't they?"

I shook my head. "They're just searching for entertainment."

He lifted the baby from the carriage.

"Darling, not here. Let's get her to safety."

"But look at this tiny frown." He pulled faces at her until she gurgled a laugh and stretched out as if trying to tug on his big ears, and I watched with yearning as I imagined us with a daughter of our own to comfort and love.

"If only we could keep her." He placed her back with a wistful sheen in his eyes that made me want to take him in my arms.

"But you know we can't. Plus, she needs to be breastfed. Our time will come, I promise."

He sighed. "I know."

From there, we cut across the park and exited through another set of gates, these ones thankfully unguarded. Women bustled down the streets, and collectively they formed a walking

3

fashion catalogue from three years earlier, colours fading and hems showing their wear. Since the invasion, everyone had learned to keep their heads lower, their movements more purposeful, and the few men in sight were prepubescent or already wrinkled, so many others afraid of venturing out, only to be rounded up in the impending call-ups for forced labour.

As we approached the address the resistance had given us, the front door of the house opened a crack, and a woman peeked out, observing the baby carriage. She recited our code in a stiff voice that wouldn't have fooled anyone. "Have you come to see my new flower beds?" On hearing our response, she checked for onlookers and beckoned us into her front hall. Inside, she bent over the baby carriage with a look of heartbreak, her eyes ringed red, her skin showing the toll of sleepless nights. "Please, come sit down," she said at last. "I'll put on the kettle."

"We can't stay, I'm afraid." I glimpsed an empty bassinet in the sitting room, a baby blanket crocheted with initials draped over the side. The sight of it made my throat tighten. "We're so sorry about your loss, *mevrouw*."

She picked up the baby and gazed down at her. "It's a dreadful time to bring a child into the world, isn't it?"

Theo and I exchanged a glance.

"Well," she said, "at least I can still be of use to another young life." Her chin started to tremble, and she retrieved a handkerchief from her pocket. "Such light hair, for a Jew. What happened to her mother?"

"Pneumonia," Theo replied. "We were hiding them in our attic, and by the time we found a doctor who would come, it was too late." He glanced at the clock on the wall. "I'm sorry, we need

4

to get going. We can't thank you enough, *mevrouw*. Please hide the carriage well. Your husband knows what to do with its contents."

I leaned to kiss the baby on the forehead and squeezed the woman's hand in farewell. Theo paused in the front entrance. "It warms my heart to see how willing you are to care for a child that's not your own." She nodded, but kept her focus on the baby, and once the street was clear, we left the house without looking back.

SHORTLY after eight the next evening, the blackout curtains went up across Amsterdam, erasing the city from the sky. The Nazis had cut the electricity again, so I lit a candelabrum and sat beside the darkened window to play the violin. Nobody went to the symphony anymore, yet I still practiced every day. My bow glided across the strings while the grandfather clock ticked like a metronome, counting the passing minutes. I put down the instrument and drummed my fingers against it, wondering what was taking Theo so long, raking my thoughts for the forgotten mention of some appointment, but all that came to me were the signs in the squares, threatening forced labour in Germany, men picked up from the streets at random and carted off in trucks. I thought of Theo's favourite student, who had disappeared the week before.

I'd set a potato-and-nettle soup to cook in the hay box, and when the aroma wafted over, I rose to go stir it. In the hope of a distraction, I surveyed the kitchen, our good Delftware, the tablecloths from my trousseau, making a mental inventory of what we'd next barter when we ran out of eggs and butter.

A key jiggled in the front door lock. With it came that balm of relief, soothing my ever-fried nerves. Feeling silly for letting my imagination get the better of me, I resisted the urge to rush over to Theo, to run my fingers through the lone wave in his hair, to chide him for keeping me on edge. Instead, I bent over the pot, humming to myself, until he came up behind me, encircled his arms around my waist and lifted me into the air, the wooden spoon in my fist dripping soup across the tiles. He whispered into my neck, "I missed you."

"You know," I said, "it's impossible to think straight until you make it home."

When he put me down, his thick eyebrows hung lower than normal, like a shelf over his eyes. "Sorry, dear. I had a few stops to make. Piet is coming by in an hour to drop off some newspapers."

"One of the resistance publications?" I took his cold hands in mine, pressed them to his chest. "Where does he want you to deliver them?"

"I'll pass this batch on to my students."

"Good idea. You can tell me more about it over dinner."

"Later; it's almost nine." He led me upstairs to our bedroom, where he reached into the back of our wardrobe, pulled out the old atlas and opened it to reveal the small radio hidden within its pages. I lay beside him on the rug as he hooked up the moffen sieve and fiddled with its modulator dials to filter out the interference from German jamming stations. The Westerkerk chimed the hour, one of the few churches that hadn't yet lost its bells to the Nazi armament factories. As silence spread across Amsterdam with each passing week, it felt as if the city were holding her breath alongside us. But then came the sound we waited all day to hear. The first four notes of Beethoven's Fifth, the Morse code *V*, for victory. *Radio Oranje* on the BBC, the broadcast from our exiled royal house.

Theo passed me a headset and held my hand while we listened by candlelight. The government spoke of the recent factory strikes, the growing Nazi retaliations, but urged us to stay calm. "Resist the pressure to answer the labour call-ups. Stand strong or go into hiding—we must persevere."

I leaned over until my cheek brushed his and tried to picture the house empty at night, Theo deported for work in Germany. I couldn't bear the thought. He turned to kiss my hair. "Don't worry, love. We'll find a way."

After the broadcast, we stayed there on the rug, with my head resting on his shoulder. I wanted nothing more than for us to lie in bed all night and all day in an armour of blankets, sheathing ourselves from the troubles of the world.

"That child will have a good life with those people, won't she?" I asked.

"They're devout Christians; they'll treat her like their own, I'm sure of it."

I looked up at him. "And do you still think we're making the right choice by waiting?"

He hesitated. "It'll be hard enough for even the two of us to get through the war with all these food shortages and wage cuts. The last thing I would want is—"

A knock came at the front door. I moved to spy under the blackout paper, but Theo was already halfway to the stairs. "No use looking; it's dark as a cave out there. That'll be Piet, right on time."

I got up and followed him, but right before he reached the entrance, there was a loud noise, the splintering crack of wood. The door flew open. I saw the guns first and then the uniforms. The Gestapo burst into the house, yelling at us in German not to move. While they searched the rooms, we stood there in terrified silence, our hands above our heads. A lamp crashed to the floor. Drawers were flung open, papers sent fluttering, my violin tossed aside with a clunk. The smell of warm soup grew nauseating. Shaking, I rubbed my thumb against my ring finger, my wedding band cool against my knuckles. I lowered my gaze along the tiled floor until this granted me a glimpse of the corner of Theo's shoe, the anxious tap of his foot. One of the Gestapo shouted from upstairs. He'd discovered the radio supplies, the secret alcove in our attic. I thanked God we had nobody left in hiding.

The moffen circled us with taunting expressions, the barrels of their Lugers staring like deadened pupils. "Hand over your identification," the head agent said. "You have two minutes to pack. No talking."

One of them escorted us to our bedroom, where my undergarments lay strewn across the rug. As Theo reached for our luggage, his face met mine. His hair was dishevelled, and behind his glasses, his eyes looked wild, all whites. We packed our warmest clothes, and I took our wedding photo off the wall, placing it in Theo's suitcase. I refused the moffen the satisfaction of seeing me cry. On our way downstairs, Theo laced his fingers through mine, sending a silent plea. *Don't tell them anything, don't let them win—I love you.* The Gestapo agent smacked him against the temple, knocking him sideways and ripping him from my grasp. When I reached out for him, they held me back, rough hands choking my wrists. I whispered his name, but it got lost in the noise. In front of me, Theo cradled his head. Then they shoved us forward and marched us out into the night.

WE Dutch girls climbed out of the frigid darkness, that nest of sickness and death. Outside the cattle car, dogs snapped at our ankles. The train whistled as it set off again and German guards shouted, pushed us into waiting trucks. When we arrived at the Ravensbrück camp compound, we were led around like parts on an assembly line. Examined. Assessed. Tagged. Sorted. We filed into a warehouse, where female guards ordered us to undress and turn in our clothes, and while I bent to remove my stockings, an SS man leaned in and whistled at the sight of my dangling breasts. Two gaunt prisoners handed out stained uniforms, and I put on the striped tunic and long, grey knickers, the fabric coarse against my thighs. The leather shoes had frayed laces and pinched at my toes, but many of the women around me were forced to squeeze their feet into bulky wooden clogs.

The Jews with their yellow triangles emerged from the hall, heads shorn, nicked and bleeding from a careless barber. Skin spotted from lice. The women sobbed as they tried to cover their scalps with kerchiefs, any shred of fabric they could find. I understood the weight of their loss, and with a wince, I fingered the red triangle that marked me a political prisoner and raised a hand to my curls, grateful I still had a fraction of my own identity.

We slept two or three to a bunk, the sneezes and coughs of strangers on my skin. The sick urinated on the straw pallets where they lay, too weak to climb down from the top bed and drag themselves to the toilets. I learned to sleep with my cup and bowl tied to my clothes. In the beginning, Dutch mothers told folk tales to their frightened daughters while a trio of cabaret stars swapped bawdy riddles across the beds, but these soon turned to quarrels over stolen bread. One woman drove herself mad, writhing on her mattress, yanking out clumps of hair and muttering to herself. Sometimes she whined like a puppy, going blue in the face with distress, while the others yelled at her to keep quiet. My pity for her became fringed with fear. Madness lurked there at Ravensbrück, tugging at us all. Survival depended on a stable mind, so I had to stay strong.

The latrines often clogged, spilling brown puddles onto the floor of the barracks block. Water became tainted from the fluids of the dead that had seeped into the camp sediment, taking on a tang and leaving many with swollen bellies. I made a constant trudge back and forth to the toilets as my body tried to purge itself of the contaminated liquid, the moulding potatoes from the soup.

I soon came to understand that camp life played out in a different key for certain groups. German gentiles had the best chance at survival, in part because they easily understood the orders thrown at us throughout the day. Some of us—the Germans, the Dutch, whichever races the moffen deemed "human"—were permitted to keep our hair, but we had to wear it combed back, tucked under caps and kerchiefs. I forged hairpins from strips of wire from the factory. One night, I sat on my bed, teasing my bunkmate's thick waves into rolls and decorating them with ribbons torn from the edge of her kerchief. She became Ginger

Rogers and I Betty Grable, and we fell asleep imagining a lavish banquet, with satin gowns and pearls and Champagne and *confit de canard*. The next morning, I woke to her body cold and lifeless against mine.

As days passed, the growls from my stomach grew louder, the sores on my hands redder. We poured the mucky ersatz coffee into our bowls to warm our cold feet, and each night, I picked the crusted mud off my shoes and polished them with the greatest care. When I found a hole growing across the right sole, I traced my finger around it and wept.

For long hours, we laboured in the Siemens factory near camp, where we made electric components for submarines. During those shifts, I made a mental list of new German words so I could learn to react without delay. They forced us to sing on the march to and from work. As we rounded the lake, my voice would grow hoarse with false cheer, and I sometimes caught myself cursing all those people Theo and I had sheltered, all the news we'd spread with our crystal radios—What had it amounted to? Half the Jews we'd helped were probably dead, and we'd become prisoners ourselves. I was Inmate 21522. But I was determined not to be worn down, not to transform into one of the skeletons that moved through the camp like the living dead. And so I clung to Theo's memory with all my strength: how he'd pleaded my innocence when the Gestapo had herded us out onto our darkened street, the bells of the Westerkerk tolling overhead. How he'd clutched my hand in the detainment cell, pressed my wedding band to his lips, his palms still blotched with grease from the radio. I thought of all the dreams we'd stockpiled throughout the war: of baking three-layered cakes again and picnicking along the Amstel River in new clothes, of me travelling with the orchestra to perform in Paris, of his history papers being published in journals as far off as New York. Of starting a family.

I promised myself I would do whatever it took to make it through the war alive.

My chance came on a cool morning near the end of June. At four o'clock, the reveille sirens woke us. An SS officer with a clipboard walked down the rows with a female guard. With a cleft chin and sagging neck, he appeared even older than my father, the type of man I'd expect to see bundled up by the fireplace in a café back in Amsterdam, smoking a pipe and complaining about the persistent rain. Whenever this officer passed a woman with light hair and fair skin, he stopped to look her up and down. Some, he pulled aside. When he got to me, he asked where I was from and when I told him, he reached out to cup my breast, rubbing his thumb over my nipple. "Good shape," he remarked.

He noted my number on his clipboard and ordered me to join the others. Attractive girls, all of them. Despite their pale, bruised skin, they looked young and healthier than the rest of the inmates. All of them had their hair. Most wore black triangles for "asocial" behaviour—sexual deviants, alcoholics, prostitutes, troublemakers. Some wore the "criminal" green; a few others, red, like I did.

We huddled together but broke into rows of five as the officer approached. I pinched my cheeks to draw some colour into them. How many times had I seen it before: women pulled out of the line, never to return? He surveyed us with a wry smile.

"Consider yourselves lucky. I'm going to offer you a rare opportunity, a chance to serve the Führer, to help promote the efficiency and operations of camps across the Third Reich."

He paused to glance at the guard and suddenly I was sure he intended to make us Blockovas—block supervisors. A despicable function. Twice, the Blockova in our block had demanded my bread ration because she claimed I was too pretty, that I needed to learn that things wouldn't always be handed to me. Other Blockovas beat women or assigned extra labour. We hated even those who did nothing but follow the rules, because they had the power to hurt us on a whim.

"Strip."

At that, I unbuttoned my shift. Goose pimples flared across my chest as it fell at my feet. Some women tried to cover themselves, but I knew well enough to keep my hands at my sides. The officer circled us, removing a shadow of a girl with a spine that stuck out like a string of beads, and two women with misshapen breasts. He ordered them back to the work Kommandos before returning to position in front of us. "I want sixteen volunteers to service the prisoners at our new bordellos. We need some ripe, willing young women."

It took me a moment to understand what he meant. My skin started to prickle, bringing flashes of an Amsterdam alley: low necklines and tawdry earrings, drunken soldiers stumbling out of doorways, smears of cherry lipstick on their chins.

"Through the Führer's generosity, you'll receive fresh food and a quarter of your earnings, and you will be released from the camp after six months of service." He grinned, letting that remark dangle.

I touched my hand to my side, yearning for the reassuring weight of my wedding band, which the moffen had confiscated upon my arrival. A pain hit my stomach, as if someone had reached in and pressed down on my gut. Six months, could it be? The girls around me shifted their weight. Perhaps their own stomachs were growling, their minds clouding with visions of hot dinners, of comfortable trains with dining cars headed away from Germany.

"Who is willing to service the Reich?"

At first, nobody moved. Eyes remained cast to the ground. The only sounds were the distant steps of marching prisoners.

"Think about it," he said. "Quarters with proper beds and hot running water."

A crow cawed, drawing my gaze upward. The bird sailed high above the compound, a dark speck against the dark sky. It swept past us, beyond the electrified confines of the camp, and disappeared.

A girl stepped forward. A green delinquent triangle marked the uniform at her feet. Her hair was the colour of butter, and she wore a certain confidence, like she'd spent years weaving her way up through the German underworld. I wondered what had brought her here, if she'd been accused of theft or maybe assault.

The officer nodded and turned to us. One by one, girls hesitantly offered themselves. Some looked as young as twenty, others twenty-six or twenty-seven. Only two had brown hair; the rest were textbook Aryans.

The officer rapped a pen against his clipboard in impatience. "If no one else volunteers, I'll select someone."

Hunger scraped at my insides. I pictured a plate of fresh fruit and even a slice of meat, imagined being granted my freedom, but I considered that the officer might be lying. He watched us without any emotion. Yet if he'd wanted to, he could have driven into camp and carted us all away without a word of explanation.

Two days earlier, on the way to the factory, I'd passed a group of women digging ditches, the roughest work of all. One stood knee-deep in water and mud, wincing as she heaved the shovel over her shoulder. She'd rolled up her sleeves to reveal a fierce rash, a clear sign of typhus. In a few days, she would be dead, her body fed to the greedy fires of the crematorium.

A heated room, a hot shower. Away from the scourge of lice and vermin, a chance to maybe feel human again.

"Where are you sending them, sir?" The woman beside me shook as if she couldn't believe she'd dared speak up.

Without a glance in her direction, he swatted away the question. "To my men's camp, Buchenwald."

That name. One that had taken seed in the transit camp at Vught, as I'd spotted Theo's back retreating into the cattle car. A rumour passed on in whispers, as we wives and mothers, sisters and daughters watched through our tears, watched our very purpose for living disappear down the rails. A name I'd also heard at Ravensbrück, but one that had never seemed like anything more than a word, a spot in my mind where I'd tucked him for safekeeping. But it was a real place, a camp with fences and a crematorium and a brothel.

Two SS men approached and stood behind the officer, leering at our nakedness. One of them winked and moved his hand to reveal the erection swelling in his trousers.

The officer cleared his throat. "Well?"

I knelt down to pick up my uniform, making sure to glance up and look that dirty mof straight in the eye. I felt the solid ground against my palm, dirt beneath my fingernails.

Then I stood and took a step forward.

CHAPTER TWO

KARL MÜLLER
JUNE 25, 1943
BUCHENWALD CONCENTRATION CAMP, GERMANY

K ARL MÜLLER ARRIVED AT BUCHENWALD JUST before dawn. The morning was already muggy. He'd spent the entire night on a train, and the rattling of the carriage and a broken window had granted him no rest.

The camp Kommandant came to meet him at the station in Weimar. In his late fifties, Otto Brandt had a high widow's peak and a hard-boiled appearance. He'd inherited the camp just a year earlier. The previous Kommandant and his wife had been arrested and were under investigation for fraud: stealing from camp coffers. As the new Schutzhaftlagerführer, Karl would be second-in-command and responsible for ensuring that such a scandal wasn't repeated.

Brandt stretched out a hand. "You must be Müller. Karl, isn't it?"

"Yes, sir. It's an honour."

"My associates in Berlin have said nothing but good things about you. But I have to say, I was surprised to hear they were sending me someone who has never set foot in a camp before. You've risen up the ranks quite quickly, it seems. Family connection?"

Karl dug his heels into the ground. "Hard work, sir."

"Very well. I'll give you a tour of the camp myself, along with an overview of your duties here. And I'm warning you, as deputy commander, you'll find yourself stretched very thin." He led Karl to a parked Mercedes, where a driver was waiting. Karl opened the back door and slid onto the seat next to Brandt. His eyelids felt heavy, and he struggled to stay focused as the car wove its way through the woods toward the camp.

"Seven years ago," Brandt said, "all of this was virgin land. The prisoners built everything: the barracks blocks, the railway, even this very road. Paving it was a terrible hassle but well worth the lives lost. The inmates call it Blutstrasse."

Blood Road. All Karl could see in the dim light was vegetation, mostly oak and beech trees, and it struck him that a camp of that capacity, one of the economic powerhouses of the Reich, could be hidden by such peaceful surroundings. They turned in past the SS garrison, down a straight street with a gas station and a painted wooden carving of inmates in uniform. Robust-looking men with stiff smiles. The flower bed at its base gave the place a quaint feel, reminiscent of some Bavarian ski resort. Another sign pointed to the zoo, which he took to be a joke until he heard monkeys screeching. A long building ran down the left side of the road. Brandt explained that this held the camp command offices, where Karl would be based. On the right, an iron gate marked the entrance to the protective custody camp, where the prisoners were detained. The driver stopped the automobile, and Brandt checked the gatehouse clock while a guard rushed to open the doors. "We're running a bit behind schedule. Reveille will start shortly."

Karl debated asking for some time to rest, but decided that the Kommandant was not the type to grant favours. Still, the camp was shaping up to be a more comforting and welcoming place than he'd anticipated. They passed through the gate, and Karl pointed to the iron message that topped it, the letters painted bright red. "Well put." *Jedem das Seine*, it stated—to each his own. You get what you deserve.

Brandt beamed like he had forged the words himself. The gate led to a huge square, the muster grounds, where thousands of prisoners assembled.

"Roll call happens twice per day." Brandt stepped out of the vehicle, motioning for Karl to join him. They climbed up to a platform at the top of the gatehouse and looked down over the camp pitch. "All prisoners must be accounted for. You may be asked to preside over this, Müller, so pay attention."

A number of SS officers with clipboards gathered nearby. More and more prisoners appeared. They formed perfect squares of perfect lines. Karl assumed that camp figures fluctuated with new arrivals and deaths, but to the best of his calculation, he estimated some fifteen thousand prisoners, virtually all male. One of the officers began to call out numbers, and certain inmates stepped forward. Karl was a bureaucrat, a stranger to this military discipline, but the order and precision of it all astounded him, reminding him of his father, who valued such things.

It was then he heard the music. The initial squeal of a trumpet. Then a drum, a trombone. He searched for the source. To his right, a brass band had set up. The musicians wore cheerful red trousers and navy jackets with gold piping, but their bony frames exposed them as prisoners. The conductor raised an arm and the players burst into tune, a lively number that Karl didn't recognize.

He looked to Brandt. "Nice touch, sir."

"We try to make the camp as civil as possible. You'll also hear music broadcasted at times."

The inmates stood still, their faces hardened like stucco. One in the front row started tapping his foot. At first, Karl thought he was marking the beat, but then the man began to sway and collapsed. Karl turned back to the band as he was dragged away.

The roll call crawled on for more than an hour and got held up at various points. Karl's fascination with it waned as he fought to stay awake. A barbed-wire fence blockaded this part of the camp, and a city of barracks, some wood and some stone, sprawled across the slope that led down from the muster grounds. Beyond the far edge of camp, rolling green hills crossed the horizon. Brandt took him back downstairs and guided him along the rows of prisoners, pointing out the different symbols on their uniforms. The Gypsies, the communists, the Jews, the Jehovah's Witnesses, the homosexuals.

"You'll notice we keep the Jews in segregated quarters to avoid spreading their filth." Brandt looked at Karl for a response, who nodded. "You do agree, don't you, Müller?"

"Of course."

Brandt leaned in to study Karl's face. "Where is it you come from, exactly?"

"I was raised in Munich."

"And your parents?"

"You'll find they're well bred and well established there. My father served as a colonel in the First World War and now works as a banker."

"A banker?"

"I assure you, the party ran a bloodline check on me, if you're implying anything." Karl cracked a smile, but Brandt didn't seem to find this amusing.

"Indeed," Brandt said. "Let's carry on. I'll show you the highlights."

Brandt led him along the front line of barracks blocks as he went on about Karl's new role. He would be in charge of the preventive custody camp, which meant responsibility for the financial administration, the performance of the prisoners, ensuring order, preventing escapes, and so forth. Karl nodded where necessary but spent most of the time studying his surroundings. The asphalt roasted under the sun. Prisoners caked in dirt slogged off to the quarry and factories with their labour Kommandos, as if they hadn't bathed in weeks. The Kommandant indicated the arm bands that identified the Kapos, the prisoner overseers. The stink of sweat was obscene, and he fought the urge to cover his nose with his sleeve. Had they no shame?

Up ahead to the right, a foul smoke curled from a high chimney, and beyond that, guards stood in the watchtowers, their machine guns aimed inward. A sandy security strip covered with long, spiked *chevaux-de-frise* bordered the fence. Karl gestured to it. "Do many try to escape?"

Brandt shook his head. "Look at the slope we're on. Building atop the Ettersberg created ideal surveillance conditions. Mind you, there are always the ones who decide to throw themselves into the fence."

"But why would—" Karl stopped himself as he noticed the electrical insulators along the wire. He tried to reconcile this gruesome image with the cheerful, robust-looking men from the road sign on the way into the camp.

"You've got a lot to learn, don't you?" Brandt halted in front of a lone, wizened tree, the only sign of vegetation Karl had seen within the prisoners' camp. "Here's a fitting place to start."

"Is this Goethe's Oak?" he asked.

"I'm impressed. You must be a man of the arts."

"A man who knows his trees." Karl stepped forward to run his hand along the knotted bark. "Do you think the stories are true? Did Goethe really sit right here to write?"

The Kommandant smiled, as if to himself. "Who can say? But what better reminder could you ask for of our noble heritage? It sends a strong message to the inmates, don't you think, reminding them of the enduring power of the Reich."

As they walked on, Karl pictured himself resting beneath the trees in the forest, just as Goethe once had. He imagined they would have had plenty to discuss and contemplate together. But Brandt gave him little time to reflect on this. He picked up the pace and identified the buildings to the right: the camp kitchen, the laundry, the disinfection facility, and the depot where they stored the inmates' personal property.

"A lot of the day-to-day business runs smoothly on its own, thanks to the prisoners we've put in administrative positions,"

Brandt explained, "but the criminals and the politicals are always fighting for favour and will pit themselves against one another like dogs if you don't stay on top of it."

A Kommando of prisoners with green triangles marched by, but Karl had already forgotten the meaning of all the different symbols and hoped Brandt wouldn't decide to test him. He drew Brandt's attention to the decrepit wooden blocks that were fenced off up ahead. "What are these?"

Brandt replied that it was called the Little Camp, and that they had converted those horse stables into a quarantine block for Jews and new arrivals. "Bring a handkerchief if you have to venture in there. The stench is awful."

Pushing on toward the northwest edge of the perimeter, they passed the infirmary blocks. "You'll hear all about the medical experiments we're pioneering here. A vaccine for typhus, among other things. Fascinating to take a look, if you have any passion for science." Brandt checked the time. "There's not much left. The cinema, the greenhouses, the factory. You'll see it all in due time. Let me show you your office."

They crossed back through the rows of blocks, encountering several work Kommandos along the way. Inmates carrying shovels and gardening tools, buckets of sod. Dark shadows marked their faces. They lowered their eyes as they passed, parting to give Karl and the Kommandant a wide berth. For the first time in his life, Karl felt what it was like to be a man of power. He envisioned himself as a great Bavarian lord of centuries past, surveying the construction of a grand estate. He had the sense that he was part of something important, witnessing the rise of a great empire.

But after crossing the pitch and exiting through the gate-house, Karl felt himself breathing more easily, like he'd returned to another world. The men on this side of the sentry line looked fit and healthy in their guard uniforms, prime examples of the Aryan race. Off to the right, a bunch of dogs started barking. He paused to pinpoint their location.

"Would you like to see the kennel?" Brandt asked. "We have some of the best-trained dogs in the nation." Without waiting for an answer, Brandt led him across a grassy patch to a brick build-ing. Along one side, open-air enclosures contained wolfhounds and Alsatians. The dogs yelped excitedly as the men approached. Brandt unlocked one of the enclosures, and an Alsatian jumped up at them, its tongue lolling. Karl bent to pet it and got covered in drool as it licked his face.

"Don't be fooled," Brandt said. "They're trained to target prisoners' stripes. At a moment's command, they can tear some-one to shreds."

"I left my dogs in Munich with my parents," Karl said. "Living without them will be an adjustment."

"You should have brought them along. The officers' dogs live like kings, spoiled with fresh eggs and red wine."

Each of the dogs' stalls stretched far back, with a separate covered area for sleeping. Far more space than any of the prison-ers must have in the blocks, Karl thought, based on the masses that had gathered for roll call. "Well, I know where to come if I need company," he said.

The tour continued in the SS command headquarters, the long building lining the road that led to the gatehouse. Next to this was the adjutancy, which contained the records department, the legal department and other administrative sectors. Karl's own office proved to be larger than his one in Berlin, letting in ample daylight through the windows. He was pleased to spot a couple of potted plants in the corner.

"Let's make one more stop," Brandt said, "at one of my favourite parts of camp."

He insisted they call the driver, even though it would have been only a ten-minute walk. They drove out the way they'd first come in, past the semicircle of SS barracks toward the south side of the Ettersberg. The sun had come out, and the clouds were giving way to blue sky.

They stepped out of the automobile by a collection of small turreted buildings, with oak timbers carved in a traditional style. As they approached, Karl realized that the buildings held cages, and together formed an aviary. Brandt explained that Himmler himself had ordered the construction of the falconry as a gift for Göring, who had yet to even see it. Karl and the Kommandant toured the various cages, admiring the sharpness of the hawks' beaks, the unmistakable intelligence in the eagle's stare. A prisoner with thick gloves was trying to drop live mice into the falcon's cage. The bird screeched from its perch and flapped its wings, sending the prisoner scuttling. He hurried off to a separate set of enclosures on the side, where Karl glimpsed the brilliant turquoise of a peacock.

"Incredible, aren't they?" Brandt said. "It's not often you get to see such powerful creatures up close." He paused to watch the falcon tear into a mouse's tail. "You know, one of my nephews trains hawks on his ranch in Argentina. I always thought that might be a nice way to spend my retirement."

"Have you been there? Argentina?"

"No, not yet. Once the war is over, I'll pay him a visit. Have you?"

Karl shook his head. "With everything we have here in Germany, I've never felt much pull to travel."

"Of course. And once we win this war, the Reich will be unparalleled. Even the Americans will be begging us to let them in," Brandt said, before gesturing for them to return to the car.

Karl looked back at a building near the falconry that they had skipped. Brandt told him it was the hunting hall, but that it was now being used to house some of the more prominent prisoners, including the former French prime minister and his wife.

"A shame, really, that those Jews get to enjoy a big open hearth and nice furniture. If I had it my way, they'd be thrown in with all the rest. But don't worry, Müller, you'll see that your villa is just as grand and finely furnished."

The driver had to go only a couple hundred metres before reaching the officers' housing. As they drove down the road, Karl counted ten charming villas bordering the wooded slope of the Ettersberg. A low stone wall with an ornamental turret wound down the lane. The driver stopped near the end, and Karl looked up at his new home. The wooden villa stood two storeys tall, and with its peaked roof and balcony, it reminded him of something he might see in the Bavarian countryside.

The Kommandant walked Karl up the steps to the front entrance. "My place is right there." He pointed. "Later this week, I'll invite you over to meet my family." He unlocked the door with a key from his pocket, which he gave to Karl.

The interior was sparsely furnished, with a few items that the previous Schutzhaftlagerführer had left behind, and simple decorations, most notably a framed portrait of the Führer. The sitting room contained a fireplace with a pair of antlers that framed the mantel. Karl's luggage sat on the rug. He had received instructions to order his own furniture, but had so far arranged only the necessities for the master bedroom.

Something rustled in an adjacent room. Karl entered the kitchen to find a prisoner polishing silverware. He was the skeletal vestige of a man, like the sorry traces that cling to the bones thrown to dogs. He stopped what he was doing and looked up, but didn't quite meet Karl's stare.

The Kommandant's voice came like a whiplash from behind. "What are you doing? Remove your cap before an officer!"

The prisoner fumbled for his cap and pulled it off to reveal a freshly shaven scalp. He scrunched the fabric into his palm while he stuttered out an apology.

"This time I'll let you off," Brandt said, "but if it happens again, the Schutzhaftlagerführer will send you to the quarry."

The prisoner nodded and apologized repeatedly. Karl felt uncomfortable with them both standing there, waiting for him to react, while all he could think about was getting some rest.

"I assume you'll be working for me," he said.

The prisoner responded that he was the cook and asked if Karl would like him to prepare breakfast. Karl shook his head.

Brandt checked the time again. "Take some time to get settled; I'll expect you in my office in an hour." He nodded toward the prisoner. "And don't hesitate to get violent with them. They need to be put in their place." At that, he set off, leaving Karl in an unfamiliar house with a manservant he wanted nothing to do with.

CHAPTER THREE

Luciano Wagner
May 2, 1977
Buenos Aires, Argentina

L UCIANO WOKE TO A THUD. AS HE WRESTLED FREE of his dreams, he felt the cold tiles against his bare legs and the thick, bitter taste of licorice incubating in his mouth. He rubbed his eyes, opening them to see the half-empty bottle of Fernet lying beside him, its neck hovering over the shower drain.

The light glared overhead. A headache sliced at his temples. How long ago had he passed out? His toothbrush balanced on the edge of the bathroom sink, topped with a glob of tooth-paste, while a half-smoked joint sat forgotten on yesterday's newspaper. All he was wearing were his briefs. He needed to clear his head, to try to forget the humiliation of the night. Rejection was a patch of nettles: it stung at first encounter, but the real suffering came afterwards as a lingering scarlet rash. He cringed, recalling Fabián's look of shock, almost disgust, the way Fabián had yanked away his hand and taken off into the crowd of protestors. How stupid Luciano had been, reading into his friend's every gesture like some sort of sign: the way Fabián had grinned at him when the student rally began, the way he'd clapped him on the back and hugged him a second too long.

Luciano rubbed his aching forehead, imagining he could still smell Fabián's scent of spearmint and aftershave, the traces of his touch. He groaned and groped for the light switch, not ready to face his shame or his hangover. But as soon as he flicked it off, there was another noise in the apartment. A crash in the kitchen, like something falling off the counter. Low, muffled words. Burglars? A rush of footsteps followed as a band of light appeared beneath the door. Luciano thought of his parents asleep in their bed and fumbled to get up. Then he heard his mother scream.

He felt around for something that could serve as a weapon but froze at the rasp of a man's voice. "Arturo and Patricia Wagner?"

"Who are you? What do you want?" Luciano caught the panic rising in his father's tone.

"Where's your son?" asked another man.

Luciano clenched his fist around the towel rack while his mind roiled. The men's Spanish sounded proper, not the slur of petty criminals. He held his breath as he heard his bedroom door kicked in and thought of his bed, still made, his satchel on the shag rug, where he'd tossed it when he came in from the student rally. They would discover the banners, the pamphlets.

A second later, two men barged into the bathroom. Luciano squinted at the sudden brightness, his eyes locked on the assault rifles in their arms.

One grabbed him by the shoulder. "Got him!" The man laughed at the sight of the liquor bottle and yanked him forward, sending him stumbling down the hall toward his parents' room.

Three men stood in the corner, training their rifles on his mother and father, who sat huddled on a mess of bed sheets. The clock on the nightstand read 4:00 a.m. His mother looked up at him through her tears. Loose strands of hair had fallen from her bun, and her pink nightgown had slipped down to expose her chest. She whimpered, mouthed his name and flexed her hand like she wanted to reach for him, but one of the gang stepped toward her and snapped at her to sit still.

The barrel of a rifle hit Luciano in the back, knocking him to the floor. He started to shake.

"What do you want with him?" His father sounded like he was at the far end of a tunnel.

One of the men stood over Luciano as two others left the room. Somewhere, they were opening cupboards, rummaging through bookshelves. Glass shattered. The floor spun around, the dusty carpet in his nostrils. Above him, thick moustaches, striped polos, a tweed blazer. Like any other men on the streets of Buenos Aires.

The man jabbed him with the butt of the rifle. "Where were you tonight?"

Luciano yelped and his mother cried out.

"Shut up, you fucking whore."

At this, his father flinched but said nothing.

Luciano's voice was shrill. "At a friend's, studying."

"You're lying."

He winced, expecting another blow, but something soft landed on him. Fabric.

"Get dressed."

He grabbed his clothes and fumbled to put them on. A pair of faded bell-bottoms and his favourite striped T-shirt. As he crouched to tug on the socks and shoes, he glanced sideways at his father. Wiry white eyebrows stretched to meet, his blue eyes frosty, unblinking. Luciano searched for some sign of worry in the deep wrinkles on his father's face but couldn't find any. His father raised a hand to his chin as he watched Luciano, brushing it once, twice, until Luciano became aware of the trail of spit that clung to the corner of his own mouth. But before he could wipe it away, the men forced his parents to get up and tied their wrists. They grabbed Luciano's arms and bound his hands behind his back with a rough cord.

"Papá, help me!" He didn't know what his father could possibly do. His father's back stiffened, but he said nothing. Luciano's mother started to cry harder, provoking a growl from one of the men, who pulled Luciano's binds tight. The look on his father's face didn't change while he nudged Luciano's mother with his foot, silencing her.

The man in the tweed blazer reached into the closet and withdrew two neckties. He fastened the plaid one around Luciano's mouth. It forced Luciano's tongue back, making him sputter, and he squirmed under their grip. Then he was pushed forward again, down the hall, away from his parents. He turned in time to get a final glimpse of his mother's tear-stained face and his father's fingers trembling against the bed sheet.

Two of the men led him out of the apartment and into the cramped elevator. The cage door rattled as it was dragged shut. When the elevator came to a halt on the main floor, a neighbour's apartment light flicked off. Luciano fidgeted with his bonds, glanced at every door in the hall, praying someone would emerge to intervene.

When they stepped out into the crisp autumn night, Luciano's heartbeat went into overdrive. Two Ford Falcons were parked beside the curb, their green hoods gleaming beneath the glow of the street lights. A man with a pistol nodded when he saw them and opened the back door to the first car.

One of the men shoved Luciano up against the side of the vehicle and fastened the other necktie around his eyes. Luciano caught the scent of fried onions on the man's fingers. Something dropped over his head. Soft, like a knit sweater. The smell of his mother's laundry detergent. The man palmed the back of his skull, forced it down and shoved him into the car. Luciano tried to yell but the gag left him rasping. His head smacked a hard edge before he landed on smooth leather.

"We're taking you for a little drive."

The door slammed. He kicked the seat and tried to yell again. Two of the men climbed into the front and exchanged hushed instructions. In a scramble for air, Luciano turned his head to the side and inhaled through the wool of the hood, but only sucked in his own liquor breath. The motor turned on. The seat rumbled against his cheek as the car pulled out and started down the road. He prayed as hard as he could for something to stop them, whoever they were, for someone to look out a window and call for help, but all he heard was the jackhammer pulse in his ears as they took him farther and farther from home.

CHAPTER FOUR

MARIJKE
JUNE 25, 1943
RAVENSBRÜCK, GERMANY

I T WOULD BE A LIE TO SAY THAT I IMMEDIATELY regretted my decision. While the other prisoners trudged off to the factories or to dig ditches under the sweltering sun, the sixteen of us were shepherded into the infirmary. A Blockova came around with an extra ration of soup. The pot was still hot and, for once, the Blockova reached the ladle down to the bottom to scrape for potato peels, examining us with a mix of deference and suspicion. I sucked all the taste from each spoonful before swallowing. When I finished, I got into line.

The doctors ordered us to remove our clothes again so they could compile our records. The female guards in the room jeered, calling us whores and night walkers and commie-lickers. While I waited my turn, I shielded my body with my arms and told myself over and over that I was a respectable, loyal wife.

35

Two doctors sat at a small table. One checked a sheet of paper and asked to see the number on my uniform. "Now then," he said, "you're twenty-three, correct? At what age did you begin menstruating?"

"When I was fourteen, sir."

"Are you still experiencing regular cycles?"

The girl beside me blushed as the other doctor questioned her, but I swallowed and looked directly at the man in front of me. "Not since I got here."

"Any chance of pregnancy?"

"No, sir."

"Have you ever given birth?"

"No, sir."

"And how would you describe your sexual experience?"

I thought of Theo kneeling to kiss my chest and something inside me ached. "Sufficient."

"You're single, I presume?"

"No, married."

He stopped writing to look at my face. "What is your husband's name?"

"Theodoor de Graaf." Perhaps he expected us to be regular women of the night, but saying Theo's name sparked my hope, making me certain I would find him, that everything would be worthwhile.

With cold, gloved hands, the doctor prodded my chest and vagina, examining them for blemishes and sores before testing for venereal disease. The wrinkles on his forehead bunched up as he scribbled something on my records. Only one woman failed the medical screening, but the staff swiftly replaced her with a slight German girl with nutmeg hair who had been given no choice about her fate. She spent that first day cowering in the corner like a wounded kitten.

After the examination, we received a disinfection bath and an injection. The Nazis were taking no chances, unwilling to let us contaminate their labour force with disease. They sent us to a room with sun lamps, and we all spent a few minutes under the glow. But the best blessing was the food. Oh, the food. All of us women sobbing at the sight of a full plate: a thick hunk of bread without mould, a piece of sausage, a boiled potato. Sausage! Never had anything tasted so decadent.

Once we had eaten and scraped our plates to catch every last crumb, the conversation began. We swapped stories, conversing in German in a strange stew of accents. Some of the girls were Polish, but most were German, though they'd been imprisoned across the country for different reasons. Some, for avoiding work, others for their political affiliations or for petty crimes. Gerda, the first to volunteer for the brothel, had received her green triangle for having an illegal abortion. The frightened brunette who had been forced to join us last minute was a communist and introduced herself as Sophia. Two girls were divorced and another had seen her boyfriend shot, his body robbed of its possessions, right down to the monogrammed handkerchief she'd given him. Edith, a heavy-breasted woman with a gap in her teeth, had worked as a prostitute before the war, as had three others. When Edith said this, we all grew quiet, realizing we would need to rely on their experience.

A hot, dry spell consumed the next two days. The SS officers responsible for our transport to Buchenwald allowed us to enjoy the weather, encouraged us to lie in the sun. My sallow complexion returned to something more human. Instead of our uniforms, they provided us with regular clothes, colourful pleated skirts and even cotton undergarments. My chest had started to shrink at Ravensbrück, but it still felt like a luxury to slip a brassiere back over my breasts.

We treated those days like a vacation, but the thought of what lay ahead kept me up late into the nights. I curled up on the thin straw mattress, listening to the snores of the other girls, which grew louder as they regained their strength, and I tried to imagine what it would be like touching a man I'd only just met. So much time had passed since I'd even thought about making love. Nothing could arouse me. I tried to fantasize about Theo—about running my fingers through the cowlick in his hair, the taut muscles in his arms as he helped my father carry sacks of flour into the bakery. But no matter what, I couldn't shake the image of his black eye, bleeding and swelling shut beneath his glasses as the moffen led us away from home.

ALMOST all of us had arrived at Ravensbrück by cattle car, boarded up in suffocating darkness for countless hours before tumbling out at the station in Fürstenberg, a picturesque town of red-roofed buildings that lay on the opposite side of the lake. The sixteen of us now left from that same station, but this time, we journeyed by truck. We clumped together at the far exit of the station for a good half-hour while the driver loaded crates of ammunition into the military vehicle. An SS woman stood around us while a guard from Buchenwald sat on the back of a nearby bench. He cupped his hand around his lighter, unable to keep his cigarette lit in the breeze. As he struck the flint, a little boy came skipping down the street. Upon spotting the guard, he stopped and dug his hands into the pockets of his knit shorts, which he'd far outgrown. He looked from the guard to the gun that rested on the bench and then back up at the guard, who beckoned him over to ask him something. The boy grinned in response. Then a woman carrying a suitcase and a bundle of brown paper packages caught up to him. She laughed flirtatiously as the guard winked at her, but when she noticed us girls, she pulled her son toward her and urged him on. I buried my fist into the fabric of my skirt and watched them continue down the road toward the water. The church bells pealed the hour, and at the strike of nine, the guard tossed his cigarette into the bushes and ordered us into the truck.

The vehicle jolted and bounced along for many hours, but I took in the fresh air and the view of the countryside out the open canvas back. How easily life seemed to carry on outside the camp walls. Farmers herding sheep, horses grazing in the pastures. The only sign of war was the occasional roadblock, a few soldiers loitering against signposts.

The guard and SS woman accompanied us all the way to Buchenwald. I lowered my voice and joked that she'd come only to keep an eye on the guard, to keep his paws off the precious cargo. This got a laugh from the girls, but no sooner had I said it, than I cringed at the meaning of those words. *Cargo.* Something to be tossed from person to person before coming out worn and battered at the other end. I apologized for my remark, but

Sophia shook her head. "We need to be able to laugh about what life throws at us. How else can we expect to press on?"

The driver stopped several times, letting us out to relieve ourselves in the bushes and to eat some stale biscuits and a can of green beans. Sophia compared it all to a summer outing, a drive out to her uncle's lakeside villa on the Bodensee, and she told us stories of long mornings spent reading *Madame Bovary* on the veranda, of crabapples plucked from low-hanging branches, and for a few blissful moments I was with Theo again, sailing on the IJsselmeer, my bow coaxing Bach from my violin. "Music like spun sugar," he'd said, as we drifted in circles, going nowhere together.

The truck hit a rut and the music dropped away.

Hours later, dusk crawled out to meet us as we turned onto an access road, signs pointing to Buchenwald. The paved road wound through a lush forest. I fidgeted as I scoured the trees for barracks blocks or some sign of the camp, but the surroundings were disturbingly serene. Part of me wanted to believe that Buchenwald meant a proper prison with individual cots and adequate toilets and rations, but if Ravensbrück was how the moffen treated women, I dreaded what awaited us at a men's camp.

After a couple kilometres, we drove past the end of a railway line, where a throng of men in shirts or wrinkled suits surged from a cattle car. I leaned forward to get a better look, curious where they had come from, if they were as frightened as I. Was this the same path my husband had followed into the camp? Had he stumbled, stopped to rub the sweat from his neck, or had he walked with his head held high, as only a few of them did?

We passed a curved row of two-storey blocks painted a deceiving sunshine yellow. Officers milled around outdoors, but we drove by them down a side road. The column of fresh arrivals ran alongside the truck, clutching their suitcases like life preservers while dogs chased at their heels. Did they realize they would lose everything in a matter of hours?

The truck made a right. Sophia and I exchanged nervous glances as it slowed to a stop. We heard a gate clang open with the understanding that we'd arrived at the prisoners' camp, and when a guard rushed to close it behind us, I tried to decipher its iron-clad message.

"Jedem das Seine," Sophia read.

THE building that would serve as the brothel stood between the infirmary and another structure, which we later discovered to be a cinema, a reward for good behaviour. We were intended as the other reward, the grand prize. A fence ran around the brothel, isolating it from the rest of the camp. The long wooden building had shuttered windows and a number of flowering plants on either side of the concrete steps that led to the entrance. The prisoners' blocks lay out of sight, and I quickly understood the slim chance of spotting Theo. He would have to come to me.

The two guards who had accompanied us ushered us forward. We filed through the door, anxious about what awaited us. Bare, cold bunks? Some twisted form of bondage? A crowd of randy men? Sophia squeezed my hand as we stepped over the threshold, but when I looked around, the tension fizzled. A vase of sunflowers brightened the centre of a long table, and a leafy plant stood in the corner near the radiator. A radiator— all those times I had woken up in Ravensbrück shivering under my thin blanket, dreading the thought of autumn and winter. We gathered in the middle of the room and admired its every detail. Framed landscapes hung on the wood-panelled walls, which were lined with chairs and benches. So civil, almost cheery.

WE had two weeks to settle in before the brothel opened for business. One of the Buchenwald doctors knocked at our door on the first day, a man with an unusually high forehead. He exam- ined each of us, chatting away as he groped our private parts. When he told me I had a lovely face, I dug my fingernails into my palm to keep myself from frowning.

Despite the discomfort of the medical exam, we had little to complain about those first weeks. The smell of ersatz coffee woke us at seven. The brothel supervisor fetched it from the camp kitchens along with our breakfast. I made a big show of parading around the day room with the Thermos, pouring out each girl's ration. Bread with jelly, even butter. Whereas in Ravensbrück we'd wolfed down our watery soup in desperate gulps, each meal at Buchenwald became a spectacle, something to be savoured. I rolled butter across my tongue until it melted.

The second morning, Sophia and I sat in our shared bedroom, which we had for just the two of us. A small vase of wildflowers stood on each nightstand, their perfume almost overwhelming in such a tiny space. A sketch of an Alsatian hung on the wall, the same dogs that had bared their teeth at us each day at Ravensbrück. But what perplexed us most were the framed photos of handsome men on each of our nightstands, men with perfect smiles and white-blond hair.

While I reclined on my bed, Sophia tried to rearrange the blossoms, plucking out the ones that had begun to droop. "Do you think they'll replace these once they all die?"

"You're talking about flowers, not their labour force. God knows why they've even bothered to dress up this place. Who are they trying to fool?"

White petals fell across her pillow. She gathered them one by one and nodded at the photo on her nightstand. "Clearly someone, judging by the presence of our imaginary boyfriends."

I shoved the framed photos into the drawer. "Don't waste time trying to rationalize their thinking. They don't deserve it."

"Maybe they had a photographer come in, propaganda photos for Himmler? Something he can show off at his banquets?"

"Or send as postcards to our parents? 'Be proud of how your daughter is serving the Third Reich!'"

She gave a throaty laugh. "My mother would rather me dead."

What would my mother think? Where did she even believe I was? What had they told her? At Ravensbrück, I'd received permission to send a letter, but maybe that had never even arrived. Whole paragraphs blacked out by the censor, it could have gotten lost in a mailbag somewhere along the German border.

"Is this all a ruse?" Sophia asked. "Will they start giving us pig feed in a week or two?"

"Who knows? The heart of a Nazi must be no bigger than a toad's."

"Just like Hansel and Gretel—do you know the story? They're fattening us up."

"I suppose nobody would visit the brothel if we all looked like ghosts."

She twisted a stem between her fingers. "The question is, why do they want a brothel for the prisoners in the first place?"

We both sighed. Then I noticed an orange wildflower sticking out of the bunch. "Look, the colour of the Dutch royal family. Last winter, my cousin got arrested after she wore an orange brooch while teaching at the primary school, and I was fined for hanging laundry out on the line in the tricolour of our flag. Soon they'll place spies at all the windows in Amsterdam."

"Here." Sophia tucked the flower into my hair. "Press it between some books so it lasts."

She went off to dispose of the wilted petals, while I stayed in the room, running my hands over the furniture, feeling out the oddities of this new, unexpected prison, and letting my mind drift back to Theo, hoping he'd also found someone at Buchenwald in whom he could confide.

That night, it was my turn to bathe. We had a proper washroom with hot running water. I sank into the tub until water lapped at my earlobes. My hip bones jutted up like mountain peaks separated by a wide valley. I stayed in the bath until the water turned cold, and while towelling off, I folded my arms across my chest, studied myself in the mirror, and wondered whose hands would next explore my naked body.

Two SS women assumed the roles of brothel supervisor and cashier. One of them was a proper Greta Garbo, with arched brows and cranberry-stained lips, but her words rushed at us like a bitter gale. The cashier stooped with a bad hunch, and three dark hairs sprouted on her chin, but she did her job and left us in peace. In private, Sophia and I referred to them by absurd names: Beauty and the Beast, Athena and Medusa, Ahab and Moby, and, simply to spite them, Harpo and Groucho.

The day the brothel officially opened, I woke with a tearing pain in my gut. I prayed it was cramps, that after two months of growing weaker, my body had switched on again. Menstruation meant a five-day break from "work," something we all yearned for from the outset. One of the Polish girls swore our cycles would resume after six or seven months of our new diet. Sophia argued that we would be freed before then, like the Kommandant had promised. I laughed. That line had lured so many of the girls, but the moffen were not the type to return their catch to the sea. They would let us flounder about, gasping for air, as we died a slow, humiliating death.

As I lay on my bunk that morning, clutching my stomach and contemplating my fate, I tried to think of Theo and why I had volunteered. Not for freedom but to find him. The more men I bedded, the more I could spread the word. Somebody out there would know him.

The tighter I clung to this thought, the more the ache subsided. I dragged myself to the dining table, where we ate in silence. Fifteen hardened faces around me.

Edith gave us a warning. "Servicing a stiff-collared businessman is one thing, but if Buchenwald is anything like

Ravensbrück, we'll be dealing with starving, lice-ridden men who haven't touched a woman in months."

While we finished our coffee, the brothel supervisor came to the head of the table to brief us. "After you clean the rooms, you're free to spend the rest of the day as you like. Indoors, naturally. Dinner is at seventeen hundred hours. At nineteen hundred hours, our facilities will open for two hours, as they will each day from now on, except Sundays, when we offer extended hours."

"How many visits should we expect?" Sophia asked.

The supervisor's painted lips twisted into a smirk. "Each man is allotted fifteen minutes, no more than twenty. No fancy positions, just man-on-top. We shall strictly enforce this. You'll receive up to eight clients each night."

The wrenching pain returned. Eight chances, I told myself— eight chances to find Theo—but even those words felt like a betrayal.

"You're only useful to the Reich as long as you're healthy, so we will take every precaution against any undesirable consequences. You shall receive regular injections against pregnancy and venereal disease but are responsible for using a rubber sheath with all clients. Use disinfection ointment to clean yourself after each visit. Anal and oral intercourse are forbidden. Is that understood?"

Her instructions passed through me. I was no longer Marijke, not even Number 21522. I was a whore.

When the supervisor left, the cashier carried in a laundry basket heaped with worn men's socks. SS socks. The other girls grabbed needles and thread, eager for a distraction, but I refused to join in and nobody minded. A sparse collection of books filled the shelves in our common room, where men would wait their turns in the evenings. The books had German authors, all patriotic and fascist, more propaganda than literature. I chose Goethe's *The Sorrows of Young Werther*, a slim novel that appeared mildly entertaining, and settled in a quiet corner.

By late afternoon, I'd given up on reading, unable to focus. Dinner consisted of peas, bread and sausage, but I couldn't eat.

Edith leaned over the table and whispered to me. "The meat will boost our energy. They want to prepare us for an assault of cocks."

Even that word made me wince.

At a quarter to seven, the supervisor led each of us into a *koberzimmer*, a cubicle. I had koberzimmer 9. We had just showered and smelled of harsh soap. The tiny, narrow room contained a single bed with a thin pillow and mattress cover but no sheets. An array of plants turned the windowsill into a potted jungle. The room had two doors, one for my use, which opened into our sleeping quarters, and the other for the client. A photograph of Hitler and two watercolour sketches hung on the wall. One showed the ruins of a medieval tower, the other a series of colourful old buildings. The name "Weimar" was written in calligraphy under both pieces, the town we had passed on our way into camp.

I paced back and forth, every muscle in my body tense as a thread pulled to its breaking point. A hesitant knock sounded at the door. I flopped onto the bed. Stood up. Sat down again and blinked back tears, bracing my body for a rough beating, a blitz of lewd remarks.

The prisoner who entered walked with a limp. Wire-frame glasses hung on his sunken face, and he wore a thin, patchy moustache. "My name is Ernst," he said. A German with the markings of a political prisoner. His handshake felt so weak that I worried my touch would leave bruises.

"Marijke."

He sat beside me on the bed and struggled to undo the buttons of his striped uniform. I slipped off my blouse, angling my shoulder to hide my chest. His cheeks flushed as he opened the final button to reveal a ladder of ribs. The scrawniness of a child. I thought of my brother, a boy of eighteen hauled off to work in German factories. The moffen made men out of boys and boys out of men.

"I . . . Marijke, I don't want to hurt you."

I looked away. "You won't."

While I began to remove my skirt, he reached out, grazing my hip. We both recoiled at the touch.

"I've never done this," he said.

"Me neither."

"Really?"

"Not like this, I haven't."

Inching toward me, he placed a hand on my thigh and stared at it doubtfully. While he stroked my leg, I tried to estimate how much time had passed—two, three minutes? He tugged on my skirt and my eyes closed as it fell to the floor.

"Look at me? Please?"

"I'm sorry. I just . . ."

"I know."

Then we were both naked. I tried not to see the growing hardness between his legs. I wondered if I'd even recognize Theo's body anymore, or if it would have also withered away.

Ernst lowered my head onto the pillow, pulled himself on top of me. Tears gathered, but I held them in.

"Marijke?"

"I'm ready."

He sighed, rolled off, and positioned himself beside me. "Just give me a minute."

We'd been warned what would happen if the client wasn't satisfied. My hand wavered as I reached between his legs. "Please, go ahead."

"No, I can't, not like this."

"What can I do to help?"

"You—no, nothing." He sat up, passed me my blouse and stared up at the ceiling. "In Berlin, there was a girl I'd known since we were four or five. Her mother used to do our laundry, and whenever she came over, we would build forts from the clean linen. She had the prettiest laugh, like handbells at mass."

I hesitated before slipping on my blouse. "Where is she now?"

He looked at me with feverish eyes. "What if I never see her again? Two of my friends have dysentery, another collapsed in the quarry yesterday. I always thought she and I would get married, have four or five children. I would have taken such good care of her."

"I know how hard it is."

"I'm not asking for your pity."

"My husband is in here, somewhere."

"Oh." He bowed his head. "I'm sorry." When I didn't answer, he pulled on his trousers. "I just assumed . . . well, it doesn't matter."

We sat quietly, wallowing in our own shame and embarrassment. His fingers twitched against the pillowcase. Unable to stand the pained desperation in his expression, I shifted to lie down, and he curled into my back with his cheek pressed to my shoulder. I held his hand and we just lay there. After a while, a dampness crept across the back of my blouse. "Don't cry," I said.

"I don't want it to end like this."

"It won't." As those words left my mouth, they drifted away into nothing, but the croak in his voice gave me the resolve to offer hope, even though I had little to spare.

"What if I never touch a woman again?"

"You can't think like that. You'll never survive if you do."

"You're right."

Like horses with blinders, we fixated on the goal of survival, but so much of it came down to luck. I pictured myself shivering on the bunk at Ravensbrück, trying to make it through the cool, sodden nights. But then the music returned. I recalled how I'd spent that time imagining my fingers around the bow of my violin, how I'd transported myself back to the auditorium in Amsterdam, where I used to practice until my fingers blistered. I turned to Ernst, whose cheeks were blotchy and wet. "What do you love more than anything?"

"Her."

"Besides her."

"What do you mean?"

"What else makes you happy?"

"Mathematics, I suppose. I used to teach."

"Good, then fill your days with mathematics. Create complicated equations and solve them. Think of formulae and geometry and algebra."

Someone knocked on the door. Time was up. We put on the rest of our clothes, and I whispered Theo's name to Ernst, begging him to spread the word of my search. Ernst paused as he left, and kissed my cheek. "Thank you."

When he was gone, I sank down against the wall. Seven more to go.

EVEN though many of the men were too weak to take control, what they managed was enough to leave me raw down below, a burning that grew worse each time as I felt myself swell and dry up, until this became an unbearable pain. While they had their way with me, I lay there like a corpse and stared at the ceiling, willing myself to vanish, to find some escape. Once, I made the mistake of looking toward the door, where I noticed an eye pressed up to a wide peephole. Those filthy moffen were spying on us, probably getting aroused by my suffering.

By the end of that first week, I could barely move. I counted each visitor, calculating the amount of time I had left before I could trudge back to the sleeping quarters. The final prisoner entered the room without a hint of excitement, and as soon as he moved to touch me, I could tell he didn't fancy women. A pink triangle, a handsome man of around twenty with girlish features.

"Why are you here?" I asked.

He led me to the bed, undid the clasp of my brassiere. "I have no choice."

"But you paid for your visit. Isn't it meant as a reward?"

"Not for me." He stripped, exposing a criss-cross of lash marks across his back, deep rope burns on his wrists.

"Oh God."

"Don't feel sorry for me, not me." He avoided my gaze. "They've carted some of the others off to the infirmary."

"The infirmary?"

"They think they can cure us. We've heard rumours of castrations, injections." He didn't flinch as he said this, but took out his penis and rolled it in his palm, studying the plants as he tried to get hard. "I don't want to do this any more than you do."

I hadn't thought there was anything as awful as being a Jew in a camp. Never before had I met someone of his type, although I'd always had my suspicions about our neighbourhood cobbler in Amsterdam. But like the cobbler, this boy had a friendly face and seemed perfectly normal. His brow furrowed in concentration. What was he thinking about, or whom?

The moment he tried to enter me, he lost his erection and began to panic. But I had no idea how to arouse a man who had no interest in me at all. I couldn't take him in my mouth. I tried to stroke some reaction out of him, and when he closed his eyes, this worked for a moment, but then he grew soft again.

We heard a loud rap and saw that beady eye at the glass.

"Hurry up in there!"

I didn't budge. The moffen didn't care if other men didn't go through with it, so why now? The boy grabbed himself, furiously rubbed up and down. He bit his lip in frustration. "Help me, please."

I pictured an infirmary block, a set of surgical knives on an operating table. With sudden strength, I pulled him overtop of me, with his back facing the door. "Just pretend. I'll hide you."

His shoulders hunched inward as I raised a bent leg to conceal his groin. He thrusted faster, faking a groan, and reached out to brace himself against me. But by mistake, he yanked my hair and I dropped my leg in surprise.

The door swung open, and an SS officer came in, a beefy man with a baby face. "What are you doing?"

We froze. My limbs trembled under the boy's weight. When he said nothing, I spoke up. "He's almost finished."

"Both of you stand up." As we separated ourselves, the officer sneered at me before diverting his attention to the boy's shrivelled penis.

"Please," the boy said, "give me another chance."

"After trying to trick me?" He grabbed the naked boy by the elbow before turning to me. "You insolent bitch. You only have one purpose here; don't forget that."

As he pulled the boy out of the room, the boy glanced at me over his shoulder, but I looked down at a spot in the centre of the floorboards, terrified of what punishment lay ahead.

FOR several days, I heard nothing of the incident and continued my work as normal. On the third evening, I was about to wash up after my last client when the brothel supervisor appeared. "You're not done. One of the officers says you have some dues to pay."

I swallowed. "What do you mean?"

She passed me fresh linen to put on the bed before leaving the koberzimmer. I sat in the corner on the floor, knees pressed to my chest, fighting to breathe.

The door opened and he strutted in, that same ruddy-faced officer. "We meet again." He pulled off his leather overcoat, draped it over the back of a chair and hooked his thumbs through his belt loops as he leaned back to examine me. "I don't think I ever introduced myself. SS-Kommandoführer Hoffmann. Bruno, if you must. And your name?"

I said nothing but stood in front of him, trying to steady my breath.

"Marijke, plucked from the streets of Amsterdam for civil disobedience. A Jew-lover from the resistance." He tugged at his belt buckle. "You're far too pretty to be here, my dear."

He approached with a sickening grin, forcing me back until I was up against the bed. His tunic and shirt came off, and his bratwurst fingers fumbled with the buttons of my blouse. As soon as he had two loose, he reached underneath, his fingernails scraping my skin as he pawed my breasts. A bulge appeared in his trousers. He nodded and I began to undress, but not fast enough for his liking. Stitches in my blouse split with his impatience.

Dropping his trousers to his ankles, he flipped me onto my knees and splayed my legs before forcing himself inside me with a searing burn. I prayed for him to finish quickly, to leave the room and forget all about me, to never look at me again. But he took his time. With every stroke, I wanted to cry out, but refused to give him the satisfaction. Instead, I tried to focus on what life would be like after the war ended. Once Germany lost, a nation wiped out like a sandcastle beneath a crashing wave. How it would feel to cycle through the market again, the calls of the fishmonger at my back. Theo and I would have beautiful, healthy children. He would ride alongside me on a carrier bike, twin girls sitting up front in the box, while I took our infant son on mine, and we would stop along the IJ to watch the freight ships docking.

The slimy mof smirked and stroked my cheek when he came. He pulled out, wiped himself on the mattress cover, his eyes never leaving me as he dressed. I pointed my body to the wall, but he came over, looming above me. He grabbed my nipple between two fingers, pinching hard. "You did good, girl. A positive report."

A sudden rush of saliva filled my mouth, and the moment the door closed behind him, I stumbled over to the sink and heaved.

CHAPTER FIVE

KARL
JULY 9, 1943
BUCHENWALD

⁂

BUCHENWALD WAS TOO FULL OF MEN. IN BERLIN, Karl hadn't minded. He could sit at the office all day, phoning men, in meetings with men, and then he would leave work and head to the beer halls, where alluring numbers in short skirts and frilly tops waited. The few women stationed at Buchenwald looked like Clydesdale horses.

Shortly after his arrival, Karl attended a cocktail party in Brandt's villa. The brass band performed, and waiters roamed through the house with trays of drinks. He asked for straight whisky and sipped it in the corner while studying the other officers. Most had paunches or shiny bald patches. Their wives must have noticed that he was one of the youngest, because they kept looking in his direction, huddling like a gaggle of geese, until a plump lady wearing an emerald brooch approached. "You must be the new Schutzhaftlagerführer."

"Karl."

She grabbed him by the arm and led him over to the others. They threw out their names one by one, which he promptly forgot, though he tried to make note of their respective husbands.

"How lovely to have you join us," the plump one said. "Why don't I give you a tour of the villa?"

Another swooped in. "Ursula, I believe your husband was looking for you. I'll show our new recruit the highlights."

"No, I just spoke with him."

"Actually, ladies," Karl said, "that's very kind, but the Kommandant already gave me the tour."

A third woman stepped forward, this one wearing a ridiculous amount of rouge. "Even better. Why not join us in the sitting room for a drink? We'd love to hear more about you."

"Yes," Ursula added. "You have to tell us what brought you to the camp. The Führer should be clamouring to have you as one of the faces of his party. And where is your wife? A man like you can't be single, can he?"

His thoughts drifted to Else, four years earlier. Lovely Else, tall and graceful, lounging on his daybed in her beret and fur coat. Her shattered expression when he'd broken off the engagement. "It's your parents," he told her as she wept into his new uniform. "It's not that I don't love you." She didn't beg him to reconsider. Last he'd heard, she'd joined the cabaret, while her parents had fled to America, though he doubted they would get any more sympathy for their Bolshevik delusions there.

A voice snapped him back to Buchenwald. "Don't be such a meddler, Ursula."

"I just thought we could introduce him to some of the eligible ladies around here."

"Eligible ladies?" The one with the gaudy cheeks snorted. "The camp guards?"

"Well," Karl said, "it's been a pleasure, but I can't stay here all night." He broke out of their circle and headed for the porch. Outside, he took a deep breath of fresh air and loosened his top button. All the schmoozing, the decrepit condition of the prisoners, it felt overwhelming. As he took a seat on the settee and looked up at the sky, the hinges of the porch door squeaked. He stiffened.

"Relax, Müller. The flock has moved on." Brandt chuckled and came over to join him. They sat listening to the crickets chirping in the woods that separated the villas from the rest of camp. There was no sign of the stars between the gathering clouds.

"Beautiful out here, isn't it?" Brandt said.

"Certainly a nicer view than my place in Berlin."

"You're a reasonable man, Müller, and I like that, but you've never set foot in a camp before. It's unusual for someone of your experience to be granted a post like this."

"I understand, sir."

"The Führer has scores of able-bodied men out there in combat, but the engine of our economy runs here in these camps. Our brains, Müller, our strict adherence to discipline. Camp life takes some getting used to, you know, not to mention a certain fortitude. Think of Buchenwald like a factory. Things can run smoothly only if every single person does their job efficiently and without hesitation."

"Well, you can count on me for that."

"Good." Brandt stroked his chin. "Now, come on in and have a cigar with us."

"Yes, sir. I'll join you in a minute."

The Kommandant went back inside but Karl sat there a moment longer, staring at the murky sky and reminiscing about Else.

A few days later, Karl was checking inventory in the depot that contained the inmates' personal belongings when he heard female voices outside.

"Did I tell you about that guard last night?"

A young woman with a Dutch accent replied. "I don't want to hear about it right now." She paused and sighed. "How about this instead? I spy with my little eye, something that is grey."

He moved to the window. A dozen women had filed past with a guard, but a few of them dawdled at the end of the line, some of them linking arms. They wore blouses and pleated skirts, so he assumed they belonged to the SS officers' brothel. A long-nosed girl spoke up.

"You spy? What are you talking about?"

"It's a game; you have to guess what I'm looking at." The Dutch girl had a small chest and stood taller than the others. Her curly hair was the colour of apple cider, and she wore it pulled back from her pretty face. "Just guess!" She spoke in a singsong voice, but something harder coated her words, a lacquer of determination.

"A game, really?"

The Dutch girl tugged at her companion's sleeve. "Come on; it will make things better."

"I don't know. Everything here is grey. That wheelbarrow?"

"Keep guessing."

Their conversation faded as they walked farther away, but he watched for another minute, curious about that girl and what had brought her to the camp.

IN the evening, he paid a visit to the SS brothel. All day, he'd questioned how he'd ended up at Buchenwald. His young age and lack of military training had set him up for desk jobs crunching statistics on economic productivity, but his superiors had conspired a different fate. Despite what he'd told the Kommandant, Karl suspected his father had played a part in getting him the promotion, probably reeling in a few favours from his prominent network. If it hadn't been for his age and declining health, his father might have fought for such a position himself. As a fellow veteran, Wilhelm Müller spoke of the Führer like a comrade, a man who understood him.

Every spring since the war, Karl's father would retreat into a stupor for the month of April, during the anniversary of some battle. His skin gave off the smell of alcohol as he locked himself in his study long into the nights. As a child, if Karl got in the way or used the wrong tone, his father would strike him. Once, he'd thrown a chair across the room. Karl's mother would comfort Karl after his father calmed down. She assured him that his father loved him but that the war had damaged him in ways they couldn't see. Still, Karl always went to bed wondering what he'd done wrong, forging plans for ways to please his father.

Every summer, his family spent time at their lake house. As a boy, Karl would pack his suitcase two weeks ahead of time, dreaming of the adventures that awaited. His father, however, could never relax on those holidays; he always had a newspaper or a book in his hand, as if he were wary of what idle hours might do to his brain. He enforced his regime of militant regulation with fervour: from the age of nine, Karl had to perform forty-five minutes of calisthenics each morning to earn breakfast. Afterwards, he was permitted to play for two hours, but then he had to read or study until it was time to swim lengths along the shore. Sometimes, his father made him lug stacks of bricks back and forth until his arms ached. "Being weak or sickly is not a condition," his father argued, "but rather a sign of indolence and a lack of character." When Karl passed afternoons in the forest, collecting plant specimens for identification, his father scoffed in disapproval. "Stop carrying around those flowers. You look like some kind of fairy."

Karl had first heard of Adolf Hitler at age thirteen. His father returned home from a late business dinner to say that he'd seen a commotion outside a local beer hall. And while the failed putsch got Hitler thrown in jail, his father never forgot that name. So when Hitler returned to the scene years later, promising a revived Germany, a restoration of glory, the Müller family had been among the first to place their trust in him. They'd seen cities growing crowded from overpopulation and worried about the threat to their properties, which were hard enough to maintain under the crippling inflation. The National

Socialists vowed to protect their land, to create *Lebensraum* for the German people, living space for the population to expand and prosper. They would take back what had been swindled by the Jews, the Treaty of Versailles. They would pull Germans from the sinkhole of humiliating defeat and economic weakness. The Reich would be great again, powerful among nations. A fresh start for everyone. And if all this happened, Karl hoped his father might also soften, return to how he'd been before the war, capable of warmth and affection.

The year Hitler became chancellor, Karl had turned twenty-three. His father had a very specific vision for what kind of man he should become: a patriot, robust, educated, cultured and fearless. So instead of pursuing his interest in biology, Karl had followed his father's path by studying economics. At university, he trained in track and field and discovered a talent for javelin. With Hitler boasting about placing the Third Reich on the world stage, Karl's father eyed the upcoming Olympics in Berlin. He pushed Karl to train harder, but the other athletes were younger and stronger. The day before the qualifiers, Karl pulled his shoulder. Unwilling to accept his resignation, Karl's father called him a pansy, a weakling, and took him to another doctor for a second opinion. The injury was as real as Wilhelm's disappointment.

A decade later and Karl had regained his father's confidence. When he joined the SS, his father had hosted a celebratory party at their lakeside estate. And after he got word of his new job at Buchenwald, his father had sat him down with a cigar and told him how pleased he was that Karl was active in the cleanse and in the advancement of the Third Reich. He would bring honour to the family name. The idea of a cleanse sounded so clinical that Karl almost forgot they were talking about actual people. He still found himself grappling with the party's views on race and the Final Solution, but the visit with his father had left him with such a feeling of pride and responsibility that he pushed these doubts away. The promotion had excited him, a chance to witness the heart of the Führer's labour force in operation.

But now, extraordinary as it was to see the inner clockwork of the economy, the camp felt dreary. A place where officers never smiled, where zoo animals and labourers wore the same glazed look. He was determined to cheer up and hoped he'd find the Dutch girl on duty.

When he inquired about the SS brothel, a bunch of officers responded with hungry grins. So, he arrived there with two men who were practically salivating. It was his first time in a whorehouse, but he kept that quiet and let the others do the talking.

"Ingeborg, now she's a fox. She can't get enough of me."

"That brunette? Haven't you seen the size of her teeth?"

"The breasts on her and that's what you stare at?"

"What about that girl from Frankfurt? She's tighter than a Jew's wallet."

"I heard she gave Bauer crabs."

Karl stepped in. "I'm certain she would have been dealt with if she had."

The officers paused in agreement. Then the girls paraded in front of them one by one. As the most senior officer, Karl got first pick. These weren't the ones he'd seen outside earlier and not one grabbed his attention. He'd always imagined prostitutes as sirens. The few he'd seen on the street in Berlin wore perfume and fake pearls. They beckoned with sultry words. But the women before him were thin and flat. Barely an ass on any of them and drab lingerie seemed to hide what curves they did have. At least Himmler knew to spend his budget outfitting his men, not his whores.

He hesitated before choosing the fairest of the bunch. She had pinned up her hair in fat rolls. With that hairstyle and her long neck, she reminded him of Else.

The staff gave them injections to ward off venereal disease before showing them to the rooms. Karl watched the girl undress before doing the same. Her ass sagged and stretch marks covered her stomach, but it had been too long since he'd seen a naked woman, and he was hard instantly. But just as he entered her, the groans of the other officers picked up. The slap of skin against skin. He couldn't escape it. The girl lay there, not doing a thing or making any noise. When he did manage to finish, any pleasure he should have felt was dulled by her indifference. She rolled off the bed and began fastening her dress. While the other officers left the brothel just as they'd come in, bragging about their conquests, he left disappointed, the sourness of her breath lingering in his mouth.

CHAPTER SIX

DESPITE LUCIANO'S ATTEMPT TO CONSTRUCT A mental map of the car's route through the streets of Buenos Aires, the twists and turns had grown far too many to count and he had no idea if they even remained within city limits. After twenty minutes—or was it an hour?—the car slowed to a halt. A window rolled down, followed by the crunch of approaching footsteps.

Someone outside asked a low, muffled question, and the man in the passenger seat responded with, "Luciano Wagner."

At the mention of his name, Luciano stiffened. He lay on the back seat, his skin chafed from the gag, his limbs aching in their contorted positions: knees curled against his torso, arms pinned behind his back. Sticky sweat gathered along the waistband of his jeans.

The person outside instructed the driver to proceed, but the vehicle stopped again a minute later. As the doors opened, Luciano sucked in the cool air. Hands snatched at him. He thrashed and kicked in panic, but his legs tingled and he struggled to stand as they pulled him to his feet.

A jab in the back sent him forward along a paved road. Ahead, the sound of creaking metal, like a door opening. His shins hit something that made him trip against a body.

"Watch it." The man struck Luciano and tugged him forward.

A different surface, hard under his feet. Before he had time to get his bearings, he was led down a staircase into a room with the cold dampness of a basement. His captors removed his gag and their footsteps faded away, but a prickling instinct told him he was being watched, so he ground his tongue against his molars until this distraction quelled his trembling.

A deep voice in front of him broke the silence. "Your name?"

"Luciano Wagner." This came out cracked. Why were they asking what they already knew? Did they have so many prisoners to keep track of at once?

"From now on you're number five-seven-four—remember that. Rank and *nom de guerre*?"

"I don't understand."

Another man interrupted. "Just answer."

"I don't have one."

A sigh and the rustling of papers. His heart beat with such madness that the others must have noticed. "I don't know what you're talking about," he insisted. "My name is Luciano. I'm a student at the UBA; I've done nothing."

"You're involved in terrorist activities. Opposing the government and provoking student disobedience. Now, if you'll give us the information we're looking for, we'll make this easy for you."

These were military men, pawns of the government. He grew dizzy, and his muscles cramped, already anticipating what was to come. Students at school, many of them more involved than he, had spread rumours of these kidnappings. Of young men and women, beaten up in their homes, electrocuted with the torn end of a lamp cord while their parents were forced to watch. Rumours of a Ford Falcon that had pulled up at a church in broad daylight, and the plainclothes officers who kidnapped the outspoken minister while the congregation watched. At the time, he'd dismissed the accusations as outrageous, telling Fabián that fear mongering was just another means to draw support for their cause.

But now he understood it was all true. His captors would demand a list of accomplices for his concocted crimes. There might be torture. It made no sense to fight back; the building probably contained dozens of armed men. He clasped his cuffed hands together and looked in the direction of the voice. "My parents have savings, a watch, gold necklaces—my grandparents own sheep and cattle. They'll give you all of it!"

A pause followed, and Luciano imagined one man signalling to another.

"What do you want? What can I give you? Please, I'll do anything."

"We have no tolerance for your petty revolts." Someone approached and pushed him into another room. Behind him, the voice called out, "Number five-seven-four, don't forget."

Heavy footsteps came at Luciano. Hands grabbed his clothes. He wrenched free and lunged back the way he'd entered, but ended up shoved against a bumpy wall lined with what felt like egg cartons. Without warning, something long and hard smacked his shoulders and calves, a pain that sent neon starbursts—green, orange, yellow—across his vision. He cried out and tucked down. Strikes against his neck, arms, an arc of spasms down his back. A loud tear, his shirt ripped along the seam. Then his binds came off. They ordered him to remove his clothes. Once he was naked, someone came over and restrained him. A blow to the groin stopped his squirming. "*Mierda!*" he cursed, doubling over at the waist. He was lowered onto a metal bed frame.

"Time for you to meet the grill."

Luciano shook as his legs and arms were splayed and tied down. He couldn't remember the Lord's Prayer, but Pablo Neruda's poetry spilled out in urgent whispers.

"What was your rank with the organization?"

"I'm not a Montonero. I'm innocent."

"Who's behind these student protests? We want names, first and last."

The past week flashed before him: brainstorming slogans after class for the rally for freedom of speech, Fabián's tousled hair as he addressed the crowd of students, his full lips glistening with spit as he delivered a passionate call to action. Had they nabbed him, too?

"I don't know anything!"

They fastened something sharp to his hands, feet and stomach, cold like metal. A switch and an electric buzz filled the room, magnifying and concentrating overhead. Rank breath like curdled milk, warm against his face. The blindfold had shifted to let in some light, so he could just make out what was suspended above him: a rod as wide as a broomstick. He tried to make up some names, but not fast enough.

"Let's see if Caroline can loosen your tongue."

Then came searing pain. The electric prod sent waves of shock from head to toe. Loud, shrill screams rose up over the buzzing, and he only half-realized they were his own. It felt like his arms and legs were being ripped away, blinding, hot-red pain. Muscles contracted and his bowels loosened, the stench of shit mixing with that of roasting skin, of rotting pork and burning mouldy leather.

The begging cries that formed at his lips gave way to screams. He felt himself float toward the ceiling, and his yells grew distant as he looked down to see himself lying naked on the bed frame. Convulsions sent his body flying up, writhing against his restraints, but he didn't feel any more pain. The torture stopped and, for the first time, he heard loud music blasting, muffling his screams. Suddenly, he understood the purpose of the egg cartons.

"Are you ready to talk?"

He started to retch, almost choking on the vomit. His jaw felt numb.

"Doctor?" the man asked.

Another voice responded. "He can take it."

They removed the clips from his body and hooked something different to his teeth, a claw that scraped his gums. He tried to move his hand, to form words through the clumps of vomit.

"Names," he said. "Montoneros: Carlos Esteban Alarcón, Daniel Corbo, Miguel Angel Herrera." No response except the pain, those coloured shapes spinning faster and faster, plunging a rainbow of daggers toward him.

The voltage hit his teeth like a meteor, burning, exploding across his head until he was sure his skull would split down the middle. "Daniel Herrera," he cried. "Carlos Corbo!" He screamed until he couldn't hear anything, couldn't feel anything, until he hovered over the bed frame looking down on the singed body that twisted and jerked on the grill.

A cold splash of water brought him back. He heard a hiss and crackle. Something dribbled from his gums, his tongue, hot and metallic. For a few minutes, nothing happened and he drifted in and out of consciousness. Shadows and pillars of light passed in front of his eyes. A cool metal object pressed against his chest, causing him to piss himself, but he heard a voice again, the doctor measuring his pulse. Muffled orders and the loosening of the ties at his wrists and ankles, then darkness.

WHEN Luciano awoke, his eardrums hummed. Something still covered his head, but this new fabric itched and dug into his skin where it was fastened. A putrid taste filled his mouth: iron and earthy decay. It felt like his skin had been peeled from his bones with a scalpel. Heavy shackles bound his ankles, and his wrists were cuffed again, his clothes back on, but it felt too warm for the basement, and he lay on a thin, soggy mattress. The air smelled like urine and stale sweat. Tilting his head back, he sensed a bright light high above him and the longer he stared at it, the more his senses returned. The pain sharpened to a point, and he saw Fabián hopping the gate at the Subte station; his mother's chiming laughter as she twirled to show off a burgundy jumpsuit; his father driving a borrowed car down the coast, humming along to the classical station on the radio.

He cursed himself for going out that night, for getting his parents involved. His mother's shattered expression, his father's cold and unreadable one. But if these men worked with the police, his parents wouldn't be able to do anything to help. He'd recently seen a crowd of women gathering near the Casa Rosada, the pink presidential building that sprawled across one end of the Plaza de Mayo like a great wall of coral. Mothers, grandmothers, all of them wearing white kerchiefs over their hair. Some held photos of their children or signs and banners. They had started to march, circling the Pirámide de Mayo while they chanted, demanding that the government, the police, give them information about their missing sons and daughters. Some of their children had been missing for weeks, some for months. Now, Luciano understood that he had become another one of the *desaparecidos*, the disappeared.

He shuffled to the right until he came in contact with a wall. Its rough texture and the almost hollow sound it made against his knuckles gave the impression of particleboard. He inched himself upward. Once he managed to sit, he leaned against the wall, which gave slightly under his weight.

Then the tread of boots across the floor behind him, slow, deliberate steps, interrupted by a click, a noise he knew from years of Clint Eastwood films—the sound of a pistol being cocked. Luciano stayed very still. A cold sweat formed on the back of his neck as he anticipated a guard taking aim, but the footsteps retreated.

Over the next several hours, he calculated that it took the guard an average of one minute and ten seconds to pace what must have been a long passageway and that the man paused every twenty minutes for a cigarette. The soothing smoke drifted over to Luciano, making him itch for a cigarette of his own. Later, he decided he was still in the city, probably near the airport, as planes passed overhead with the low rumble of takeoffs and landings. But there was something more surprising: on all sides, voices let out muted cries and chains clinked, marking the presence of other prisoners. He tried to picture them suffering alongside him and wished they all shared a cell so they could talk. His throat burned, and when nobody responded to his cries for food or the toilet, he soiled himself on the mattress. The effort of sitting had grown unbearable, so he reclined again, slipping in and out of a restless sleep. Later, he jolted awake, alert, but with a blank mind. He was left to run his swollen tongue over his tender gums, counting the passing seconds.

At 4,532 seconds, he lost count. A door close to his cell clanged and a guard barked out a command: "Get up."

"No, please," a girl responded, "not again!" Her pleas made Luciano shiver. Something told him she'd been through far worse than he had. Shackles clanked, and the guard pulled her from her cell. Once they were gone, Luciano perceived nothing around him but darkness and felt very alone, but when she was brought back much later, he had to listen to her soft, broken whimpers, which made him long for the silence again.

The space must have lacked windows as the quality of light stayed constant, and the absence of planes told him it was late at night. Pangs gnawed at his stomach, but he couldn't remember when he'd last eaten. He saw himself grilling midnight steaks with chimichurri on a family camping trip, savouring the last bites of his *nonna*'s baking.

The incident at the student rally came back to him. The expression on Fabián's face when Luciano had reached for his hand after misreading a tight embrace. For a second, Fabián let his hand linger, but his eyes widened and then hardened as he broke away. The rest of the evening, Fabián kept his distance, his only remarks centred on the lettering of the protest banners, the need for a proper audio system. He had left without saying goodbye.

Luciano brought his bound hands to his head, willing the image to disappear. He tried to picture his friend in the safety of his own bed, the sheets cast to the side in the midst of a dream, but found himself wondering if Fabián wasn't trapped somewhere nearby, with nobody to comfort him. The possibility took over like a migraine.

Later, faint noises woke him: honking cars and the squeal of brakes. Enough traffic to be a major street. Then something else, something that seemed impossible amid it all: the ring of children's laughter.

He cocked his head, waited for it to stop. But there it was again. A group of children, laughing and playing. There had to be a school close by. He sat up to get a better sense of its location but felt himself go faint, and by the time he came to, the students had disappeared. He pictured them in their classrooms, busy with spelling tests, oblivious to what was unfolding metres away.

All day, he cowered in the corner of his cell. His eyes gummed shut from lack of use. The blindness haunted him, conjuring demonic creatures that circled him, drawing closer and closer and baring bloody fangs. Later, he saw cannonballs shooting in slow motion from all directions. They never hit, but the anticipation made him claw at his exposed skin, twist his wrists against the handcuffs until they bled.

Each time the guard came by, he prayed for the door to open, for a bullet to the head. A quick death. Or perhaps he would just starve. Time had vanished in the black nothingness of his cell, and for all he knew, it could have been days or entire weeks since his capture. He had no recollection of eating. Long hours dripped into one another, and he grew so light-headed and weak that he could no longer raise his face from the mattress.

When the door did open, he was ready. "Just shoot me," he said, but a garbled mumble came out, and instead of the release of a trigger, he heard something drop onto the mattress. The door clanged shut. When he reached out, his hands closed around a stale bun.

AT first, he'd had no way of relieving himself, but he had so little in his stomach that it seldom mattered. Later, a guard brought him an empty cola bottle, but in his fumbled attempts to use it, he spilled it across the mattress. Before the fabric dried, he had to go again, but this time he needed more than a bottle.

He waited until the guard came back down the hall and then whacked the door as hard as he could. When he got no response, he repeated this and pointed to the bottle that rolled between his feet on the off chance the guard was looking.

"Wait."

By the time the guard returned, Luciano's gut had cramped up, and he was so surprised to hear the door open that he didn't move.

"Hurry up, you piece of shit."

He struggled to lift himself, his legs flimsy and useless. The guard hauled him out of the cell and positioned him so he was standing; his hands were placed on the shoulders of someone in front of him. Another door opened and a few seconds later, Luciano felt a pair of hands grasp his shoulders. A heavy grip, with long, wide fingers and rough palms. The guard ordered them forward, making two more stops farther ahead. Luciano estimated that the chain must have included at least six or seven prisoners, based on its slow, caterpillar movement. They slugged on: right at a corner, forward again, the shackles around their ankles jangling. There was a downward step that he could feel coming from the dip in the prisoner before him. The bathroom was on the right. The guard guided them into the room. Countless footsteps echoed across the tiles. He felt his way through the open space, the jostling bodies, until he hit a wall. When he found a toilet, he tugged at his pants, which fell down without unfastening the button. A few days earlier, he would have balked at the idea of using the bathroom so publicly, but now he took his time, savouring the comfort of human presence. The pad of feet against the floor, the unzipping of zippers, the sniffles and dry coughs. At one point, there came a loud smack, a cry, and a thud against the floor. "No talking," the guard said.

As they fell back into line, Luciano felt the warmth of that body beneath his hands, the limp collar of a shirt and skinny shoulders. He imagined another student, maybe a historian-in-training, or a political scientist like Fabián. Someone who loved to swim and play soccer. Before the guard led the guy back into his cell, Luciano gave his shoulders a squeeze.

The walk down the hall left him exhausted and sore, but instead of praying for a bullet to the head, he wished for another trip to the toilets. This time, he wanted to measure the distance in hopes of calculating how many other cells lay between him and the bathrooms, how many people were trapped there.

He started paying closer attention to the noises around him—the din of traffic, the comings and goings of the school-children, and the dawn chorus of a nearby bird—until he could construe the start of each new day. Every morning before the onset of rush hour, the cell to his right opened, and the guy whose shoulders he'd squeezed left for the day.

In the beginning, Luciano's gums were so inflamed that he could only suck on the dry bread he received, but after the trip to the toilets, he made the effort to swallow it all. The guards began waking him for meals with the other prisoners: polenta, chickpeas. Never enough to banish the hunger pangs. He started to notice the change in the guards, the switch in their voices, their approach. Some prodded, some beat him; others let him move on his own.

One morning, he worked up the courage to speak. After going to the toilet, he fell into line behind the guy with the nar-row shoulders, the one who always left his cell during the day, yet never returned moaning in pain.

They ate in a small space next to the bathroom. The guards uncuffed their wrists and permitted them to raise their hoods in order to eat, but his eyes were sore, his vision blurry. Most days, the guards brought in sugarless boiled maté and tossed hard chunks of bread that sent them all scrambling. Today, they had a deep bowl of plain boiled lentils. It circled around the room, each prisoner allowed one mouthful before passing it on. Luciano had trouble chewing; the lentils had been over-salted, likely as a cruel joke, but he still felt a tug in his stomach when the bowl began a second round. It made it to the prisoner beside him, the same guy who kept leaving the cell. Only one spoonful remained.

The prisoner dipped the spoon into the bowl and lifted it to his face, but the spoon was empty. He passed the bowl to Luciano, who poked at the lentils to make sure his eyes hadn't been playing tricks on him. A warmth settled in Luciano's fingers and toes as he ate the last bite, sucking on the lentils, rotating them with his tongue until all the salt disappeared.

A guard came to collect the bowl and spoon and ordered the prisoners to lower their hoods. Once the guard began organizing and cuffing everyone, Luciano edged toward the prisoner.

"Thank you," he whispered.

"You need it more than I do."

The surrounding prisoners fell into line, but the two of them stayed put.

"Where do you go every day?" Luciano asked.

"I work."

"What?"

The guard approached. "Get moving."

As Luciano stood to join the others, he strained to catch the guy's hushed reply. "I'm Gabriel."

◐◑

AFTER this encounter with Gabriel, he was taken back to the basement for another round of torture. This time, it didn't last long. Or perhaps it did. He passed out within the first few minutes of shocks, and when he came to, he was back in his cell. His bones felt limp. Although he heard Gabriel's movements, his tongue was useless, doubled in size.

But Gabriel's remark encouraged him. Maybe there was a way to escape this horror. Another week of solitude and he would lose his mind. Questions piled up—where did this guy work? What did he do? Every hour, Luciano would wave his arms to the passing guard in hopes of being escorted to the toilets. Most times, the guards ignored him, and when he did get the chance to go, Gabriel was never there, and Luciano was left to form the last link in the chain.

Soon, the guards came to fetch him. Fearing the basement, he began to tremble, but his body relaxed once his hands fell onto narrow shoulders in a worn, collared shirt. He squeezed them twice in greeting as they approached the bathroom.

"Get undressed," the guard ordered as he unlocked their wrists. "Time for a shower."

Visions appeared: the history book he'd read in his journalism classes, photos of emaciated naked bodies, the words "gas chamber" in bold letters. Luciano swallowed. The ground seemed to slip away beneath him, filling him with dizzying fear, but then he felt a tugging hand.

"Come on," Gabriel whispered.

Luciano resisted the pull and was about to warn him when he heard the splash of spraying water. The guard told them to remove their hoods, and the prisoners entered the room together, discarding their soiled clothes in heaps by the doorway. Feet shuffled past in the hall, and he wondered if the women were marching off to another set of showers.

The brightness hurt Luciano's eyes; the icy water stung his skin, and the sliver of soap they gave him smelled of chemicals. He scrubbed himself as if he could slough reality away. But his wounds burned, his bruises still felt tender, forcing him to abandon the soap as he flinched in pain and shock. It looked like his body had gone through a grater.

He squinted across the room and noticed the guards' backs were turned. "Gabriel," he whispered. "What sort of work do you do?"

Some muscle still clung to Gabriel's thin arms and torso, which bore only a few faded marks. Gabriel's nakedness drew Luciano's eyes downward, but he quickly looked away.

"I compile military documents."

"You mean you help them?"

"Better than this inferno."

Luciano rinsed the suds from his hair as he considered this. He leaned in. "Could you get me a job?"

Gabriel ran his hands across his scruffy jaw. "What do you study?"

"Journalism."

"Oh, me too."

"Please, I—"

A hand came down hard on Luciano's back. "I said no talking!" The guard smacked him, knocking him against the wall. He shoved Gabriel, who tumbled into Luciano, and they fell to the floor in a slippery mess of limbs while cold water battered their eyes. As they got up, Luciano kept his head down. But once they had dressed and put their hoods back on, Gabriel managed a single word. "Number?"

With his head still spinning, Luciano couldn't figure out what Gabriel meant. But it came to him as they trudged down the hall: the instructions from the basement. *Number five-seven-four. Don't forget.*

Just before they returned to their separate cells, Luciano traced the three digits on the back of Gabriel's neck.

WHEN the traffic outside had grown still for quite some time, Luciano understood that night had fallen. Soon, two people walked down the hall, stopping at the next cell. The guard locked the door to his right, and through the thin wall partition, Luciano could hear someone slide down onto the mattress. He eased himself up against the partition, flexing his toes over and over as he waited for the guard to be out of earshot. "Gabriel?"

"I'm here." Gabriel paused. "You're in."

Luciano clutched his hands to his chest in relief. "Doing what?"

"Translating documents. You speak English, don't you?"

"Well, I've studied it a bit."

"Shh!"

The guard paced past their cells, trailing fresh cigarette smoke. The boots halted in front of his door, but Luciano feigned sleep. Even after the guard left, he kept his mouth shut, unwilling to endanger Gabriel's life more than he already had.

"Luciano? They'll get us at six thirty. Be ready."

Given that he had no change of clothes, no way of grooming and no alarm clock, Luciano wasn't sure what "ready" could mean, but he thanked Gabriel. They both fell silent, and soon he heard soft snores beside him. Only then did he realize that Gabriel had found out his name. He lay down on his back, imagining he could see through the hood, through the ceiling, straight up to the Southern Cross in the starry sky.

CHAPTER SEVEN

MARIJKE
AUGUST 2, 1943
BUCHENWALD

SOMEONE WAS SHAKING ME. "MARIJKE!"

Certain I was dreaming, I rolled over, but the shaking persisted.

"Marijke, wake up!"

I opened my eyes to find the brothel supervisor standing over my bed. A light shone in the hallway but Sophia was whistling through her nose in her sleep.

"I need you right now," the supervisor said. For once, her tired face looked soft, almost friendly.

The brothel had closed hours earlier and the prisoners were all asleep in their blocks, which could mean only one thing. "Is someone here?"

She nodded. "Get dressed."

Suddenly, I was wide awake. "Kommandoführer Hoffmann?"

"Somebody far more important, the new Schutzhaft-lagerführer. Go freshen up and don't keep him waiting."

I put on my heels and white pleated skirt and hurried to the koberzimmer. That familiar pang returned to my stomach while I stood over the sink, trying to smooth out the wrinkled fabric and rinse away all traces of sleep. With a fresh coat of bright lipstick, the face in the mirror looked like a pitiful version of myself, like I had wilted under heavy rain. This feeling of self-disgust grew stronger every day; a hundred prisoners would have been more tolerable than another SS officer.

When the Schutzhaftlagerführer stepped across the threshold, the first thing I noticed was his stagger. Neither Theo nor I drank, but I'd seen alcohol transform men on the streets back home—provoking catcalls and heated brawls—and was terrified of what it could do to someone who was a monster from the start. He grabbed my arm and hooked me in. The beer on his breath stank as he smothered me with a kiss, but his voice sounded crisp. He said hello and leaned back to look at me. A scar carved a slight gap in his right eyebrow. That's when I caught the shade of his irises, a brilliant, striking blue—the colour of gas flames. "You," he said, "you're going to help me forget a rough day." He brushed a curl from my face with startling tenderness.

I took a step back.

"Are you afraid of me?" he asked.

"No."

"Are you sure?" Amusement danced in the faint creases around his eyes, an expression that chased away my sense of caution. He looked like the boys in the village where I grew up, teasing, begging for admiration. For a moment, my fear disappeared.

"The Führer has already taken everything away from me. I have nothing left to lose."

"Don't be foolish. There's always something left. You have your looks, this perfect body." He motioned for me to take off my clothes and spin in a slow circle. I obeyed, trying not to shiver as he smiled, measuring me up. His gaze left no part of me untouched. "The most beautiful girl I've seen at Buchenwald."

"There's no need to flatter me, sir."

"Don't you appreciate it?"

"With all due respect, you're not here to court me."

He smirked, his face full of desire. "You know, I could have you killed for that mouth of yours."

I winced, wondering if I'd misjudged him, but his tone sounded more flirtatious than threatening. He stepped forward, grabbed my bottom as he kissed me. He took off his cap to expose a head of dirty-blond hair, parted neatly to the side. There was something urgent in the way he kissed me, as if he were the one that death had in his sights.

Compared to Bruno, he was gentle. At one point, he stopped thrusting to bend toward my neck, scattering soft kisses that sent a pulsing shock down below. His lips rough and chapped against my skin. "Do you like that?"

None of the other men had shown any concern for me, any awareness that I was more than just their toy, so I didn't know what to make of this. He just wanted to feel powerful, that he could control my pleasure as well as my body. A small gasp served to stoke his fire, to hurry things up. His thumb pressed hard into my arm as he pushed himself deeper. I waited for it all to end, for him to get up so I could return to my own bed and try to slip into the comfort of dreams. Closing my eyes, my violin in my hands. The piece I was practicing the week the moffen arrested us, Theo reaching out to touch my waist, tea steaming beside us on the kitchen table.

He finished with a deep grunt and collapsed on top of me, trapping me under his heaving chest. But he didn't leave, not right away. When he pulled out, he lay beside me, cradling me in his arms. Drops of his sweat clung to my back and I tried hard to ignore the growing wetness between my legs as he stroked the dip of my waist. For a few long minutes, he said nothing. His breath grew so shallow that I thought he'd drifted to sleep, but as I twisted to look at him, his eyes snapped open.

"You are gorgeous," he said. "What's your name?"

He smiled when I told him. "Such a lovely name. I'm Karl, Karl Müller."

His touch on my spine, vertebrae awakened one by one. Shivers. I tried not to notice.

"You know, I've seen you before," he said.

"Isn't that the type of line you ought to save for some girl in town?"

"I mean it. You immediately struck me as being different from the others."

"Probably because they have experience."

"No, something more than that. You're the only one who still has some light in her. Even the girls back home wear the war on their face." He sighed and rubbed a finger across my knuckles. "Tell me, Marijke, what is it you do back home?"

"I'm married."

"Ah, I see. Well then, is there anything you do just for yourself?"

"No."

"Nothing?"

"Music, then. I play violin and used to play with the symphony."

"Violin? Classical? I prefer cabaret. Have you heard Zarah Leander playing over the loudspeakers each morning?"

"I hear nothing in her songs but endless love for the Reich."

He laughed. "Well then, what would you rather hear: Wagner? Beethoven?"

"Schubert."

"Not a second's hesitation? If only my men spoke with such conviction." He laughed. "I'll see what I can arrange."

He wrapped me tighter while I debated the meaning of that, puzzled over his feigned sense of interest.

"It's been so long since I've lain next to someone," he said. "Isn't it unfortunate to have a large bed in a splendid villa but nobody to share it with?"

My mind flashed to the bunks at Ravensbrück, to lifeless limbs pressed up against mine, and angry retorts built up in my throat, eager to spill out. He didn't even appear to notice the lash of his remark, and that was the worst part. His breathing grew deeper as he drifted to sleep. I had trouble relaxing in his arms.

Later, after he woke up and got dressed, he lingered at the exit. "I want to see you again."

I said nothing, thinking only of the cool fabric of my pillow, Sophia snoring beside me.

"Do you agree to that?"

"Does it matter? I thought the officers had their own brothel."

"You're right." He opened the door and took a step before turning to look at me once again. "Next time, I'll bring you a violin."

THE following morning, once we had finished all the cleaning, the brothel supervisor came into the day room with a bag of yarn. "Winter comes early to the Eastern Front," she said. "I want a pair of socks from each of you by tomorrow morning."

After she left, we all sat down around the long table, and Sophia passed out knitting needles. I unwound a ball of yarn to cast on.

Edith twirled one of the needles between her fingers with a grunt. "By tomorrow morning? Clearly, the only thing that woman ever knits is her brow!"

The others snickered, but I focused on counting stitches and found myself drifting away from the room, back to the night before. That SS officer, so unlike the first, the flashes of gentleness in his touch. His talk of music had surprised me, leaving me with the inapt notion of a refined man. I had flushed my memories of every other visit, of the men's prickly chests and moles and bodily fluids, but the images of this officer refused to be erased. They settled there, making Theo feel even farther away.

"Marijke. Did you hear me?" Gerda said. "I asked what's wrong. You look like you didn't sleep."

Sophia gave the others a sober look. "Marijke had to take care of an SS man late last night, and not just anybody either—the Schutzhaftlagerführer."

Everyone turned to me. "What was he like?" one girl asked.

"Did he brag about all the Jews he's killed?" asked another, with a mix of curiosity and contempt.

Edith raised an eyebrow. "Was the gun in his trousers as big as the one in his holster?"

"Eighteen," I counted, raising my voice. "Nineteen, twenty, twenty-one." I didn't meet their stares until I finished knitting that row. "He wasn't what you would expect."

"What does that mean?" Edith asked.

I shrugged. "I don't know."

Sophia gave me a pitying look and tried changing the subject. "Tell us, Edith, what's the trick to getting the smell of sex off your skin? No matter how much soap I use between visits, I still feel the sweat of those men caking on in layers."

Edith hesitated for a second, as if she wanted to push me more, but she took the bait. We had already gathered how much she, more than the other experienced prostitutes, loved to show off. "Lemon," she responded. "A dab of lemon behind the ears and some rosewater. Of course, that's a little tough to come by here."

Sophia looked like she was sucking up every word. "And how about some lines we could use to make things more tolerable?"

"You mean, you want to speed things up a bit?" She winked. "The key, ladies, to making a man squirm with desire is flattery and fakery. Whether or not they'll admit it, every fellow has an ego that needs stroking as much as his member." She grabbed a tall glass from the table and held it to her mouth suggestively. "Mm, *Herr* Kommandant, two hands just aren't enough for a cock like yours. Look at the way you fill me up! Why, yes, of course I came!"

Sophia blushed and even I had to laugh at her ridiculous performance. She carried on with exaggerated exclamations until we all reached a fit of giggles. I chucked a ball of yarn at her head. "Now I've completely lost count."

"There was a man who kept coming to see me in Berlin," she said. "He visited on Sundays, when his wife saw her Latin tutor, and he loved to be dominated. He would travel a full hour to come see me. The next thing I knew, he wanted to buy me a house. A house! So he could always drop in, any time he liked."

"And what happened?" Gerda asked. "You have a secret palace you haven't told us about?" She touched her hand to her throat, like she was feeling for a long-lost string of pearls.

"No. The war came and he enlisted straightaway. I heard he returned from Russia a year later without any legs. He never came back to see me, so I have a feeling that's not all he lost, either."

We were quiet then. In the other room I could hear the brothel supervisor gossiping with the cashier. I noticed a hole where I had dropped a stitch. "I'm worried these socks might end up too small."

One of the Polish girls tsked. "My mother once made me a pair of socks that were too tight. They gave me blisters so raw I had to hobble home from school."

I put down my knitting and leaned in, lowering my voice. "Actually, that may not be a bad thing. What do you say, ladies, up for a little sabotage?"

Sophia tapped her fingers against her lips and gestured toward the other room. "What if they notice?"

"We'll be subtle. Just tighten them a bit in the heels and we'll have part of the Wehrmacht limping its way across Russia."

The others grinned. Sophia nodded, and then she also joined in. Our knitting needles clacked away, and for the first time all morning, I could close my eyes without seeing a stranger's body overhead.

CHAPTER EIGHT

KARL
AUGUST 2, 1943
BUCHENWALD

I N THE BEGINNING OF AUGUST, THE KOMMANDANT decided the camp was overflowing with "undesirables," men no longer fit for hard labour. Karl agreed to oversee their execution. The execution room lay in the basement of the crematorium, a spot he tried to avoid. The smell of burning flesh was overpowering, like sulphur and charred liver, so thick he could almost taste it. As he entered the building that morning, shards of bones and a thin layer of ash covered the floor like dirty snow.

A Jew loaded a corpse onto the steel trolley cart. Rigor mortis had taken hold of the body, and one leg jutted out to the side, preventing it from sliding into the oven. The Jew tried to adjust it before picking up a wooden mallet and bringing it down on the limb. The leg broke with a crack.

"You there," Karl said.

His head snapped up as Karl pointed to the floor.

"Get this filth cleaned up."

The inmate went to retrieve a broom and Karl walked past him, avoiding the bodies stacked nearby. A tangle of pale limbs like raw chicken legs. Some had begun to rot, and the skin was a greyish green.

Three guards waited for him downstairs. The execution room consisted of a long hall, divided by concrete pillars. Streaks of red tarnished the white walls.

He turned to the guard closest to him. "When was the last time you painted here? I want this place kept tidy."

The man, short and apish, stood with his weight cocked to one side. "With all due respect, there's no sense in painting over it. We wouldn't be able to keep pace."

"Take that as an order. And straighten up—show some respect."

The man nodded at another guard who appeared in the stairwell and then left. Moments later came the pounding of footsteps overhead. A single, high-pitched wail. Karl's gaze rose to the metal hooks that lined the walls, two and a half metres high, the kind a butcher would use to hang a pig carcass. A hollow clang brought a tumble of prisoners down a chute and the three guards approached them. Wooden clubs bashed at the blue-and-white stripes, clobbering the prisoners. Men with white whiskers, boys too young to grow a beard, all of them so gaunt and brittle they hardly looked alive. The cries grew louder, and one inmate glanced straight at him: the look of an ensnared rabbit. Karl turned away.

Once they had drawn blood, the guards dropped their clubs. They grabbed for the prisoners one by one and together hoisted each up against the wall with the help of a stepladder. Not one inmate struggled. Karl hated them for that. Resigned to their deaths. The guards slipped nooses over their necks and fastened these to the meathooks. Most of the prisoners suffocated slowly. As they dangled there, some looked at Karl. He saw no pleading in their eyes, no desperation. Emptiness. A rush sent his head reeling, and he could feel himself starting to gag. He turned on his heel and moved for the stairs.

"Everything all right, Schutzhaftlagerführer?" one of the guards asked.

"You've done well. I've seen enough."

KARL had no appetite for the rest of the day. Not wanting to be alone with his thoughts, he decided to eat at the SS officers' mess, which was serving his favourite supper, schnitzel with spätzle, but he consumed nothing but water. Each time he reached for a piece of bread, a potato wedge, he thought of those dangling bodies. He fingered the skull insignia on his hat and reminded himself that he believed in Brandt's approach to the camp labour. He believed in the Führer, in the Reich.

His lips cracked where he had bitten them. Water did nothing to hide the taste of blood. One of the other SS officers came by with two steins. Beer sloshed over the brims as he set them down. "Looks like you could use this, Müller." The guard was a redhead named Ritter whose spectacles were always dirty.

Word was that he'd spent some time living in America, where he'd picked up a bad habit of casual address.

Karl opened his mouth to reprimand him but thought better of it. "Exactly what I need." He took a swig, savouring the smooth coldness. He took another sip and another, until the day's events slid into the bellows of his stomach. He was back in a beer hall in Munich, laughing with friends, women at their sides.

Ritter put his elbows on the table. "How are you at cards?"

"I don't gamble."

"Eight o'clock in the officers' lounge. Come join us."

His beer was half-empty, but his appetite had returned, and he wondered if the cook had any leftover schnitzel. "I should eat something."

"As you like." Ritter stood and reached for his beer. "But coming from someone who has been here a while, it's a good distraction."

THREE tankards of beer rolled around Karl's empty stomach. He fanned out the cards in his hand. Two pairs: kings and sevens. The other four men looked down at their lot with poorly masked disappointment. All of them his inferiors. He considered that he ought to have spent the evening with the Kommandant, drinking wine and bathing him in charm. At least he had a decent hand.

He pushed a stack of poker chips into the centre of the table. Ritter's chair creaked as he leaned back, and Karl's own seat felt wobbly. Another officer, Kommandoführer Hoffmann, counted out chips until his stack was as tall as Karl's and then added three more. He had the mug of a bulldog with heavy frown lines. The corners of Hoffmann's mouth twitched as Karl debated his move.

"You think I'll fold," Karl stated.

"I haven't said a word."

"How long have you been at Buchenwald, Hoffmann?"

"Since it opened."

Karl rotated a chip between his thumb and forefinger, its grooves digging into his skin. "And based on your experience, what is your opinion of the camp?"

"I don't know how you expect me to answer that, sir."

"You seem like the type of man who would be happier out at the front, charging against the Tommies, blowing things up."

Hoffmann hesitated. "The work we're doing here is essential to German prosperity."

"Indeed, and I suppose you do still get some excitement, with the occasional execution."

Ritter and the others exchanged uneasy glances while Hoffmann cleared his throat. "They get what they deserve."

"Yes, we all know they're here for a good reason. Tell me, have you ever had to kill anyone yourself?"

A shake of Hoffmann's head gave way to silence, so Karl took another sip of beer and counted out the extra chips. They clinked together as they fell. The men leaned in as the two of them flipped over their cards. Triple eights. Karl clasped his hands and shoved the chips toward Hoffmann, who gave a nod of recognition while the others stayed quiet.

"You have me beat," Karl said. "What else do you do for fun around here?"

The men threw out options: go into town, the cinema, drink, the brothel.

"I've tried the brothel," Karl answered. "Dull girls, nothing like the ones back home."

Ritter clapped Hoffmann on the back. "Our man here tested out the new brothel last week."

"New brothel?"

Hoffmann looked like a boy caught stealing apple pie. "It just opened. Pretty decent girls, but the good part is that they're a fresh bunch. They're meant for the prisoners, but the supervisor will look the other way if you slip her a few marks." He reddened. "Not that you would need to, of course."

Karl raised his stein to his lips and swished a mouthful of beer as he debated the idea. Brandt had mentioned the prisoners' brothel: *Himmler's pet project*, he'd called it. Himmler believed that the best way to increase the productivity of the camp labourers was to introduce a reward system for the more privileged prisoners. Cigarette vouchers, visits to the prisoners' cinema. The brothel was the top prize. Those girls Karl had seen outside the property depot had to belong to this new brothel.

Between drinks, the image of those bodies returned. Bruised, gasping. He needed to erase those thoughts for good and decided a fresh, ripe girl would do the trick. "One more drink," he said.

Hoffmann jumped up to get the beers. After he left, Ritter laughed. "He doesn't know how to handle a superior who looks him in the eye."

"Just because I'm playing a round of cards doesn't make you my equals."

Ritter shut up. Nobody spoke until Hoffmann returned. The cards lay discarded on the table, so they sat and drank while the conversation stayed on women and sex. Ritter went on about a girl he'd left back home, worried she was straying. Karl stopped listening. The fizz in the beer was making him belch, and he kept blinking to bring the table into focus. Everything felt fuzzy. A naked woman, that's what he needed. A round ass to squeeze, breasts to fondle.

He swallowed the last of his beer and stood up. "That's it for me."

Ritter raised his stein. "Enjoy your nightcap."

BY the time Karl found the prisoners' brothel, tucked near the back of camp and across from the infirmary blocks, it was past eleven. Only one of the brothel windows was illuminated, and he paused at the entrance, bracing himself against the concrete stairs while he banged on the door.

A curt female voice called out, "We're closed."

"Open up."

The door opened a crack. A tall vixen of a woman stood there, red lips pursed. She looked him up and down before inviting him in. "Schutzhaftlagerführer Müller. I don't believe we've had the pleasure."

Her hand was cold, but he held it an extra second. He would have happily taken a turn at her as well, but there was something hostile about her he didn't trust. "I've come to see one of your ladies."

"Are you aware there's an officers' brothel?"

"I am."

"The girls are all sleeping." Her eyebrows peaked, but the buzz that had set in told him not to back down.

"Bring me the most attractive one. No, wait, is one of them Dutch?"

She looked like she wanted to say something but instead rushed off. Karl took a seat in the waiting room. Five minutes later, she returned. "She's ready for you, although we normally require visitors to get an injection."

"I'll have none of that."

"The doctor isn't here at this hour, in any case."

"Aren't your girls clean?"

"We take every precaution, sir, and they are new recruits, but you understand there's always a risk." She led him down a corridor filled with doors, stopping at the one labelled "9." "Here you go."

He pushed open the door. The Dutch girl stood in front of him in a low-cut blouse and slim skirt. She smiled coyly, folding her hands in front of her like a woman in line for ration coupons. The same girl he'd hoped for, all right, but he hadn't anticipated some show of virginal modesty. He walked over, pulled her in to taste her. She blushed, and colour flared down to the beauty mark left of her chin. Her lips parted, asking for another kiss. That morning—the broken limbs and suffocating gags—blurred into the background.

"You," he said, "you're going to help me forget a rough day."

Karl brushed aside her dishevelled hair to get a better look. The beer lurched in his stomach. A pretty girl, but nothing spectacular. Flecks of gold sparked across big green eyes. Her breasts swelled from the neckline of her blouse. Modest, but the perfect size to cup. That inviting cleft between them. His blood started rushing, but she shrank back and fiddled with her skirt.

"Are you afraid of me?" he asked.

"No."

"Are you sure?"

She raised her chin and made some snide remark about being swindled by the Reich. Had one of his colleagues been in his place, they would have given her a well-deserved lashing, but she spit those words with venom, that same alluring determination he'd caught the other day. A flash of colour in all the grey.

"Don't be foolish." He granted her a chuckle before waving at her to undress. She turned in a circle to show off a slim figure, pearly legs that stretched on and on. Her ribs poked out at awkward angles, making him wonder why they couldn't even feed the whores a proper diet, but a splatter of freckles on her lower back pointed down to a peachy ass. He wanted to grab it but tried to calm down, hoping to draw out the night's distraction as much as possible.

When he tried to compliment her, she bristled and gave a saucy reply. But that just made him want to kiss her again, to feel the heat of her tongue against his skin. His hands felt empty without her breasts. "You know, I could have you killed for that mouth of yours."

She went quiet, and he reached for her, pleased by the power of his words. His lips ran up her shoulder, but on meeting the tender spot at the back of her neck, his erection flagged. The sharp point of those meat hooks. Five, six dangling bodies. How easy it was to take a life.

He reached round to spank her and pulled her close, kissing her hard to fight off those images. He drew her hand under his belt, her touch cool against the heat of his body. Her fingers were the type you'd see in a cigarette ad, long and slender, but she fumbled with the buckle, chewed her lip, pushed instead of pulled. His hand closed around hers, guiding it up and down until a groan escaped him. Under the harsh light, her legs glowed. Clutching her shoulder, he entered her, bit the lobe of her ear, bent to kiss her chest. The scent of soap clung to her skin. He was desperate to keep going, speed up and give in to the pleasure. But he needed to last, to take his mind away from that camp.

His hands on her hips. Sweat gathering on her collarbone, at his temples. Kissing her, thrusting deeper, faster, hungry for her. Her legs tensed, spurring him on. He pulled them wider apart, buried his face in the crook of her neck, licked her there and growled into her hair as a pulse within him shuddered into a quake, the heat leaving his body. Finally, he let it all go.

Two days later, rain poured down outside his office window, and the light flickered as he tried to get comfortable in his straight-backed chair. A stack of papers sat in front of him, cataloguing the latest output from the camp armaments factory, but as he scanned the budget, his thoughts kept returning to the prisoners' brothel. The night played over and over. He'd slept with far more attractive women, but this one, Marijke, stayed on his mind. Her bare body in his hands. Goose pimples on her breasts. It was her lips that kept drawing him back to that moment, lips spewing angry, prickly words—such a mouth for a feeble-looking girl. She was the first prisoner at camp who treated him like a regular person instead of someone to fear, but he couldn't take her seriously with that adorable, guttural accent. She had pluck but wasn't cold like the brothel supervisor. Something about her kept him permanently aroused, the way she'd erased those unpleasant images from his head. Karl reached for his schedule. Thursday night he had an officers' dinner, and Friday a meeting in Weimar. Saturday, he would see her.

ON a quiet morning, Karl left his office before lunch and walked over to the camp sculpture studio. The air inside was thick with dust, a welcome change from the sour rot and decay that hung outdoors. His boots trampled over wood shavings and powder as he approached the work table, where an eagle was emerging wing-first from a block of marble. He could tell it would be a majestic creature and pictured the swastika it would soon clutch in its talons.

An inmate chipped away at the stone. He watched from a distance of a few metres until the sculptor glanced up and his fist stiffened around the chisel. Although the sculptor's shaved hair was barely greying, he hunched like an old man, with spectacles perched at the tip of his nose. White smudges covered his cheeks and the blue-and-white stripes of his uniform, which bore the Star of David.

"I've seen some of the work the artists here have done for other officers," Karl said. "You have an eye for detail."

"Thank you."

While any other inmate would have avoided his gaze, this man met it without hesitation. Karl thought there was something familiar about his stare, something hard but hollow, eyes like machine gun shells.

"I need a statement piece for the entryway of my villa."

"What did you have in mind, sir?" The sculptor took a step sideways, revealing a row of projects in various stages of completion. Two carvings, a porcelain platter, an enormous canvas filled with a family tree. An old oak, by the looks of it. The branches stretched outward to let prominent Aryan names nest on the limbs. Brandt's name wrapped around the trunk with a flourish. A centrepiece for his study, Karl imagined.

"I'd like a statue." At his family's summer home in Bavaria, a bronze nymph danced between the garden hedges, overlooking the lake. He and his friends used to slide their hands along her curves, rub her breasts until the bronze wore off at her nipples. When his mother noticed, she had gone straight to his father, who had given him a stern look across the wire-rims of his spectacles and then winked.

He realized it was his father the sculptor resembled. Those curved shoulders, the droop of his eyelids, and the deadpan expression that seemed to mask some darkness. That day in the garden had occurred only weeks before his father had set off for battle on the Western Front. He had returned home with trench foot and a long bar of medals on his lapel but had never smiled at Karl again.

"A statue that pays tribute to our great German forefathers," Karl added.

"Perhaps an eagle?" The prisoner lowered his eyes to Karl's waist, and Karl looked down to find his fingers fidgeting absently with the holster at his belt, where his Luger sat loaded and ready. He patted the gun and leaned in as a side door opened. Five prisoners entered. At the sight of him, they moved to their places, one behind a half-finished bust, and another three beside a large kiln. The sculptor shifted as if to hide the fifth person, who bent low over a table cluttered with pens and ink.

"Who is that?" Karl asked.

The sculptor began to twist one hand around his wrist. "My son."

"Bring him here."

The figure rose and came forward. The boy was probably no more than fourteen or fifteen, but his body caved in upon itself, making him appear almost half that age. The skin of his cheeks looked as thin and transparent as the tissue paper that the department store in Munich used to wrap shoes. Karl couldn't help but pity him, although he felt guilty for thinking that. "You work here?" he asked.

"Yes, sir."

"Is that so? A young body like yours is better suited to the quarry. Show me something you've made."

The boy pointed to the family tree. "I painted most of that."

The brushstrokes were assured, the design solid, so unlike Karl's schoolboy endeavours: snow dogs that had toppled over as he tried to sculpt a tail, a lopsided sketch of the Reichstag.

"Tell me," Karl said, "if you could carve anything, what would it be?"

"Sir?"

"Do I need to repeat myself?"

The boy's voice wavered, and he stood up straighter. "Wood or stone, sir?"

Karl thought of the forests in Bavaria, of towering silver firs and pines. "Wood."

The boy played with the cuff of his prisoner's uniform as he considered his answer. "I would think," he said at last, "a bird would be nice."

"I don't want an eagle, something different."

A faraway expression consumed the boy, as if he had left the confines of the camp and returned home. For a brief moment, Karl wondered where that was, although it didn't matter anymore.

"No, not an eagle. An owl."

Once, in the dead of winter, a tawny owl had crossed Karl's path. Even though it was a quiet evening, he hadn't heard a sound as it swooped down on its prey. The owl left a perfect outline of its wings in the fresh snow. A feeling of calmness and awe had passed over him as it retreated into the trees, leaving with the same stealth and grace as it had appeared.

Karl cleared his throat and turned back to the sculptor. "Excellent, you will carve me an owl—a strong, dignified one. And your son will help."

THE following evening after roll call, Karl went to inspect one of the blocks in the Little Camp. The wooden barracks blocks there lacked windows, and almost a thousand inmates crammed into the one he was set to inspect. On the shelves that served as bunks, men packed together like matchsticks. Rampant dysentery depleted the incoming labour force before it even arrived at the munitions factory.

The block reeked like stale sweat and vomit. Covering his mouth with a handkerchief, he completed the inspection as quickly as possible, avoiding the throng that parted as he crossed the creaky floorboards. He tried to replace their pocked faces with scenes from Leni Riefenstahl's films—bearded rabbis swindling honest men, ragged Gypsies snatching from German pockets. After briefing the Blockführer on how to handle the dysentery outbreak, he ducked out of the block and circled around it to leave the Little Camp. He checked his watch, already counting down the time until he could return to the brothel, to Marijke's soft legs and warm, inviting mouth.

That was when he noticed the painting. A mountainous landscape spread across the lower-right corner of the outside block wall. The remnants of a castle turret caught the light of a morning sun and the blue paint glistened against the damp, rotting wood. With a frown, he touched the outline of a foothill. Who had painted it? His initial thought was an artist from the sculpture studio; they were the only ones with easy access to paint, but a barbed-wire fence separated the Little Camp from Buchenwald proper. Someone in quarantine must have somehow pilfered art supplies. The rich earthy palette reminded him of the beautiful peaks and hiking trails in the Bavarian Alps, the smell of freshly baked pretzels after a day of skiing. He turned away from the block and continued on without any investigation. After all, it was just one painting.

BRANDT called Karl into his office the next day. Karl stood in front of his desk and waited for him to speak, trying to ignore the itch of his officer's tunic, which was far too thick for the summer heat.

"Well." Brandt stopped to take a puff of his cigar. "What did you think of Monday's executions?"

"It was quite an experience, sir."

Brandt tapped off the ash. "All week, you've looked very . . . anxious. Are you sure you're cut out for life here?"

Karl thought of his father, how much he was counting on him to perform well, to make the family proud. "Of course. I've just always been behind a desk, up until now. Give it another week, and I'll have made the adjustment."

"I hope so. On a different note, what's the status on the new camp vandal? Have you found him?"

"What do you mean, sir?" As soon as the question left Karl's mouth, he recalled the painting. He'd hoped the maintenance Kommando would remove the artwork but should have known the matter would come back to haunt him.

"That graffiti made a mockery of me." Brandt sat up straight and smacked the stack of papers in front of him. "Next they'll try to smear the block walls with their Zionist hogwash."

"What would you like me to do, sir?"

"Deal with it." He motioned for Karl to leave, but stopped him at the door. "Make an example out of the culprit. I don't want to see any more of this in my camp."

Karl walked back to the officers' quarters, his Luger heavy against his hip. His pace slowed with each step. As he approached the villas, he glanced at the place next to his. The children of another officer played house on the balcony, their dolls spread out around them as they giggled.

HE found the boy kneeling outside the entrance to the sculpture studio, whittling away at a large chunk of wood. When the boy saw him coming, he moved out of the way. "Your owl, sir."

The bird perched on a jagged stump a half-metre high. It was still a crude outline, but the tail feathers had taken shape. Karl's attention turned to the boy, whose hands were blistered from the knife. The rusty blade lay on the ground. "What happens to these carving knives when you aren't working?"

"They are taken at the end of each day."

"And the painting supplies?"

The boy stiffened. "Those too."

"Why do you think we keep an art studio at Buchenwald?"

"I don't know, sir."

"Give me an answer."

The boy squinted into the sun. "Maybe everyone needs a bit of beauty in their life."

"Everyone worthy of art, you mean. Those loyal to the Reich." Karl thought of Marijke, her love of the violin, and how much pleasure it gave him to anticipate her reaction to the surprise he was arranging. But that was different; she was different.

The boy dug his toe into the dirt. He'd been issued a bulky pair of wooden clogs. "Yes, sir."

"Good." Karl gave him what he hoped was a threatening look. "That owl better be in my sitting room within twenty-four hours."

Karl left the boy and continued his morning round. A thought came to him while passing the Little Camp. He worked his way around the perimeter of the fence, pushing aside tall stalks of weeds, searching for troughs in the dirt. His trousers snagged on one of the barbs, and on loosening the fabric, he nicked his finger. Searching in his pocket for something to act as a bandage, he spotted a pile of scrap metal and an old tire a few metres down the fence. As he rolled the tire away, a colony of ants scattered out over the toes of his boots. Sure enough, behind the debris was a gap in the wire just big enough for a boy.

As Karl left the brothel that evening, the clouds parted to reveal a full moon. Aside from the warm breeze that shook the trees and the howls of dogs in the kennel, the night was quiet. He removed his hat to wipe his brow, which felt slick with sweat. His mind was trapped in the lazy trance that follows a good fuck, and he already ached to see Marijke again as soon as possible.

He cut across the compound in the direction of the main gate. The sound of movement came from around one of the two-storey blocks. A glance at the watchtower told him the guards couldn't see the block from their post and he rounded the corner in time to see someone darting away.

"You, there." He switched on his torch. "Stop!"

The prisoner halted, but Karl swore under his breath as he turned around. Even from a distance, the boy's outline was clear. He shone his torch to the side. On the wall to his left, still wet, a field of wildflowers in pink and purple.

The boy stood on the spot, blinded by the light. As Karl strode toward him, his expression shifted from fear to horror. "Did you really think you could keep doing this undetected?"

The tendons in the boy's neck rose until Karl could see his throbbing pulse. "No, sir."

"Why would you risk your life? And that of every person in this camp?"

The boy looked down at the dirt.

"Get out of my sight."

"Pardon?"

"Go."

Without a word, the boy ran off. Karl returned to his villa and asked his servant to run a steaming bath. The servant also set out a fruit basket and a bottle of brandy. For a few private hours, Karl relished the fantasy that he was back home, in a place where the women he bedded were eager, the air pure and alpine fresh, the artists as valued as the art, and where the only orders he had to follow were his own.

IN the morning, he rose to find the owl sitting on his veranda, along with a message from Brandt: *We have the culprit. You're to supervise punishment in the sculpture studio.* He leaned against the wooden pillar of the veranda with the message crumpled in his fist. The owl leered, mocking his stupidity. The Third Reich had risen on the backs of powerful, decisive men—not cowards.

An hour later, two officers accompanied him to the sculpture studio. Upon his order, they lined the artists up against the wall for a flogging. The boy was missing.

Karl pulled the boy's father out of line. "Where is he?"

The prisoner focused on Karl's chest, the corners of his mouth quivering. "He was selected for special treatment."

Karl's throat tightened as he stepped back, knowing full well what that meant. The guards raised their clubs. He opened his mouth to call out and revoke the punishment, but thought of

Brandt's orders, of his father, the highly praised officer. The guards looked at him, and he nodded.

He heard a smack and the shattering of glass as the sculptor's face hit the wall, watched the sculptor's body jerk with each strike. Afterwards, the man knelt to retrieve his spectacles, his shirt torn and bloody as he fumbled around on the dusty floor.

Pushing past the other officers, Karl stepped outside into the glaring light of the sun. A jackrabbit bounded across the gravel road before disappearing into a copse of trees on the other side of the fence. Karl stared ahead at the smoke that poured from the chimney of the crematorium. Then he turned away.

CHAPTER NINE

LUCIANO
MAY 9, 1977
BUENOS AIRES

THE GUARD CAME FOR LUCIANO IN THE MORNING. As usual, Luciano went to eat with the others, but all they received for breakfast that day was a chunk of bread and a lukewarm gourd of maté. He nibbled on the bread, wishing he could stow a piece in his pocket, but he was far too hungry and couldn't risk getting caught.

After they ate, the guard called out a series of numbers: 341, that was Gabriel. At the sound of his own number, Luciano rose. With the hood back on his head, he stumbled over something, probably a foot. Someone grabbed him by the arm. This guard had thin fingers but a taloned grip. Luciano imagined him as a hawk. A friend of his father's used to train hawks outside the city. Luciano had visited once and would never forget the morning he'd woken up to discover a mouse in the aviary, its neck twisted in the hawk's beak as tufts of fur flurried down onto the lower branches.

The small group of prisoners—he'd counted twelve—fell into file. Hawk led them down the corridor until they stopped and started down a long flight of stairs. At the landing, they turned and descended another flight and then another. They came to a flat spot, moved forward, before dropping a few more steps. There was a loud clang in front of them and the creak of hinges. They proceeded across the hard floor and the sudden cool, moist air made Luciano stiffen. His muscles twitched, everything in his body urging him to run. But he had no hope of escape, not with his blindness and guards everywhere, and, besides, Gabriel's hands on his shoulders showed no sign of tension, so he told himself that there must be more to the basement than torture chambers. Noises came from all sides, but without any echo, which made him wonder if the basement contained a series of rooms.

"Workers in the photography lab, step right," Hawk ordered, speaking with a mild lisp.

The person in front of Luciano shifted. Luciano tried to picture prisoners gathering around cameras and film but didn't understand what purpose there would be for photography in such a purgatory. Hawk marched off with that group and different footsteps approached. Without a pair of shoulders to hold, Luciano didn't know where to move, and Gabriel had to push him forward until the guard took Luciano and led him into an abrupt left turn. Then the guard yanked him to the left again. Luciano banged his elbow on something hard. After a few more steps, he felt a tug on his shoulders as Gabriel stopped behind him.

A jangle of metal ran down the line, the guard removing handcuffs. Luciano twisted his wrists, rubbed the skin until the numbness disappeared.

"Hoods off," the guard said. "Take your seats."

Luciano did as he was told. The air felt chilly against his skin after the damp chamber of the hood. He shut his eyes, allowing them to adjust to the light. Fluorescent bulbs overhead buzzed like wasps in a glass bottle. Partitions formed a small room that contained only a few cupboards, a desk and a large table with typewriters where the other prisoners gathered. The far wall had two high vents, which he assumed led outdoors. No daylight pierced the dense metal grilles, but he longed to pull over a chair, to climb up and inhale the smells of autumn: rain-pattered soil or rotting leaves or whatever might lie on the other side of that wall.

Luciano hurried to take the seat next to Gabriel and slumped into the chair, his legs tingling from their sudden use. There were four other detainees. The woman and two of the men looked to be in their twenties or thirties, but the man at the far end was much older. He had a distinguished air about him, even though his face was no less gaunt or grimy. All the men had scruffy beards, but Gabriel's was by far the sparsest. This struck Luciano as odd, but he assumed Gabriel had spent less time imprisoned. The woman sat across from Luciano. Her blank face reminded him of a plaster death mask he'd once seen in a museum.

They stopped fidgeting and straightened up when a balding man in military uniform entered to replace the guard. He carried a stack of documents under his arm, which he distributed systematically. It became clear each person around the table possessed a particular skill. Once everyone else had a file folder, the man came up to Luciano, towering over him so the brass buttons of his uniform were at eye level. He had a wine-coloured birthmark on his neck shaped like the boot of Italy. "Well, it looks like more coward scum knocking at my door. You speak English?"

Luciano swallowed and nodded, fixating on those gleaming buttons in the hope of hiding his nervousness. The braided design of a rope encircled each one like a noose. He swallowed, picturing this tightening around his neck. In exchange for a little relief from torture, he was offering himself as a collaborator.

"Good. So you can translate? We can't afford any sloppy mistakes."

"I'm a journalism student, sir." He tried to keep his voice steady. "But I've studied English literature for years."

"Consider this your test." The man placed a paper-clipped booklet and pen on the table before moving to his desk in the corner.

The others shuffled through their documents. Some fed paper into typewriters, and the room filled with the clicking of keys and a series of chiming dings. Their supervisor sipped a cup of coffee while flipping through a newspaper. Luciano grabbed a fresh sheet of paper and uncapped his pen. The lid bore an anchor with a Phrygian cap and the Sun of May, the emblem of the Argentine navy. At the sight of this, the weight that had lifted when the guard removed his handcuffs returned as a heavy yoke. He realized the orders for these assignments, their very imprisonment, must have been sanctioned by those people working right at the top of the Casa Rosada. As he reached for the booklet, he imagined his hands and feet dangling from strings, flapping in the air as General Videla peered down and grinned beneath his thick moustache. And there, in the audience in front of him, his parents and grandparents and Fabián all watching with shame and disappointment. Luciano hesitated, but the long lesions on his forearms, green with infection, reminded him that collaboration could save his life.

He scanned the letter in front of him. The words slipped away as he stared at the page, wishing he were back in his favourite café, where he composed essays while the candlesticks beside him tapered into waterfalls of congealed wax. The name at the bottom of the letter was John Baxter, the address a street in Washington, DC. Luciano had heard rumours that the American government channelled money to Argentina, blind to the evil of the military junta, but this document contained perfect Spanish. *For the purposes of official business . . . authorized visit . . . United States of America. . . .* He read it over twice before understanding that they needed a translation to create a forgery so they could filter more of their contacts into the United States. Next to him, Gabriel adhered a set of matching photos to various passports: one Uruguayan, one Spanish, one Brazilian. Luciano recognized the person in the photo from the news, a prominent navy commander.

A guard came in with a *medialuna* and a fresh cup of coffee for the supervisor. The two men conversed in low voices, and Luciano took the chance to get a good look at the guard. The hooked curl of the guard's hands and his thin fingers told him it was Hawk. When he turned around, their eyes met. He was probably only eighteen, the type of guy Luciano might run into at the cinema or a rock show. Hawk cocked his head and left the room.

Luciano tapped the pen to get the ink flowing and started on the first sentence of the letter. The language looped itself into knots, and the sentences took time to untangle. *Based on the information submitted by the petitioner, Dr. R. L. London, on December 21, 1976, I take pleasure in informing you that the beneficiary, Mr. Jorge Emanuel Castrol, has been granted a multiple-entry visa for business purposes, effective April 19, 1977.* He skipped over the few words he didn't know in English and was finishing off the second paragraph when music picked up in the hall. A soothing recording of something classical, piano and woodwinds. Luciano pushed aside his surprise and tried to let the music settle his nerves, imagining himself writing a report at the kitchen table to his father's favourite sonata.

The scream came like the glowing tip of a hot poker. A woman's anguished cry followed by another, this one a deep, bellowing moan. "God, no."

The others stayed bowed over their work, pasting and scribbling away while the balding man watched them in amusement. Luciano tried to catch their eyes, but their faces were blank, unreceptive, like he was watching them on a television screen. He lowered his head and stared at his translation. The word "travel" blurred into a fog of blue ink as the woman's screams filled the air, growing louder, more desperate, until at once they cut off, leaving only the sound of the classical recording playing on.

FIFTEEN hours of daily labour, without breaks. On his first day, Luciano learned to estimate time by the television on the other side of the wall partition, which the guards used to muffle the sounds of the tortured if they didn't turn on the music. They raised the volume for the soccer matches and lowered it for the evening news, and so, at certain hours, it served as a clock.

For three days, Luciano threw all his energy into the translations, hoping diligence would distract him from the persistent screams. Three letters of invitation, two visa approvals, and one long-winded article destined for the Associated Press, which boasted about the great strides Argentina had made in extinguishing "the abomination of communism." The article let him practice his journalism skills, and he took some liberties with the translation in order to create what he hoped was elegant, self-assured prose. Once or twice, the tapping of typewriters and the scratching of pencils managed to trick his mind into believing he was back in the university library working on a paper. Between tasks, he dwelled on the meaning of the work he was doing and stole peeks at Gabriel, hoping for reassurance or some acknowledgement of their shared guilt, but Gabriel concentrated on the passports, dabbing a stamp in ink and carefully applying the American seal to visa after visa. Luciano tried to cut through the brambles of guilt, tried to convince himself that translating propaganda wouldn't cause any pain, that a few English sentences couldn't kill anyone, not directly.

When he returned to his cell on the third night, he couldn't sleep. Gabriel's soft snores came from his right and silence from the girl to the left. The footsteps of the guard drifted across the floor, along with the sweet smoke of his menthol cigarette. Luciano took shallow breaths to keep his hood cool. After every shift, he felt like he was entering a sticky Amazon night, where poisonous insects and yellow-eyed creatures hid in the canopy. He felt trapped, unable to run or move at all.

A nearby prisoner called out to the guard, whose strides echoed back down the corridor. A cell opened and something hollow landed on the ground—probably a bottle to piss in—before the door closed again. He rolled onto his back to catch the muted ball of light above him, glowing like a far-off sun. He could still feel the grooves he made on the paper while transcribing the government's lies. With the clench of his jaw, he pushed beyond those thoughts, fumbled around the corners of his mind for something else. A ladder appeared. After propping it up against the basement wall, he unscrewed the cover of a vent, slithered through the hole, across the grass, over the flower beds, down the road, through the city until he reached the steps of his apartment. Standing up, he withdrew the key from his pocket and walked through the front door.

A whimper from the right snapped him from the haze. His muscles tensed again, and he pounded his fists against the mattress, handcuffs rattling. No matter how he tried to lose himself again in memories of Fabián, of his friends and his mother and father, everything hovered around him like those swarming insects.

The night before, he'd rapped on the partition and asked Gabriel if he knew where they were being held. ESMA, Gabriel told him, the Naval School of Mechanics. Luciano had ridden past it on the bus before. The academy formed an enormous complex of white stucco buildings with red-tile roofs, surrounded by a perimeter fence.

Focus. The instructors at journalism school stressed the importance of reporters channelling their ideas. Already, he felt things slipping, memories obstructed by those yellow eyes and shifting shapes. If he couldn't hold on to his own thoughts, he would go crazy. He needed focus.

Long before enrolling in his program, he'd sought his father's approval on one of his early attempts at reporting, a piece about a neighbourhood park overrun with petty crime: bike theft and a vandal who kept painting swastikas on the trash cans. For almost a week, he carried the article around in his book bag, hoping to catch his father in a good mood. That Thursday, his mother took a night shift at the hospital, leaving him and his father to their own devices. Of course, this meant *asado* at the steakhouse a few blocks over. Luciano drummed his fingers anxiously against his chair until the waiter brought out the bread bowl. Then he slid the article across the table. "It's just something I've been working on. I thought you might like to read it."

His father took it without comment and scanned the first paragraph before he stopped, removed his reading glasses and held out the article. "Fascist brainwashing and baby carriages? What are you trying to say here? You can't write anything coherent if you don't know your audience."

Luciano nodded and stuffed the pages back into his bag. They ate the rest of the meal in silence, until his father mumbled some excuse about needing to hurry home to finish checking over his factory reports. Shamed by his father's apparent lack of interest,

Luciano had sulked for days and vowed never again to show his writing to his father, who in turn had never asked.

Luciano lay still in his cell as he considered his father's remark. He imagined the weight of his favourite jade-coloured fountain pen between his fingers, a pad of lined paper in front of him. In his mind, he began to write.

Dear Father,
How could you . . . Dear Father, honestly, what were you think-ing? Dear Father, when they came to take me away, you, you just sat there. Your eyes were so cold, like glaciers. Dear Father, when they came for me, why didn't you try to bribe them, or lie and say I'd spent the night at home? Why didn't you do anything, anything at all? You coward.

The evening of the rally, Mamá had worn her nursing shoes under her skirt as she set the table, making sure to arrange the silverware exactly perpendicular to the table's edge, as Papá liked it. Her hair was tied back the way Papá liked, everything just as he liked it. She kept checking the clock, and when he finally came home from his job at the Opel factory, he pecked her on the cheek and nodded at Luciano before sitting down to eat. Tuesday meant pasta, his nonna's special recipe, which she'd learned to cook as a child in Italy. The aroma of olive oil and thyme filled the kitchen while Mamá prayed, but Papá was fixated on the soccer match on the living room tele-vision. It distracted him for most of dinner, so he probably hadn't noticed how little Luciano ate. When Mamá had asked Luciano about his plans for the evening, Papá had interrupted by slamming his fork down on the table—Boca Juniors had gotten a penalty.

Always caught up in your own world, aren't you? You never . . .
I debated telling you about the rally. But that would have just,
you would have sworn and called me an idiot for sticking out
my neck. "Getting involved will bring nothing but trouble," you
would have said, or "Reckless protestors are asking to be killed."
You would have reminded me of people you'd known in Germany,
the fate of those politicians and artists who tried to defy Hitler.
That might have been enough to make me hesitate, convince me to
stay home. Instead, I left right before the match ended, but you
didn't notice. You didn't even fucking look up as I headed out the
door. I wish I could say that was unusual.

Did his father think Luciano had brought this fate upon himself? He wouldn't be wrong. When Luciano joined the Peronist University Youth—the JUP—he hadn't understood what they were all about. The members treated each other like family, a type of unity and respect he'd never felt at home. They called each other by nicknames—he became "Liebre," because they said he ran like a hare on the soccer field. It was Fabián who had talked him into everything. Luciano knew as much as anyone that Argentina needed change, but he'd seen enough headlines about the Montoneros—parkade bombings, assassinations, gunfights—to be wary of the JUP's tactics.

Dangerous business, taking a stand. You've said it a dozen times.
But, Father, these students have such a strong message. They

promise that, they claim we can initiate change, starting with
students, that universities can serve as a platform to engage the
masses. Instead of just sitting back in fear, watching the country
fall apart, we can act.

Some students organized weapons, just in case, but Luciano had limited himself to the occasional rally. The evening of his capture, they had chanted and marched outside the Congressional Palace until their voices grew ragged. "No more fear!" Sparklers waved around them as Fabián moved to the head of the group to deliver his speech, calling on the military to give the power back to the people. The night had crackled with energy; everyone believed they were on the brink of change.

Father, you don't want to know what . . . Father, I'll spare you
the details of what they've done to me. But I bet you'd be surprised
to hear where they're keeping us—and I say "us" because there
seem to be hundreds of us here, but I couldn't guess the exact
number. It's crazy how many thousands of people must pass this
building each day unaware. The student in the next cell says we're
being held in the officers' quarters, at ESMA. Apparently, there's
another floor of people imprisoned above us in the attic. But I
don't get how these officers live on the floor below us. Some have
their wives and children with them. It just doesn't—how can they
go about their daily lives knowing what surrounds them? Father,
you once said that nobody in this world is truly evil, that it's all
a matter of circumstance. I wonder if you tell yourself that so
you don't have to come to terms with what happened in your own
country. Because how can anyone hear the screams of tortured

women and still sleep at night? How can anyone eat steak and drink Champagne while we starve overhead in soiled clothes? If that's not evil, what is?

Father, they call our floor La Capucha, probably because of these damn hoods. Yesterday, when I called out to go to the toilet, a guard kicked me, fucking kicked me in the head! "You're nobody," he said. "No one is looking for you; nobody cares if you're alive."

Now, tell me: How many times can you hear something like that before you start to believe it?

CHAPTER TEN

MARIJKE
AUGUST 21, 1943
BUCHENWALD

O N HIS SEVENTH VISIT, KARL ASKED IF I ENJOYED
sex with him.

I stared at his bare feet as we lay on the bed. "Yes, sir."
It was only a half lie.

"Sir?" He trailed a finger across my back. "Why won't you
ever say my name?"

At first, I didn't understand. I was showing him the respect
he believed he'd earned. But then I thought of the prisoners, so
many of whom just wanted to be touched, to feel the warmth
of a woman's embrace. Perhaps the life of a Nazi was also lonely.
Karl always entered the koberzimmer with a flinty stare and
rigid movements, but within minutes, something in him would
soften, the warmth returning to his eyes. The gentleness that
followed felt like it belonged to a different man, someone he'd

buried within. Even if that were the case, no one who could tear apart a family or kill the innocent deserved to be treated as an ordinary man.

Karl cleared his throat. "There's a reason I keep coming here. I'm not visiting any of the other girls, not here or in the SS . . . facilities."

"Whorehouse."

"Marijke."

"That's what it is, whether or not you're paying for it."

He turned my chin to meet his. "Do you think of me as the sort of man who's chasing a piece of meat?"

"Do you want me to answer that honestly?"

With a sharp sigh, he dropped his hand from my cheek. "I don't know why I even care what you think."

On the floor across the room, his pistol lay on a pile of clothes, the barrel pointed right at me. How would it feel to pick it up, to line up all the guards, the top SS men, and avenge the innocent one by one? The idea was as tantalizing as it was unnerving. Karl got up, but I watched the angry motions of his wrists as he fastened his boots, as he turned the doorknob. "Next time, you might not be so lucky. There are a lot of wolves out there."

Two weeks later, I awoke to faint music playing over the loudspeakers. Roll call. But it wasn't Zarah Leander. That day, they were playing Schubert. I smiled despite myself. Surely, it was no coincidence but a gesture from Karl. At breakfast, a package arrived, wrapped in brown paper and marked with my name. In it was a violin.

Never before had I seen such a beautiful instrument. I refused to play on my own accord. My fingers glided over the varnished spruce and I even went so far as to raise the violin to my chin, but the bow stayed at my side. I was afraid of what it could unleash. Tilting it sideways revealed the inscription on the inside and my breath faltered the first time I read and reread it. Made in Naples in 1761 by the renowned luthier Nicolò Gagliano. A priceless instrument, one every violinist would have dreamed of playing. Yet it had slid into my lap, likely ransacked from the home of a Jewish heiress or a flamboyant opera singer, and this realization made me tuck it away out of sight.

KARL made a habit of appearing late at night, after I'd made my way through a line of prisoners, each thinner and more pallid than the last, and none of whom had heard of a quiet history professor named Theo de Graaf. Each passing night weakened my hope of finding my husband, but I never stopped asking. Only privileged prisoners received permission to visit the brothel, meaning our clients had somewhat better health and hygiene than most, which we counted as a small blessing. The other girls had grown used to the brothel routine: the primping, the faked pleasure, the endless swabs for venereal disease. Sophia acquired a sort of beau, a fellow communist named Friedrich, who requested her by koberzimmer number and who smuggled her sausages and flasks of gin. She gushed about him to anyone who would listen. However, the brothel supervisor had caught on and began shifting around our assigned koberzimmers with the hope of stopping such relationships from developing any further.

Karl's visits no longer frightened me. Sober, he acted civil, and there was something that intrigued me in his austere manner, a hidden vulnerability. But he was still the enemy.

I waited for him in the koberzimmer in a lavender silk robe that had arrived the day after the violin, more an expectation than a gift. When he came in, he no longer rushed at me as he had in the beginning. He would tilt my chin, drawing my gaze to his, and kiss me.

In bed, he made no demands. Some nights, he was a wildfire and thrusted with a crazed fury. Other times, his movements were slow and savoured. If I flinched in pain, he would pause until it subsided, and when it was all over, he'd linger, his head on my breast as he recounted his life story. He told me about his rise up through the ranks, his favourable encounter with Himmler, but I preferred memories from before the war, stories about his family estate in Munich, his two wire-haired pointers, Axel and Faust, and his broken engagement. I spent a lot of time trying to imagine his former fiancée, trying to understand what kind of woman could love a man capable of overseeing so much terror.

THE day the first autumn leaves tore from the branches of the trees outside, I caught myself thinking about Karl. There was something so dreary about those orange leaves, the way they flapped in the wind, only to be whipped across the road to the infirmary blocks, where dozens of men were taking their final breaths. I thought of his arms around me, the way they seemed to block out everything until nothing existed outside of that tiny koberzimmer: no battlefields, no camps, no husband. With the other visitors, I could coax myself into some type of trance, a reality far away, but Karl made distraction difficult with all his questions, his unpredictability.

Perhaps he sensed this effect he had on me, for that night he stayed longer than usual, lying at my side and stroking my hair. He was massaging the nape of my neck when he stopped, separating a coil of curls from behind my ear. "My mother used to say grey hair was a crown of glory, proof of a righteous life."

"What are you talking about?"

"You have a few strands of grey."

"I'm not surprised."

"You're far too young for it."

"At Ravensbrück, a twenty-six-year-old went white almost overnight after her sister died of typhus."

He rolled onto his back. "I'm sorry."

This caught me by surprise; it was too late for apologies. "For what?"

"That this is happening to you."

"To me?"

"To your people."

I sat up and glowered at him. "And the Jews? The communists? The Gypsies? What about them?"

"I didn't put anyone in this camp. I just follow orders."

"But you joined the party, so what do you really believe?"

"You know, I used to think—" He stopped short.

"What?"

"No, nothing."

"You can be honest with me, you know."

He hesitated, started to say something and paused before beginning again. "My best friend in primary school was a Jew. Aaron Stein. We sat together in the back row and pierced our fingers with needles so we could be blood brothers." His face clouded. "I shouldn't be saying this. Nobody here knows."

"You think I'm going to turn you in to the Kommandant?"

Karl smiled a little but looked trapped in his own memories. "He was always braver than me, a better explorer. Back then, I wanted only to sit and play with toy soldiers, to charge into battle like my father. Aaron was the one who would scramble onto rooftops and lead us on spy missions through old warehouses."

"What happened to him?"

He swallowed. "I don't know. I don't want to know."

I tried to strain my thoughts, draining away those of Karl and leaving only memories of Theo, but it was no use. Much as I tried to avoid it, his gaze kept locking on to mine, with such intensity in those gas-flame eyes.

"Will you play something for me?" Karl asked.

"The violin is in my bedroom."

"Go get it."

I fastened my robe and slipped into our sleeping quarters. Sophia raised her head curiously as I reached for the violin, but didn't say a word. When I returned, Karl sat against the wall and I noticed he'd put on his underdrawers. He gestured to the instrument. "Do you like it?"

"It's beautiful."

A pleased look passed over his face.

"What would you like me to play?"

"Anything."

As I raised the violin, the trees outside groaned in the wind and the floorboards creaked, seemingly in anticipation. He watched me tune it. I took my time, wondering whether I could still play after so long without practice. But when I closed my eyes and my bow met the strings, the music returned like a summer storm. Chopin: Nocturne, op. 9, no. 2. A piece I'd been working on before we were captured. Soft, gradual notes, like floating in the middle of a lake at twilight, fireflies overhead. The smell of applesauce warming on my mother's wood stove. The rough wool of Theo's sweater as we skated along the canals.

With the bow in my hand, something came back to me, and for a few minutes, I was gone, away from the camp. I felt innocent and indestructible, the woman I had once been. I didn't look at Karl until the piece ended, until the violin was back in its case. The corners of his eyes glistened. He reached for my wrist, coaxed me into his arms and rested his chin against my hair, while I grappled with a mixture of loathing and comfort.

CHAPTER ELEVEN

THE CAMP CINEMA STOOD NEXT TO THE SPOT COR-
doned off for the prisoners' brothel. Like most of the
buildings in the camp, it was long and drab and made of
wood, with nothing to identify it, none of those rows of lights,
the gold lettering or velvet carpet that marked the cinemas in
Berlin. As Karl stood in front of it, he tried to picture Else tugging at his hand in excitement on one of her visits, her mother's
stole wrapped around her shoulders as she scanned the film titles.

To his left, a couple of haggard prisoners lined up at the
steps to the brothel. All of them political prisoners or criminals.
Himmler would never let Jews near the brothel.

Like it had so many times that day, his mind flashed to
Marijke, the flick of her tongue in his mouth, the deep arch of
her back under his fingertips. Something inside him clenched

at the sight of that crowd, the idea that he'd touched the same woman as those delinquents. But he brushed aside the thought, straightened his hat, and went into the cinema. Clusters of SS officers gathered inside the entrance, while others sat on the rows of chairs. The lights were dim, the interior as plain as the exterior, and the hot, stuffy air buzzed with chatter. Brandt called to him from across the hall.

When Karl walked over, Brandt passed him a glass of genever. "Glad to see you, Müller."

Nobody else had a drink. Some of the officers in the back row watched Karl and leaned in to speak amongst themselves. Karl felt a twinge of paranoia, the same apprehension that had once mocked him when he'd joined Boy Scouts late in the season, the only one in the troupe who couldn't build a fire. But the men turned away, shifting their attention to a wooden whipping block that had been shoved into a dark corner between the brooms and an old projector.

Brandt followed his line of sight. "There's not enough storage room for everything this camp needs to run. If our numbers keep swelling, we'll need to think about installing some permanent stocks and gallows."

Karl nodded and took a sip of his drink. "So which film are you screening tonight?"

"One of the great masterpieces of German cinema. We may be far from Berlin, but that doesn't mean you have to miss out on the finer things in life." Brandt swirled the genever in a circle and looked up at Karl over the rim of his glass. His lips were moist. "I'm sure you've seen it, but it would be good for you to watch it again."

Karl debated the meaning of that. "Of course, sir. It will be an honour."

The Kommandant finished his drink and puffed out his chest, the lapel of his uniform splitting to reveal his shirt. He signalled to a man nearby, who hurried off. A moment later, a bell rang, and Brandt ordered everyone to a seat. Karl followed him to the two empty spots in the front row. The lights dimmed and the screen crackled on.

Jud Süss. He had seen part of it before with colleagues in Berlin but had been forced to leave partway through on account of an upset stomach, punishment for a late night of drinking the evening before. The opening credits started rolling to a dramatic musical score. A message appeared: "The events portrayed in this film are based on historical fact." Then a date and place: 1733, Stuttgart—the coronation of Karl Alexander, duke of Württemberg. Banners and garlands covered the city streets, and the commoners cheered, ran to greet the duke as his carriage rolled past. Fancy clothes, a luxurious palace. Soldiers marched by in perfect unison. The music grew eerie and the scene cut to a sign in Hebrew script in the middle of the crowded ghetto. Men with long, unkempt beards, shifty stares. The plot came back to him. The Jew, Süss, agrees to help finance the duke on the condition that he be allowed entry to the city, where Jews had long been banned. Süss shaves his beard and sidelocks, dresses himself like a Christian, and weasels his way up into the duke's inner circle. Tricking and conniving.

He glanced at Brandt, who leaned back, stroking his chin and watching intently while the councilman's beautiful daughter begged the Jew to save her imprisoned husband. Karl hadn't seen this part, and his hand tightened around the arm of his chair as the Jew dragged beautiful Dorothea to his bed, pinning her down and raping her.

Behind him, a couple officers grumbled. "Filthy Jewish pig," said one. "Kill them all," said another.

After the film ended and they returned to their villas, Karl changed into his robe and slippers and retreated to his bedroom with a glass of brandy. In bed, he reached for the book on his nightstand. *Plant Life in Bavaria*—well-thumbed and full of bookmarks for all the trees and shrubs that had caught his attention on his evening walks back home. He flipped through a few pages, trying to find a sketch that resembled the bush that had taken over the veranda of his villa, before putting it down with a sigh.

The door to his wardrobe jammed as he tried to open it. With a little jerk, it came free and he reached for the book that lay in the bottom of his suitcase. The pages weren't as worn as those of the plant guide, though he'd received both the same year. He opened the front cover to study the inscription on the inside:

Karl, we can expect great things from this man. Read this with care. He's the answer Germany has been searching for; I'm sure of it.

Merry Christmas.

Love, Papa.

The closing line was written in his mother's flowery script, as if she had decided to make up for his father's shortcomings in affection. With a sip of brandy, he turned the page and began to read. *Mein Kampf,* by Adolf Hitler. *Volume I: A Reckoning.*

FOR a week, he locked himself in his office night after night, poring over a stack of books and old newspapers at his desk. Articles on the Führer's rise to power, copies of his edicts, of Goebbels' essays and Himmler's speeches. Pamphlet after pamphlet: "The Jew as a World Parasite." "What Does Bolshevization Mean in Reality?" He examined the racial wall charts designed for doctors' offices and read the SS booklet on racial theory twice through. Just as plants and animals differed in species, it claimed, so did humans. Different races inherited different characteristics, which made some more adept for survival than others. The booklet showed a photograph of a German farm on terrain reclaimed from the sea next to a shot of a Russian one on fertile Ukrainian soil. The German farmhouse appeared expansive and sturdy, while the Russians had managed to build only a rickety shack. The text explained that the Jewish race had sprouted from the mixing of a multitude of races, and that the negative traits of these races had come together and magnified through the generations. The Jews were parasites without a home: they latched on to host countries, and adapted to blend in with the locals, adjusting their language, sometimes dressing like Christians. Trying to control the local economy, corrupt bloodlines. Just like Süss had in the film. And Germany was far from the only country to recognize this truth. He recalled the ship overflowing with Jews that had tried to dock in Cuba a few years earlier. The Cubans had known better than to let them overrun their country, to sneak in with their conniving ways. Even the Americans had turned them away. Countries all the way down to Argentina were closing their doors to immigration. From what he had heard, German officials in Argentina were doing a particularly good job of drumming up Nazi support and educating the locals about the dangers of Jewish parasites.

The word "parasite" sounded harsh, but he thought back to his plant guide, the trees he knew from childhood. Colonies of *Heracleum mantegazzianum*—giant hogweed—had invaded the land around the lake, choking out the smaller plants that couldn't compete for sunlight. Nasty weeds, those things. Their sap could burn your skin if you got too close. But Germans were unlike the smaller plants. They were the silver fir, standing tall and proud.

When broken down to a science, racial theory made sense. For centuries, the Nordic race had proved its superiority. Beautiful architecture, glorious music, strong, capable rulers. And when the existence of their people was threatened by an invasive species, wasn't it only natural for them to protect the very foundation of the Reich? This world war, the booklet concluded, was not simply a war against nations, but the German people's battle to save their race from turmoil and decay.

His research turned to war correspondent reports from the *Völkischer Beobachter* that told of courageous German efforts at Stalingrad, of Churchill's desire to thwart their people, to make them suffer as they had after Versailles. The more he read, the more he thought of the many comrades his father had seen collapse at his feet on the battlefield. The Triple Entente had acted just as ruthlessly during the First World War, but after its end, they had treated Germans like the only aggressors. Kicked them at the knees and laughed as they buckled. They robbed them of good men and then left them to starve as they raked in their reparations. And after seeing how Germany could rise up again and make the nation stronger than ever, the Allies were afraid. As Goebbels himself said in his speech on the Führer's birthday, the Führer had done everything he could to prevent another clash of nations, to end the war as quickly as possible. But Britain thirsted for power.

"Confidence," Goebbels stated, "is the best moral weapon of war. When it begins to fail, the beginning of the end has arrived." Karl thought hard about this and considered his own hesitation when faced with the executions, the sculptor's son. Was he too weak to embrace the position he'd been granted? The duties? The Führer needed all of them to play their part in ending the war, in preventing the spread of Bolshevik chaos, in restoring the Nordic spirit to its former glory. The Führer needed Karl.

IN his first year with the SS, Karl had formed a bond with two of his colleagues in Berlin, Rolf and Dietrich. When the three of them got leave during the same week, they went mountaineering together in the Bavarian Alps. In the tent, they'd huddled together against the cold while they slept. But the second night, Rolf's hand drifted under the blanket, coming to rest on Karl's neck and stroking the curve of his jaw. Karl brushed him off but said nothing, assuming Rolf was lost in some dream. The final night, it happened again, but Karl didn't want to start a fight or give Dietrich the wrong idea, so he pushed Rolf away and left it at that. Rolf was, after all, their superior. On the way back to Berlin, the three of them stopped at Karl's parents' for lunch. Between courses, his father pulled him aside.

"You shouldn't associate with this Rolf. I would have hoped you could at least spot the signs."

Karl didn't respond.

His father said it was indisputable: Rolf's soft, effeminate features, the pitch of his voice, the delicate way he cut up his beef. "You have to report him."

Karl protested that he couldn't betray a friend, especially without real proof.

"Children have friends; men have comrades. Don't let some womanish emotions distract you from your duty. Besides, if you'd choose to keep a man like him in your circle, I'd worry about how that could reflect on you."

Three weeks passed before Karl acted. But he did, and it turned out he wasn't the only one Rolf had accosted. Rolf was sent to a correctional facility for treatment and never returned to Berlin.

AUTUMN came early to Buchenwald. By late October, the trees around Karl's villa shivered in the night, growing as scrawny and sorry-looking as the prisoners. Each evening after sunset, the wind began to howl, and the officers wouldn't stop complaining about the cold. Karl escaped as often as possible. Marijke's arms, the heat of her kisses, took him away from it all.

On a brisk morning, he awoke to frost. It formed thin layers of ice over the puddles and gave a satisfying crack under his weight as he made his way toward the muster grounds. Camp numbers had swollen above thirty thousand, though that figure fluctuated daily. Some died off; some were transferred elsewhere, and they occasionally had to eliminate those who were a "burden to the system." Brandt acted like spouting off vague terms could make the guards forget what they were doing.

While Karl stood listening to the roll-call officer bark out an endless list of numbers, he grew conscious of how detached he'd become. He no longer flinched at men collapsing in front of him from the morning cold. The corpses that littered the grounds seemed little more than a nuisance, forcing him to step out of his way, the countless rows of prisoners mere numbers. Economic input, the currency of the Reich.

A scream broke out from the detention cellblock that stood beside the gatehouse. He stood still, careful not to let any emotion show as the cries of the tortured grew. The smoke from the crematorium mixed with the crisp air, a foulness that had worked its way into the wool of every uniform he owned. He may have grown blind to the sights of death, but the smells and sounds were impossible to avoid.

Several of the inmates in the front row cringed at the noise. The breeze picked up, and one of them shuddered, his toes poking through the tip of his left shoe. The sight made Karl think of Marijke shivering in her bed. The roll-call officer puttered through his duties, so Karl told him he had business to attend to and went to the equipment depot to see about an electric heater for the brothel.

After arranging its delivery, he crossed the prisoners' camp again. The band was playing to march the inmates off to their work details, but the music sounded flat and tired, and the tuba player seemed to choke on his notes, like he didn't have the breath left in his lungs. The rising sun hit the frozen ground as the muster grounds began to clear out. When Karl cut in between two sets of blocks in the quiet northwest corner, he stopped. Two men stood at the far end of the buildings, wrapped in an embrace.

"What in God's name are you doing?"

The prisoners broke apart and spun around. Their faces were ashen. Sure enough, they wore pink triangles on their uniforms. They cowered like street dogs while Karl marched over to them. "Where are you supposed to be right now?"

The older of the pair stepped forward. "I was saying goodbye, sir." He hesitated. "I'm being transferred."

"Now he's late for work."

"I'm very sorry, sir."

The other man hunched over, afraid to look at Karl.

"And you." Karl pointed to him. "What Kommando are you in?"

The inmate spit out the name of the munitions factory with an accent that marked him a Berliner.

"From now on, you're digging ditches."

The inmate nodded, still focused on the ground. Karl noted their numbers and was about to let them go when he spotted a group of guards who had gathered to watch. An officer walked past the end of the blocks before doubling back. Hoffmann.

"Is everything all right, Schutzhaftlagerführer?" Hoffmann asked. "Do you need any assistance?"

"Everything is under control."

"These fags acting up again?"

"I've dealt with it."

"You know, sir, I caught the shrimp touching the bigger one just last week." The gleam in his eye suggested he was lying. "The Kommandant says there's no room for second chances."

Karl cleared his throat. "I know very well what the Kommandant said. You can leave, Hoffmann."

Hoffmann stalked off, but the other guards stayed within earshot. The prisoners' shoulders fell in relief, which made Karl bristle. They took him for spineless, probably thought he'd let them off, even with everyone watching.

"Can one of you tell me what Himmler has to say about fags?" he asked.

Neither responded. The fear returned to their eyes, driving him on. They were nothing but weaklings, pansies. Degenerates going against society, against science.

"Homosexuality is polluting the Reich, impeding the rise of the Aryan race." The guards moved in, so he kept talking. "The two of you are like weeds, contaminating our garden. Tell me, what does a good gardener do with weeds?"

One of the men buckled like he'd taken a shot to the gut. Karl nodded to the guards. They circled the prisoners, raised their batons, the butts of their guns in the air and brought them down hard. Part of Karl wanted to turn away, but he watched every hit. Dirty fags. Those damn, filthy fags. He repeated the phrase over and over in his head. The smack of metal against flesh muffled the men's cries.

When they could no longer stand, he held up his hand. "Enough. Take them away. Put them both on the next train to Auschwitz and make sure they get sent straight to the showers."

For all Marijke had heard about Karl's life, he knew little about hers. He preferred to think of her as having always been waiting for him, of her story starting when her path crossed his.

His little violinist, his Roman candle.

One Sunday, he thought about her as he sat in his drawing room with his morning coffee, what it would be like to have her sitting beside him in her dressing gown. Else used to fuss over him, rising to refill his drink before he'd reached the bottom. But Marijke? She would be absorbed in the newspaper, reading out the latest symphony reviews, speculating about why the cellist had gone flat. He chuckled thinking about it.

The double doors opened, and a hunched prisoner shuffled in with a stepladder. He jolted as he spotted Karl. "I'm very sorry, sir, I was told to change these light bulbs." He pointed to a pair of overhead lights, which had weakened to a dull glow. "I'll come back later."

With a wave of his hand, Karl instructed the prisoner to carry on and tried to return to his fantasies of Marijke. The inmate set up the ladder near the bookshelves and clambered up to unscrew an old bulb. He looked the same age as Karl. When he bent to set the faulty bulb on a shelf, Karl pictured Marijke's husband, leaning over to pass her a book. A man without a name, without a face, but the thought of him wouldn't go away. There they were, sitting hand in hand on the settee, Marijke gazing at him with a saccharine smile.

The light bulb squeaked as it twisted into the socket. Karl became aware of a stagnant taste in his mouth and took a big sip of coffee, debating whether it was too early to break into his liquor cabinet.

The prisoner noticed Karl watching and doubled his speed.

"Enough," Karl said. "You can finish the job later."

The inmate hurried down from the ladder, almost dropping it against the wall in his rush to pack it up. Karl waited until he had left, put down his coffee and headed over to the records office.

"I need information on a Dutchman," Karl said to the inmate clerk. "The name is De Graaf."

"Yes, sir. Do you know his number?"

"He arrived from KZ Vught late in the spring. That's all I know."

"Shall I send the information to your office, sir?"

"I'll wait."

The clerk left the room. Five minutes passed before he returned with some files. "Two men with that name arrived in the spring."

The first record card showed someone with a heavy overbite and wrinkles, but his wife's name was Johanna. Karl flipped to the second card. Theodoor de Graaf. Age twenty-five. Love of Marijke's life. The man stared up at Karl through his photo. Spectacles and a square face. The records listed his hair colour as brown and his height at 185 centimetres.

Karl held up the file. "This one."

The clerk brought him another card that covered De Graaf's labour details. De Graaf had worked as a university lecturer in Amsterdam. Had his brain seduced Marijke? Certainly not those sailboat ears. As a Dutch political prisoner, he hadn't been assigned hard labour. Instead, he belonged to the Camp Protection detachment: inmates responsible for guarding the depots at night and supervising camp cleanliness, the type of labour that could grant someone access to the camp bonus system. To the brothel. The file noted him a hard worker. Karl tugged to loosen the collar of his uniform and gestured to the clerk to come closer.

"How else can I help you, sir?" the inmate asked.

"Make me a copy of these records. Every word you have on him."

CHAPTER TWELVE

Luciano
May 13, 1977
Buenos Aires

THE WOMAN TO LUCIANO'S LEFT WAS GROWING louder. He often woke to the sound of her retching, and she murmured strings of nonsense whenever he returned to his cell. One night, her stomach rumbled so loudly that Luciano could hear it through the partition. She wept, a sound like the wind shaking rain from leafy branches.

He inched up against the partition. "Are you all right?" He couldn't think of anything else to say.

Her cries stopped. "He needs more food," she whispered at last.

"Who?"

"My son."

"Your son is here?"

Someone approached. He moved away from the wall, and the

footsteps ceased. A soft noise came from the other side of the particleboard, like the woman had placed her hands against it.

"I'm pregnant."

Luciano touched his own side of the partition. He thought of all the times she'd rested her hands on his shoulders during the chain-gang slog back from breakfast. Her fragile touch. She blended in with everyone else in the dining room, like a hand-me-down doll worn to the stitching. Maybe she used to be very pretty, but in any case, he hadn't noticed any bulge at her belly. "How far along are you?"

"When I arrived, I was six months, but I think it's almost time." She paused. "His father is dead. They showed me his bloody shirt."

Luciano withdrew his hand from the wall and dug his nails into the thin fabric of the mattress. "Jesus."

She grew quiet and he considered telling her he was sorry to hear it, but that meant nothing.

"Did they take your wife?" she asked. "Are you married?"

He thought of Fabián, his plump, bowed lips, the scar on his knee from the time he'd tried to slide down the banister at the campus library, the crinkle of his rolling papers. "No."

The footsteps returned, marking an unfamiliar pace.

"Do they know about the baby?" Luciano asked, once he dared to speak.

"I don't know."

Two nights later, her cell was silent. Luciano pressed his ear to the partition, tapped softly, but got no response. And when the guard came to lead everyone back from breakfast, a new pair of hands fell on Luciano's shoulders.

That afternoon, as their documentation supervisor stepped outside to get another coffee, Luciano nudged Gabriel's foot. "The pregnant girl in the cell near us, she's gone."

Two other labourers looked up, but they continued working with mechanical movements.

"If she's pregnant," Gabriel replied, "she's done for."

The long-haired girl stopped typing. "No, you're wrong. They've taken her to the maternity ward."

"So they'll let her keep the baby?" Luciano asked.

One of the other men interjected. "And miss out on an opportunity to flaunt their omnipotence? They must kill the unborn babies along with the mothers."

Gabriel glanced at the doorway before turning back to Luciano. "No, they'll keep her there with the other pregnant women, but when the baby is born, they'll take it away."

"Then they'll kill the mother," the other man said, "electrify her to toast."

The girl went pale and started chewing on a strand of her hair. "You're sick. Talk like that just makes them win."

The man stared back with his lined face. Then the supervisor reappeared, pausing in the middle of the floor to scrutinize them. As Luciano turned back to his translation, he realized he had never bothered to ask the pregnant girl her name.

Dear Papá,

That music. The music is tormenting me. The operas. The piano and the—what are they? Flutes. Dear Papá, the piano and the flutes play on and on, but all I can think of is what they're trying to cover up. The pleas, the screams. Wretched screams. I can't take it anymore. It's so, it's so . . . Papá, somehow the music also reminds me of you.

What time was it? If his father was already home from work, he would be sitting in the teak armchair with a glass of Fernet and cola, listening to Brahms or Schubert. And whenever the violin picked up again, Papá would tilt his head and smile, his eyes glazed over with some secret memory. Luciano had grown up to those sounds. According to Arturo Wagner, nothing trumped the splendour of music. Not just classical, either. As a kid, Luciano had lain on the linoleum floor, gazing up at his parents as they circled the room in a tango. While Carlos Gardel crooned about his love for Buenos Aires on the record player, his mother would rest her head on Papá's shoulder. Their feet gave the illusion of moving on their own: pivoting, crossing, and now and then swishing into a little kick, Mamá pausing to wink at Papá.

No matter how much of an asshole mood you're in when you walk in that door, once the LP starts crackling, everything changes. You lean back in your chair and close your eyes; your face relaxes. It's like you become someone else. What do you hear in that music? Where does it transport you? I need to know. I need to see something beautiful again.

CHAPTER THIRTEEN

MARIJKE
DECEMBER 14, 1943
BUCHENWALD

EVERY DAY THE SAME CYCLE: CLEANING, DARNING, primping, all leading up to that horrible finale. The other girls began to measure our days in the number of men they bedded. I refused to count. On Sundays, we suffered through extended hours, but that was at least shower day for the men. On tolerable days, business was slow. On exceptional days, a camp speech or electricity outage might shut down the brothel. But those instances of relief were few and far between, and for the most part, I was forced to spread my legs each night from seven to nine, when I would count down the minutes until I could try to scrub the shame from my thighs and slip back into my own bed.

Aside from Karl's visits, the only interruptions to this miserable routine were our camp walks, which grew more sporadic as time progressed. The young guard who often led us had a stout build and a face that was squished in like a bat's. He was one of the same guards who peeped on us at night, and I would have despised him if he weren't the only one who permitted us to talk amongst ourselves while we walked.

One afternoon, he showed up later than usual, near the end of the workday. We filed out of the brothel and followed him two by two, passing the enclosed area of the Little Camp, where several Jews stared back at us. The way they looked at us reminded me of something I'd seen shortly after Theo and I had joined the resistance. We'd walked over to Nieuwmarkt with forged ration coupons stuffed under our clothes. A barbed-wire barricade sliced through the square, cordoning off the Jewish quarter. While I kept a lookout for our contact, Theo gestured to the old weigh house with a sigh. "Just think how small Amsterdam must have been when they built this city gate some five hundred years ago." He lowered his voice. "And now the damn moffen have gone and cut it all up again."

Across the barricade, a little girl was studying us. She began tugging at the yellow star on her coat, fascinated by its brightness. Her mother chided her and checked around for nearby soldiers before kneeling to straighten the star.

Theo was still admiring the building's turrets. "Look at this beautiful city of ours. This is what we're fighting for, Marijke."

"Indeed." I looked back at the girl, who had waved to me over her mother's shoulder. "If we don't stand up for her, who will?"

Unlike that child, there were few signs of humanity left in the men standing behind the fence of the Little Camp. Thin skin draped over their bones like a shroud. A week of relentless rain had turned the clay ground in the enclosure to mud. One of the men knelt, and the feet that jutted from his wooden clogs looked black with rot. I resisted the urge to turn away, giving the man what I hoped was a look of solace.

As the guard led us on toward the depot buildings, we began to talk in low voices. The sun shone above us, but thunderheads gathered on the horizon. Edith tauntingly pointed this out to Sophia.

"Don't be cruel," I said. "You also wouldn't like thunder if you'd suffered through half the air strikes she has."

"Don't talk to me about suffering," she retorted. Like many of the girls, she'd become catty, prone to bickering about small things, about who got the best portions at supper, who got the seat in the sunlight after our chores.

My attention shifted from her as some of the gardening Kommando came out of the greenhouses to our left, carrying hoes and trowels. I scanned the group, but they were almost all green triangles and I knew Theo would be red like me. The Kapo cursed at them, waving a bludgeon over his head. When a prisoner slipped in the mud, the Kapo went over and smacked him on the back.

I looked down at my feet, and Sophia sighed. After a moment, she took my hand. "Think of how nice it will be to have a garden again, once all this is over. Tell me, what will you plant in yours?"

"I thought it was my job to distract you," I said, "not the other way around."

She carried on. "The first thing I'd want is strawberries."

"Oh?"

"When I was little, I would help Mother tend her garden. She always let me water the flowers, and I pretended to hold court in a fairy-tale kingdom, with strawberry blossoms as my ladies in waiting."

I smiled, trying to picture her as a laughing little girl. We continued on in silence, but I could feel the warm reassurance of her presence beside me, and I wondered how I would ever have managed at Buchenwald without her.

The clouds darkened, bringing cold air. The first raindrops fell on my head, and the guard lifted the collar of his jacket to protect his neck. As we started our circle back, two prisoners stepped out of the crematorium with baskets full of clothing. Mostly uniforms, but also men's shirts. One of these fell from the basket, but the prisoner didn't notice and kept walking. As we passed, I reached down to pick it up, spotting the large *X* painted on the back. I had seen this mark on some of the women at Ravensbrück. When there were shortages of uniforms, the moffen used an *X* to distinguish the prisoners from civilians. It could be seen at a distance, the perfect target on an escaping back.

The smell of sweat still clung to the fabric of the dress shirt, and I tried to imagine the man who had worked and died in it. Had he come from another camp, another country? Was he Hungarian, Polish, or maybe Dutch? A husband, a father? I fingered the button on the right cuff, reminiscing of languid Sundays at home, the mornings when we had raisin buns and coffee in bed, when I wore nothing but Theo's dress shirt to wash the dishes. Those echoes of what was lost felt heavy in my chest.

I didn't notice our line had stopped and I bumped into the girl in front of me. Sophia yanked the shirt from my hands and passed it to the guard who had come over to see what I'd found.

He beckoned to another prisoner, ordering him to bring the shirt to the laundry. He narrowed his eyebrows at me in warning. "Keep up."

Water began to stream down my neck, under the collar of my blouse, and into my shoes. I started to shiver. The guard took us back through the heart of the blocks while the rain soaked through our shirts to our undergarments. It was almost dusk, and labour Kommandos were returning from work. They marched in five by five, heads low and feet dragging. Some could hardly walk. Mud splattered their uniforms and raindrops dripped from their eyebrows. These were the men who had once played soccer with their friends, competed in breaststroke at local swimming pools. The men who had run down city streets, children bouncing on their shoulders in laughter. Men who had carried their wives across the wedding threshold, who had promised nothing but happiness and love. As we passed by, many of them watched us with smiles or the sadness of their own memories, but others looked ahead, their eyes vacant, unseeing. Those were the *Muselmänner*, the walking dead.

As we neared the end of the blocks, the camp band started up, announcing roll call. I glanced back. A group of inmates was cutting across in the opposite direction, toward the throng of the muster grounds. One of the men had removed his cap to wring out the water, and as he put it back on, I caught a view of his profile. I felt a sharp, sudden twist in my stomach, my breath trapped still in my chest. Theo.

Without thinking, I stepped out of line, and I ran. But his head had already disappeared into the crowd. The guard shouted after me. I called Theo's name, but the rain and the brass band and the sounds of hundreds of footsteps swallowed my voice. Twenty metres from the edge of the throng, an arm reached out like a blockade, and I stumbled into this other guard, his body obstructing my view.

Our guard yelled at me to get back in line. The one who had stopped me grabbed me by the elbow and brought me there. When I craned my neck to see the muster grounds, he slapped me across the face.

"You dumb whore. Do you want to be sent back to Ravensbrück? Or straight to the crematorium?"

My cheek stung, and I felt the stares of the other girls on me, their fear and worry. But I could think of nothing except Theo. Behind us, roll call had started, the face I'd seen lost somewhere amid thousands.

The brothel guard addressed the other one. "Take her to the detention block. The brothel supervisor will come by to arrange her punishment."

THE Bunker, as we called the detention cellblock, took up the left wing of the gatehouse. The jailer was uncomfortably handsome, with a nose that spread wide and flat, like it had been broken in his youth. As the guard led me in, the jailer grinned. "I guess today's my lucky day." He pointed to a cell on the right. "This one's free."

The cold cell contained nothing but a bare sleeping bench, which the jailer folded up into the wall. I moved to sit against the back wall, but he prodded my legs to keep me from doing so. "No sitting and no leaning during the day. A whore like you should be used to standing on street corners all night. You'll feel right at home."

The steel door slammed shut. He waited a minute before checking the peephole to make sure I was still standing. Then he left me alone in the dark.

Shivers and the torment of my thoughts kept me awake throughout that first night. I lay with my cheek pressed to the cold surface of the bench, and though my stomach cried out for food, my mind kept replaying that moment. The slope of the prisoner's nose, the deep *V* of his jaw. Those protruding ears. His long strides. I swore I'd seen him, but had it actually been him? This man had looked older, perhaps too old, and the shape of that shaved skull looked unfamiliar. Had I wanted it so desperately to be him, that for a single moment, a stranger had become my husband?

Theo. His floppy hair that never lay flat, the rough spot on his left middle finger from the friction of his pen. The adoring look he would give me as he drifted to sleep. How I longed to wake up in his arms, to feel his warmth against me, to sail together down the Amstel, listening to the silly rhymes he would make up about the brood of children we wanted to raise. Our vow to grow old hand in hand, watching the seasons change, year after year after year.

The click of a lock woke me the next morning. The jailer nodded when I asked to use the toilet, but while I did, he banged on the door for me to hurry up. The odour in the hallway told me that not everyone in the cellblock received that privilege. Back to the cell I went. I had to fold the bed and stand again, all day, with nothing but water. My legs grew numb; my head started to spin. Again I doubted our decision to get involved in the resistance but kept trying to reassure myself that we'd made some sort of difference, that we'd helped others to safety. When I looked down at the concrete floor, I saw my skull cracking against it. To stop myself from fainting, I tried to keep my mind alert. Like a film reel, my thoughts wound back through my fondest memories of Theo, every little detail. The day we'd met, four years earlier. The frost that clung to the handlebars of the bicycles parked along the frozen stretch of the Keizersgracht. The dusting of snow that sparkled in the afternoon light, while the city ventured onto the ice. The table my father and I had set up with a tray of fresh *stroopwafels* from his bakery. And then that handsome university student who stopped by with friends to buy hot cocoa. The way his eyes kept darting to me, how he stayed to chat until his third mug was empty. How I'd known, even then, that he would become my world.

Theo. His face grew fuzzier the more I thought about him. His eyes, the particular shade of brown, or were they hazel? All I could see clearly was the bright blue of Karl's. My feet, my shins, my knees, the arch of my back—everything swelled and ached. My head throbbed. Every few minutes, a guard checked the peephole, but otherwise I was alone in the darkness. But I heard the jailer, heard the others, heard their screams, their pleas, the crack of a flogging whip. I covered my ears with my hands and hummed, but I felt myself swaying, slipping, like someone had pressed a finger to my forehead, pushing me back toward the floor. And when I couldn't take it any longer, I reached an arm out to brace myself against the wall, and the door opened again.

I woke to someone stroking my hair. Sophia. She held out a cup of coffee and a piece of dry bread. "Eat this."

My chin felt stiff with drool, my eyelids with sleep. When I tried to rub my face, a slicing pain struck my shoulder. I cringed, trying to remember how I'd gotten back to the brothel.

"You're lucky," she said. "The Schutzhaftlagerführer cut your punishment short. You were delirious when you returned. You've been mumbling in your sleep, something about your husband."

"Sophia, I think I saw him. Out there, with one of the Kommandos."

"I assumed as much. Either that or you'd gone completely crazy, trying to sprint off like that. It's a miracle nobody shot you on the spot!"

Her words sizzled with anger, and I realized how worried she must have been. I clasped her hand. "But I was so certain, at least for those few seconds. Now I don't even know."

"You think you're safe from harm because you're one of us. None of us is safe, Marijke. What would have happened if Karl hadn't stepped in? How many days would you have lasted?"

The noises came back to me, the horrible tortured cries. I tried to respond, but this turned into something half-cough, half-shudder, and I shut my eyes again, desperate to wake up and find myself back at home.

Sophia paused. "I'm sorry. I can't imagine how bad it was. I didn't mean to upset you. Please, you need to eat."

I took the bread and bit off a corner, chewing slowly while she rubbed my back. The dizziness faded, that shred of sustenance bringing the brothel back in focus. When I finished it, I propped myself up on my elbows and considered what it meant that Karl had intervened. If one thing was certain, it was that he had some power to protect me, so long as I made sure to keep him happy.

AFTER that, my desperation grew, the need to find out about Theo complicated by Karl's increasing signs of affection. When a blizzard covered the camp in ice, Karl sent fur-lined mittens and a cashmere scarf. I didn't allow myself to wear them on our walks. I kept an eye out for Theo and detested the thought of him seeing me with luxuries I couldn't even have afforded back home. Sophia asked to borrow them, but I didn't like the idea of her using Karl's gifts either, so the mittens and scarf stayed wrapped in tissue paper in a box under my bed, alongside the violin.

One night, instead of pulling me to him, Karl bent to kiss my thighs, to touch me, to taste me, and I hated myself for how my body responded, coursing with pleasure, making me cry out. I shut my eyes and repeated my wedding vows to myself, trying to summon every word, every line the minister had said. After Karl left, I curled up in the warm imprint of his body and sobbed. I found myself struggling to hold on to the smell of Theo, the taste of his lips. These had blended deep into the pot of many others. Never had I been anything but honest with him, but I was starting to understand that shame is the very best secret keeper, for I had no idea how to ever face him again. Rationality was slipping away as my emotions took over. And despite my fears of offending Karl, I'd resolved to ask him about Theo. None of the other prisoners I'd met had heard of my husband, and I had to learn the truth. He could find out if

Theo was well, but I didn't know how he would react to the reminder I wasn't his. I dwelled on how to ask this, how to time it. With so much at stake, the wrong phrasing, the wrong tone, could be disastrous. Karl might have him transferred, or something worse.

I waited until I couldn't bear it any longer, until my dreams of Theo became so vivid and tormenting that I couldn't sleep at night.

My request came on a chilly January evening, as snow fell outside the window. Karl must have expected my question, for he took it without any sign of surprise.

"Please," I begged. "I need to know he's still here."

"I'll see what I can do." He looked past me out the window, making no attempt to hide the char of jealousy on his reply.

I prayed I hadn't made things worse by asking. But after everything that had happened, a persistent voice in my head whispered that I had to know, that as painful as news of his death would be, it could also free me from the heavy guilt that followed me around.

Later that night, I huddled in a ball on my bed, certain I'd sentenced my love to more suffering. I tried to block out images of his back, bleeding and scarred from lashes, of his shoes, sunken in mud, of his hands, calloused and numb.

A week passed before Karl came back to me. For days, Sophia had to hide all the SS socks I'd darned, so shoddy a job I'd done. When he strode into the koberzimmer, I clutched the end of the bed sheet, pleating it into my palm. He kissed me and stepped back to brush the snow from his cap onto the floor. "Eight centimetres today and it doesn't show any sign of letting up. Luckily this servant of mine has years of experience cooking for long

Polish winters. He's learned how to prepare all my favourite dishes." He winked and checked for my reaction, but his words passed through me. "Now tell me you haven't been too cold today."

"No," I said, "thank you."

He proceeded to comment on the state of the roads leading into camp, all the delays in deliveries, and despite being more talkative than normal, he said nothing about Theo. My fingers twitched, eager to reach out and pry the answer from him. Off came his overcoat and boots. When he straightened up again, his lips brushed mine, but I was too anxious to meet this kiss and he pulled back with a creased brow. He unfastened the top button of my blouse before stopping to look me in the eyes. "Aren't you even going to give me a proper greeting first?"

"What do you mean?"

"Don't try to hide what you're thinking. It's all over your face." He walked over to the sink, gripped its sides in long contemplation. The power he held over me filled the room like mustard gas, and I had to force myself to breathe, fearing my husband gone, his body a pile of ash, death by starvation or punishment for some trifle. Karl turned around and stared at me. "I can't lie to you," he said at last, "much as I'd like to. Your husband is alive."

My eyes welled up, but I swallowed and bit my lip to keep the joy from spilling out. "Thank you, thank you so much."

Karl said nothing.

I took a deep breath. "Is that everything?"

"He's at Ohrdruf, a satellite camp around fifty kilometres from here."

"And for work? Do you know what he does?"

"He builds roads."

I wanted to ask for more—could he ensure Theo's safety, have him transferred to a better work detail? Yet I had to watch my step. With a single word, he could have my husband killed.

Karl acted rougher that night, pinning my hands above my head, pounding against me. Once he came, he collapsed on my chest, hair pasted to his forehead in sweat, but his lips strayed to my nipples, his fingers between my legs. Later, he drew spirals on my back. "One way or another, this war will end. The question is, will that take you away from me?"

We both knew the answer I had to give, the only answer that made any sense, but I couldn't find a way to wrap my tongue around it. "What are you trying to say?"

"I have this fantasy of us running away together, finding ourselves a small cottage somewhere in Bavaria, somewhere in the middle of the woods, away from everything." He paused. "I guess what I'm asking is, if we lose the war, will I lose you?"

Before I said anything, he placed a hand on my shoulder, his grip heavy and unyielding, holding me firmly in place.

CHAPTER FOURTEEN

KARL
DECEMBER 24, 1943
BUCHENWALD

B EFORE KARL KNEW IT, CHRISTMAS HAD ARRIVED. Shreds of red, green and gold interrupted the monotonous grey. The wives of the SS officers threw endless dinner parties, dressing their children in festive ribbons and ties embroidered with swastikas. To raise money for the celebrations, Brandt withheld rations from the prisoners for twenty-four hours. The SS ordered the bakers to make dozens of stollen. They brought in crates of Champagne. They roasted geese. Nobody mentioned the Soviet advances or the recent bombings in Berlin.

On the morning of December 24, Karl took an automobile into Weimar. Women and children crowded the streets, and a large tree had been set up in the square. He wandered past market stalls selling chestnuts and tapered candles. The classical

Weimar architecture, muted in colour but bold and assured in presence, the monument to the poets Goethe and Schiller—all this reminded him of what they were fighting for. He crossed the square to stand in front of the Haus Elephant, where a balcony hung over the hotel entrance. Hitler had made many speeches from that spot. In the photographs, he leaned against the iron bars of the balcony, arm raised in a salute, promising to make Germany great again. But when Karl looked up at those bars, all he could see were the ragged faces of dying men behind them.

A little girl in a patched coat appeared beside him on the cobblestones, clutching a pile of spruce boughs. "Christmas garland, officer?"

He prodded her bundle. "Garland? These are just branches. Where are the decorations?"

Her face fell. "This is all we have this year."

Only then did he notice how empty the stalls looked, when compared to the Christmas markets he knew from before the war. "Very well. And where should I put a Christmas garland, young lady?"

She smiled as he pressed some reichspfennige into her palm. "Your wife will know what to do with it."

Karl opened his mouth to object but thought better of it. He patted the girl on the head and turned away with a smile, his preoccupations disappearing as his mind returned to Marijke.

BACK at Buchenwald, he traipsed through the woods by his villa. Patches of snow covered the ground, but he searched until he found a rowan shrub that still bore some berries. He cut off a sprig and carried it home with a pocketful of pine cones. The Kommandant expected the officers for dinner. After showering and polishing his boots, he sat at his dining table with a pair of tweezers and glued the pine cones onto the spruce bough. A tedious task that demanded a certain dexterity, a skill he hadn't used since building model gliders as a boy. It amused him how Marijke brought out this side of him, stirring up interests and passions he'd long neglected in favour of duty. But while her feisty spirit energized, it also warned of the danger in thinking with your heart instead of your head. By following some foolhardy impulse, she'd landed herself in the cellblock, and if he hadn't fished her out in time, she might have returned to him unfeeling and broken.

When the glue had set, he tore the ribbon from the package of a scarf his mother had sent and wound it through the branches. The smell of the forest clung to his fingers. The finished product lacked a woman's touch but still looked cheerful enough.

BRANDT was all too eager to make a spectacle out of Christmas dinner, boasting about the plumpness of the ducks, the age of the Chianti and all the trouble he'd had getting it shipped from Tuscany. Karl chewed slowly and drank plenty, avoiding thoughts of the man he'd seen throw himself into the electric fence the day before. They had granted the inmates some concessions—extra rations for two days and the chance to receive packages from their families—but only the privileged, of course.

Once the table was cleared, Brandt presented the officers with SS cufflinks and slipped an extra-large bottle of brandy onto Karl's lap. He handed out toy Viking ships for the officers' sons, which bore the detailed craftsmanship of the camp sculptor. Karl closed his eyes, wanting to forget him and his son. As a start, he broke into the brandy.

A short while later, he crossed the camp pitch under the stars, his belt buckle lax after the hearty meal. One of the guards in the watchtowers was taking swigs from a flask, but the muster grounds were empty. At the edge of the prisoners' blocks, Karl heard a low sound. Men's voices, rising up in Polish, then in Czech. Another song began, this one in German. A shiver ran down his neck as he caught the tune. The music drifted between the rows, growing louder, more determined with every step he took. *Stille Nacht, heilige Nacht! Alles schläft, einsam wacht.*

When he got to the brothel, he arranged to enter the koberzimmer ahead of Marijke. The brothel had closed an hour early and the women were getting ready to sleep. He laid the garland on the bed and pulled a number of candles from his satchel, lighting these and arranging them on the floor.

The door to the girls' quarters opened, and Marijke stepped into the room in a simple green dress.

He approached her, lifting the garland over their heads like mistletoe. "Merry Christmas, my dear."

She swatted at the spruce bough and dodged his kiss to examine it. One of the pine cones had gotten loose and dangled from a piece of hardened glue. "You did this? And the candles?"

"Your gift is on its way but got held up in Berlin." Karl snuck in for that kiss, removed his jacket and boots and guided her by the hand toward the bed.

She shook her head. "Enough presents. What am I supposed to do with them?"

"But it's Christmas. I want you to be happy, even for an hour or two. Please." The sleeve of her dress had shifted so he leaned over to kiss her bare shoulder. "You look radiant."

From his satchel, he pulled out a bag of nuts, some oranges and apples. Her face perked up.

"I have wine, too," he said.

"This is plenty."

She waited, expecting him to undress her, but instead he passed her an orange. The peel fell off into her fingers in a single piece, stirring his excitement as he thought of what else those hands could do. But he didn't want to rush the night. "Why don't you get your violin?"

She nodded, pleased by the suggestion. When she re-entered the room, the neckline of her dress hung lower, and she pointed to the garland with a shy smile. "Did you really make that?"

"The first thing my mother did every December was fill the house with greenery. It's not Christmas without it."

"It's not Christmas without family."

He tried not to grimace, hoping she wouldn't ruin the mood, but she sat on the edge of the bed and stared into the candles, the flames reflected in her pupils like embers. Then she raised the violin to her chin and started playing "Adeste Fideles." He rested his head against the wall and reached out to touch her knee. The music was a salve. It numbed everything: the image of the sculptor's son in his oversized clogs, the prisoners' screams from the detention cells, her husband's name and number. There were no bombs. No orders. No bodies. Just an image of him and her by a fireplace, a chicken rotating on a spit, mulled wine, Axel and Faust asleep at their feet.

The song ended, cutting off his fantasy. Marijke looked at him. "When the war broke out, did you ever imagine it would still be dragging on four years later?"

"How could anyone have? There's a good chance this won't be our last wartime Christmas either." He studied her. Her back arched invitingly, and the candlelight flattered her skin. In that light, she was flawless, a Renaissance beauty. "At least I get to spend it in your arms, rather than with a pistol in my hand."

His father's stern voice returned, memories of him sitting in his armchair, reciting the one story he told over and over. "You know, my father was stationed by Ypres in 1914. On Christmas Eve, they placed candles along the trenches and brought in a scrawny tree covered in tinsel. It stood there in the mud, and they gathered around to sing Christmas carols. He said the shooting stopped on both sides and the Tommies poked their heads out into no man's land to join in."

Karl's chest tightened as the prisoners' carols echoed in his head.

"A sign of hope, then," she said, "that people are still people despite it all. It probably becomes much more difficult to shoot a man once you've looked him in the eye and shared a Christmas meal." She stared at him like she intended to go on but instead reached for her violin again. A cluster bomb of sharp, grating notes. Then she exhaled and started over with something slow and soft and soothing.

"That was just the first year. Father said it didn't happen again."

After a few minutes, she put the instrument back in its case and grabbed a handful of nuts. "What did you do last Christmas?"

"I got a week's leave, so I spent it in Munich with my parents. Nice as it was to see them, too much had changed. Father kept pestering me about work, challenging all my decisions and pushing me to ask for a promotion. Mother always looked forward to preparing a big dinner, but with rationing, well—she wasn't made to suffer through two wars. She's taking it quite hard."

A hazelnut split open with a large crack. Marijke set down the nutcracker and popped the nut into her mouth without responding.

"And you?" he asked.

"We intended to go to my parents as well, but there was a blockade on the trains that week. Normally, we might have cycled—though, of course, we had no bikes anymore."

"Oh?"

Her fist tightened around a handful of shells but then she sighed. "It was fine. We stayed home. I practiced my music and we listened to the Christmas broadcasts on the BBC."

The word "we" boomed. Of course her husband had heard her play countless times. He'd probably stood behind her, tracing the delicate spot where the violin met her neck, just as Karl had.

"What?" she teased. "Are you thinking of arresting me on account of our illegal radio?" As she tended to do, she inched in but left just enough space that he would need to move to touch her. Like she was afraid of admitting what she wanted, of letting herself go.

"Come here." He pulled her in, kissed her neck. Her arms, her wrists, her lips. She kissed him back. While he tugged at his socks, she unbuttoned her dress. Her fingers paused at her chest, and she kept looking at him as she took her time unclasping her brassiere. He threw his trousers on the floor, cupped her breasts, wanting to feel all of her, to hear her cry out his name.

But when he moved to touch her thighs, her husband's number came back to him. The face from his photo: Inmate 31224. Karl stopped and smacked his fist against the pillow. Only the weak lost control of their thoughts and emotions. And no man in his position ought to feel anything for a whore. She was, after all, a prisoner.

"What's wrong?"

"Nothing." He pulled himself on top and grabbed her ass as he entered her. She sucked in a breath, her body tense. Her hand reached for his, but then the man was there again, taunting him. De Graaf's hands on her skin, reminding Karl who had claimed her first.

AFTER that, Karl couldn't stroll through the prisoners' camp as he had before. Any time he spotted a tall man with big ears, he paused to examine his face. Once, he followed someone half-way to the prisoners' canteen until the stranger turned around. De Graaf haunted him in the brothel, while he got ready for the day, while he worked in his office.

The bitter rogue in Karl's head told him to have the man killed, assigned to the ditch-digging Kommando. Better yet, to an extermination camp. More than once, the possibility kept him up late into the night as he studied her husband's records, searching for signs of weakness in his face.

De Graaf belonged to one of the two-storey stone blocks near the Little Camp and the disinfection building. Karl made his way there on a Sunday after lunch. His cook had prepared a savoury pickled dish with the roast, and the taste of brine was still making his mouth water.

Wet snowflakes fell over the camp pitch, the first heavy snowfall of the new year. He tried to imagine himself as a boy, careening around the blocks, packing hard snowballs and dodging attacks. But the scattered prisoners outside ignored the snow. It piled up on their caps as they plodded around with wheelbarrows, bare ankles poking out of their clogs.

He climbed the stairs of the block to the upper level. A good hundred inmates filled the day room, passing their free time. Some talked at the tables; others lay sprawled across the floor, but it was absurd they could sleep through the racket of voices. Wet uniforms hung from the rafters, adding a damp mustiness to the terrible body odour. A shirtless inmate squatted near him, tugging on his suspenders and muttering to himself. In the opposite corner, a group bickered over something. Karl moved closer. They'd made a checkerboard from a scrap of wood and played with cigarette butts and pieces of stale bread. They jumped up when they saw him, and within a few seconds, everyone was standing at attention. One inmate brushed crumbs from his sleeves as he rushed over. His arm band identified him as the Blockältester responsible for the block's daily operations. "Good afternoon, Schutzhaftlagerführer."

"Surprise inspection," Karl said. "Line them up."

The Blockältester shouted toward the bunks while Karl started down the line in the day room, but he reached the end without stopping. "Number three-one-two-two-four," he called. No movement, and no one looked at him when he repeated the number.

The Blockältester consulted a clipboard. "Inmate three-one-two-two-four received permission to visit the library."

"Very well." Karl frowned, frustration tugging at his nerves. He glanced at the bunks in the corner, searching for something to fault. On spotting a mug and bowl that had been left on one of the beds, he walked over and knocked it to the floor. "Straighten up those mattresses. Half rations for everyone tonight."

THE inmates' library took up part of Block 5, the same building that contained the records department. Thousands of volumes crammed the shelves, which the camp had stocked using money from the inmates' pockets. Sometimes, the families of doctors or political dissidents sent novels. He was sure it eased their consciences to pretend their husbands and nephews were curled up in a corner after a day's work, thumbing through *Moby-Dick* by lamplight.

A prisoner sat at the front desk of the library, sorting a set of encyclopedias. A large sign was posted behind him: *Juden verboten.* Someone had sketched a prisoner with a hooked nose to clarify, likely one of the camp artists. He again recalled the sculptor's son but redirected his thoughts to Marijke, her smooth skin and feisty laugh.

"Can I help you, officer?"

He moved past the librarian and into the high wooden book stacks. The first row was empty. A pair of green triangles huddled in the third row, whispering over the pages of a thick leather-bound volume. His palms were clammy. He paused, cursing himself, cursing her husband. Then he saw him. Bent over a table, his shoulders towering above the back of the chair. De Graaf flipped the page of his book while Karl stood there watching. His fingers drummed against the book's spine. Karl's muscles grew tense as he pictured those fingers grazing Marijke's naked back, as he heard her moaning his name: *Theo.*

The floorboards creaked under Karl's weight. De Graaf glanced up from his reading, and his look of entrancement dissolved as he hurried to stand up and bow his head.

"Look at me." Karl crossed his arms. "What were you reading?"

De Graaf's eyebrows hung low over stormy eyes and his voice cracked. "A biography of Rembrandt, sir."

"So you think that's the best use of camp time."

He held up his library pass. "I have permission."

"You missed an inspection. And we've received reports that you've been neglecting your work."

His giant ears flared red.

"What do you have to say for yourself?"

"My apologies, sir, but I swear I haven't missed a day."

Karl couldn't hide his satisfaction at De Graaf's grovelling tone. "Get back to your block. And no more library visits."

"Yes, sir, thank you."

De Graaf kept his head low as he retreated. Karl smiled to himself. Despite his confidence that the Nazis would win the war and that this would sever their marriage forever, he resolved to do something to eliminate any last chance of that man ever making Marijke happy again.

For two weeks, the possibilities weighed on him. He could have her husband shot, whipped, hanged in the crematorium, deported. He could tell him about Marijke, but that might also instill in him a will to survive. The more Karl's feelings for her escalated and she entered his plans for after the war, the more he asked himself how he could torment her like that. What that would make him.

In mid-January, she asked the question he'd been dreading. She wanted to know where her husband was, if he was alive. Her request was bold, but the anxious twitch in her cheek betrayed her. Karl ground his teeth, unprepared for the bite of hearing the man's name from her lips. Sensing his jealousy, she curled into him, offering her body as a sedative. But he couldn't stay hard, because there De Graaf was again, drumming his fingers against her hips. Laughing in Karl's face as he hovered over a brood of children, all in matching outfits. She tried her best to distract Karl—teasing, caressing, licking—but he became irritated by her efforts and left the brothel early. By morning, he had a plan.

AT dawn on January 16, De Graaf was rounded up at roll call and sent to the infirmary, where he was charged to the care of Dr. Fischer. It was an open secret that Fischer had forced some inmates to write his dissertation in order to get his medical licence at Buchenwald, and he now oversaw medical experimentation. Tests on the typhus epidemic, lethal injections, hormone transplants in homosexuals: groundbreaking projects that would lead to scientific advancement and serve a greater good.

According to the report Fischer sent Karl, Inmate 31224 entered the experimentation room at approximately 08:00 hours.

Fischer instructed the patient to remove his trousers and lie on the examination table. He took out a syringe, put on his gloves and explained that he was providing a vitamin supplement that would enable the patient to work longer hours, to thrive off a limited diet. The patient winced as Fischer administered an injection to his genitals. Over the next few days, Fischer repeated the injection, noting swelling, bleeding and substantial pain. The procedure ceased on January 19. On January 21, the swelling began to subside, with high expectations for rapid healing. After subsequent verification, Fischer deemed the experiment a success: Inmate 31224, Theodoor de Graaf, was completely sterile.

After De Graaf was discharged from the infirmary, Karl had him transferred to one of Buchenwald's sub-camps. Nearby, but just out of reach. De Graaf got assigned to a construction detail, building tunnels and roads—tough work, yet nothing lethal. Karl promised himself to control his jealousy from then on, to let fate step in and have her way. But when he returned to the brothel and told Marijke her husband was alive, the joy on her face gnawed at him for days.

"DON'T you ever tire of the same girl?" The brothel supervisor stood at the threshold of the prisoners' brothel, holding open the door as Karl approached.

"What are you implying?" he asked.

When he reached the top of the steps, she smiled. She'd removed the jacket of her uniform and unbuttoned the top of her blouse to show off her cleavage. "You know, you're the only officer who stops by but doesn't try to coax me into bed." She slid her arm up along the door frame and studied him. Heat crept up the back of his neck.

She laughed. "I'm sorry, Schutzhaftlagerführer. She's a pretty one, but why settle for butter when you could have Chantilly cream?"

"You laze around in the brothel all day and that's the best line you can come up with?" He shoved aside her arm and stepped past her. "Stop flattering yourself."

He had arrived at the brothel earlier than normal and found it still open for business, with the last round of visitors filing into the waiting room. A couple of prisoners stood in line to pay at the table, but he pushed ahead of them. "I'm here to see Marijke."

The cashier chewed the end of her pencil. Of the handful of female staff he'd seen at Buchenwald, she was by far the ugliest. Heavy folds hung from her neck like melted wax, forming a double chin. When she didn't answer, he repeated himself. She gestured to a bench in the waiting room. "I'm very sorry, Schutzhaftlagerführer, but you'll have to wait."

"You can't be serious. For how long?"

"She's occupied right now. Another girl, Sophia, is available if you prefer."

He swallowed and ground his heel against the floorboards before taking a seat. The cashier's tone rattled him, and he cursed his oversight in showing up during regular hours. For some time, he'd toyed with the idea of banning the prisoners from visiting her, but he was wary of the Kommandant finding out. Brandt prided himself on the productivity of the brothel system and on the crop of women he'd selected, and he wouldn't understand why Karl wanted to tamper with these or why he would sleep with a tainted woman. Whether Karl liked it or not, duty took priority, which meant gaining Brandt's trust and respect, and keeping his involvement with Marijke as quiet as possible.

A few prisoners waited on the seats across from him. Carcasses, the lot of them. Sunken eyes and patchy hair. The idea of any of them touching her infuriated him. He debated leaving to save himself the humiliation of waiting, but was too anxious to feel her body, to get a break from the ration reports and Blockführer appointments that had clogged up his day. Five minutes passed. Six or seven prisoners came out of the hallway that led to the koberzimmers. He studied each face, searching for some sign that they'd been with her, although he didn't know what he expected to see.

The brothel supervisor strolled into the waiting room. She had put her jacket back on, but as she leaned over to speak to the cashier, she smacked her red lips together, daring him to stare. Karl rose and went right up to her. "Enough waiting."

"As I've mentioned before, sir, there's no queue at the SS brothel." Her tone was condescending, even haughty, and he felt his authority slipping from his grasp. The heat returned to the back of his neck, this time prickling with anger.

He struck his hand against the tabletop. "This is outrageous! Tell me what room she's in!"

The cashier sat very still without blinking, while the brothel supervisor's lips pressed into a straight line. "Right away, sir." She reached for the papers on the floor, checked the room numbers listed on them, and nodded for him to follow.

At the door to Marijke's koberzimmer, he took a deep breath and then entered to find her sitting on the bed, smoothing out the mattress cover. A calm spread over him, like the relief from a cold compress applied to a wound.

"Hello, beautiful," he said.

She rose and let him take her in his arms, but made no effort to return his embrace.

As he removed his tunic and folded it, he pointed to the plant that hung from the ceiling in a knotted contraption. "This is a cheerful addition. What's this called again?"

"Macramé." She started to strip off her clothes as if undressing for a medical examination.

"What's wrong, dearest?"

"I've had a rough day."

His fingers stopped unbuttoning.

"Aren't you going to ask why?"

"I don't want to hear the details."

"You don't like the thought of what happens when you're not around?"

He walked over to the window. The other potted plants obstructed the view and withered from the frosty air that leaked through the thin glass. "You think I could forget?"

All of a sudden, the room felt stuffy. He lifted a handful of soil from one of the pots, squishing it in his fist. He reminded himself that nobody had forced her to join the resistance or help those Dutch Jews, just like nobody had pushed her into prostitution.

Her arms slid around his waist. He turned around to see a thin trail of sweat clinging to her hairline, her cheeks mottled red.

"I'm sorry," she said.

She guided him to the bed and raised his fingers to the collar of her dress. As he undid the clasp, she tilted her head to expose the nape of her neck. When he kissed it, she pulled him in, sucking his lip. With his free hand, he parted her legs, but she winced at the touch.

"What is it?"

Her eyes clouded. "Nothing, go on."

He tried, but her body wouldn't respond, so he leaned back against the wall.

"You don't have to stop."

"Tell me what's wrong."

She tucked her knees to her chest and sighed. She looked tired, and the light that had first drawn him to her had dimmed. "It hurts."

Thoughts of those prisoners in the waiting room came back to him, and he tried to ignore these while his erection ached against his thigh. He brought her toward him and rested her head against his shoulder. "Nothing has to happen. Don't ever feel like I'm forcing you." He kissed her forehead. For the next half-hour, they sat together. The only sound was the slow pattern of her breathing against his own.

LOSING the promise of sex should have discouraged him from visiting. But every morning, he woke to visions of her heart-shaped face, her slight but tempting curves, the faded sunspots on her shoulders. Each song the brass band played became another story to share. The first buds on the trees, the party for the Führer's birthday—he tried to capture every detail for her. He filtered out the heavy bits, of course. He wouldn't bore her with the progress of the war, worry her with the growing camp death toll. He didn't want to burden her with his complaints, his own fears.

By late spring, Karl could no longer ignore the fact that Marijke wasn't his to keep. She dominated his thoughts, and for months, he had been sending a steady stream of gifts. Dried meats, wine, even a gold watch. But no matter what, she was still a prisoner, and he was one of many men.

It had been almost a year since his arrival at Buchenwald. Brandt remarked he was pleased with how Karl had taken to camp life, that he seemed to have found the backbone for it. A month earlier, Karl had revoked Ritter's holiday leave after he'd tried to crack a joke about Karl's leniency toward the prisoners, and since then, Karl's SS inferiors had showed him more of the respect he deserved. The officers had stopped inviting him to their card games and gave him a buffer of space. He held no objections. Aside from Ritter, they were a thick-headed bunch. They swore and smoked tirelessly, chugged Champagne as if it were beer, and had no interest in music or opera or nature or anything that didn't contain a trigger or a fuse.

Most of the officers followed the rules and used the SS brothel, believing that the girls were far prettier, and for the most part, they were right. Karl had gotten rid of the haughty SS supervisor at the prisoners' brothel and her sidekick. Not only was he sick of their disdain, but he also knew that they let any guard or officer into the brothel who would offer up an appealing bribe. He found two middle-aged female prisoners to take over the administration of the brothel, hoping it would keep his men away from Marijke.

He made up his mind to take further action the day the Allies invaded Normandy. Berlin gave them little information about the attacks. All morning, he stayed in his office with the radio turned up loud, but he couldn't get a good hold on the facts. The reports spoke of countless ships, paratroopers, amphibious landings, but assured them that the Wehrmacht would have no difficulties stifling the attempted invasion.

Lunch and dinner passed without stoking Karl's appetite. As he pushed his cut of beef across his plate, he debated what to say to Marijke. News of the invasion would excite her, but the termination of the war would mean the end of the two of them. He didn't know what had gotten into him. What they had was no relationship. If he never returned to the brothel, she would probably be relieved.

He stewed all afternoon, trying to distract himself with a visit to the kennels. One of the Alsatians jumped into his lap, which calmed his nerves as he sat there petting it. But this was only a temporary bandage, and by eight that evening, he'd worked himself back into a panic. The Allies would advance on them, and who really knew how long that would take. Months, weeks? He refused to lose her so quickly. But he knew he should have been more worried about his own skin. An Allied victory would plunge Germany back under water; Uncle Sam would hold them under, laughing while they thrashed and struggled to stay afloat. Luck might take them to a POW camp, although he doubted the Americans would look on him with sympathy. Not when they grasped what they were doing at Buchenwald. Maybe it would be smartest to run, he thought, but his father had warned him about that before Karl left for Buchenwald.

You may not be fighting right on the front, son, but you must show the strength and bravery of a soldier no matter what. There's no room in the Reich for cowards.

Karl told himself it was pointless to dwell on the invasion. He had to stay strong, stay dedicated to the cause. It was his duty, to his family, to his people. The Wehrmacht had insurmountable power, and he trusted the Wehrmacht generals to launch a fierce counterattack. Hitler would lead the Reich to a magnificent victory.

KARL had planned to stop by the brothel at nine as per usual but couldn't wait any longer. He checked with the radio operators for updates one last time and made his way over there. The evening felt cool, even though the sun still rested over the peaked roofs of the blocks. He thought of how nice it would be to bring Marijke out to watch the sunset, but that would be taking a big risk. Rumours about Marijke could reach Brandt, and there was no telling how he might react.

The new cashier—a plain but friendly woman—nodded as Karl entered. He glanced at her clipboard for the koberzimmer number, but the cashier asked him to wait while she checked to see if Marijke was ready. A row of prisoners stared down at their shoes when he entered the waiting room. Green triangles and a pink one. Red grooves ran across the back of the queer's wrists, evidence of a recent whipping. Himmler had sent a memo to the camps on updated Reich procedures for dealing with homosexuals. The problem had worsened, he argued, and they had to crack down. The Jews were one thing—a pest, as Himmler saw them—but the pink triangles were eating away at the German race from the inside out.

The prisoner must have noticed Karl's staring, because his leg started to vibrate against his chair. The noise irritated Karl. He rose and marched into the hallway, ignoring the cashier who turned to call out to him. As he rounded the corner, he stopped. A guard had his piggish face pressed up to the peephole of Marijke's koberzimmer, while one of his hands jerked up and down in his trousers.

"You—get the hell out of here!"

The guard spun around and sputtered out an apology as he wrestled his hand free and did up his zipper.

"You're a disgrace."

The guard hid his hands and stood at attention. "A few pink triangles came in tonight. I was told to make sure they were doing what they were brought in for."

"You're despicable, you know that? What's your name?"

The guard paled as he told Karl, but as soon as he had scurried off, his name dropped away and all Karl could think about was the man in there with Marijke. His fingers curled around the doorknob, but then he stopped himself. She would feel humiliated if he walked in on that, but there was no way in hell he wanted it to go on another minute.

The new brothel supervisor appeared in the hall to investigate the commotion.

"I sent the guard away," Karl said. "This one needs to get out of there." He gestured to Marijke's door but the woman didn't move.

"They have three more minutes."

"Now."

She rapped on the door, and he moved a few metres to the side until the inmate emerged, shutting the door behind him. The man didn't look like someone who'd just fucked. His hair was shaved too short to appear dishevelled and he was so pale that Karl expected him to keel over at his feet.

She pointed down the hall. "Please go see the doctor for another injection."

The inmate kept his head down as he walked away. A flash of worry struck Karl. All those men, it must have been hundreds by now. Even if these prisoners were cleaner than most, did he really want to be sharing her at all?

The brothel supervisor gave him a curious look. "Are you going in?"

"Send the rest of her clients to someone else." As soon as the words left his mouth, he knew he didn't mean for that night alone.

CHAPTER FIFTEEN

Luciano
May 15, 1977
Buenos Aires

L UCIANO STOOD IN THE BASEMENT WAITING TO FILE into the Documentation Office. Hawk called out to him, "Number five-seven-four, step out of line."

Luciano's heart fluttered like a caged hummingbird as he moved to the side. A door at the other end of the basement creaked, and he almost pissed himself at the idea of more torture.

"Three-four-one, you too."

Gabriel moved behind him. They waited while the other labourers filtered into their respective rooms. Luciano could hear Gabriel's teeth chattering nervously. He squinted through the hood, trying to see what Hawk was doing. Hawk took him by the elbow and guided him forward. Gabriel fumbled to match the pace. They crossed the basement and stopped farther down. Hawk led them into a room, undid their handcuffs and instructed them to remove their hoods.

"Five-seven-four, you've been reassigned to go through these files." He placed a folder on the desk. "Three-four-one, show him what to do."

Luciano blinked a few times to bring the room into focus. A smaller space than the Documentation Office, with a single desk and a wall of metal filing cabinets. In the hall, someone cried out in protest. Hawk strode over to the doorway to check what was going on. He glanced back but paused only a second before disappearing.

Luciano and Gabriel didn't speak. They listened, waited. When Hawk didn't return, Gabriel approached the folder and opened it. For the first time, Luciano was left without super-vision for more than a minute and had a chance to speak to Gabriel openly, to study his friend from head to toe. It was fine to call him a friend, after everything Gabriel had done to arrange the translation job, but they knew so little about each other. As Gabriel picked up the top file and began to read, Luciano noticed how long his eyelashes were. Dark curls spilled over his ears, and a few sprang loose against his brow like escaping thoughts. The unbuttoned collar of his shirt exposed a triangle of an almost hairless chest, and Luciano wondered if somewhere out there, Gabriel had a lover pining after him, a girl who liked to dance her tongue over the contours of his skin.

Gabriel looked up and caught Luciano staring. They both lowered their eyes. Luciano ran his fingers over the marks on his arms, the scars of the Machine, reminding himself they had a job to do.

"They had me organizing these files when I first got here," Gabriel mumbled, so Luciano went over to the desk to stand right next to him. From outside the room came angry shouts and a loud thud.

"Do you think he's coming back?" Luciano asked.

Gabriel chewed his lip and glanced at the door. "I wouldn't give it more than five minutes." He held out the folder for Luciano to see. It contained a list of prisoner numbers and a pile of index cards as thick as a matchbox.

"How long have you been here?"

"They nabbed me in February. The first two months, I got nothing but the hood and the Machine. Then they had me scrubbing the blood from the torture rooms. You don't know the luck you had to get a job right away and a good one, too."

Luciano lifted up the top index card. Attached to the back was a black-and-white shot of a woman in her late thirties, with information about her background and capture. The woman wore a striped shirt that draped like a nightgown and faced the photographer straight on. Listed under her name was her profession: schoolteacher. "What university do you attend?" Luciano tried to distract himself from her haunting stare.

"I dropped out." Gabriel paused. "What's the point in being a journalist if your mouth is taped shut?" He took the index card and held it so Luciano could see. "We need to file these by prisoner number." He opened a cabinet drawer that contained hundreds of index cards. From the top of the cabinet, he pulled out a hefty record book and flipped through the sheets of numbers until he found the one that matched the index card. Columns covered the page: name, personal data, date of entry and exit, and a final one with annotated letters. "Look," Gabriel said, pointing to the letter *T*. "She was 'transferred' last week. They transfer twenty people every Wednesday."

"Transferred where?"

Gabriel shook his head. "You still have a lot to learn, don't you?"

Luciano scanned the names in the first column as the truth twisted through him. He pulled the drawer all the way out and flipped through the cards.

"What are you looking for?"

"A friend." He rustled through the cards until he got to where Fabián's name would have been. Then he snatched the registry from Gabriel, found his own prisoner number and checked the other entries from the same week.

Gabriel looked suspicious. "This isn't the only detention centre, you know. Dozens are hidden throughout the city."

Luciano nodded but let out his breath before laying the registry open on the desk. In the background, the music began, a soprano's aria, and he braced himself for the screams that would leak through her song. "They can't get away with this."

"They already have."

"If people knew what was going on in here."

"What do you expect to do about it? Rattle your chains a little louder, hoping someone on the streets will hear? Every day they pick up more and more of our comrades, the people who are already trying to make a difference." Gabriel checked the door again. "Anyway, I wouldn't have pinned you as a revolutionary."

"All we need to do is survive." The first scream broke through the music. Luciano winced and closed his eyes, picturing the way Fabián seemed to grow taller as soon as he got in front of a crowd. "This can't go on forever. And when we're free, we can rip off that tape."

"They won't ever believe what we've gone through. The military will do everything they can to make these places vanish." His gaze fell on the book. "We'd have to remember every last detail, down to the number of steps it takes to get to the toilets." He started to add something else, but someone entered the room. Like Hawk, this guard was still a teenager, with a wiry frame and long sloth-like limbs. A thick pair of glasses took up most of his face. He had the look of a guy who had always eaten his lunch alone at school.

The guard reached for his waist and pulled out a pistol. "What are you doing in here?" He walked toward them with the gun pointed, his lip curled into a practised sneer. "Well?"

"I'm—I'm showing him the filing system," Gabriel stammered. "One of the guards just left."

The guard scrutinized Luciano, making him feel like he was laid out on a table for dissection. "Is that true?" His accent sounded provincial.

Luciano nodded. The guard lowered his gun and ran his finger along the barrel as he considered their answer. Luciano wasn't sure what frightened him more: the flash of pleasure in the guard's grin or the fact that someone he could have babysat was toying with their lives.

The guard stayed for what felt like a minute before taking a step back. "Get to work, then." He retreated to the doorway, where he pulled out a cigarette, his eyes still on Luciano.

Gabriel turned back to the index cards, but they shook between his fingers. The music played on as they bent over the files, and Luciano flipped through the cards, trying to block out the vacant black-and-white faces, trying to ignore their fates. He heard a low discussion behind him, but didn't dare turn around. When he finally had to reach for the registry book, the guard with the glasses was gone, and Hawk stood in his place.

AFTER they returned to La Capucha, Gabriel scratched on the particleboard between their cells. Luciano shifted as close to the partition as possible before scratching in return.

"You know that guard with the glasses?" Gabriel asked.

"Yeah?"

"We call him Shark. Watch out for him."

"Why?"

"He likes to prey on guys, you know, ones like you."

A guard passed by and banged on their cell doors. "Shut up in there!"

Luciano's throat went dry as he rolled over to the centre of the mattress; all the possible meanings of that phrase flew through his mind. *Ones like you.* Again, he pictured some girl caressing Gabriel's shoulders, the same spot Luciano touched every day on the march downstairs, kissing the small of his back, which Luciano would never feel. He should have known Gabriel would guess the truth, as Fabián had. A flicker of relief passed through him, the realization that he wouldn't have to pretend, wouldn't have to lie, make up stories of girlfriends and sex as he had so many times before. But then he cringed, overcome by shame, worrying what Gabriel thought of him.

Dear Father,

I've tried making a list of the times you've hurt me most. Disappointed me. But maybe it's easier to think about the few times you've surprised me or left me wondering. The older I get, the easier it is to—you're a complicated man, Father. All iron, like a knight whose armour has rusted around him. But I know there's more to you than that. I keep thinking about that spring we took the road trip through Patagonia. Do you remember seeing the glacier in the middle of that cold snap?

Between the bouts of rain, the wind had wailed so hard it stung their ears. With half the contents of their suitcases layered on, Luciano had thought they resembled sausages, except for his mother, who always managed to appear graceful.

As the tour boat took them toward Perito Moreno Glacier, his mother kept trying to get them to pose for a photo in front of it, but his father stood at the bow railing, his neck craned up toward that looming, jagged wall of ice. Two hundred and fifty frozen square kilometres of shocking bright blue.

"That, son," he said, "is the type of power man will never have." He turned to Luciano in awe before staring back out over the water. Waves sloshed against the glacier's edge a hundred metres from the boat, and a patch of sunlight emerged, the reflection against the ice so dazzling that they had to look away.

His father's nose had gone pink. He clapped his hands together to warm them and asked Luciano's mother if she'd packed the Thermos of coffee. As she crouched to get it out of her handbag, they heard a loud boom. Luciano knew it was only a falling chunk of ice, but his father lunged toward them, shoving them against the deck, his arms spread to shelter them. Mamá cried out in surprise and told Papá to calm down. The moment he realized his mistake, he got up, but Luciano could see his frantic panting. A laughing crowd had gathered beside them, and his father had turned crimson when the tour guide came over and launched into a lesson on glacier calving.

You stayed in a bitter mood all day, but I replayed that incident over and over. I couldn't—I was obsessed with the panic and concern in your eyes. All my life, you've judged Mamá for picking me up after school, for phoning my teacher when I was bullied. "A boy needs to fend for himself," you said. So why did you finally sense the need to protect me? And since when is a man like you afraid of loud noises?

After that trip, his father's hair had turned from dirty blond straight to white, like a reminder of that glacier ice. He'd never seemed to care about appearances, but in the days that followed, he stayed slouched in his armchair, lost in his music, and kept muttering some strange proverb about a crown of grey hair.

Tough and callous as you appear, Father, you, too, show your cracks. A big part of me felt pleased to see that.

CHAPTER SIXTEEN

MARIJKE
JUNE 7, 1944
BUCHENWALD

NEARLY A YEAR HAD PASSED AT BUCHENWALD, and I was worn out and deflated. My figure had almost returned to normal, thanks to our decent rations and Karl's gifts of food and sweets. I normally split these among the girls, except once. The first time he'd given me a cake piled high with berries, I kept it to myself, devouring it in the bathroom like a brothel rat. That same night, I'd found blood in my panties, and from then on, my period randomly came and went.

The visits from the prisoners had lessened over time, which we took as a sign that the men were dying off. We met this with a mix of relief and sadness. Sophia lay in bed after hours, grieving for Albin the counterfeiter and his soft, woollen voice, or for the French actor, Henri, who had lived beside her favourite brasserie in Paris. I'd long grown numb to the visits; the chalky faces and warped limbs all began to look the same, painful reminders of a time I yearned to forget, of a husband who seemed like the faint glow of a lighthouse on the horizon. Although I still asked each visitor about Theo, the question had become habit, with little hope for a response. To the inmates, the girls at the brothel were perfect examples of femininity. Girlfriends, not whores. They clung to us with such desperation it became difficult not to look on them with pity, to feel guilty at our inability to fulfill their fantasies. How they wanted to feel loved. I barricaded myself from them, providing the necessary comfort and nothing more.

At first, we girls had tried to alleviate our shared misery. But after months of being cooped up like hens, we'd begun to peck at one another, searching out each other's weak spots. We fought over who got the biggest slice of cheese, whose turn it was to scrub the toilets. Gerda snapped at Edith for bragging so much, calling her a lush and a harlot. Edith, in turn, accused Gerda of stealing her hairbrush and spare thread.

No matter how much the sun shone outside, the brothel felt gloomy—a prison for our minds as much as our bodies. Even I felt my patience dwindling. The way Sophia clicked her tongue against her teeth while she chewed irritated me beyond reason, and although she would never have said a bad word against anyone, she seemed more and more absent, like she was only half-listening to me, and I sensed her growing exasperation whenever I went on about Karl.

Dinnertime became unpredictable. Some days we chatted and gossiped, sharing stories from home, marvelling at the differences between our customs: how we tied our scarves, how we celebrated the birth of a baby. Laughter became our own brand of courage.

Other days, Edith and Gerda swore back and forth across the table, while the Polish girls argued in their own language.

One morning, after another spoiled breakfast, Edith gestured to me as she emerged from her bedroom. Her face had the greenish tinge of unripe fruit.

"What's wrong?" I asked.

She led me into the bathroom and shut the door behind us. I'd never seen her so serious.

"You can tell me," I said. "I won't say a word; that's a promise."

She tugged on her lip as she debated what to say. "A week ago, I found a sore, and now there are more of them."

"A sore?"

"You know." She started to whisper. "Chancre sores."

My gaze dropped to her waistline, as if I expected to see them through her dress. She blushed in embarrassment, something I'd thought her incapable of.

"Oh God, Edith." In the mirror, my expression shifted to match hers. I reached out to hug her, but she pulled away.

"That's not all." She withdrew her hands from her pockets and flipped them over to reveal a fierce rash across her palms.

"Is that—?"

"Syphilis."

"Are you sure? It could be something else, maybe scarlet fever?"

"No, I've seen it enough times before in Berlin. There's no doubt about it."

What settled over me then was an icy feeling, the same sensation as when cycling up onto the dike on a February's day, the type of damp cold that wriggles into your core. I feared not only for her, but for all of us. We'd known something like this would happen sooner or later.

"How did the doctor not notice?" I asked.

"I don't know. During my last checkup, he seemed rushed, distracted. But now it's inevitable."

"It might go away, if you rest all day. I'll take over your chores."

"And then what? I infect all the men who come tonight?"

For a second, I thought they deserved it. After all, one of them had gotten her sick. They happily visited the brothel knowing the hell they put us through. But then my sensibility returned, and I reminded myself that most of those prisoners had it far worse than we did.

"We'll think of something," I said. "For now, don't draw any attention to yourself."

"Me, not draw attention to myself? That'll be a challenge." She forced a laugh as we left the bathroom. At least she was still acting like herself.

SHE lasted until dinner. When someone asked her to pass the water jug, I caught a glimpse of her palms, which had grown even redder. Gerda watched Edith with disdain, and later, while we cleaned up our plates, the brothel supervisor pulled Edith aside and asked to see her hands. Edith glanced at me, and we both knew it was over. She was sent straight to the infirmary blocks.

She didn't return that night, nor the next. When I told Sophia the whole story, she agreed there was a good chance Gerda had spotted the rash and reported it. A cruel thing to do if it were true, but we decided not to rush to any conclusions, lest we create more of a rift between us all.

Several days later, Sophia and I lay on our beds, contemplating Edith's fate. I assumed she'd been taken back to Ravensbrück. Sophia's guess wasn't as optimistic.

"She's dead, she must be."

"Don't say that."

"We're all thinking it. She's no good to the SS anymore. They have no reason to keep her alive."

"Maybe she's still recovering in the infirmary."

Sophia shook her head. "I know you don't believe that." She sounded so weary, defeated. "Marijke, I've had enough. All of these men, I don't feel human anymore. I can't go on like this."

"Please, you can't talk like that." I said this even though I heard my own echo in her words. The feeling that we'd become objects, the way everything had dulled: my senses, images of home, of the people I loved.

"Some prisoners have found a way out, you know. They take their lives into their own hands."

I sat up. "Sophia, listen to me. We'll get through this."

"Why, what's the point? What good awaits us, even if the war does end in our favour? We return home to find our cities destroyed, half our family missing? How do you expect me to ever marry after this? We're tainted."

Tainted. She was right. Theo, if he survived, would never look at me the same way. What would become of our marriage? That sick ache came back, that dread, the fear—the only emotions that stayed sharp.

I gripped the corner of the nightstand and looked her in the eyes. "When the Allies win, you'll go home to loving parents, your brothers. They will survive, just like you. And you'll have friends, like me, and one day, you'll meet someone who can look past all of this." I moved to sit beside her and placed a hand on her knee. "Please, you need to hold on. Trust me that it will be worth it."

She closed her eyes and breathed in, her fingers closing over mine. She squeezed my hand and didn't let go. "All right," she said, "I trust you."

SUMMER solstice came and went and still Edith did not return. Karl did, though, and his visits were both a reminder of my suffering and a welcome distraction. Whenever he came by, I took extra care to fluff the pillow, to pinch some colour into my cheeks and tease the curls and rolls in my hair. I found myself telling him things I'd only ever told Theo: my fears about how I'd never be let through the same doors as the male violinists in Amsterdam, my worries that I was too selfish to make a good mother. With these confessions came the nervous anticipation of his response, but he always kissed my wrists and told me I had nothing to worry about, that I was strong and brave and beautiful. Later, I berated myself for these moments of weakness. I knew I mustn't lower my defences, mustn't forget who he was. Any time another Nazi crossed my vision, my anger prickled, threatening to lash out like slippery tentacles. Who knew what Karl was capable of, how much happiness he'd crushed, how many lives he'd extinguished.

Docile and concerned as he acted around me, he had a temper that fired up like an engine when he'd had a long day. One minute, he'd praise the meticulous nature of the prisoners tending the camp garden, and in his next breath, he'd accuse them of hoarding potatoes and threaten a flogging. This gave me the sense that he was trying to be two men at once, and I worried what could happen if he ever turned on me.

As we lay on the bed one night after closing, he pressed into me, his chest sticky against my back. "Seeing you is the best part of my day," he whispered, his voice lost in my hair.

"It's not every day."

"I wish it were."

I sighed. On his last visit, he hadn't even wanted sex, claiming he'd come only to see me. But when he didn't want it, I did. I was afraid of what I'd become, something half-woman, half-animal. I'd always taken pride in being sensible and loyal, so who was this stranger who'd betray all that for something as primal as desire?

Karl nudged my shoulder. "I've been thinking." He scratched. "Perhaps it's selfish. I don't want you to see other men."

"Like who? Bruno?"

"Who's that?"

"Kommandoführer Hoffmann. He pays the brothel supervisor to arrange a girl now and then."

"That brute? He's got shit for brains." He scratched his chin. "Well, no, not him—not anyone."

It felt like he had struck a match inside of me, a hesitant, flickering glow. "What would I do all evening?"

"I want you to myself."

"You are selfish."

"I love you."

I closed my eyes. "Don't say that."

"It's true. Whether you want to believe it or not."

After slipping out of his arms, I went over to the sink and let cold water stream over my wrists. I tried to picture Theo, his scent, the sound of his voice, but the image was blurred around the edges. Karl's presence remained in the koberzimmer long after he left, his smell of leather and pine, his voice solid and thick as an old elm. If I admitted to having some sort of feelings for Karl, would that mean I accepted what he had done as part of the SS? I wished there was a way to separate one version of him from the other. I turned to him. He sat up in bed; the mattress cover had sprung loose and gotten twisted between his legs.

"Can you actually do that," I asked, "keep the other men away?"

"I can do anything." He flushed. "Well, a lot of things."

"Can you get me out of here?"

"No, not that. Sadly, that's beyond my powers."

In the pause that followed, I became very aware of my nakedness, my nipples hard and inviting. I returned to the bed and sat down, wrapping my arms around my body.

He reached for my hand, his eyes teeming with concern. "You would leave me if you were free, wouldn't you?"

Water dripped from the faucet. I paused. The sound tugged at something, a memory of one rainy day the winter before our capture. The house had grown drafty and cold, and our attic was newly empty, as the resistance had found a safe house in the countryside for the elderly Jewish couple we'd been hiding. Theo wanted to take in someone new right away, but I was hesitant. With the Gestapo on constant patrol and certain neighbours ratting one another out for so much as humming "Het Wilhelmus," the risk was higher than ever.

That morning, Theo had brought something down from the attic, a mahogany backgammon set the couple had left behind as a gift. We sat there for hours, listening to the drizzle outside and drinking tea while racing our pieces around the board. I teased that it was the luck of the dice that made him win. He winked, waving those Midas hands in the air. "That's where you're wrong. You see, over the course of a game, luck tends to balance out, and it comes down to strategy." He explained how you could approach the board in different ways. "It all depends on those opening rolls of the die. If you're not rolling high, you'll need to start building walls to block your opponent. At any moment, everything can shift, but strength lies in knowing when to maintain your defences, and when it's safe to make a move." I tightened the faucet to stop the dripping. Karl waited for my reply. "You know," he added, "I would never force you to do anything."

"You did the first time."

"That's different."

"How?"

"I'd had far too much to drink; I wasn't myself. I love you, Marijke. Did you hear that?"

"That's not some magic phrase."

He grabbed my arm, almost roughly, but softened his grip and kissed my cheek. "Well, what would you like, then? Would you rather continue your regular schedule?"

"Of course not."

"What is it you want?"

"I want to be left in peace."

He withdrew his arm. "Does that include me?" His mouth sagged into a frown, a sad, sorry look that made me crumple again. More and more, simple gestures and an ounce of vulnerability could deceive me into seeing him as an everyday man, a lover. I thought back to Theo's explanation of that backgammon game, and I envisioned all those brothel visitors wiped away like game pieces from my board. Keeping Karl happy, allowing him to believe whatever he desired, could serve only to protect me, to help me survive and find my way back to my husband.

I sighed and touched the creases in his cheeks. "Make the arrangements, then, and I will be yours."

He smiled.

"For now."

"I'll sort out a private room for you and better rations."

"That's not necessary."

"But I want to."

"The other girls wouldn't understand. I'm surviving as is and I wouldn't feel right about it."

Karl tousled my hair, his fingers catching in the knots. "Always worried about everyone else." He stood and took an ivory flask from his overcoat pocket. "This calls for a celebration."

"I told you I don't drink."

"Not even for this?"

"I'll find my own way to celebrate."

CHAPTER SEVENTEEN

AFTER KARL CAUGHT THAT GUARD LEERING AT Marijke, he rounded up the SS officers who visited the prisoners' brothel. He didn't need to worry about the guards. That troublesome brothel supervisor, greedy as she'd been, wouldn't have let any of them visit the girls, but he wanted to set the officers straight before they started bribing her replacement for that privilege. As far as he knew, only three or four officers, all well below his rank, had made it a habit: Ritter, a couple of his drinking mates, and Hoffmann—"Bruno" to Marijke. He should have suspected that mongrel was after her. When Hoffmann entered the officers' lounge that night, Karl felt the urge to go over and bust in his teeth.

Ritter took a seat and pulled out a cigarette. "Well, we're all curious what this is about." He held out the pack in offering, but when Karl responded with a cold look, he stood up again. "I'm sorry, Schutzhaftlagerführer, do you mind?"

"Go ahead." As the other men lit up, the atmosphere in the room relaxed, and with it went Karl's sense of his authority over them. He paced back and forth. All week things had been jetting from his mouth faster than he could think. The day before, he'd told Marijke that he loved her. Words that could lead to nothing but problems. He'd only ever said that to Else, and he wasn't even sure if he'd meant it then. But, try as he had, he couldn't quash the feeling.

The stinking cigarettes made his nose itch. He let out a cough to seize the men's attention and began the little speech he'd planned. "I'm bringing this up in private so Brandt won't get after you, but that doesn't make it any less important." His voice escalated with each word, and he gripped the sides of the table as if it were a podium. "It's about the prisoners' whores. I know we've had some fun and games, but it's time to end things. From now on, that brothel is for prisoner use only."

The men shifted. Ritter and Hoffmann exchanged sly looks.

"The Kommandant hand-picked the girls at the SS brothel," Karl added. "It's an insult to him if you sneak off and use the second-rate ones. Besides, do you really want to be fucking the same women as criminals and communists?"

Ritter broke a grin. "Not to mention those fags."

"Right, the last thing you'd want is to catch one of their diseases. Do I make myself clear?" Karl let go of the table and examined the men.

Hoffmann met his gaze. "Does that apply to all officers?"

Karl felt his temper flickering hot. His voice sharpened. "It applies to you—understood?"

Hoffmann's lips pinched to hide his scowl. Karl could have hit him right then, but then he might have run to Brandt with the whole story. Much as the Kommandant liked Karl, he wouldn't be happy to hear that Karl had gone behind his back about the brothel ordeal.

"That's settled, then. If I hear any more reports of visits to the prisoners' brothel, I'll have to report it to the Kommandant straightaway."

The officers nodded. When Karl dismissed them, they gave quick "Heil Hitler" salutes and dispersed.

THE muggy heat of summer and the spike in camp numbers gave rise to a new problem. Death hung around like never before, and the crematorium couldn't keep up. Flies swarmed the piles of waiting corpses, while the sun went to work on decaying flesh. Karl had started to take a detour to get to the depots. The output of the crematorium proved to be as much of a headache, although it was nothing like the truckloads of ashes the SS at the extermination camps had to deal with, thank God. It took a man with an iron stomach to handle a camp like Auschwitz. Still, something had to be done about all those ashes.

The solution came to him on one of his strolls near the grounds of the falconry. Deep craters formed among the trees there, like the devil had reached up his claws to pull the earth down into hell.

Within a week, they began dumping ashes at that spot. Karl passed by again one morning at dawn. The first pit was already filling up. Even though the sky was still a murky grey and the inmates had yet to leave their blocks, it was far from quiet at the edge of the woods. Squirrels scurried around clucking at one another. A breeze caught the forest canopy like a sail, mimicking the soft roar of the sea. Far below in the crater, the topmost ashes whirled up, refusing to settle in that Devil's Hole, and for some reason, this disturbed him far more than those rotting bodies, the flies. He stayed there that morning for a very long time, transfixed by this movement, the way the ashes spun like they still possessed life.

SHORTLY after lunch on a hot August day, the type of hazy afternoon that pastes a shirt to your back, Karl was on his way to a meeting at the DAW arms factory at the camp's eastern border. He kept thinking back to those ashes, the unpleasant feeling the image had left in his stomach. Since that day, he'd adjusted the route of his morning strolls to a different part of the woods.

Now as he neared the sentry line, a pebble scuttled across his path. The ground started to rumble. His chest tightened as he looked up to spot a *V* of long white slashes across the horizon. One bomber, a mere speck, flew at the head of the pack, approaching closer and closer. Then came a loud roar. Not the uneven *wow-wow-wow* of Luftwaffe engines, but a deep drone.

There was nothing nearby for cover, the only air-raid shelter ten minutes away. The noise grew deafening, accompanied by a high-pitched whistle. The air-raid sirens started to wail. He broke into a sprint, just in time to see a plume of red smoke appear at the edge of camp. A flare to mark the DAW factory as a bull's eye. The sight brought him to a halt. Too stunned to move, he watched, dread hardening in the back of his throat.

The planes were right overhead. He pushed on, his feet smacking the pitch. On all sides, prisoners yelled, ran or dropped to the ground. He changed his course to cut away from the factory, back toward the sea of prisoners' blocks. Marijke. There was no bomb shelter for the prisoners, not even enough for the SS. Something pulled at him, the need to protect her. He hesitated but kept moving in the direction of the gatehouse. There wasn't time, and he'd be a clear target darting to the opposite end of camp.

Bombs screeched through the air, scattering explosions all around him. Dirt flew into his eyes. Metres from the gate, a bomb landed right behind him. He threw himself against the gatehouse, ducked and covered his head with his arms. The cement wall vibrated against his back while pieces of debris hit his shoulders, narrowly missing his head. Another explosion. The impact slammed him back. Metal sliced his arm. He saw red before feeling anything. Brandt's briefings on emergency protocol came back in fragments, useless to him now. The planes circled, and the horizon erupted in white flashes. Incendiary bombs. He struggled to his feet, clutching a hand to his arm, blood dripping between his fingers.

He ran on through the gate, alongside the SS barracks. Between some buildings, craters had gutted the lawn. One of the barracks had split open down the side like a dollhouse. Amid a mass of wood and slabs of concrete and metal bed frames lay an SS guard. He was sprawled dead in the middle of the floor, a razor clutched in his hand and half of his jaw still lathered with soap, the other half blown clean off. Karl covered his mouth, trying not to vomit. Somewhere, the wounded screamed—SS men. A nearby bomb detonated in flames, the heat licking at Karl's hair. He could taste sweat. Ignoring the cries for help, he pressed on. All he could think of was getting underground.

His stomach twisted with cramps by the time he made it to the air-raid shelter, a bulge of stone and earth hidden between trees. He scrambled down the steps, banged on the heavy door and hollered for someone to open up. Another piercing whistle. His arm throbbed. He slammed his weight against the metal and fell inward onto another officer. The door shut behind him. He got up to look around while his vision adjusted to the dim lamplight and found Hoffmann crouched in shadow with a handful of other officers. Seven SS wives huddled together, pale and trembling, children clinging to their skirts. An infant wailed, but nobody spoke. No sign of Brandt.

The sky boomed for another half-hour, the children whimpering all the while. The heat in the shelter grew unbearable. While Karl made a bandage from a corner of a baby's blanket, he thought of the blast by the crematorium, how it had just missed him. He thought of the streak of flames through the treetops. Of Marijke.

Soon, everything fell still, and his ears rang in the silence. Everyone looked to him for instructions. He cleared his throat. "The women and children should stay here until I send a messenger. The rest of you, let's go."

BUCHENWALD still smouldered at sundown. Smoke crept through the camp like a fog, choking out the orange sky. Injured figures limped in and out of sight. Embers kept blazing up in the trees, and they'd put half the prisoners to work at helping control the fire. Others built makeshift stretchers out of fallen trees, and both the infirmary blocks and the SS hospital overflowed onto the steps outside. Karl and Brandt met by the SS barracks to compare findings on the damage.

The Kommandant noted that a couple of their administration buildings had burned to the ground, along with the isolation blocks where they kept the prominent prisoners, politicians and an Italian princess. A year earlier, they would have gotten flak from Himmler for such losses, but now the Reich's cloak of invincibility had slipped and reality was setting in.

The factories had suffered the most. Karl informed Brandt that only two buildings from the Gustloff Works were still standing. A long row of tables covered with half-assembled K98k carbines was all that remained of one of the main halls. The DAW factory had fared better, but enough explosions had hit its grounds to leave it filled with broken glass and dented machines and probably close to a million marks' worth of damage.

Although the Allies had crippled Buchenwald's armaments production, they'd spared the labour force. Karl assumed they had lost a couple hundred inmates with the destruction of the factories and had yet to determine the number of wounded, but estimated approximately one thousand. To verify this and thwart any escape attempts amid the chaos, Karl ordered an emergency roll call. But no bombs had touched the prisoners' blocks, the brothel. He noted this with bitter relief; the only one that had landed in the prisoners' camp was the one that had injured him. No doubt, the Allies had targeted their attack. Which meant they knew about the prisoners in the blocks, about the thousands and thousands of lives the SS controlled there. Their continued advancement would reveal the truth, the crimes the Nazis were committing without any remorse. It would expose them all as murderers.

Brandt folded his arms and sighed. His face was set in a deep frown, his neck smeared with ash. "And then there's our men. I've called in all the doctors from Weimar and the neighbouring towns, but that still won't suffice. We're going to lose more overnight."

Karl recalled the screams, men impaled by splinters of wood. The way they had writhed amid the debris, a foot or an arm lying metres away. He flinched, ashamed of how he'd ignored those cries for help. "What are the numbers at?"

"At least seventy-five killed, a good two hundred wounded. But some are still unaccounted for." Brandt fixed his gaze on the casern behind Karl, where a crew of men tried to clear away the rubble. They lined up bodies on the road, one or two Karl recognized. The night tasted of iron. "The worst is that we failed to protect their families."

"They're safer here than in Berlin at least." Karl started coughing and waved a hand to clear the smoke between them. "Thank God for that air-raid shelter. Though we'll need to build a couple more closer to the villas."

"Have you been back there?"

"Not yet."

"We were lucky, Müller; others not so much." Brandt rubbed his forehead, but then his brow hardened with resolve. "They won't get away with this. We'll rebuild the factory, of course, but before we start on that, we'll see to it that the prisoners pay for every life we've lost."

"Of course, sir. Just tell me what I need to do."

BRANDT'S comment about the villas got Karl worrying, so as soon as he returned to his office, he made his way back. Breathing became easier the farther he got, but dusk had masked the forest with shadows, and the buzz of the rescue squad faded to nothing. Even the frogs had gone quiet.

The stretch leading to his villa was brighter than usual because the house belonging to the head of the political department was missing its roof, and lights from the building behind it shone where its second storey should have been. He stepped up to the edge of the man's property. The veranda had collapsed, and the mound of bricks and mortar on top of it looked like a mountain slope after a landslide. A bookshelf tilted out of the front window, while books spilled across the garden, the bindings charred, spines split with loose pages caught in the shrubs and fluttering between the leaves like white flags. But some volumes lay intact and their gold-embossed titles caught the light: *Don Quixote, Uncle Tom's Cabin, The Atlas of the Modern World.*

As he moved on to his own villa, he raised his hands to his temples, trying to keep the iron band of his headache from tightening further. But the building's silhouette remained complete, even up to the stone chimney. Once in front of it, he spotted a couple of broken windows by his study and a small hole in the roof. There was debris strewn across the veranda from the hit to the other villa, but nothing major. He exhaled and closed his eyes.

Brandt's place didn't have a single mark. The gardens of two others had been torn up from a nearby blast to the road, which had sunk into a shell hole almost a metre deep. But apart from some missing chunks in the walls, they had survived. These villas also had lights on, but Karl couldn't see anyone inside.

He had a sudden desire to find Marijke, to hear her comforting chatter, her warm laugh. As he turned around to head back to the prisoners' camp, something up ahead caught his attention thirty or forty paces down the road from the crater and out of the villas' glow. He turned on his torch as he neared. There, at the edge of the trees, lay one of the model ships Brandt had given the officers' sons at Christmas. Its mast had snapped off and hung to the side, the ground beneath it splattered with blood.

He spotted Marijke crouched along the path that ran between the brothel and the infirmary blocks. Finding her unharmed brought on a rush of relief so strong that it took him a moment to realize he'd never seen her outside before. She leaned over a prisoner with a bandaged head. A couple dozen others were arranged on the ground around her in some haphazard queue to the infirmary, and several other girls attended to the wounded nearby.

"What are you doing out here?" he asked.

She'd rolled up her sleeves, and wisps of hair fell across her jaw. There was something calming and beautiful to her disarray, to seeing her outdoors. For a second, he allowed himself to imagine that she was out tending to their flower garden on a Sunday afternoon.

She stood up, and Karl could have sworn she looked just as relieved to see him. "So many men haven't had a chance to see a doctor yet." She nodded toward a guard who lurked behind her. "He's supervising us."

Karl straightened up and took a step away from her. "I'm bringing you back."

Marijke paused, scanning the scene around her, but she bent down to squeeze the wounded man's hand before following Karl inside. The waiting room hummed with disorder: inmates exchanged celebratory grins, clapped hands and spoke with frenzied gestures. One seemed to be mimicking something exploding. When they noticed Karl, the movement stopped.

"What is this? Why is the brothel even open?" He ordered the brothel supervisor to free up one of the koberzimmers and then turned to the prisoners. "Keep your mouths shut."

They looked to the ground. The image of the model ship came back to him, the way his neighbour's son had exclaimed in excitement as the families gathered in the drawing room at Christmas and the boys ripped the wrapping paper from their packages. Whose boat had it been—whose son? Karl studied the prisoners with a glare, searching for those traces of smug joy. Had they no respect for even their own dead?

"All of you, leave," he said. "Back to your blocks."

Marijke went rigid as the men filed out. Karl hoped she could see he was doing the other girls a favour, giving them a night off. The brothel supervisor led Karl and Marijke down the hall. The room still smelled of sex, but it was better than the thick air outside. Once alone, they fell toward one another, and the tension in her body relaxed in his arms.

He let out a breath in her ear and leaned to taste her neck. "God, I need you."

"Karl." The first time she said his name, it was a whisper, the second a command. "Karl. What happened?" She opened his tunic to examine his arm, and he realized he'd been wincing. "Does it hurt a lot? Did the doctor bandage it? What is this, cloth?" The knot had slipped undone, and the blanket looked about to unravel. Marijke peeked beneath it and scrunched up her nose. "Let me find the brothel doctor."

"I don't need him." He struggled to refasten the bandage. "Just tie this for me."

The pain kicked up again when she tightened the fabric. He gritted his teeth and swore, causing her to pause. That spark he hadn't seen in ages had returned to her face. She wrapped her hand around the back of his neck and kissed him.

"What were you saying before?" she murmured.

That loud whine returned like a headache. The firestorm by the factory, everything shaking beneath him.

With surprising force, Marijke guided him back onto the mattress. She slipped her hand under his shirt, but his mind kept drifting to those cries for help, the ones he'd ignored. The broken rigging on the mast of that ship. Her fingers curled around the hook of his belt, the button of his trousers, and as she slipped them off, he realized he wasn't going to be able to get hard. When he raised his eyes to find her smiling down at him, he saw those prisoners in the waiting room again, their obvious glee.

He sat up and shoved her off him, biting resentment coating his words. "Since when are you so eager? And why are you grinning like that?"

She leaned back to look at him. "Grinning? I'm just in shock that after all of this, I'm somehow still alive."

"Men with families were killed, even some of their children."

He swung his feet onto the floor and bent down for his trousers. She tried to rub his back, but he turned and wrenched her by the arm. "Innocent, good German children. How can you be celebrating?"

"I'm sorry," she said. "But—"

"But what?" When he let go of her, she shuffled back against the wall, pressed her knees to her chest and rubbed her wrist.

"Nothing." Her voice grew timid. "It's horrible, that's all."

How desperate she seemed, curled up there, waiting for his attention like a pathetic lapdog. "What do you know about what it was like? You, idling the day away while men died all around me? What if I'd been killed?"

A strange expression flickered across her face, but he refused to consider what she might have been thinking. She got up to stand in front of him. "Don't you think I was terrified locked in here? And can't you tell I'm happy to see you?"

"Maybe I've spoiled you too much. Look how good you have it."

Goebbels' speech came to mind, his declaration about confidence, a weapon with as much power as any bullet, when wielded by the right person. Some people were born to lead. Others were weak and couldn't see past the end of their noses. They'd drag down society if they were given free rein. That was why Germany needed the camps.

He put on his hat and adjusted it in the mirror before turning back to her. "You can all stop celebrating. We'll rebuild and rearm. And each and every prisoner at Buchenwald will help Germany win the war."

CHAPTER EIGHTEEN

Luciano
May 17, 1977
Buenos Aires

SOMETIMES, LUCIANO SWORE HE COULD HEAR BELLS
tolling. He pictured his mother dressing up for mass, the
communion wafers, the sheen of gold from the altar. That
church smell: musty air, flowers and competing eaux de toilette.
Hands fluttering between pages of hymn books. Mamá would
stay long after the pews emptied, praying urgently for his return.
His father would not be with her; that, Luciano knew for sure.

Dear Papá,
Why did you make me stop going to church? Dear Papá, I miss
Sunday mass with Mamá. Dear Papá, did you ever go to church,
even as a boy? Did you—well, I know you never cared for reli-
gion. What is it you always say? Hell is, no—heaven is a place,
heaven exists only for people who don't have their feet planted on

the ground. Yes, that's it. But don't you think . . . I wonder if that would change if you knew what it was like here in this darkness. Papá, the man who now has the cell to my left, he talks to himself. Recites things. In Hebrew, I think. His devotion makes me wish, I wish I had something to make me stronger, to give me hope.

Luciano strained his ears, listening again for those murmurs, but heard nothing and tried to call back the hushed, guttural sounds. Did his father remember when Luciano was eight or nine and they had the Austrian family over for dinner? One of Luciano's friends from school, Michiel Rosenberg, and his parents. They weren't friends for long, but Michiel had just arrived on a steamship from Europe. Mamá claimed it would be nice for the whole family to meet new people; she probably thought Papá would enjoy the chance to talk about the "Old World."

You came home late. You came home late and sat down at the table in that alpaca sweater Nonna knit. The one you complained itched at the collar. With your knife, you lined up your potatoes rank and file. You were quiet and barely said a word.

Señora Rosenberg had asked if his father missed Germany. Papá told her he was glad to have gotten away in '38, that he'd left just in time. She nodded emphatically, remarking that she'd wished they'd managed to do the same, but that no country would accept their people in those days. Luciano remembered the silence that had settled over everyone then. His mother stood up and made a big fuss clearing the dishes while his father stared coldly at the table, at some invisible centrepiece.

Later that night, after the visitors went home and Luciano was in bed, he'd heard his parents yelling.

Mamá called you a brute, or was it callous, inhospitable? You— you threw something, something that smashed against the kitchen tiles, and you forbade her from inviting over guests without your permission. Everything needs your permission, doesn't it?

For the longest time, he hadn't understood why everyone was so uncomfortable at dinner. But lately, when his neighbour whispered those prayers, he thought back to that night. Unlike many of his friends, he'd never heard his father say a bad word against Jews, but he had a suspicion that their background was at the root of that tension.

Papá, you never talk about life in Germany. What was it like with everyone in Europe bracing for war? Men with guns, gathering in the beer halls, boys running foot races with the Hitler Youth? Did Munich fill with fear like Buenos Aires? Even though you had no . . . even though you left before the war broke out, it must have affected you. I get the feeling you're harbouring some dark feelings. Did you feel guilty when the Rosenbergs visited? Maybe you felt terrible for what your people did, but that comes to those too cowardly to take a stand. Don't forget, you also failed me when they came to take me away. Do you regret that, too?

THE guards arranged a bunch of chairs around the television set, which they cranked to full volume. Luciano, Gabriel and a few other prisoners passed by on their march back from the bathroom. The sports commentator announced that Luciano's favourite soccer team, Boca Juniors, was playing a tournament match against River Plate for the first round of the Copa Libertadores. It must have been May 18, because he and Fabián had bought tickets to that match. He frowned at the thought of the two empty seats in the stadium. What an afternoon it could have been—just the two of them, laughing and drinking beer and snacking on *choripanes*, with no girlfriend around to distract Fabián.

Someone let out a belch and called out, "Who are you rooting for?"

No one replied, but Luciano recognized Shark's voice. He was sure it was a trick.

"Take off their hoods," Shark added. "I want to see their faces."

A guard came around and removed their hoods one by one. Squinting into the light, Luciano saw for the first time the basement hallway, the plain pillars that ran down it toward the torture rooms and the large square floor tiles. It was a frighteningly inconspicuous room.

"You." Shark nodded at Gabriel. "You a Bocas fan?"

A trumpet sounded on the TV. The spectators in the stadium rose for the national anthem, and something tightened in Luciano's chest as the crowd began to sing.

Gabriel blinked nervously. "Yes."

Hawk came over to take an empty chair. "Which of you cheer for River Plate?"

Two of the other labourers slowly raised their hands.

"Good. Our boys will be cleaning their cleats with Boca tears by the end of this."

Shark cracked his knuckles. "Are you willing to bet on that?"

"I'll wager Friday's shift and a pack of cigarettes that River Plate wins two to one."

"Friday is my sister's birthday. Make it tomorrow's. Three to one for Boca Juniors."

The other guards went around the circle offering bets. Luciano shifted, eager to get back to work and out of their sight, but Shark turned to Gabriel. "Well, *boludo*, what's your bet?"

Gabriel fidgeted with the pocket of his jeans. "I, uh, I don't know."

"Hurry up."

"I don't have anything to offer."

The group of guards laughed.

"Give me a score," Shark said.

"One to nothing, Boca Juniors."

Luciano chewed his lip, certain he was next. Even though Shark cheered for Boca, he didn't want to piss off any guard, didn't want to know the consequences of losing. Shark turned to him.

"A draw," Luciano said. "Nil-nil."

Shark shook his head. "What a bitch answer."

The other three labourers gave their scores while the match got going. Luciano waited for the guards to order them back to work, but their focus stayed on the game. Gatti was goalkeeper, his long hair dangling in his eyes as he darted out to join his teammates on the field. Parts of the crowd tossed blue and gold confetti whenever he made a save. Shark hooted and pumped his fist into the air, but Luciano and Gabriel stood still, not daring to make any noise.

Shark waved a hand toward them in irritation. "What kind of fans are you? Cheer, damn it!"

Luciano let out a weak whoop. Hawk laughed and pulled a box from his bag. *Medialunas*, apple lattices, *alfajores* dipped in chocolate. Luciano's mouth watered while the box made its rounds among the guards. Shark helped himself to three, emptying out the box.

It felt like the longest match Luciano had ever seen. He watched the guards, trying to gauge their moods.

When the ref called a disputable penalty against River Plate, Hawk and Shark started yelling at the ref, then at each other. "What was that, *hijo de puta*? Is your fat head too stuck up your ass to see the lines?"

"Shut up. Just look at the way that *maricón* is nursing his ankle!"

Luciano ran his tongue over his lips, imagining the flaky dough of those *medialunas*. In the final few minutes of the game, he tried to imagine himself and Fabián in the stands, arms draped across each other's shoulders, singing and chanting as hard as they could.

The ref blew his whistle, calling the end of the match. A nil-nil draw. The players walked across the pitch to shake hands, and the guards grumbled, lit up cigarettes. Nobody mentioned the bet.

Shark glanced up at them and crossed his arms. "What are you still doing here? Get out, you sons of bitches."

Luciano lowered his head to accept his hood and led the line of labourers back to the Documentation Office, still thinking of Fabián, his huge grin, his cheeks painted blue and gold.

Two days later, when the prisoners were filing out of the eating area, Hawk hooked his fingers around Luciano's shoulders. Luciano shook as he followed Hawk blindly to the stairwell, trying to figure out what awaited him. A new job? More torture? Something worse?

But Hawk didn't take him all the way down to the basement. They stopped one flight of stairs early. Luciano had never been on this level, not since first entering ESMA, but had heard it contained military offices and the officers' dining hall. The air smelled faintly like coffee.

Hawk stopped Luciano a few metres from the landing and raised his hood just enough to free his nose and mouth. "Your reward." He picked something up and passed it to him: a telephone receiver.

Luciano felt his way down the phone cord to touch the rotary dial. The dial tone droned in his ear, making his heart beat faster. He wondered if it was really true or something to mess with him, to raise his hopes.

"You have one call. Tell your parents what good care of you we're taking. Say anything else and you'll regret it."

Luciano opened his mouth in disbelief. What would he say; what could he say? He counted out the holes in the dial with his finger but paused when he found the number six.

"Excuse me," he said, "can you tell me what day it is?"

"Friday."

Friday morning, just after breakfast: his parents would both be at work. More than anything, he wanted to hear his mother's voice, her gushing love. But if he had only one call, he risked getting stuck on hold with the hospital. Maybe they wouldn't find her in time, and then he wouldn't get to speak to either of them.

"Come on," Hawk said, "you have one minute."

Luciano dialled. His stomach did acrobatics as it rang. Two, three, four rings.

"Hello?"

Luciano didn't answer, suddenly overwhelmed and unsure what to say. He wanted to reach out through the phone, to hug his father the way he hadn't in years.

"Hello?" His father sounded gruff, fatigued.

"Papá."

"Luciano? Son, is that you?" His father coughed and raised his voice. "Where are you? What have they done to you? Are you all right?"

Never had his father asked so many questions. Beside him, he heard Hawk's loud, steady breaths. Luciano paused, trying to carefully phrase his answer. "They're treating me well here. We get enough to eat and lots of rest. Please don't worry about me."

A muffled noise, silence. Then a heavy sigh. "They're monitoring the call, aren't they?"

Hawk tapped Luciano on the shoulder.

Luciano swallowed, pushing back tears. "I'm just fine, tell Mamá I'm doing fine. I have to go now, I'm sorry. Take care of yourselves and don't worry."

"Luciano, wait. I—"

But before Luciano caught whatever his father wanted to tell him, Hawk pressed the switchhook and the line went dead.

CHAPTER NINETEEN

W HEN THE BOMBS STARTED FALLING, WE HAD nowhere to hide. We froze. Ran to the windows. Huddled under the table of the day room, all of us together. Some of the girls shrieked; others cried. Sophia rocked back and forth, and Gerda prayed. The roar of the planes, the smell of smoke and chemicals, the sense that the world was crashing down around us. If I'd had my thoughts about me, I might have had visions of home: 1940, the Luftwaffe criss-crossing our skies, the centre of Rotterdam flattened in an afternoon. Friends left homeless, acquaintances killed, and Theo clutching me in our neighbour's cellar in Amsterdam, surrounded by half a dozen faces as frightened as these.

Instead, I sat there in the middle of the brothel, unable to move, to speak, to think. With each explosion, the chairs rattled against the floor. Men screamed in the distance. I covered my ears and squeezed my eyes shut, whispering Theo's name over and over, the one thing that could keep me sane.

There reached a point when the sky fell silent, and so did we. We waited, hesitated, before inching back to the windows. Trees obscured our view, but smoke billowed toward the brothel. Wilhelmina and Bertha moved across the room to the front entrance. They were the new brothel staff, middle-aged prisoners recruited from Ravensbrück. Nobody knew why the SS women had been replaced, but I hadn't failed to notice how the timing had coincided with Karl's decision to save me for himself. Wilhelmina opened the door and called out to a guard who was running by. He shouted back that the bombers had passed, but the factory and SS barracks had been hit.

We girls stared at one another, all of us stricken, unsure what to feel, how to react. Sophia, normally so quiet, was the first to speak up. "They say Göring will soon need to go on a diet if he wants to fit in between the two fronts!" A joke she must have heard from Friedrich, her brothel beau. She punctuated it with a little laugh, empty and tinny, but this grew until she truly was laughing, and tears of relief trickled down her cheeks.

As the minutes passed, we shed our fear. We began talking of the Allied approach, realizing they had spotted the prisoners' blocks and knew of our existence. Hope bubbled up like uncorked Champagne, but in the hours that followed, it became tempered by the moans of the injured lining up outside the infirmary blocks. Some of the girls had first-aid training and begged Wilhelmina to be allowed to go help. She debated this until a nurse from the infirmary came over to ask us himself. All of their doctors had been directed to the SS hospital.

The wounded filled the space between the brothel and infirmary, some propped up against the walls of the blocks, most lying on the ground. They held their arms, their legs, where the shrapnel had left deep gashes. A few had lost a limb. It might have resembled a battlefield, were these men not in prisoner stripes and too emaciated to ever climb out of a trench. We brought them pitchers of water, applied gauze to quell the bleeding, while I tried to keep my queasiness at bay. It didn't take long before one of the girls called out to Sophia. She was standing over a man who was motionless, his uniform stained and torn. Sophia ran over and knelt beside him, pressed his lifeless hand to her lips, and I knew it was her Friedrich.

Two days after the air strike, Sophia turned twenty-five. Given everything that had happened, and the peculiar brew of grieving and relief this had fostered, I didn't know whether it would be appropriate to mark it, but I hoped it might cheer her up after Friedrich's death. I'd been planning a celebration for weeks and had convinced the girls to save the sausages and flasks of alcohol they'd received from the prisoners for the occasion. When I'd first mentioned my plans to Karl, he brought me some pens and scraps of paper and promised to look into arranging a cake from the SS canteen, but I didn't dare ask if he'd remembered that promise. Right after the bombing, he'd come to the brothel absorbed in bitter thoughts, seeking nothing but reprieve.

On the afternoon of her birthday, luck paid us a visit. One of the waterlines had burst during the air strike, and the new brothel supervisor announced that it still hadn't been fixed. We all grinned, aware that a water shortage would guarantee a night off. While Sophia tidied our bedroom, I enlisted some of the girls to help decorate. We covered the day room with signs to remind her of her beloved Paris: the south wall became the Champs-Élysées, the windows the Seine, the table a patisserie.

As we finished our preparations, Wilhelmina entered the room to set out our dinner, and the corners of her mouth turned up in amusement. I took another look at the signs and blushed. They were crudely drawn in pen without a speck of colour. Childish, not festive. But when Sophia came in, her face lit up at the sight.

I gave her a hug. "Happy birthday!" The rest of the girls filed in and gathered around. For once, everyone was smiling.

They fed us a meagre dinner that night, nothing but boiled turnips and potatoes. Meals from the SS canteen would be postponed until things returned to normal. For Sophia's sake, I tried to conceal my disappointment. After we ate and cleared up, Wilhelmina and Bertha left the room, and we sat in a circle, some of us on chairs, others on the floor. I pulled out my violin in front of the girls for the first time and played the most joyful pieces I knew.

They applauded when I finished. "Oh, Marijke," Sophia said, "do you ever belong onstage."

I smiled and took the opportunity to bring out the sausages and gin. "Here you go: the men at Buchenwald send their best wishes. Let the celebrations begin."

The others laughed, while Sophia poured everyone a drink. I held a hand over my cup. "None for me. I can't stand the stuff, and we don't have any water to wash it back. But let me propose a toast: to our dearest Sophia on her birthday, may she always find beauty and happiness in life."

"To Friedrich," she added, "and all the other good people the world lost this week."

We nodded, and the others shot back their drinks, lips curling at the bitterness. A moment of soberness followed as the air strike played out again in our heads. The crackling of fire, shooting sparks into the air. The wounded holding our hands as they cried. But most of all, the fear, the uncertainty.

Gerda leaned forward. "You know what I heard?" She paused. "Goethe's Oak was hit in the bombing."

Several of the German girls gasped. "Really?" Sophia asked.

"One of the prisoners told me. He said it was a stray fire bomb, that it burned all night."

"What?" I asked. "You mean that old tree by the laundry building, the one with a girth the size of Göring's belly?"

"Yes, that's the one. Goethe penned some of his best work under it," Gerda replied. "And legend says that whenever Goethe's Oak falls, it will signal the fall of the German Reich."

"Aha," I said. "Confirmation that the end is near." But inside, I questioned how it would feel to know that the collapse of your own country would be the one thing that could save you. The air strike had brought all of us hope, even the German girls, yet I couldn't help but think of their families scattered in cities and towns across the map and what the approaching Allied bombers meant for them. I stood and went to the bedroom to clear my head. My mind drifted to Theo again, and for the umpteenth time that week, I wondered if he was safe, what he was doing, what he was thinking.

Sophia appeared in the hall. "Everything all right?"

"Yes, I think so. You know, I'm so sorry about Friedrich."

She sighed. "Maybe, in another life, he might have made a good husband. He was married, though; did I tell you that? I keep asking myself if his wife will ever find out how he died, although maybe she's dead herself."

"All the suffering this week, yet somehow we feel the need to rejoice in it."

"I've stopped trying to make sense of things." She extended her hand. "Look, why don't you come do my hair? Gerda wants to watch how you braid it."

I followed her back into the day room and got her to sit cross-legged in front of me. The tension filtered from my mind as I sifted my fingers through her thick hair.

"Tell us, Sophia," Gerda said, "how will you celebrate your next birthday as a free woman?"

"As a free woman? Why, I'll eat and eat, of course! Stuff myself silly. Chocolate tarts, marzipan, macarons, lemon custard. Perhaps Marijke's father can teach me a thing or two about opening a bakery."

I smiled. "Then the first thing you'll need to learn is how to make proper Dutch *boterkoek*."

And then the game began again as it did so often. While I twisted Sophia's hair up into a crown around her head, we all swapped recipes, our favourite meals from childhood, the dishes we'd mastered, down to every little detail. The way icing sugar melts on your tongue. The tart juices from freshly picked black-berries. The taste of ocean as you slurp down pickled herring. The butter-richness of old Gouda cheese sliced over warm rye bread. Our mouths watered and our stomachs grumbled as we pretended we were dining in fine restaurants with white-gloved waiters or, as I imagined, at home by candlelight, with my hus-band at my side.

The game ended when Wilhelmina came back in and ordered us to get ready for bed. As we turned out the lights, Sophia leaned over to whisper her thanks, for making her feel a few hours of happiness, for turning her back into a young girl who knew nothing of hunger or air strikes or brothel madams.

SUMMER slid into autumn, and as Karl had affirmed, the camp rose up again on the backs of the prisoners. The SS buried their dead and burned ours. They forced the prisoners to repair the damaged buildings and keep making weapons. Yet something at Buchenwald had changed. The Nazis became rabid with ven-geance. We heard of a guard who had thrown a man's cap into the electrified wire and demanded he retrieve it; of an officer at evening roll call who made the prisoners sing without pause until dawn; of a jailer who hanged inmates by their wrists until their joints detached. News of the jailer made me nauseated, a reminder of my own stint in the Bunker, of what might have happened, had Karl not intervened.

These stories came to us in whispers over the brothel mat-tresses, but we saw little of it ourselves. The men in the waiting room looked thinner and paler by the week, but we had gone back to receiving many of our meals from the SS canteen, and with Karl claiming me for himself, I was freed from that vicious cycle of man after man. Instead, I had to help Bertha with the cashier duties, so she and Wilhelmina could take long smoke breaks on the front steps.

Karl took advantage of my idle time, calling on me more and more often until seldom a night went by without him. Since the bombing, he'd stopped sharing news of the war and boasting of the German progress, and switched to topics he called pleasant: nights at the opera, his boyhood hikes in the mountains, his dreams for a life with me at his side.

JUST before dusk one day in early November, Sophia came into our bedroom, where I was changing. "Your presence is demanded outside, Madame." She winked, a faux loftiness to her words.

"Outside?" I didn't need to ask whom to anticipate. Cold air radiated from the windowpane beside me, so I put on her sweater overtop of my own and pulled the mittens Karl had gifted me from under my bed.

He was waiting beyond the fence that encircled the brothel, his hands in the pockets of his leather overcoat. I hesitated at the top of the stairs, having never ventured from the brothel without a line of girls behind me.

"Come, Marijke, hurry."

I obeyed. He checked behind him before placing his hand against the small of my back. "This way."

He led me to the right, down the hill and away from the main pitch of the prisoners' camp to an area I'd never seen before. My breath escaped in clouds, the winter air tickling my lungs. Above the forest, a deep blush tinged the grey sky. I waited for another command, something to indicate what he expected of me, but when we passed the stables, he wrapped his arm farther around my waist. "I want to show you something."

"What?"

But he didn't reply until we reached a patch of meadow and a path that must have led out of the camp. He stopped in the middle, pointing to the treetops. The branches formed silhouettes against the horizon, so thick they appeared to bear leaves.

"I don't see anything."

"Look harder."

A movement in a far-off copse caught my attention.

"Aha, birds."

"Wait." He stood behind me, holding me with his chin resting on my hat. We waited for several minutes, and for the first time in months, I felt the stillness of my surroundings. No girls snoring. No men groaning or panting. No sirens, no orders. His embrace was relaxed. It felt almost like Theo's.

A bird took off from its perch, followed by another. Karl squeezed my elbow. "It's happening."

And the sky filled. Birds poured from the trees. Hundreds of them—no, thousands. They soared in unison, shifting together into shapes. I couldn't tell one from another; beating wings swooped en masse, their movements growing, contracting.

"Starlings," he whispered.

They rose and fell, dove and swirled like one long, winding ribbon. I had both the feeling of a deep calmness and the sense that something in my chest was floating up, like part of me wanted to leave my body and twirl with them beneath the wisps of cloud.

I turned to gaze up at him. "This is what music looks like."

He smiled as he stared at the sky. Then he began to hum. The opening bars of Pachelbel's Canon, off-key, but still recognizable. He stepped back with a slight bow, raised his arm and spun me in a slow circle, his throat snagging on the high notes. Above us, the ribbon twisted and rippled, and behind it, the sky bled indigo. He turned me around and around, and when the moment felt right, my voice picked up to match his.

The starlings danced into the twilight. But as they began to settle and return to their roosts, we stopped to watch. And in that briefest of moments, he became just a man, and I just a woman. There was no master, no slave. He held my hand, and the clouds of his breath disappeared alongside my own. And everything I thought I knew—home, my dreams for after the war, my love for Theo—wavered, like the ground beneath me was no longer solid.

I took Karl's gloved hand and pressed it to my lips. "Thank you; that was beautiful."

We walked back in silence. My feelings for him were growing sticky, harder to tame, the sense of wanting more and unbidden thoughts that proved impossible to ignore. As we neared the brothel, the distance between us widened and I slowed my steps, reluctant to return to my prison within a prison. I considered what we'd witnessed, the mesmerizing force of the birds' choreography. It was easy to see the comparison between the starlings and us prisoners, the strength in numbers. But having faith in this idea was another matter.

At the edge of the fence, Karl stiffened and stood up straighter. The Kommandant was coming out of the infirmary. He stopped in front of us. "Müller, there you are. I've just been to see Fischer. All the frostbite this week has been a nuisance for our labour capacity. They're lopping off toes and fingers faster than you can count." He raised an eyebrow as he noticed me.

Karl replied in a callous, unfamiliar voice. "I found this one wandering along the camp perimeter. Seems she thought she needed an evening stroll." A look of apprehension crossed Karl's face as he registered what he'd said. I bristled and stared at his feet, the moment we'd shared slipping from my grasp.

The Kommandant seized my wrist, his thumb pressing against my pulse. He tugged off my fur-lined mitten and let it dangle from his fingers. "Someone is taking good care of her."

Karl cleared his throat. "She must have found a suitor from the clothing depot."

Inside I was seething, furious at how quickly he would betray me but also at my own surprise at seeing this happen.

Karl grabbed me by the shoulder. "I'll make sure she doesn't feel tempted to pull anything like this again."

"Good, and find out where she got those mittens." The Kommandant paused, and I felt him taking me in. "Such pretty Aryan skin. She looks familiar, don't you think? Who does she remind you of? An actress?"

"I—that's a good question. I can't quite place her."

"Whatever the case, I think I had a good eye, choosing our brothel women from the herd." He turned and started off toward the camp gate before calling back over his shoulder. "Come by my villa in an hour, Müller. My cook is preparing a nice veal tonight."

Karl didn't move until we were alone. His expression had hardened, the same shielded look he wore whenever he arrived at the brothel. He clenched and unclenched his fist as he debated what to say. "Go back inside," he mumbled at last. "I'll see you tomorrow."

AT the end of March 1945, rumours began to trickle into camp. The Allies had made incredible progress, and victory seemed inevitable. Talk of the American advancement stirred the SS guards into a panic, but uncertainty about the future frightened us even more. There was no telling what the moffen would do when cornered with defeat. A Dutch prisoner had told me about the reprisals for the resistance activities back home. After a resistance group took out two big Dutch collaborators, the Nazis raided a few universities and executed civilian hostages. At least fifty, he'd heard. The story made me sick, knowing that these were innocent students, that Theo might have taught some of them.

One piece of good news was that the Soviets had started to liberate camps in the east, but the moffen were doing everything possible to keep the prisoners from freedom. Recent transfers from the newly liberated Auschwitz warned us of what they called death marches. Was that what awaited us at Buchenwald when the Allies drew nearer? Gruelling treks on foot for days on end? Mass shootings? We were certain they wouldn't concede to losing their labour force, nor would they allow us to survive as witnesses to their crimes.

On Easter Sunday, the guard who accompanied us on our strolls decided to switch up his route, leading us girls along the western edge of the camp, taunting us with glimpses of the forest of budding trees that lay beyond the barbed wire. Near the edge of the blocks, a white mound stood a metre high. Corpses. My stomach rolled. We marched single file along the fence, and our escort warned to stay at least five metres from the wire. But the guards in the watchtower weren't concerned about us. They had their machine guns trained on a large circle of men who had gathered up ahead.

Our guard tried to lead us out of the way, but we had a good view of what was unfolding. A group of SS officers taunted and kicked three inmates wearing pink triangles. I could tell right away that Karl stood at the head of the group, overseeing the abuse without a flicker of remorse. As we got closer, I realized one of the prisoners on the ground was the handsome young man I'd gotten into trouble on my first day of work at the brothel. Welts covered his forearms, and a purple shiner bloomed around one eye.

I stepped out of line, ready to cry out, but Sophia clapped her hand over my mouth. "Goddammit, Marijke," she said. "Remember your place."

So we turned and carried on back down the pitch toward the brothel. The yelps of the prisoners faded away, but I could still picture Karl, the sternness of his expression, the sober reserve of a minister presiding over a funeral.

WHEN Karl came into the koberzimmer that evening, I lay on the bed, clothed and facing the wall.

"Hello, beautiful." He bent to kiss my cheek. When I didn't respond, he started undressing. I waited until he had removed his boots and tucked away his gun before I flipped over to face him.

"Oh, there you are." He winked and tried to cuddle up beside me, but I sat up.

"I saw you beating those prisoners today," I said. "How could you?"

Karl jerked back his head. "You saw? Were you girls out for a walk?"

"Just tell me."

"I didn't beat them myself."

"You gave the order!"

He grimaced. "Some things are necessary, Marijke, but I wish you didn't have to see them."

I curled away from his touch. "Necessary?"

"We have to control the spread of that disease before it takes over the nation. Himmler is very concerned."

"One of the first prisoners who visited me was among those men. There was nothing perverse about him."

"If he came to visit you, that's a sign of progress."

"What do you mean?"

He went on to tell me about the medical experiments Dr. Fischer carried out at Buchenwald. The doctors had been injecting these prisoners with testosterone, trying to realign their sexuality. "We're fixing them, my dear. It's the best thing for them, for everyone."

"What if you can't convert them?"

"Then we have to take care of it another way."

I stood up and backed away from him. When he beckoned me over, I didn't move. He shot me a bewildered look.

"I don't do it myself, Marijke. I'm not a killer."

"Look me in the eyes and tell me nobody has ever died at your hands, at your command."

He slouched, dropped his chin to his chest. "I do what's best for my people."

"Your people? How could you want to be part of this?"

"Germany is my country. I'm not ashamed of that."

"A nation of executioners."

"Stop."

"Why? Are you afraid of the truth? Are you scared to admit that you're like all the others? You act like you have this halo over you because you knew a Jew as a child. One single Jewish friend— as if that excuses you from everything. All this time you pretend you're better than them, but you're just as cold and bloodthirsty."

He put on his shirt, missing buttons in his haste. "Don't you talk to me that way. I have no choice."

"You're a coward, Karl! A filthy coward." Saying his name felt powerful, a reminder that he was no less flesh and blood than the rest of us.

He was dressed then, everything but his boots. He clutched my shoulder, his fingers digging into my collarbone.

I wrenched free. "How could anyone ever love you?" I moved for the exit.

"Marijke, don't. Please come back. I'm sorry. Listen to me."

Sophia's warning returned to me as I walked through that door, and I realized the grave risk I took in treating him like any other lover. In the hall, I waited for him to call out again, to drag me back, to exact punishment. But he didn't, so I returned to the sleeping quarters more frustrated and repulsed than ever.

CHAPTER TWENTY

KARL
APRIL 1, 1945
BUCHENWALD

O N APRIL FIRST, KARL AND A NUMBER OF OFFI-
cers were having Easter lunch at Brandt's villa when
his telephone rang. The American army had reached
the vicinity of Eisenach, roughly seventy-five kilometres from
Buchenwald. Brandt hung up the call, pushed his chair out from
the table and locked himself in his study, where he spent the
next half-hour on the phone with Berlin. Ritter cut into his
piece of lamb, but the rest of them pushed away their plates and
called on the butler for a bottle of strong schnapps, which they
drank to the bottom.

That afternoon, the prisoners were quieter than normal, but
a strange, tense current ran through the camp. Karl's nerves felt
raw, and the schnapps wasn't sitting well. He kept checking the
horizon for signs of smoke and bombers. A group of men huddled

together around the prisoners' canteen, whispering. He planted his feet wide apart to watch them. They knew something; he could sense it. They were probably trying to organize, conspiring, foolish enough to think they could make a stand against the SS. A month earlier, a secret radio transmitter had been discovered in one of Buchenwald's sub-camps. Karl's orders for a thorough search at Buchenwald had left them empty-handed, but he had a nagging feeling the inmates were getting information from the Allies.

At the same time, a few lower-ranked officers appeared and ordered the inmates to get back to their blocks. They, too, looked flushed with drink, and Karl debated which of his lunch companions had spread the news. The prisoners broke apart, revealing the markings on their uniform. Three of them pink triangles.

He walked toward them, his hands twitching at his sides. "Whatever you're planning, it's useless. You won't get out of here alive."

The prisoners halted and looked to the ground, while the officers turned to him, waiting for his next move. He gritted his teeth as he heard a plane overhead, thought of those Americans marching in, throwing grenades at his villa, shooting at them, showing no mercy. He jabbed a finger at the pink triangles. "You three, stay here. The rest of you, leave."

As the others scattered, he nodded to the officers, who grinned. They circled around the fags, moving in closer, knocking them to the ground. With each kick, each cry of pain, Karl felt his nerves settling, felt himself growing stronger. They weren't defeated, not yet. They wouldn't let their enemies win.

AFTER an unpleasant Easter Day, all he could think of was Marijke. She never failed to distract him, to calm his anxious mind. But when he arrived in her koberzimmer, she seemed about as pleased to see him as a Jew served a pork roast. Her lips slumped into a sour frown, and she started in on him about those damn pansies. Granted, no part of him wanted her to witness him like that, but work was work and she failed to grasp that.

In all his years at home, he'd never heard his mother talk back to his father. His experience with women in Berlin was limited to pretty things in stockings and aprons that did exactly what was expected of them. Even Else, who had her strong opinions, had never once lashed out at him. But Marijke had the look of a lit fuse as she stormed out of the koberzimmer, slamming the door behind her.

He got up and marched over to the exit, ready to yell out her name and order her back. But he stopped himself, worried about how that would look to anyone within earshot: the brothel doctor, the guards. Plus, if he went back on his word, the two of them would go back to being slave and master. For four long minutes, he waited. The door stayed shut. His temples pulsed in his ears. Another minute passed.

His boots sat beside the sink, laces spilling onto the floor. As he stepped toward them, his head brushed the dangling vines of the plant hanging from the ceiling. He tore the pot from its mount and whipped it at the wall. It smashed, splattering dirt across the wood panels.

"Self-righteous whore."

He knelt to do up his boots, but his fingers shook, and the bow he was tying slipped apart. Still no movement at the door.

He couldn't waste the night defending himself to some prisoner, some irrational woman. It was beyond her capacity to examine reality like a man, like a responsible citizen of a powerful nation.

As he left the brothel, he cursed himself for having gotten so soft with her. He didn't know where to go from there. The wool of his uniform itched his throat, and for the first time in years, he craved a cigarette. He walked around the brothel and alongside the cinema. A biting wail came from the trees beyond the watchtowers. He stood still to listen. A baby rabbit, he was almost positive. He'd heard that cry many times in the forest near his childhood home after his father would come home from an afternoon hunt. His father used to ridicule Karl's eagerness to identify the flora and fauna in that forest. "You can't be a Boy Scout forever," he'd said, as he tapped the ash from his pipe.

The wail picked up again. He found it chilling, the thought of a fox or some other carnivore attacking a burrow in such close proximity. When the calls stopped, Marijke's hot cheeks and furious glare came back to him, and he realized that, to her and so many others, he himself was that ruthless predator.

He kept walking. After twenty-five metres, he stopped again and turned around, prepared to go back and set her straight. Or maybe apologize. But he wouldn't run in circles for some hard-headed woman who seemed to forget her role. Instead, he trailed the barbed-wire fence that led in the direction of the gatehouse. A crescent moon had risen on a bed of clouds, but the searchlights from the watchtowers lit his path. The guards' voices drifted toward him. In the distance, truck engines rumbled, signalling the arrival of a late shipment of supplies and fresh labour.

A faint peal of laughter broke out somewhere nearby. Farther ahead, he discovered the source. One of the doors to an outer block stood open a few centimetres. When the noise continued, he approached. The crack in the doorway was wide enough to glimpse inside undetected. Hundreds of inmates covered the bunks, legs dangling into the centre aisle. Everyone had his back to the entrance. Lamps burned in the common area at the far end of the block, where a few men clumped together, but one stood in front of the others, singing a Polish song. Every few seconds, part of the audience would start chuckling, a weak, muffled laugh. Karl shuffled a step over to get a better vantage point. For once, he didn't see timid prisoners cowering before him. These men's eyes held something different. Not fear. Not the weary look of resignation, but a flicker of something else, the same spark Marijke wore.

After a round of hushed applause, two new men stepped forward, both political prisoners. One wore a toothbrush moustache of charcoal. The other had on wire-rimmed spectacles and adopted Himmler's stiff-lipped pose. At this point, Karl knew he should intervene, but he kept watching with amazed curiosity.

"Well, Hindelmeer, we've lost another battle on both fronts. Tell me, what does your third eye say: Am I going to lose the war?"

"I'm afraid so, Duke Adolin."

"Will I die?"

"I'm afraid so."

"Who is going to kill me?"

The man adjusted his glasses and gave the crowd a knowing look. "A Jewish celebrity."

"Which Jewish celebrity, Hindelmeer?"

"Any Jew who kills you will be an instant celebrity."

At this, the prisoners chortled and nodded and called out in a mix of European tongues. Even Karl had to suppress a chuckle, struck by how perfectly they'd captured Himmler's mannerisms, his strange fascination with the occult. Just like an old schoolmaster. He'd been lucky enough to meet Himmler at one or two party functions, but never the Führer, who seemed unable to do so much as take a piss without being swarmed by eager followers.

The Himmler impersonator removed his glasses and started reciting a limerick. He waved his arm as he spoke, gesticulating like a raving Italian:

> *Ten men in a row in one bed*
> *All fighting for soup and some bread*
> *But here come the lice*
> *So take my advice*
> *And cover that poor fuzzy head!*

A particular flick of the wrist jumped out at Karl. He pushed the door open a little farther for a better look. Where had he seen him before? The man ran a hand over his scalp and let out a raspy laugh. Then Karl placed him. A famous actor from Bavaria, a family friend of Else's. A communist. They had dined together numerous times before the war, and unless the actor got on the subject of Bolshevism, he always made pleasant company. He was also a better match at chess than anyone Karl knew. A well-dressed, stocky man, now thin and aged twenty years. Even his eyebrows had fallen out.

Karl was so busy observing him that he didn't realize how far he'd inched forward and pushed open the door. One by one, heads snapped toward him and a whisper ran through the crowd. The men at the front stopped performing to stare. It felt like a grenade had just been lobbed, and he held the pin.

A rat scampered across nearby feet, but nobody moved. A sickly boy wiped his nose on his sleeve, and somewhere someone stifled a cough. Karl told himself to shout an order, to pull out his Luger. He touched a hand to his holster before looking back at that actor, who squinted at him from across the block. When shocked recognition crossed the man's face, Karl turned and walked away, leaving the door open behind him.

LATER that night, he sprawled across his bed, still stinging from Marijke's accusations. On the nightstand, his alarm clock counted out long, wasted minutes. When the ticking had fried his patience, he got up, made himself a cup of hot milk with a generous shot of brandy and settled in the armchair in his study.

He couldn't separate his fight with Marijke from the sight of that old acquaintance in rags. He tried to tell himself Else's friend had chosen that path by refusing to give up his political dogma. The pansies had earned blame by going against nature. But then there was Marijke. Beautiful, passionate, innocent Marijke, who didn't deserve to be torn from her home, didn't deserve to be used by man after man, like a pump at a petrol station. All because she had tried to help out a few neighbours, fix up some petty radios.

Karl took a sip of his drink and let the warm brandy trickle down his throat. A hairline crack ran through the porcelain cup, and he traced his finger along the line but couldn't detect the groove. Those actors in the block had reduced Hitler to a simple man with a moustache. He began to doubt his understanding of the Reich. Were the Allies right to hate him? Was he supporting a nation, a dream for the resurgence of the German people, or supporting one man's beliefs?

He thought of Aaron Stein, his Jewish friend from primary school. Those drops of blood from his finger mixing with his. For years, the two of them had constructed forts together, played pirate explorers at his family's summer home. When Karl's father returned from the war, Aaron sat on the front porch with him, waiting for his father to appear down the block. When Aaron's father returned from the war, Karl stood at Aaron's side in the rain, watching the coffin slip into its muddy grave. The last time Karl had seen him was in 1938, three weeks before Kristallnacht. He had just joined the party and was hurrying down the streets of Munich to tell his father. At an intersection, Aaron waved from across a crowded street. Karl was about to run over to him when he considered the party papers tucked under his arm, the loyalty these demanded. Instead, he lowered his head and crossed the street in the opposite direction. For seven years, he'd avoided thoughts of him, refusing to acknowledge Aaron's probable fate. It wouldn't take much to find out: a few calls and his name would turn up on one list or another. He'd never bothered to inquire.

The bottom of his cup contained more brandy than milk. He swallowed it back and reached for the bottle. The problem of the pansies remained. He'd seen the medical experiments, watched hangings performed at Brandt's orders, and although he had nothing personal against them, the thought of what they did left a nasty tang in his mouth. But Marijke had a point—surely that didn't create enough reason to despise them, to take their lives.

After one final slug of brandy, he screwed the lid on the bottle and returned to his bedroom, determined to fix things with her before it was too late.

CHAPTER TWENTY-ONE

LUCIANO
MAY 23, 1977
BUENOS AIRES

Dear Papá,

What were you trying to tell me on the phone? Were you—you sounded like you wanted to get something out, something I needed to hear. I could sense it in your voice; it was a voice, it was a tone you've never used before. Dear Papá, I can't stop thinking, your voice, it was so choked, so strained, but full of emotion. Something I want so badly to believe in but I—I keep wondering if I imagined it all because when have you ever—when have you ever—sounded like you cared, like you were genuinely upset, like you actually, maybe truly love me. That call keeps playing over and over in my mind, and I keep hoping to pick up on something else, to be able to dig deep down into the meaning of every word, every breath, every pause.

I want to believe you're sitting at home right now in the chair by the window, with music and the TV on, but that for once you're not watching the game. Instead, you're sitting there worrying about me, where I am, if I'm okay, maybe even, just maybe, wishing you'd treated me a little differently.

Papá, do you remember Orión the Owl? Do you remember sitting there all evening to make him for me?

Luciano sighed. He could still see the campfire's glow that had painted his father's face amber, could smell the smoke on his father's jacket. They'd been at Nonna and Nonno's ranch to celebrate Luciano's sixth Christmas. Earlier that afternoon, his father had taken him on a long walk, past the bougainvilleas and the adobe shed, through the copse that led down to the stream. His father pointed out the different species of trees and flowers along the trail, and when an owl swooped across their path, he crouched to help Luciano find it. As it perched on a low branch, his father held him close, and there was something about the lost look in his eyes that made Luciano feel like they needed one another.

Papá, the way you held me when we spotted that owl, I can still feel the comforting strength of your arms around me, the way you bent to kiss my hair. I can count on one hand the number of times you've ever hugged me. But that moment, I wanted it to last forever.

His father had carried him back to the ranch on his shoulders, showing him the sheep and cattle and asking him to name them. When Luciano also tried to rename the cat, his father laughed and claimed the new name was better. For years, they called that cat Paco. Later that night, his father sat at Nonno's workbench, the fire crackling beside him as he carved a toy. Almost in a trance, he kept to himself, ignoring everything but his hands. The knife skimmed along the wood, coaxing out curls that fell at his feet, and when he finished, he presented Luciano with the little owl and asked him to name that, too.

Orión the Owl. It was the only time I saw you carve anything. The tail is crooked, and it looks stunned, but I've always liked its flaws. At six, I didn't know any better. Now it just feels good to know you're not perfect at everything yourself.

Orión had gone everywhere with Luciano until his eighth birthday, when Papá announced that real boys didn't carry toys around like a security blanket. But did his father realize that it sat on Luciano's bookshelf even now? For years, Luciano would wish it good night, until this became as much a habit as saying the Lord's Prayer. He lay in bed, thinking about what he could do to make his father proud of him. And whenever his father scolded him for spending too much time in the kitchen with Mamá, for wearing "women's colours" or having a weak stride, he'd pull that owl down from the shelf and hold it in his fist, trying to recall the concentration on his father's brow as he worked to shape the wings just right.

All those times I would dig Orión's beak into my skin, my palm, my wrist, slicing it across and imagining it were a razor blade, like I could feel your disapproval trickling out of me. Like poison. Do you ever stop to think how much you've hurt me? You're so blind;

you don't care about anything but yourself. You don't notice what's going on around you, what Mamá and I need from you.

At one point, Luciano had taken the pair of scissors from his desk and driven them into Orión's eyes. Had his father ever noticed the pattern of nicks on the wallpaper from where he'd whipped the owl across the room? Like the traces of a game of darts played after one too many beers. The angrier Papá had been with him, the more days the owl would stay hidden wherever it had bounced, until Luciano felt guilty enough to crawl under the bed or search for it in the piles of dirty clothes.

Every time, I ended up putting it back on the shelf, because, no matter what, I couldn't throw it away. I don't think I ever could. All I want is to hear your voice on the phone again, to hear you say you miss me, that you care.

CONDITIONS began to improve for Luciano after another week of labour. He spent more time without his hood and received permission to have his meals with the other forced workers in the basement. They ate together in silence, but he felt an air of solidarity as they exchanged furtive glances, pretending to keep their focus on the soccer or telenovelas playing on the nearby TV. The volume was always maxed out, but it didn't take long to learn that whenever the screen flickered to static, someone had turned on the cattle prod in the next room. His appetite waned, and his pants continued to sag more at his waist with each passing day.

One evening, a group of them sat around, waiting for their dinner. Shark entered with a big pot, which he placed at the head of the table. He pushed his glasses up on his nose and gave Luciano a long look before leaving a new guard to supervise the meal. Even with the lid on the pot, Luciano could almost taste the charred bits that must have been stuck to the bottom.

Hawk wandered by and wrinkled up his nose. He stopped, lifted the lid and scowled. "This is what you're serving?" The new guard shrugged his shoulders and reached for a bowl, but Hawk pushed away his hand. "Don't dish it out. I'll see if there's anything else in the kitchen."

He was gone a long time. Desperate faces eyed the pot, but the guard followed orders. Hawk returned carrying a paper bag stamped with the name of a bakery. The bag opened with a crinkle, releasing the mouth-watering scent of ground beef and onions.

As the group divided the five empanadas, Hawk laid a stack of paper napkins on the table and left. Luciano bit into his half-pastry, savouring the taste of the spices. The steaming meat burned his tongue. For the second time since his abduction, Luciano smiled.

Later, he wondered if Hawk had used his own money to buy the empanadas, and if so, why he would have done that. But when five days passed without feeling Hawk's sharp grip on his arm or hearing his low voice, he assumed the guard's actions hadn't gone unpunished.

Dear Papá,

I hate how much control you have over me. Everything I do, every time I come home from school, every decision: you're in the back of my mind. I always wonder whether you'll be proud of how I'm acting, if you'll approve, if you'll respect me a little more if I do things the way you'd like.

Dear Papá, I think you're ashamed of me. Actually, I know this for a fact. I can see it in the way you lower your eyes when I come into the room, the way you never ask me questions about what I'm up to, about my friends. I bet you don't even know the names of most of them. Camila and I dated for months, and yet, the one time you met her on the street, you behaved like you'd never heard of her before. Sure, maybe I didn't talk about her all the time—maybe that's, well, maybe there's actually a good reason for that, but still. Mamá asks questions; she shows interest.

Papá, do you remember Bariloche last year? That first night of our ski trip, you said you felt like you'd returned home. There was . . . you seemed happy in a way, content for once.

Luciano breathed in, imagining the sharp resin of evergreens, steam from apple cider thawing his eyelashes. Log-framed buildings with wooden balconies, the crunch of fresh snow under their skis. The night they arrived, his father had taken them out for fondue and grinned as he told tales of skiing in the Alps with the grandparents Luciano had never met. Stories about mulled wine and bringing three pairs of socks out snowshoeing because one was never enough. He even told a few jokes. For a few hours, they acted like a normal family. The next day, however, his mother had returned to the hotel early with a headache, leaving Luciano and his father on their own.

It was too good to last. When you and I walked back through town together . . . fuck, was that ever awkward. We had absolutely nothing to talk about. I kept trying to think of something to say and ended up making some dumb remark about how we had good snow for snowmen, like I was still a kid. You gave a snort and nodded, and stopped to pet one of those massive dogs that paraded around the square for the tourists. The really big ones with the barrels, St. Bernards.

His father had spent a good minute with that dog, crouching to scratch its ears, praising its thick coat, calling it a *braver Hund*, as if it could understand German just because the breed came from the Alps. Luciano watched, transfixed, as the creases in his father's face softened like wax in the sun. Papá had thrown back his head and laughed as the dog's paddle of a tongue smeared across his chin.

While I stood there trying to come up with some interesting fact about those dogs to tell you, I felt like an intruder, like I was spying on a private moment through a one-way mirror. You didn't even notice when I ducked into a chocolatier's.

He had helped himself to the samples: alternating bonbons with white-chocolate logs. Now, his mouth watered as he thought about that tiered fountain spewing hot dark chocolate. He had just reached for his fourth piece when he glanced out the window to see that his father was no longer alone.

Then those men showed up. Old men, even older than you, with friendly eyes. They acted like they knew you.

Luciano had shoved one last bonbon into his mouth and stepped out of the shop. The men were speaking German. His father nodded and responded, but when Luciano went over to greet them, his father warded him off with a flick of his hand, so he waited by the display of truffles until they laughed, clapped Papá on the back and carried on.

When I asked who they were, you said "old friends" and left it at that. Ashamed of me once again . . . isn't that right, Papá? Embarrassed by my baby face, which you think is too soft for a man. Embarrassed by the way I wear my hair long and loose around my forehead. Or were you afraid I'd make another stupid comment, complaining about how my calves ached from skiing, or telling them that I aspire to be the country's next great poet? You made me wait out of sight in the corner like an unwelcome dog. Actually, no, even that dog was allowed to hang around your heels, nuzzling your legs as you patted its head. Good boy, you said, good boy.

WORK dragged on at ESMA, and while this gave Luciano some sense of routine, it was a routine that was never short of pain or suffering. Even those words no longer sufficed. He would have to devise a new vocabulary to capture the normalcy of terror.

Throughout his life, he'd told his mother around dinnertime that he was hungry. But "hungry" failed to capture what he felt at ESMA, an ache that wormed its way through his body, attacking every corner, leaving his dry tongue with a revolting taste, his limbs weak and every movement an effort, like he was being consumed from the inside out.

When he wasn't fantasizing about steaks and passion-fruit ice cream and pastries oozing dulce de leche, he anticipated his next shower. He tried to remember what it was like to feel clean, to smell of soap and watch his skin turn pink from the spray of hot water.

LUCIANO stood beneath the showerhead, shivering from the icy drizzle. The temperature roused his tired bones, made his veins sing. The sensation transported him to a Patagonian lake, where he dove from a dock and broke through the water's mirrored surface. He clung to this daydream while scrubbing himself and stared at the concrete walls until they became foothills thick with pine trees, a lone boat bobbing along the shore.

The shower shut off automatically. Luciano wiped the drops from his eyes and let the bathroom come back into focus: the fluorescent lights, the slick floor, the curve of asses rising off skinny frames, penises hanging shrivelled and limp. He glanced at the other men. Gabriel reached for his shirt, wet hair plastered to his legs. Their bruised bodies were wasting away from disuse, but something inside Luciano still stirred. He tried to imagine what it would be like if Gabriel were to come up from behind, pull him in for a kiss, holding his warm body close while they grew hard together.

As he dried off, he felt someone watching him and looked up to find Shark leering by the sink in the corner. Luciano swallowed and finished getting dressed, trying to hide himself as much as possible in the open room. His arms tingled as he pushed them through his shirtsleeves and bent to tie his shoelaces. A guard cuffed him, but right before the hood slipped over his head, Luciano spotted Shark staring in disgust.

The other guard arranged the prisoners in line. Handcuffs rattled as the prisoners shuffled out of the bathroom, but a tight grip pinched the back of Luciano's neck, holding him back.

Shark shut the bathroom door. "You're a *maricón*, aren't you?" His low voice hissed in Luciano's ear. "You think I can't see that?"

A blow to the shoulders knocked Luciano to the ground. His hands flew out but failed to brace his fall, and his head smacked the tiled floor, sending bright colours kaleidoscoping across his vision. He curled up to shield himself from the kicks to his ribs, his stomach, his balls.

"Get up!" Shark pulled Luciano to his knees and yanked off his hood, tearing out a few hairs along with it.

In the sudden brightness, Shark was standing over him, undoing his belt buckle, his fly. He pulled Luciano by the hair, shoved his face into his stiff cock. "You'll like this. Show me you're good for something."

Luciano's scalp roared. Everything went foggy, but he did as he was told. Shark thrust into him, clenching a fistful of his hair, rocking onto his toes and letting out staggered grunts. "Faster."

Pressure against the back of Luciano's throat. Flashes of the older man who had once eyed him invitingly from the other side of the Subte platform, Gabriel's wet body, and Fabián, sunbathing shirtless in the park, the trail of hair on his stomach leading down into his shorts. Fabián. He closed his eyes, pretending this was Fabián, that he finally had the chance to touch him, to pleasure him.

His teeth scraped skin, prompting a hard smack. Luciano began to gag and tried to pull away, but Shark held him there. Then he wanted to scream, but deep down, he knew he deserved to be punished. Punished for his urges, his secrets. For watching the guys change after soccer, for collecting fantasies about Fabián while he was supposed to be dating Camila. He deserved this. All he could do was stare down at the mildewed grid of grout between the floor tiles and try to block out the guard's groans.

Soon, Shark's body grew tense, his breathing fast and heavy. With one hand, he leaned to brace himself against the wall. Luciano didn't look up, but sensed the guard's face twisting in pleasure. With a sudden jerk, Shark pulled out, yanked Luciano's head back and came with a deep groan. He zipped up his pants and pushed Luciano to the floor, kicking him in the shins. One blow after another. Blood trickled down Luciano's forehead. Shark started to yell, but the words blurred beneath the pain as Luciano's body curled against the impact. He begged for help as loudly as he could, with the hope that someone would come and put an end to it all, but no one did.

LUCIANO sat at a white desk in a small, white room. He held a pen in his hand, but otherwise the desk and the room were empty. The door opened and two guards entered, dragging someone who was also in white, his face covered by a white silk hood. The guards dropped the prisoner in the centre of the room and slunk out, leaving the man in a heap on the floor.

"Get up."

Although he hadn't moved his mouth, Luciano heard his own disembodied voice. The man stirred and magically rose in a single, fluid motion. He stood with his legs wide, hands bound behind his back, and from this movement alone, Luciano knew who it was.

An index card covered in Luciano's handwriting appeared on the desk. *Name: Fabián Sanmartino.* The clatter of the handcuffs against the floor made him look up, but nobody had entered the room to unlock them. The hood followed the path of the handcuffs, drifting like a leaf caught mid-air.

Fabián stared at him hollowly. His jaw looked freshly shaven, his complexion flawless, but one eye had swollen almost shut. "You did this to me."

Luciano shook his head and tried to rise but felt weighted to the chair. "No, no, I didn't. Don't you have any idea what you mean to me?"

"They think I'm just like you, but I'm not. You betrayed me."

"No. Impossible." He tossed the pen aside, but it stayed poised above the desk, and he watched as another line materialized on the index card. *T,* for transferred. Dread seeped into his core. "Please, you have to understand; I would never do anything to hurt you."

Fabián took a step backward, his dark hair stark against the whiteness. From the neck down, he blended into the sterile surroundings.

"Please, believe me!"

Another step, and another. Fabián's outline grew fainter, but he kept walking back and back and back until, finally, he became part of the walls themselves and vanished.

Luciano blinked hard, willing his beloved to return. When he opened his eyes, he was still alone but had returned to the confines of his hood. His head throbbed. A scab at his temple chafed against the fabric when he tried to roll over, making him curl into a ball. Somewhere, the sound of a door opening. Lifting his hands to cover his face, he tried to protect himself from the expected beating. This sent a shooting pain down his arms. His ribs felt like they'd been crushed and were floating around his stomach. The blow never came, but he thought he heard a stadium full of voices laughing, singing, crying.

The jagged corner of his chipped front tooth nicked his tongue. He parted his lips. "Please, water." Once, twice, he asked, but he couldn't tell if he was yelling or whispering.

The sounds around him faded. Then came the strike of a match in the far corner of his cell, and shadows emerged through the darkness. A flame flickered before a hand rose up to shelter it. The clinking of glass followed. When the hand dropped away, the flame had grown to a soft glow. The light came from an oil lamp, and the shadowy figure holding it perched on a stool in the corner. The stranger raised the lamp, while his free hand slipped off the hood that covered his head. Luciano realized the stranger was himself. It was him as he had once appeared: unmarred, tanned and fit, his gaze calm, pensive. And while he wore the same clothes as Luciano did right then, the fabric bore no stains, no rips or missing buttons.

Luciano sat up and pulled himself into the opposite corner, pressing his knees to his chest. The pain was gone. He waited for his other self to make a move, but nothing happened.

"What are you doing here?" he asked, certain he was dead.

The figure placed the lamp on the mattress between them and adjusted the brass knob to raise the flame, casting shadows on the opposite wall. Luciano looked to the left to find another figure sitting there, a small boy with thick hair and grass-stained shins. The boy smiled up at the darkness with Luciano's own electric-blue eyes.

In awe, Luciano extended his hand, but when the boy turned his head, he stared right through him. A great sadness welled inside Luciano, but before he said anything, the first figure pulled a cigarette from his pocket and lit another match. The smoke whirled, clouding the space between them with the aroma of cinnamon and lemon, his mother's scent.

When the smoke cleared, a third figure crouched in the final corner. This time, a far older man, a Luciano with hunched shoulders, spidery hair and a large mole on his cheekbone. Leaning on a wooden cane, he looked to the floor as if searching for something.

This older one frightened Luciano. Unlike the others, he had never been real and might never exist in the future. Luciano noticed his shackles were gone. Luciano got up, moving toward the others, seeking their comfort. The figures turned to him, but suddenly appeared vapid, like they had no souls, and the colour drained from their skin as the light in the cell grew dimmer. The lamp had run out of oil, the wick burned to its end. Luciano fixated on its final murmur, watching the flame shudder until the instant when everything disappeared again.

CHAPTER TWENTY-TWO

MARIJKE
APRIL 2, 1945
BUCHENWALD

ANASTY BOUT OF NAUSEA FOLLOWED MY ARGUMENT
with Karl. I woke up the next day with the feeling that
someone was trying to scoop out my insides. At breakfast, the others drank our ration of coffee substitute, which
had grown tasteless as the war dragged on. But that morning,
I couldn't get within two metres of my cup without making a
staggering run for the bathroom. Every half-hour, I sat down to
relieve myself and bit my tongue to cut off my nervous whimpers. Edith had never returned to the brothel after falling sick,
and two other girls had disappeared since then. Would I meet
the same fate?

All morning, I lay in bed, clenching the bedpost and wiping
the sweat from my forehead. While the others cleaned the brothel,
I tossed from side to side, curled into a ball, but nothing calmed

the nausea. Karl haunted my thoughts, begging me to listen, telling me he wasn't the man I thought he was. *I love you, Marijke.* The words reverberated, growing louder until they blocked out everything else.

As Sophia entered the bedroom, she saw me struggling and hurried over. "What's wrong?"

I sat up, clutching my belly. She grabbed an empty wastepaper bin and thrust it in front of me, but I pushed it to the side.

"It's Karl," I said.

"Karl? That's why you're sick?"

I made room for her to sit beside me. She folded her darning into the pocket of her skirt and waited for me to speak. "Don't feel you have to tell me, Marijke."

There was a quietness in her tone, a sort of hurt that made me realize how little attention I'd paid to the other girls since Karl had freed me from the other visits, how focused I'd been on myself. Every night, when the brothel closed to the prisoners, the girls returned to the sleeping quarters, muttering complaints and swapping shreds of gossip over the night's men: who had lasted the longest, who was the most attractive. Time had twisted those nighttime visits into a sort of game, but this did little to mask the repulsion that lay beneath it all. I hadn't taken part in that post-coital ritual for months. By the time Karl left the brothel, the other girls were asleep.

"Do you think," I asked, "do you think that the Nazis are all evil? I mean, truly, deep down?"

"I know what you think."

"What?"

"You talk of Karl like he's some Romeo, like you could live happily ever after if the Allies and Axis powers could just put aside their differences and make up."

"Karl is different. He barely believes in the Reich. All he wants is to be back in Bavaria with his dogs, a quiet life. And he's sweet to me, he says he loves me."

"He's infatuated, Marijke; he loves the idea of you. They're ruthless, those men. They care only about people who look and think exactly like them. If I didn't know better, I'd say it was all switches and gears under those uniforms. You saw what he did to those prisoners."

I swallowed, remembering the colour of that man's beaten face. "I know. That was awful. Beyond awful. But he wasn't beating them himself. What if he was just following orders? He would be in just as much trouble if he tried to defy the Kommandant."

Sophia shook her head. "Listen to what you're saying. Even as a German, I won't defend those barbaric men. He's bewitched you."

Hearing that launched me into another dizzy spell. I reached for the bedpost. His face was there, those beautiful blue eyes, darkness rising up behind them like flood waters. Was I going mad thinking like this? Nobody but a fool would look at Mr. Hyde and see only Dr. Jekyll. What was stopping me from hating him?

Sophia brushed her hand through my curls, her skin cool and soothing. "Think about what you really believe, what you expect to happen when the war ends." She got up off the bed. "But for now, just lie down. I'll cover the rest of your cleaning duties and figure out what to tell the others."

She tucked me in and I rested my head against the wall, wishing I could block out the feelings that swarmed around me and fall asleep dreaming of Theo.

When I woke an hour later, the nausea had faded. Afternoon sunlight pierced the windows, shining spotlights on the floor, and the sound of chatter drifted into the room. I pulled myself out of bed, pushing thoughts of Karl to the back of my mind.

The girls sat around the table in the day room, telling stories of life in Berlin before the war: of felted, feathered hats, of silk gloves and secret affairs spilled over glasses of brandy. They talked of cabaret and jazz, a daring music that challenged so much of what I'd learned in my classes at the conservatory. But Sophia said the jazz musicians had disappeared; Hitler didn't like the blacks, either.

I told Wilhelmina I was sick and requested the night off. She nodded and made a note on her clipboard before going off to fetch me a cup of hot water.

THE illness I'd thought I'd overcome reared up like a tidal wave, and for days I was frail and out of sorts. I woke up feeling like someone had tied me to the back of a truck and driven around camp, dragging me through the mud and potholes. I lay in bed for hours. Even water was too much to handle.

Wilhelmina and Bertha tried to send me to the hospital, but I wouldn't hear of it and begged Sophia to keep me safe. Karl had said that disease and infection ruled the infirmary blocks, and his stories of medical experiments had haunted my nightmares. Still, I saw the word clinging to the other girls' lips, the terrifying fate they'd predicted: pregnant. If that were true, they would mark me as "spoiled meat" and send me back to Ravensbrück. Or worse.

The sixth morning, I received word that Karl would come by in the evening. By then, I was desperate to see him. But I could hardly move, save for the trip between the sleeping quarters and the facilities. Sophia ran a bath for me, and I wallowed in the warmth, covering myself in a thick layer of soap. When I got out, the water ran down my skin and puddled on the tiled floor as my stomach gargled. My breasts were sensitive to the touch. I refused to accept the possibility. After all those contraceptive injections, months without being strong enough to menstruate and even then only scattered periods—it seemed impossible.

As the day pressed on, I tried to make myself useful, lest Wilhelmina or Bertha judge me as too weak to receive Karl. I had to see him, to ensure his protection from whatever danger the illness could bring. I pulled the broom from the closet in an attempt to sweep, but found myself stopping every few steps to lean on it for support. The other girls filed out for an afternoon walk, leaving me on the settee with a book, but my thoughts kept fluttering away. I stood to open the window in the reception room. The fresh scent of spring wafted in, enough to send me reeling yet again. But the air carried something else along with it: harsh, frantic shouts. I couldn't spot the source of the racket, and the words were muffled but sounded like orders. Heavy feet: running, not marching. Back on the settee, I sat on my hands and stared at the window.

On cue, the girls returned, wild-eyed with answers. "They're coming!"

"Who?"

Sophia rushed over and threw her arms around me. "The Americans! They must be advancing; the SS are in a panic."

"They know this is it," Gerda said.

"And what will become of us?" I asked.

Wilhelmina and Bertha slid into the room, their expressions a scramble of excitement and dread. Wilhelmina stood in the corner with her hands clasped against her chin.

"My guess is, they'll shut us down," Bertha said. "They have better things to focus on than keeping their prisoners' dicks wet. Rumour is that the Americans still have to advance quite some way. At this point, anything is possible."

"We just need to hold off," I said, but I heard the tremor in my voice and I latched on to Sophia's wrist.

"Yes," Wilhelmina replied. "Who knows what the Nazis will do when cornered?"

That night, I went to the koberzimmer early to wait for Karl. I kept my clothes on, knowing I was far too sick to make love to him but hoping that wouldn't matter. More than once, he had stopped by just to sit beside me, to stroke my hair and kiss me as his words bridged our separate worlds. But I hadn't seen him since our argument and didn't know how to patch things over with the weight of the Americans interfering. Sophia's accusations, her condemnation of Karl grew like a nettle in my mind, spiny and eager to choke out any pleasant thoughts of him. My gut told me she was right; through my plan of keeping him pleased, stirring up his will to protect me, I might have stumbled backward into my own trap.

The nausea returned, so I lay down to rest my eyes. A wall of blackness seemed to rush toward me, and any moment, I would crash into it.

The door opened without a knock.

"Karl, darling."

But when I looked up, it wasn't Karl towering over me. It was Bruno. His jaw clenched tight. A maniacal glint in his stare.

I shut my eyes, praying he was a hallucination, but those heavy breaths continued.

"Do you remember me?" He grabbed my shoulder, forced me to look at him. "I asked you a question. Or do you still not know how to obey your superiors?"

"Please, Schutzhaftlagerführer Müller—"

"I don't have to listen to his orders anymore. Haven't you heard? It's all over."

My buttons popped open as he yanked at my blouse. Stinking breath: vodka and hot mustard. His fingers tangled with mine as I tried to wriggle out of his grip. He pulled me forward, tossed me to the side like a doll. Clawed between my legs.

"No, stop."

A hard slap across my face. My cheeks stung; the dark wall came closer. His trousers unzipping. One hand on my shoulder, turning me. Bent over. Ripping holes in my stockings.

"No!" My own voice, but the cry seemed to come from far away.

The jangle of his belt as it hit the floor. Shadows growing closer, closer. I reached back a hand, sunk my nails into his skin. His yell. Curses. And then, blackness.

CHAPTER TWENTY-THREE

BAD NEWS KEPT FLOODING IN FROM THE FRONT AND the phones wouldn't stop ringing. On Monday morning, Karl got word that the radio operators had intercepted a transmission requesting that the Allies drop weapons for the prisoners at Buchenwald. He had a hunch that it had come from the communist resistance cells in the camp, and the idea of them arming themselves kept him up late at night. Dreams of bombs exploding at the gatehouse, being woken up with a gun to his head. He also feared how the Americans would react when they got wind of what the SS were doing at Buchenwald, how much faster they would try to advance. At least the number of civilian prisoners might save them from further bombing.

More than once that afternoon, he caught himself staring at a blank wall in the office, the coffee beside him cold. To make things worse, the women at the brothel claimed Marijke was sick. He was sure that was a lie and worried he'd fucked it all up but decided to give her time to cool down while the camp demanded his attention.

His focus turned to making plans for handling the prisoners. He ordered the Blockführers to scour the blocks for any radio transmitters and had the guards check the adjacent buildings. The SS garrison contained several thousand men, all heavily armed, and even though the prisoners had strength in numbers, their weak, malnourished condition meant they wouldn't be able to put up a strong fight, even if the Americans responded to their appeal for weapons. Yet the inmates had found ways to sabotage SS plans through the one thing the Nazis relied on them for—their labour. In February, the workers in the armament factories had met only one-quarter of their production quotas for infantry vehicles, and the output of gun carriages was almost as dismal. The factory managers reported that the inmate technicians and foremen were ordering the wrong parts and tampering with repair jobs, but the ensuing investigation proved that the managers were too corrupt and disorganized themselves to pinpoint the source of the problems. As a whole, Karl didn't trust the prisoners. Any dog locked in a crate all day will have the nastiest bite.

ON Tuesday, the Americans sent a warning. Leaflets fluttered down over the streets of Weimar, landing on the cobblestones, on chimneys, in women's purses. One of Karl's men brought a stack of them back to Buchenwald and left some on his office desk. A German message printed in bold typeface: *We promise harsh retribution for anyone who commits atrocities against the prisoners of Buchenwald.*

Karl crumpled up the leaflet and threw it at the opposite wall. It bounced off and landed on one of the windowsills, where it remained for the rest of the day. He avoided looking at it, but couldn't block out the image of a firing squad, of a hood slipped over his head.

The Blockführers hadn't located the radio transmitter or any receivers. He considered asking Marijke about her work making crystal radios for the Dutch resistance, how she and her husband had learned to conceal them. But she would see right through his questions and would despise him even more for trying to trick her into helping. Instead, he went to speak to Brandt about the search, who promised to do something about it personally.

An hour later, Brandt barged into Karl's office, shaking a fistful of files. "You were supposed to approve these changes!"

Karl glanced at the papers, an order about increasing staffing at the infirmaries, which had been overflowing for months. He realized he'd signed the wrong line, but didn't remember ever seeing the form. "I'm sorry. It's been a long week."

"You'd better be ready for a whole lot more, Müller. The Americans have almost reached Ohrdruf. We're marching those inmates here, and we'll ship them on to Dachau once they arrive." Brandt crossed his arms while Karl sat there envisioning that firing squad. "Get that look off your face. Don't you have any faith in our boys at the front? We'll push them back in time."

"Of course." Karl's voice cracked.

"Pull it together, Müller. I need you to keep everything under control here. We have to crush any signs of resistance."

"Have you heard from Berlin?"

"Himmler hopes to get the prisoners as far away as possible, but the Americans keep bombing the railways. However, we can count on him to find a solution; he always does."

Karl's thoughts flashed back to that crumpled leaflet. It would take days, maybe weeks for the evacuees to make it to Dachau. They wouldn't survive being crammed back into those boxcars, not even the march to Weimar.

"We'll lose thousands en route," Karl said. "And what about the rest of the prisoners?"

Brandt gave him a strange look. "We'll deal with them if the time comes."

BRANDT'S idea for handling the masses was to give a speech, and he summoned one of the German labour Kommandos to the cinema to listen. He promised he wouldn't evacuate the camp but would continue to operate things as usual, as was his duty. After declaring that he knew about the radio transmitter, he accused the foreigners and Jews of trying to spread their vengeance to the German prisoners through their appeal for weapons. But Brandt claimed he would help the German nationals, provided they co-operated, behaved civilly. The men in the crowd exchanged glances but didn't look convinced. Suddenly, the roar of machine-gun fire interrupted Brandt. He tried to carry on, but stuttered and had to repeat himself while the guards ran outside with their weapons raised. Karl followed them. The noise clattered in his ears like it was coming from all sides. A plane swooped down overhead, its fuselage glinting in the sun, dipping low enough that he could make out the star-and-bar on the underside of its wings. It circled back again, spraying the area near the camp kitchen with bullets, a building he'd walked past only ten minutes earlier. Then the rumble of the propellers faded into the distance.

Later, after Brandt had finished his speech, Karl headed back across the camp while a crew of prisoners cleaned up the debris— shards of wood and punctured cans of beans that leached brine into the dirt. While surveying the damage, he thought of his father, bullets whistling past his ears each morning as he scrambled up into no man's land, armed with more courage than Karl could ever hope to have.

BRANDT'S orders ate up the next several days, giving Karl no time to make amends with Marijke. He slept only a few hours each night and ate his meals at his desk, leaving sticky fingerprints on files and telegrams. Word of the approaching troops had passed through the camp, and more and more blocks grew resistant to the guards' commands. The officers called the Jews to the muster grounds over the loudspeaker, with the hope of transferring them to another camp, but no one showed up. The inmate functionaries didn't enforce the order either. A senior Kapo reported that the Jews didn't want to be killed, but Brandt assured him that they planned to turn them over to the Red Cross.

The Gestapo in Weimar sent Karl the names of forty-six anti-fascists who had been accused of being saboteurs, but these men also disappeared and went into hiding, and the Kapos and Blockältesten made only a weak effort to find them. Eventually, the guards succeeded in rounding up some Jews at roll call, but according to camp records, the numbers were off by hundreds. Karl cursed at the roll-call officer and demanded the prisoners stand at attention while they re-counted. He ordered armed SS men to hunt down the remainder, with little success. Brandt told him not to worry, but Karl knew better. With the inmate functionaries ignoring their demands, the camp hierarchy was rotting away beneath them.

ON Sunday, Brandt called Karl into his office after lunch. Brandt had heavy bags under his bloodshot eyes.

"You look terrible, Müller." Brandt folded his hands on his desk. A bronze writing set shaped like a jester with a fiendish grin sat between them. Brandt pulled a pen from the holder and started jotting down a list. "I'm ordering an immediate evacuation to Dachau. Get as many prisoners as possible out of here, starting with the ones from Ohrdruf. Try to keep the guards in check. The prisoners may revolt if they get wind of the news."

"They're already banding together to stall the evacuation. We'll never get them all out in time."

"We have to try." Brandt continued with his list of instructions, and Karl tried to note them all, but he was sweating in his tunic and itchy all over as he realized that Brandt had lost faith in the Wehrmacht.

"Everything clear? Good. I'll check in with you in a couple of hours."

Karl moved to leave, but Brandt put out his hand to stop him. "We're the ones with the guns, Müller. Don't let their numbers intimidate you."

Back in his own office, Karl paced the room. A pair of planes flew low overhead, but they didn't drop anything, so he assumed it was a reconnaissance mission. He checked his wall calendar, trying to guess how much time he had left as a free man, before he would be shot in the head or hung from the gallows, depending who got to him first. His mouth went dry. He reached for his chair, gripping the armrests while weighing the options. Nowhere was safe anymore: not Weimar, not Berlin. Switzerland perhaps, but even that was uncomfortably close to the Allies. The only refuge lay far away, outside of Europe. Brandt's remark about Argentina returned to him, the content life his relative had there. Karl could either try to escape and face execution for desertion, follow orders and wait and hope, or count down his remaining hours with Marijke.

KARL sent a message to the brothel, making plans to see her at seven. He tried to conceive a plan to keep them together. But in the meantime, the prisoners needed organizing. A few dozen armed SS men would help facilitate the evacuations. They'd sort the Ohrdruf inmates and march them out by priority: Jews first, foreign prisoners, and then the Germans. After passing on instructions to Ritter about the evacuation, he waded through a mess of files about labour allocation and the Jewish evacuees and placed calls to the Gestapo in Weimar about the denouncement of those anti-fascists.

Officers ran over every ten minutes to confirm his intentions or inquire about the evacuation plans, panicking as they caught shreds of news about the weakening Wehrmacht defence. The air-raid siren had gone off that morning, and the hum of planes in the distance grew louder and more constant. To boost their spirits, Karl told them that Brandt had heard that the Germans had gained some ground and forced the Americans on the defensive. That, and Karl had all the cigarettes from the prisoners' canteen delivered to the SS garrison for the officers. With each passing hour, the racket around the administration buildings grew louder, the smell of booze stronger. While Karl was grabbing a file from the records office, a drunk guard stumbled in, tugging down his fly. Upon spotting Karl, the man turned red. "S-s-orry, sir. Wrong room."

"If the Americans catch you with your trousers down, you'll walk away without any balls," Karl said. "Get out of my sight."

Dusk fell across the camp. His stomach began to growl, reminding him that he hadn't eaten since breakfast. He looked at the clock: quarter past seven. He still needed the final evacuation list from Ritter, who wasn't in his office, so he hurried across the compound to the SS garrison, checking his watch to estimate how long it would take him to get back over to the brothel.

When he entered the barracks, Ritter's nasal drone drifted over from the mess hall. Raucous laughter bounced off the walls. Eleven SS men, all of them stinking of beer. At the end of the table sat half-eaten plates of sauerkraut drowning in mustard.

"Ritter, where in God's name is that list?"

Ritter looked startled but scooped some papers from the bench and brought them over. "My apologies for the delay, sir."

"Damn it, don't you understand how urgent this is?" Karl's words fell flat as he spotted the full jugs of beer. Ritter passed him one, but he pushed it away. "You think the Americans are sitting around getting soused right now?"

Ritter's cheeks drained of colour. "I'm sorry, sir. None of us knows what to do. We just sit around, waiting for them to march in here and cart us all off to POW camps? I bet they'll kill us all."

"Don't be so dramatic."

"With all due respect, sir, we're fucked."

Those words echoed in Karl's head, and he realized they were the same ones he'd been repeating to himself all afternoon. But the Allies wouldn't give a shit about anyone as low-ranked as Ritter.

"Nothing's over yet." Karl turned to address all the men. "Sober up. The Kommandant is calling a meeting of head officers in an hour. Inform the others." He paused to recount the men. "Where is everyone?"

Ritter fidgeted, but one of the others piped up. "A few ran off to the brothels."

"Goddammit."

Karl left the SS barracks and broke into a jog. A handful of prisoners turned as he ran past, his boots pounding against the gravel and dirt. He thought he caught looks of malice on their faces and decided to sleep with his Luger on his nightstand that night.

It took three minutes to get to the prisoners' brothel. He arrived out of breath. Pushing past the cashier, he moved straight for the koberzimmers. He ran from one to the other to check the peepholes. Naked, uninterested girls, skeletal men. Another guard touching himself, almost drooling. Karl stopped at the second-last door. Inside stood Hoffmann, his trousers around his knees. Marijke at his ankles, still dressed. Karl yanked open the door and rushed at him with his fist raised. The amusement on Hoffmann's face turned to shock, and Marijke looked up at Karl with glazed eyes. Karl swung at Hoffmann, who ducked out of the way, knocking Marijke aside.

"Get the fuck away from her!" Karl swung again, but Hoffmann was already moving toward the door. Then he was gone. Karl ran over to her, tried to shake her awake. Her skin was grey and beads of sweat covered the back of her neck. "Marijke, it's me. I'm here."

He lifted her onto his lap, but she still didn't move. Her pulse flickered like a fading light bulb. The brothel supervisor and cashier watched as he carried her out of the brothel.

A girl poked her head out of the sleeping quarters and rushed toward him. "Sir, where are you taking her?"

He didn't waste time on an answer. "Marijke, love. Wake up. Talk to me." Her hip bone jabbed into his stomach but she didn't move. As he approached the infirmary blocks, he told her about the Americans, about the evacuation list. He told her he wanted them to stay together. "We'll find a place in the middle of Bavaria, somewhere in the forest by a lake. I'll build us a little chalet and we'll live there in peace, just you and me and maybe some children one day. No war, no politics. Stay with me, darling."

Her body remained limp. As he reached for the door of the infirmary, a yellow glow fell over her face. Her lips were parted, like she wanted to say something, but her eyes stayed shut. Her eyelashes looked almost white.

A nurse in a blood-spotted shift glanced up as he pulled open the door. "Schutzhaftlagerführer. Good evening. Is everything all right?" He stopped bandaging the prisoner in front of him and came over to examine Marijke.

"She fainted," Karl said. "She needs attention."

The nurse looked around as if trying to direct his attention to the lack of beds. Dying prisoners in every corner. The stench of piss and death. Karl brushed past him and carried Marijke toward the end of the hall.

"Where's the doctor?"

"Dr. Fischer is in the operating theatre. I'll tell him you're here."

Karl looked down at Marijke. "Isn't there a different doctor available?"

"Dr. Wagner is scheduled to begin his shift in half an hour."

"Find him," he said. "Tell him it's urgent."

The nurse hurried off. Karl scoured the hall for somewhere to place Marijke. He didn't want to pack her in with all those dying men, but he relented upon finding an empty cot with proper bedding between some of the bunks. He laid her on it and squatted beside her, stroking her wrist. Within minutes, Dr. Wagner arrived. When he saw Marijke in her brothel clothes, he seemed surprised but started to examine her without any remark. "She's probably suffering from exhaustion. I'll have to check her further. I suggest you leave her with me."

Just as Karl was about to refuse, he remembered Brandt's meeting. He stepped forward. "Listen, Wagner. She needs to be taken care of, just as you would any woman of good German blood. Just as you would your wife. I don't want any questions."

Dr. Wagner rubbed his temples, and Karl noticed the fatigued lines on his face. "Please," Karl said, "just make sure she gets better. I'll come back in a couple of hours."

WORK tied him up for the rest of the night. The communists had grouped and were putting up a good fight, trying to thwart the evacuations by refusing to work or to show up at the muster grounds for roll call. The evacuation list Ritter had compiled contained twenty-five thousand names, but a good six thousand were in blocks that showed mob resistance, so it was going to be impossible to get everyone out. Karl signed his approval and set off to find Brandt for a final check. But as he carried the stack of pages, he couldn't ignore the weight of the lives in his hands, those words on the leaflet. He knew he was diverting these people from liberation, and if the conditions en route were as harsh as he imagined, a great many would die. He flipped through the stack of paper, scanning the list of prisoners from Ohrdruf until he found De Graaf's name. Visions of Marijke came to him, of the future they could have together, of vacations in Paris, of pushing a baby carriage alongside a Bavarian lake. He slipped the page back into the stack and proceeded into Brandt's office with the first sliver of satisfaction he'd felt in days. If Buchenwald was going down, at least Marijke's husband would go down with it.

KARL took Marijke's hand in his. Her forehead radiated heat, and she was still sleeping. It was two o'clock in the morning, so everyone in the infirmary blocks was asleep, except for the doctor, who had locked himself in his office with a bottle of gin. The rancid body odour was inescapable. Karl debated the risk of taking her to the SS infirmary. Brandt would be too busy to notice, but Karl had to admit she'd be much safer among the prisoners when the Americans arrived.

He bent over her and stroked her cheek. Her curls knotted around her face. He thought about lying down next to her, but what would the medical staff think? Besides, the cot was far too small. For a few hours, he stayed by her side. She stirred, though never woke, but other patients did, and the sight of their withered limbs stretching out from the bunks terrified him. How had it come to this?

Just before dawn, he returned to his quarters. An hour or two of sleep and then he had to be up to report to Brandt.

CHAPTER TWENTY-FOUR

I T MIGHT HAVE BEEN DAYS THAT LUCIANO LAY THERE in his cell, fighting off hallucinations, or it might have been a week. He tried to pray, tried to compose a letter to his father, but thoughts passed through him like coloured bars of light. When he did break past the delirium, he remembered what Shark had made him do and wished he could return to that hazy state of madness, because in the real world, the world of the prison, he could no longer hide what he was.

In the fifth grade, he'd run a three-legged race beside the lake in Parque Tres de Febrero as part of his best friend's birthday party. Luciano was paired with one of Héctor friends from swimming, a boy named Ricardo. Ricardo had tugged Luciano along the path, had laughed as he stumbled to keep up. They crossed the finish line with a face-plant, beating Héctor and his partner by half a metre. Ricardo rolled over, his arms covered in grass stains, and gave Luciano a huge hug. Luciano knew right then that the warm, tender feeling that rose up in him wasn't supposed to happen.

For the most part, he assumed he'd done a good job of hiding it, joining the soccer team like his father wanted, checking out car shows and going on about hot girls, dating a few of them.

One Saturday in January, he and Fabián had gone out cruising in Fabián's mother's car. A heat wave had settled in, and the line at the local ice cream parlour stretched down the block. Two girls huddled together, licking their ice cream cones as their bronzed legs and bare shoulders caught the sun. Fabián slowed down and whistled, making them giggle, and they came up to the car as soon as he pulled over. A flick of Fabián's head sent Luciano into the back seat so one of the girls could take the front. The other one slid in with Luciano. Within a few minutes, Fabián was cupping his girl's thigh, and the girl in the back had her arm around Luciano, who sat stiff and awkward for the entire ride, without taking his eyes off Fabián's hand. Later, once they had dropped off the girls, they drove home in silence. When they passed a strip of love motels, Luciano nudged Fabián. "Boy, the things I'd like to do to her." Fabián kept his eyes on the road and didn't answer.

Another time, Fabián left a corduroy jacket at his place to give away with a pile of Luciano's old clothes. Instead of donating it, Luciano left it hanging on his bedpost so the smell of his friend was always close. He thought of how he'd gotten hard watching the sweat drip off Fabián's back on a school trip to the rainforest, his frantic rush to cover himself with his backpack.

How badly he wanted something to happen, anything. Then he thought of Shark, of the dream of Fabián in the white room. He curled up in a ball again.

A tap came on the partition. "Luciano?" Gabriel whispered. "Are you okay?"

"How long has it been?" It hurt to speak.

"Two days, I think."

"Have they given away my job?"

"Not yet, but they will soon. Can you sit up?"

He used the wall to pull himself up, gritting his teeth to kill the groans, and once he was sitting, he felt a small victory.

"Luciano?" Gabriel paused. "It doesn't matter, you know. They leech on to anything they think can destroy us."

Luciano shifted uncomfortably. "What doesn't matter?"

"You're a good person, that's all. Don't let them win."

Dear Papá,

I need your advice. Papá, I can't stop—I've been lying to you, to a lot of people, trying to fake too many things. Like Camila. You met her outside our apartment one Sunday, remember? She's tall and freckled. She's always laughing. A tango instructor and a psychology student. We dated for a few months. Fabián kept bugging me to ask her out, so I did.

In the beginning, she and I hung out on the weekends—dinners, movies, walks in the park. We held hands, kissed a bit, but nothing else. Papá, I couldn't pretend I had feelings for her. She felt like a friend. I started helping out at her tango classes, so we'd spend less time alone, but when Fabián asked how things were going, I told him everything he wanted to hear.

Luciano sighed, picturing Fabián's sly grin as he stuck out his hand for a high-five. "*Che,* I told you she was into you. I knew it," Fabián kept saying, while Luciano admired the taut muscles in his friend's neck, tried to pinpoint the perfect stubbled spot to kiss, to swirl his tongue against.

But Papá, I couldn't—every time I looked into her eyes, I felt like a liar. Like I was betraying myself.

He knew Camila had sensed this whenever he touched her, had seen it in the gap he left between them in the booth at the pizza place, the way he'd looked away when she changed clothes after class. When she had ended things, he wasn't surprised. She deserved someone who would fall for her, but he didn't know what he deserved after so much deception.

And, you know, the worst part of hiding things is that it makes me feel so isolated, like nobody out there really knows me. Not you, not even Mamá. You all see pieces of me, the parts you want to acknowledge.

But you know, I think you have your own secrets, secrets hiding behind your blank face.

A few weeks before his capture, Luciano had cut through the Rosario on the way back from soccer practice. A storm was rolling in, and the swans that swam between the paddleboats moved for shelter as the park cleared out. When he passed through the gate to the gardens, the buzz of insects picked up and the air took on a perfume. There were roses everywhere—red, pink, yellow—lining the walkways in tidy rows and creeping up the arbours. The first raindrops began to fall, and he was about to break into a jog when he saw his father sitting alone on a bench, surrounded by tulips so dark that they appeared black. His father hunched, staring into a growing puddle, a newspaper clutched on his lap. His hand had twitched against the headline.

Papá, you didn't see me in the park the other week, but I saw you. When the thunder started, I expected you to get up, but you didn't move. You sat there while the rain fell harder, soaking you, dripping from the brim of your fedora. Still, you didn't move. I debated calling out to you, but instead I stood and watched. You looked like a stranger, a very old, lonely man.

That's what I'm afraid of becoming.

Tell me, Papá, what is it—how do you manage to keep track of all your lies? How is it possible to lead a double life for so long without going mad?

ONCE his wounds had healed more, Luciano listened for the footsteps of any guard but Shark and asked to work again.

When they brought him downstairs with the other workers, he became suspicious of the guards' willingness to accept him back and spent the first morning shaking in the photo lab. Gabriel had the task of creating microfilm copies of files in the archive. Because Luciano had used microfilm for university research, the guards told him to help.

They stood in an area that had been sectioned off as a darkroom. Other prisoners around them leaned over photos and documents. Nobody talked or looked at them. Luciano pulled out the first file, which contained information about a girl who also belonged to the JUP. Although they had attended different schools, the file mentioned one or two names he recognized, other members with whom she was associated. Her file ended with a letter *L*, which, according to Gabriel, stood for "liberated." The next document concerned a twenty-year-old boy, a Montonero who had been captured three months earlier in an ambush at his home. When he had failed to come home, they took his mother hostage until he showed his face. Luciano's insides crumpled as he saw the letter on this file. He had to stop checking.

Gabriel showed him how to position the file under the microfilmer, how to set the exposure and how the images came out. The whirrs and clicks of the microfilmer soothed Luciano, brought him back to his university library, but every time he heard a guard marching in the hall, he paused, terrified that Shark might appear in the doorway.

At one point, a guard came and escorted them to the bathroom in the basement. On the way back, Luciano spotted Shark. He stiffened and watched as Shark half-helped, half-tugged a woman across the basement. Her pants were wet at the crotch, and she cringed as she held her huge belly. The other guard pushed Luciano toward the photo lab, but Luciano turned in time to see a man in a white coat open a door and usher her into a room. Her shrieks filled the basement in bursts for what must have been hours, until, after one long, gasping moan, Luciano heard the howl of a baby.

The noise picked up, turned into high-pitched sobs, until everyone paused to listen. But it sounded misplaced, unreal.

He tried to picture the baby in the other room, the tiny fists unfurling, but all he could imagine were those metal bed frames. He thought of his cousin's birth, how he'd been allowed to watch while his mother helped with the delivery. The doctor had snipped the umbilical cord and cleaned the baby before placing her at his aunt's breast. Luciano imagined that happening with this newborn, but then he recalled what Gabriel had told him. Once the mother had nursed the baby long enough for it to gain an ounce of strength, the doctor would take the child from her arms and give it to the navy, which would adopt it out internally. By the time some navy family brought home the infant, the mother would be dead, and that child would grow up swaddled in secrets and lies.

The baby's cries abated but kept echoing in Luciano's head. He thought of the pregnant woman who had been in the cell next to him, about her dead husband, and he wondered how long she had left. Plenty of young married couples had joined the insurgent groups, including a bunch of his friends in the JUP, but he hadn't considered that many of the women would be pregnant or already mothers. Did they understand the danger they were putting their children in by getting involved? Or had they believed that they had to act for the sake of their children's future?

He grabbed another file and stared at the stack that awaited conversion. His hand tensed around the document, the paper creasing under his thumb. So many names, so many faces that would be written off as "missing."

He unrolled the end of a coil of film and fed the long brown ribbon into the microfilmer. On the table beside him sat two full rolls of government secrets. While waiting for the machine to start up, he picked up those rolls, considered their size and weight. Small enough to be stashed away, tucked into the waistband of a pair of pants, the lining of a bra. Nodding to himself, he positioned the first record, another victim marked with a *T*. He took a shot of it with the microfilmer, put it to the side and readied the next one. But when he had filled up the entire roll, he didn't switch to a new batch of files. Instead, he reached for a fresh roll of microfilm and secretly started again on the same set, making a second copy of each file.

> *Dear Papá,*
> *Borges once called this city a place "as eternal as air and water."*
> *But it seems like we're bringing it down upon our heads, doesn't*
> *it? Soon there will be nothing, nothing left to his Eden but rubble.*

Luciano tried to picture the lecture halls at university, the soccer pitch, his neighbourhood. He longed to wander the streets again, beneath trees with corkscrewed trunks; he longed for spring, when blossoming jacarandas rained purple over the city, for maté sipped between friends, for bookstores that smelled of must and ancient mysteries.

> *Papá, when this ends, when the military is defeated, the truth*
> *will come out. The people—no, we—we will restore this city,*
> *this country to its rightful state. And the dead, the missing, we'll*
> *offer them whatever shred of honour we can. You think it's best*
> *to stay quiet, stick with the flock, even if the flock is headed in*
> *the wrong direction. You're wrong. We have to fight. We have*

to do something; we have to do anything we can, to show them
they won't succeed with their plans. That we won't let them win.
Argentina needs us, all of us.

GABRIEL no longer had to wear the hood. The officers said he
was "recoverable," that they planned to reintegrate him into
society. They either tried to turn their prisoners into their little
pets or put them down. Dogs, a hawk, a shark—Argentina was
no longer a country of people but a fighting, snapping, growling
pack of wild beasts.

After the beating from Shark, Luciano's clothes had become
starched with blood, but he wore them to work several times
before anyone said anything. During a bathroom break on the
third day, one of the military officers passed through the basement and frowned at the sight of Luciano. "You've been working
in this?"

Luciano stared at the crisp uniform in front of him. The officer waved at the guard who had accompanied Luciano to the
toilets. "Take him to find some decent clothes."

The guard brought Luciano to fetch his hood from the
photography lab. Gabriel looked up as they entered, a stack of
files in his hands, but pretended to be busy as the hood fell back
over Luciano's head.

As they started up the staircase, Luciano tried to breathe
through his mouth. The hood hadn't been washed since his
arrival, and the stink of it made him nauseated. They climbed to
the third floor, the level of La Capucha, but instead of turning
left toward the cells, they went right up a small set of stairs. A

door clanged right behind them and then they descended a few steps. The guard pulled off Luciano's hood.

"Choose something."

Luciano looked around in shock. The room overflowed with furniture: chairs, nightstands, sofas, lamps, a gilded mirror, ornate hat stands, framed paintings of the Andes, a four-clawed umbrella holder—it was as if someone had run a rake across an entire city block and collected all the contents of the houses. In the centre, amid everything else, sat two giant mounds of clothing. While the guard watched, Luciano approached the closest pile. It dwarfed him, stretching almost twice his height and at least three metres wide at the base. Polo shirts, sports jackets, worn blue jeans, a red sundress with white flowers, a cable-knit sweater, platform shoes, a necktie wrapped around a suede boot. He felt the weight of the clothes on his chest and inhaled the faint smell of sweat and mixed perfumes.

The guard shifted. "Hurry up."

Luciano reached his cuffed hands into the pile. The clothes shifted as he tugged at the sleeve of a checked shirt, and something fell into his hands along with it. A baby bonnet, a soft lemon-yellow. As he held it, he spotted the matching shoes, with soles no longer than his thumb and laces still tied in perfect bows. He dropped the bonnet, blinking hard to keep himself in check, and started looking for a pair of pants. He stepped around to the other side of the mound and grabbed the first pair that looked his size.

CHAPTER TWENTY-FIVE

MARIJKE
APRIL 9, 1945
BUCHENWALD

GROANS AND WHIMPERS, THE SMELL OF ROT AND feces, and amid it all, something sterile and cold. My vision crept back, and a minute passed before the blurred shapes found their edges. I was surrounded by the dying. Around me stood tiers of bunks, men stacked like loaves in an oven, sometimes two or three to a bed. They clung to their thin blankets and gingham sheets as they murmured or stared into space. Figures in white coats wandered around but ignored those who cried out for help. The infirmary was a long, wooden block with windows every four or five metres, but these did little to brighten it up. I lay on a cot in the centre of the hall, the only female and one of few with a heavy blanket.

I sat up with a nagging thirst, but dizziness hit and forced me back down. The blanket smothered me with its heat, so

I tried to tug it off. The last thing I remembered was Bruno, the mud on his polished boots as he pulled at my clothes, but how much time had passed since then? In place of my skirt and blouse, a long shift covered my body. I slipped a hand beneath the blanket and checked between my legs. Not a twinge of pain.

A doctor with a clipboard entered the infirmary blocks, stooping in front of a bed where a leg dangled to the ground. He lowered his stethoscope to the man's heart before scribbling a note on the clipboard and gesturing with his thumb. Two prisoners came up behind him, dragged the corpse off the bunk and tossed it by the door. By the time the doctor reached the end of the hall, there were three piles, each five bodies high. Karl's stories came back to me: the attempts to develop a typhus vaccine, to cure homosexuality, using patients as test subjects. I pulled the blanket around me. The motion caught the doctor's attention, and he approached. A tall, thin man with a thick moustache that curled upward. His feet stuck to the floor as he walked, the wood covered in a pinkish layer of fluid. "And she awakens," he said.

I eased myself onto my elbows. "What am I doing here?"

"Do you recall anything?"

"Not very much."

"You need rest."

He left before I could ask anything else. A few flies started to hover around the piles of bodies. I shuddered, wishing I were back in the brothel, listening to the girls' idle chatter or the clink of their coffee cups as they ate breakfast.

One bed over, an old man's groans grew into sobs as he

called for anyone and everyone to save him: his mother—probably long dead—the Lord, some woman named Francesca. I lay back, counting the ceiling boards above me in an attempt to ignore him. A split in the wood began in a patch of light by the window and ran down into the shadow. I debated whether Karl knew what had happened, whether he'd shown up to find an empty koberzimmer or had forgotten, distracted by lager and playing cards.

Another prisoner came round with a vat of soup, pushed on a gurney with a squeaky wheel. He stopped in front of each bed to dole out a portion. When he passed me mine, I turned up my nose: clear broth with just a few chunks of potatoes. Ravensbrück all over again. Then I noticed the hollowness of his cheeks as he smiled sadly. I bowed my head and thanked him for the soup before he moved on.

A nurse walked by when I was two spoonfuls in and halted at my bed. "No, no. You're on a special diet." She whisked away my bowl, and I sat bitterly, certain she'd robbed me of a meal. Ten minutes later, she returned with a small tray that she placed on my lap. "Someone must be watching out for you."

Milk, bread with jam and a slice of cheese. I took greedy bites before noticing the stares around me. I shoved one piece of bread to the side and, when the matron wasn't looking, ripped it into two chunks that I passed to the men beside me.

The afternoon crumbled away. The hard mattress hurt my breasts, forcing me to sleep on my back. When I awoke, the stacks of bodies had disappeared. I could guess what had happened to them. Corpses were carted to the crematorium, gold yanked from their mouths and the bodies tossed into the ovens like firewood. Over the months, Buchenwald's secrets had poured out onto the beds of the brothel.

The nurse came by with a tin cup and pointed to the corner of the room, where a pair of buckets served as latrines. "Bring it back half full."

I wobbled as I got up, a rush to my head. She put her arm around my waist and guided me to the corner before leaving me in privacy. I squatted in full view and struggled back to bed without help. My eyelids felt heavy and sleep found me again.

I woke up when someone cleared her throat. The nurse stood at my bed, holding out my dinner. At the other end of the hall, that prisoner wove through the rows with his pot of soup, but she offered a bowl of stew, with chunks of meat amid the potatoes. Maybe Wilhelmina or Bertha had arranged it, ensuring I got well enough to return to work. More likely it was Karl. Whenever heavy boots crossed the floor, I perked up, but it was always the same pockmarked guard. Each time he entered the hospital wing, the medical staff swarmed him, their voices buzzing. I caught snippets of their conversation—"advancing . . . evacuation . . . Dachau"—but it left me confused. Who were they evacuating, themselves or prisoners?

The wails of the other patients died down as dusk swept over the hospital wing. The nurses gathered in a side room, smoke from their cigarettes floating into the infirmary. That bastard was probably doing the same, lounging in his villa with a bottle of brandy, not a single concern.

But when I fell asleep, I had a dream about a life with him, an estate in Munich, Sunday dinners with his parents—the table adorned with roast beef marinated in vinegar, red cabbage and raspberry custard—automobile rides and a little boy playing fetch with Axel and Faust.

In the morning, talking pulled me from my dreams. The female voices sounded like they were coming from the foot of my bed. Feigning sleep, I listened.

"We'll need to terminate it."

"Is there any point? There's nothing to send her back to."

"Give it a few days and she'll no longer be our responsibility. It's our own skin we should be worried about. We could end up like her, but working for the Yanks."

The starched fabric of their uniforms rustled, and their voices faded away. I wrapped my arms around my belly. The past months, my body had seemed as frail and dormant as a little girl's. A tear slid down my cheek. How could I carry and bear a child in the middle of a war? And how had I let Karl sneak into the chamber of my dreams, that one sacred spot where Theo and I could still be together? I touched my empty ring finger, aching to know if Theo was still alive, where he was. Questions and worries churned my thoughts: whether he'd heard the guns of the approaching Allies, if he understood the end was upon us. Had he managed to hold on, and could he hold on that little bit longer? My fingers, my toes, my skin, my eyes, my lips, my ears—every part of me pined for him: wishing to hear his quiet laugh, to return to Sundays drinking tea along the canals together, to see his face beside mine at sunrise every morning. To give him a child he would love.

If the Americans arrived in the coming days, I imagined they would march through the camp gates, bewildered at their discovery. Hopefully enraged. The moffen would flee at the bark of American orders, the loaded guns. Maybe some would try to fight, but they would be no match for the storm of soldiers. The prisoners would spill from the blocks and start running, walking, even limping toward wives and children and home.

CHAPTER TWENTY-SIX

WHEN KARL WAS YOUNG, HIS MOTHER USED TO organize party games in their garden for his birthdays. She would set up obstacles for a relay and drive a short post into the ground. The children had to spin around it with their heads bent to touch the tip. After ten spins, Karl would stand up and race forward to tackle the obstacles, but the grass tilted toward the sky as he stumbled sideways, unable to tell up from down.

His final day at Buchenwald felt like that. Beginning at six thirty in the morning, he ran around without a second to think of himself or Marijke. That afternoon, he succeeded in evacuating two batches of inmates, a total of 9,280, although this happened well behind schedule. He travelled to the train station in Weimar to oversee their departure. They had to march ten kilometres from the camp, down the same access road that some of them had helped pave years earlier. Many dropped dead in their feeble state, and others had to step over the scattered bodies. Karl's driver honked to get past the columns of prisoners, but the officers in the automobiles in front started shooting at anyone who failed to keep pace, and the road became stained with bright blood. The evacuees hobbled into the station in clumps, looking as if all their willpower had drained away. As the guards herded them into the cattle cars, Karl tried not to think about the fact that they were sending these men, so close to freedom, to certain death. He imagined Marijke, the way she smiled in her sleep, her girlish, sputtering laughter, and he asked himself whom they were taking these men away from.

They spent the rest of the day covering their tracks. Karl had the hooks removed from the execution room, the resulting holes filled in and the walls covered with a fresh coat of paint. A group of Jews collected stray corpses, though there were far too many for the crematorium to handle. The more orders he gave, the more conscious he became of the futility of the efforts, and he started to understand how much blood was on his hands. He saw it in the scrap of fabric snagged on the electric fence, in the raven that picked at a rotting finger, in the buckets of ashes they dumped in fresh pits. These images refused to leave his head.

Between duties, Karl managed to send a message to the hospital to inquire about Marijke. He'd dropped by to check on her again the night before, but had found her fast asleep. The doctor's latest update was that she was still mostly sleeping, and he would keep her there while he ran some tests. Karl debated what the doctor meant by "tests," but as he composed a reply, Brandt called on him to produce a number of files.

The Kommandant kept all of the officers busy well into the night. At midnight, he summoned them to his office for the latest dispatch. Hoffmann stood at the back of the room, as far away from Karl as possible. Karl gritted his teeth and tried to listen to Brandt's speech, but all he could think of was what he planned to do to Hoffmann once the war ended.

Brandt rose to survey the group. "I'm afraid we've reached the end. The first team of Patton's Third has reached Grumbach and Wiegleben. Barring some miracle, we have less than twenty-four hours."

The beef Karl had eaten for dinner rolled in his stomach. The other officers shifted. Ritter's knuckles went white from balling up his hands. They waited for Brandt to say more. Brandt took off his cap and rotated it by the brim, exposing the ebb of his grey hair. Over the course of the week, the lines on his face had deepened and the skin on his neck sagged. There was something both dignified and weary about his appearance, but it made Karl doubt whether he would live to have wrinkles himself.

Ritter piped up. "What's expected of us, sir?"

Brandt gave Ritter a sharp look. "What do you think? You're officers of the Reich as long as you're still standing." He sighed and ran his hand through his hair before replacing his hat. "I'm taking orders as much as you are. Hoffmann, Ritter, I need you on duty for the next few hours. The rest of you, get some shut-eye."

The officers exited the room single file, but Brandt motioned for Karl to stay. He locked the door and pulled a bottle of brandy from the cabinet under his desk. Karl sat across from him and took two long sips, letting the drink slide down his throat with a satisfying burn. Brandt drank his snifter dry. "What am I supposed to say to our men, Müller? Who knows where we'll be this time tomorrow."

"This is what it comes to, then," Karl said. "The Reich breaking apart beneath our feet, while the Führer sits back in Berlin and measures the tremors."

"The prisoners will overrun us the moment they hear machine-gun fire. We should kill them all now."

Karl ran a brandy-soaked finger over the rim of the snifter until it began a high whine that sent him back to the brothel: Marijke teasing out the first notes of a Brahms violin concerto, the cool touch of her feet on his lap. "Maybe we should let them go."

"Let those swine terrorize the countryside? Are you daft?"

"The Americans will do it anyway. If we make the first move, they might go easier on us."

"I doubt that. Even if they did, Himmler would try us for treason. There's no avoiding it, Müller. The Grim Reaper is knocking." Brandt reached into his breast pocket and pulled out something small, which he slid across the desk. "You'll need this."

A brass vial shaped like a lipstick tube. Karl knew what it contained. Visiting officials had handed out cyanide capsules like party favours at SS events for the past month, although he'd never accepted one. With a nod, he slipped the vial into his pocket. Brandt took off his tunic and latched his thumbs under his suspenders as he leaned back in his chair. "I'm sixty years old, Müller. I'm in no shape to do this myself, but I'm telling you because I like you: get out of here. Run and hide—stay away until this war is long over and they've given up on the little fish.

Find your way to South America if you can. I'll give you the contact information for my nephew."

Karl's palms tingled. He rubbed them against his thighs, but that just made them itch. Brandt poured them each another glass of brandy, even though Karl had barely touched his. This one he drank like the Kommandant: in three quick slugs.

"Just be glad you don't have a family to think about." Brandt poured yet another round. "Müller?" He looked concerned. "You seem lost. Can you keep it together?"

Karl nodded but refused the offer of more brandy. "I'm going to catch a couple hours of sleep. You'll notify me if any more news comes in, won't you?"

INSTEAD of going to sleep, Karl visited the zoo. Koch, the camp's first Kommandant, had built the small enclosure for his wife and the families of the SS officers. Although it was near Karl's office, and he'd sometimes seen monkeys scrambling around their enclosures from behind the barbed wire of the prisoners' camp, he'd never visited. Even as a child, zoos had made him uneasy. His mother had taken him to the one in Munich in 1916, and he had left the elephant house in tears after seeing the great mammal up close. Such a noble beast, but she had paced her enclosure with a heavy sadness in her eyes.

The zoo was deserted. A torch guided him through the trees, but he could still see the light from the nearby watchtower. There came a crack like a gunshot and then another. He halted before concluding it was dead branches falling from the trees. Then he heard a sound like a scream and paused to listen, but this was just the monkeys screeching. At the main compound, he stopped. Four brown bears in a rocky pit. His torch hit one of them straight on. The bear squinted and yawned, revealing a string of saliva that bridged its sharp incisors. He took a seat on a nearby boulder. The yawning bear got up and circled the small pit before lying back down, like it wanted to show Karl how much it longed to escape its confines.

The spotlights of the camp watchtowers passed by in intervals, lighting up the shadows between the bare trees. The rumble of artillery had finally settled down for the night. As Karl fingered the buttons of his tunic, his father came to mind: all the times as a boy Karl had run his hands over his father's old military uniform, mystified by the thought of him chasing the enemy like a modern-day Achilles. But there was nothing glorious or heroic about what lay within a barbed-wire world.

He wanted to be at Marijke's side, desperate to believe in a future together, but his own future risked termination at any hour. Even if she were to run away with him, she faced a life of danger and uncertainty: her hands would be caked in dirt, shredded by brambles, while she shivered through the damp nights. But he couldn't allow himself a goodbye either, knowing it would be so difficult to leave that he would end up sitting at her side until the Americans marched in and looped a noose around his neck. He had to let her go.

A low growl knocked him out of his stupor, but the bears were asleep. His pulse spiked as he got up and flashed the torch in all directions. His hands grew clammy, but he forced himself to cross the camp complex at a controlled pace. Plenty of running awaited him.

BACK in his villa, he deliberated over the luggage that lay on his bed: a sturdy, old suitcase that his father had picked out for his graduation, which had seen him through many trips around Germany and all his years with the SS. But instead, he rummaged in the wardrobe for a rucksack. Taking one of the cars from the SS garage would be too risky with all the reconnaissance patrols that were bound to be out; he would have to travel on foot. He tossed two spare shirts into the rucksack, along with a pair of trousers, his torch, a water canteen, a blanket, a flask, an extra Luger with bullets, and a few emergency provisions he'd filched from the officers' mess. The brass vial was still in his pocket. He unscrewed the lid, trying to imagine himself biting into the capsule as he sat in solitary confinement in some Allied prison. With a shudder, he packed the vial in the rucksack, but then changed his mind and slipped it back into his pocket, safely within reach.

Five minutes later, he was packed and left to consider his fate. He poured himself a shot of Dutch gin, which he slammed back while picturing Marijke walking down the aisle of the church, his parents beaming in the front pew, not a uniform in sight.

Once he'd emptied a third of the gin, he capped the bottle. From his nightstand he took out an unopened wooden cigar box. He lit a cigar and tossed the lighter into the rucksack. Long, deep puffs to settle his nerves. The tobacco had a rich flavour, with a hint of something nutty, walnut or almond. When the cigar started burning his fingertips, he stubbed it out on the headline of a month-old newspaper: "Offensive in Hungary: Hope for a Comeback on the Eastern Front."

The clock read 3:30 a.m. He held back a yawn and rummaged through his things in search of a map, but the only one he could think of was pinned to the wall in his office. Leaving the rucksack in his room, he made his way back to the office, keeping a careful watch for Hoffmann or anyone who might report his departure. He lowered the window shade to block out the office light. The map showed only the vicinity but contained topography markings, and he'd used it to plot the American advance. He slumped as he turned to look at his desk. A small picture frame sat on the corner, a Christmas photo of his parents. For a moment, the idea of bringing it along tempted him, but he couldn't leave any sign of his disappearance. A pile of files also sat there, all mentioning his name and rank. He started to shred them but gave up after a handful. The camp had no shortage of proof of his existence.

On his way out, he stopped at the clothing depot. He picked out something from the prisoners' garb, trousers and a shirt marked with a painted X. When he returned to his villa, he spread out the map in an attempt to formulate a plan. By then the gin had caught up to him. He studied the forest surrounding the camp and crossed off the no-go zones, but the pencil felt like rubber between his fingers, and he kept nodding off, so he rested his head on the desk for a few minutes of sleep.

He woke up at five thirty. The sun would appear within an hour, and the Americans wouldn't be far behind. He pulled the rucksack over his shoulders, turned off the lights and left the bedroom without looking back. When he locked the front door, he pocketed the key. If nothing else, it would keep those Allied paws off his things for an extra few minutes.

Outside, he made his way down the lane along the dark, mossy edge of the forest. He stopped to listen. The first morning birds were chirping, and somewhere a squirrel chattered. Once he felt certain that nobody was around, he turned on the torch and ducked into the underbrush.

CHAPTER TWENTY-SEVEN

FOR WEEKS, LUCIANO SECRETLY MADE AN EXTRA COPY of each of the files he was converting. He couldn't hide his actions from Gabriel, but Gabriel was eager to take part, and together they developed a system for hiding their work, tucking the microfilm into a ridge on the underside of a table at the end of each day.

While Gabriel worked at the microfilmer, Luciano would act as a lookout, but the guards were often busy with a newspaper or the television and paid little attention to the labourers. The two of them proceeded without a solid plan. They had no clue how they could conceal the files long-term or how they would get the information past ESMA's walls, but Luciano was soothed by the simple knowledge that his collaboration with the oppressors could turn into sabotage.

The air in the basement grew colder, a sign of winter, the weeks that had passed since his arrival. The navy men kept a small radiator near the TV, but the lab lacked heating. During a particularly chilly shift, Luciano had to keep rubbing his hands together to stop his fingers from going numb. When their guard stepped into the doorway to chat with one of the others, Gabriel motioned Luciano to come close. He leaned over the microfilmer as he positioned the file.

"Can you realign this for me?" he asked. Once Luciano had crouched down, Gabriel continued in a whisper. "That girl with the new clothes? We call her Lashes. She's sharp as an arrow, got captured at the same time as me."

At first, Luciano had no idea who Gabriel meant, but he remembered he'd noticed a change in one of the other workers in the lab, a busty girl a few years older than him. Her auburn hair looked fuller and glossier, like it was being washed, and her cheeks had taken on a rosy tinge. He glanced around for movement. "Why are you telling me this?"

"They're planning to release her, trying to reintegrate her into society, part of this recovery program."

Luciano didn't ask how Gabriel knew so much. "You trust her?"

"As much as you can trust anyone here." Gabriel adjusted the focus on the microfilmer and clicked the shutter. "She's committed to the cause."

Luciano thought of the girl's angled features, the high cheekbones that made her resemble his mother. "She could be perfect."

The machine made a strange noise, and Gabriel leaned back to investigate. "I'll make the arrangements."

THREE days later, Lashes smiled at Luciano when they entered the photo lab, flashing him a subtle thumbs-up.

But in the darkroom, Luciano couldn't focus. He kept staring into the red safelights, fiddling with a paper clip. Gabriel winked, which only made him more anxious. Strange smells floated through the basement: fried wires, coffee, a guard's musky aftershave. Luciano flipped through the files—all marked "Transferred." He spotted a familiar name, a girl his mother babysat when he was little. María Josefa used to wear her hair in pigtails and would ask his mother for fried pickle sandwiches. Her mug shot looked nothing like the girl he remembered. He prepared her file for processing and moved on.

When he returned to the main area of the lab to fetch a binder, he noticed the guard slip away from his post for a bathroom break. They had two minutes to act. After signalling to Lashes, he hurried back to the darkroom. Gabriel started to ask something, but trailed off and shifted to block the view of another worker while Luciano reached for the microfilm he'd hidden. He tucked the rolls into the waistband of his pants and returned to the area where Lashes waited, photographs of navy officials fanned out in front of her. She seemed conscious of his every movement. He walked over to the filing cabinet, where he splayed his legs to keep his knees from knocking, and listened for the guard before opening the drawer to slip the microfilm between two folders. Then he returned to the darkroom with a random file.

Once shrouded by shadows, he shifted the black curtain that covered the entrance to spy. The guard had returned to his post. Lashes held up a photograph, pretended to study it and brought it over to the cabinet, where she retrieved the files containing the microfilm. But they dropped from her hand. Luciano cringed and let go of the curtain, certain they were screwed. He felt blood coursing through his veins like rapids. But when he peeked out again, Lashes was casually picking up the files. She restored them to the cabinet with the trace of a smile, angling her body toward the darkroom to reveal the bulge beneath her right breast.

LUCIANO lay awake thinking. He thought about his deteriorating body, about the chances of seeing his family and Fabián ever again. About risk, the meaning of the word, what it had meant to different men across time. Ordinary men, heroes. Argentina, he decided, had been wounded so many times, its gashes so deep, that time could no longer guarantee recovery. In the middle of the battle, Argentina called for help, but any comrade who hoped to save her faced a shower of bullets.

Dear Papá,

You think I have no courage. Dear Papá, maybe I was a coward before, but you can't judge me anymore after what I've lived through. Horrendous things, impossible things. And even though when I joined the JUP, even though I joined only because Fabián convinced me, I'm ready now. I'm ready to place my own branch on the fire.

Papá, tomorrow they're releasing someone. A girl. She's . . . she'll carry the truth Argentinians need to hear. She carries answers, answers to the question everyone is asking: Where is my son? Where is my daughter? Where is my husband, my wife?

I'm sure you don't—well, maybe you believe my role is minor, not enough to feel redeemed. You probably think I'm scared shitless. You're right. I'm terrified. Terrified of pain, of the darkness, of death, but more than anything, terrified I'll live out the rest of my life in shame. Shame that in trying to save myself, I somehow played a role in someone else's suffering.

I need to be honest. With you, with myself. I need to be honest about who I am. I've hid the truth for so many years, out of fear, out of the sense that what I've been feeling is wrong. That you'd hate me for it. I hoped to be the son you've always wanted: a strong, brave man. But I'm not that. Maybe you already can see this, but you have to hear it from me—Papá, I'm in love with Fabián.

CHAPTER TWENTY-EIGHT

MARIJKE
APRIL 11, 1945
BUCHENWALD

I KEPT WATCH FOR THE DOCTOR AS I LAY IN THE INFIR-
mary, determined to stay awake. My stomach was back to tossing on high seas. Years earlier, my mother told me that while
I was in her womb, she'd sung to me every day while preparing
breakfast. She believed it stopped the kicking, that she could
feel my tiny legs relax. I wasn't about to sing, not in the middle
of hundreds of prisoners and a handful of Nazis, and not to a
baby that was probably no bigger than a pea. Instead, I closed
my eyes and imagined picking up that beautiful Italian violin.
Lifting it to my chin, the polished wood of the neck against my
fingers. The bow began to glide—careful, elongated movements.
The notes pooled around me, rising higher and higher until the
music pulled me under. I dove deep, searching for the bottom
until I found a concert hall floating amid fog, a stage set with a

single chair. In the pit, the orchestra awaited my signal. Then it joined in, faceless musicians raising their instruments to back me in a soft adagio movement. The flutter of the flute, chasing birds over autumn trees. The pluck of the harp, moss-covered trails running along a brook. The scales of the piano, climbing up a snowy mountainside. The music built, peaked to a crescendo, and then the orchestra cut away, leaving only my violin to fill the theatre. I played on. Somehow, I felt that child in my belly, guiding my bow. I played until my hand grew sore, and when I lowered my instrument and stepped over to bow, the lights flickered on. The theatre was empty, save for a pair of seats in the front row. Two men: one in a pressed SS uniform, the other in tattered stripes and glasses. I began to shout.

A noise jolted me back, but I couldn't tell where it was coming from. A guard burst into the infirmary. His hair stuck up all over, and even from across the hall, I could see the sweat on his forehead. "They're coming!"

The doctor tossed his clipboard on a gurney and ran out after the guard, the nurses flocking close behind. I heard a surge of confused, frightened yells, muffled commands. Inside the infirmary, all the moaning seemed to stop. Dozens of heads turned to the entrance, as if we expected to hear "The Star-Spangled Banner" playing in the distance, the clatter of machine-gun fire. But there was no sign of them, and even the yells of the medical staff subsided, leaving only the sound of the breeze that flowed in through the entrance, scattering loose sheets from the doctor's clipboard across the bunks.

Fifteen minutes passed. Mouths began to open, and whispers filled the hall. A few people struggled out of bed, but most could walk only a few metres before reaching out for help. Two boys made it as far as the door. They peered out and gestured that there was no one in sight. I watched them take three steps outside before passing beyond a white wall of sunlight.

When they returned, the shorter of the two knocked on a bedpost for attention, but he already had a captive audience. At first, his words came out as a croak.

"Speak louder," I called out.

"The camp is empty," the boy said.

"Empty?" a man asked.

"The guards have disappeared."

"And the prisoners?"

"They must be out at work or hiding in the blocks."

A siren sounded and an announcement rang out over the camp loudspeakers. "All SS officers, evacuate the camp."

We waited. I gripped the edge of the bed, my stomach somersaulting in a mixture of euphoria and fear. Nobody wanted to venture out into camp, to be shot down at the brink of liberation. Soon, the medical staff returned. The doctor flitted around the hospital, making no effort to hide his dour mood as the staff collected their tools, broke test tubes filled with fluids and shredded stacks of paper. He left with a small box of belongings, and three of the nurses followed. One turned to us, hesitating. For the rest of the afternoon, she stayed in the infirmary, wandering between the rows of beds and handing out water and what meagre rations were left. I ate cold soup like everyone else. It did nothing to ease my hunger, but I felt better than I had in days, so I sat on the edge of the bed and tested out my feet. They tingled as they brushed the floor. The nurse came over and guided me as if I were a toddler, but within a minute I could walk to the end of the hall and back without pause.

"Didn't the Schutzhaftlagerführer bring you here himself?" she asked, as I pivoted for a second lap.

The surprise made me pause, as I tried to hide my smile. But if he had brought me here, why hadn't he returned to check on me? The nurse looked at me for an answer, making me wary. She was a plain woman, with thick, unbecoming eyebrows. Her chewed nails looked raw at the corners.

"Yes." I noted the curtness in my tone, and lowered my voice. "Are you frightened?"

She took a seat on my bed, slowly nodded and began biting her nails. I sat down on the far end, but we both looked straight ahead at the entrance to the infirmary.

"So am I," I said.

"Why? This is your happy ending."

"Is it that simple?"

"The Americans will kill us."

"You're just a nurse. They'll be more worried about the SS men at the top."

The remark rushed out before I had a chance to understand its meaning, and the thought of a gun at Karl's head made my chest ache.

"If I were one of them," she said, "I'd run while I still had the chance."

My mouth tasted sour. The nurse and I sat quietly until a raspy cough broke out nearby. I brought the man some water. He tried to pat my arm, but I barely felt his touch. His sallow skin had clusters of scars and inflamed sores. When he returned the cup, the men next to him stretched out. I tracked down a sink. The nurse joined me, and we ferried water to beds for much of the afternoon. Some men had the strength to thank us; others couldn't even lift the cup to their lips, so we had to pour for them, a stream trickling down their chins as they tried to swallow.

The nurse stopped to wipe her bangs from her sticky brow. She stuck out her hand. "I'm Emma."

"Marijke."

We continued on down the rows, and I stopped a few times to hold men's hands or sit by their sides. I was serving Row 7 when the Americans arrived. Outside, people shouted. Someone fired a shot. English, the first I'd heard in two years, since late nights huddled around the secret radio in our bedroom.

Two soldiers opened the door. Americans. Their eyes bulged and their faces paled in astonishment and disgust. They lowered their guns. "Holy fuck."

One of them spun around to wave someone in. An older man in a well-decorated uniform pushed through the soldiers and strode into the centre of the infirmary. He stopped to survey the room and looked at Emma. "You speak English?"

She pinched two fingers together. "A little."

"Where are the doctors? Who is in charge of this place?"

"They are gone."

Up until that point, I had stood on the spot, too stunned to think. But when Emma had to grab on to a bed frame for support, I stepped forward. "The staff fled. This woman stayed out of her own goodwill."

The officer turned to the group of soldiers that had gathered behind him, and flicked his head in our direction. They fanned out, wrinkling their noses at the stench as they approached, their eyes round as guilder coins as they picked their way through the swamp of prisoners. The strongest of the patients climbed off the bunks to launch a wave of feeble cheers, while one teetered forward and opened his arms to embrace an astonished soldier. A handful crowded together and tried to lift a young private into the air, but they couldn't raise him above their shoulders and he tumbled back onto his feet, shaken and embarrassed.

The man in charge came over to me, the first officer in two years to address me without any hint of desire. A broad, muscular soldier. He took off his helmet and held it under his arm while surveying the beds around me. His mouth hung open as he stared at half-dressed patients whose jutting ribs shuddered with their coughs. Men with purple hollows around their eyes weeping with joy. "Christ almighty." He turned back to me, reached into the breast pocket of his uniform and withdrew a thick bar wrapped in paper, "Hershey's Tropical Chocolate" stamped on the front. "Take this. It tastes like shit, but it'll do you some good."

I unwrapped the corner and broke off a small chunk. Chewy and bitter, nothing like the chocolate I remembered, but I didn't care.

"Don't bother saving it. There'll be plenty more coming your way, for all of you." He continued down the hall, stopping every few metres to peer at a prisoner or relay an order to his men. Emma appeared at my side again, white as porcelain, and I slipped my hand into hers. We shuffled to the door and stood in the entrance. Even this late in the afternoon, the light outside made me squint.

"Do you want to go out?" she asked.

I shook my head. The idea of wandering around freely was too strange to grasp, and I wasn't sure how far I could make it yet. Still, I couldn't look away. A whole world lay out there, beyond the prisoners' blocks. Amsterdam, Europe, America—I could have walked through that gate and gone anywhere. "Maybe I should stay here," I said. "What if the Schutzhaftlagerführer comes looking for me?"

"Why would he do that?"

I looked away, unable to decide whether to feel disappointed by the truth in her question or embarrassed for expecting more of him. "I suppose I've spent so long wondering if I'd even survive that I don't know anymore what comes next, what I even want to happen."

"For you, the hard part is over."

As the soldiers milled around, clearing away the dead and trying to give the living a chance of survival, I considered tracking Karl down, with the thought that we could leave the camp together. If the Americans protested, tried to trap him for his crimes, I would defend him. I lay back down on my cot and buried my face in the sheets, ashamed and confused. What was wrong with me? What had he done to make me capable of such doubt, such irrationality? A thought crept up on me, the nagging worry that, in some small way, I was also complicit, for who could possibly feel any affection toward a Nazi? When we had first met, I couldn't comprehend what his ex-fiancée had seen in him; now I had the same question to face myself.

The Americans filtered through the block during the evening, bringing us tins of corned beef and hard biscuits, which was too much for most of the prisoners to stomach. Several more passed away during the night, and I mourned for them, for losing the battle at its very end. A vision of Theo came to me, huddled in one of the blocks, his spirits ripe with hope. I wondered if he believed I'd survived, if he would take me back when I told him the truth about my time at Buchenwald and my baby. But what if he was already gone himself?

IN the morning, I was in bed chewing another hard chunk of chocolate when the American sergeant returned. He paused at my cot. "How's the patient today?"

I sat up. "Better. Well enough to get out of here."

"Now, there sure is no doctor around to tell you otherwise. But let me assure you, a walk through these grounds is no stroll in the park, so make sure you're ready for it." He made a move to continue on.

"Wait, please, I'm looking for someone."

"I'm afraid we haven't sorted through any of the prisoner lists yet."

"It's not a prisoner I'm looking for. An SS officer. Schutzhaftlagerführer Müller. The deputy director."

"What a tongue twister. Müller, you say? Sorry, ma'am, haven't heard of him." He gave me a quizzical look, but I didn't volunteer any more information, so he continued. "We sent a truck of girls home yesterday. If you're feeling up for it, another transport will depart in two days, this one heading west."

"Girls from the brothel?" I asked.

"Could be, but I'd have to check with someone on that."

The sergeant wished me luck and said goodbye. I thanked him and forced what I hoped was a grateful smile as I tried to unravel what he'd said. After eating a little more, I decided to venture outside. Emma had disappeared during the night. I looked for her around the infirmary and was disappointed when nobody had seen her, but I trusted the sergeant would keep her safe.

Scrounging around the nurses' office, I found a plain, brown dress that I changed into. My nerves hummed as I exited the infirmary, half-expecting someone to chase after me and order me back to my place with the swat of a gun. Instead, the American guarding the entrance waved and lit up a cigarette. The compound of the camp stretched out before me. I took a tentative step onto the gravel path.

Much of the camp looked familiar from our regular walks: the neat rows of blocks that curved around the muster grounds, the warehouses tucked away in the back. On all sides, cadaverous men wandered about, aimless in their newfound freedom. One or two stopped to watch me pass, and I found myself lowering my gaze, afraid I would find my husband peering at me. I kept watch for the grey of the SS uniforms, but the few Nazis I did see were being paraded around in handcuffs by Americans and prisoners. One prisoner carried a withered, white-haired man, perhaps his friend or his father, holding out the limp body to anyone with a water canteen.

My first instinct was to return to the brothel. It lay right across from the infirmary blocks, but I walked in the opposite direction for a few minutes before convincing myself to turn back. The closer I got to it, the more I slowed down.

All of the shutters were closed and the plants that lined the front walk had been trampled. The door stood ajar. I entered and became immediately aware of the stillness within. The brothel was dark. One of the chairs lay on the floor, feet pronged in the air. In the sleeping quarters, all traces of the girls had vanished. The colourful blouses and skirts, Sophia's stash of gifted alcohol and shoes. I knelt to check under my bed, but dustballs rolled around the spot where my violin had lain.

In the washroom, long strands of blond hair looped around the shower drain, but the soap and the toilet paper were gone. A commotion in the reception area startled me, and I tiptoed out of the washroom. I peeked around the corner to find a pair of American soldiers rifling around.

One glanced up. "Hey, get a look at this."

The other soldier approached me. "Why, hello, ma'am. What are you doing in here?"

I stiffened. "I—I came for my belongings."

"We're scouting out possible spots to bring a bunch of sick kids. What was this place? It's nothing like the other buildings."

I waited for him to crack a grin. "Someone must have moved my things. Goodbye."

"Why don't you stick around? As soon as we're done here, we'll take you down to our transport and rustle you up something to eat."

After declining their offer, I left, forcing myself to keep walking until I was out of sight, resisting my impulse to turn and take one last look at what I was leaving behind.

My feet led me all the way across the compound, past a comb lying in the dirt, the long line at the prisoners' canteen, a body draped over the barbed wire. All around me, the Americans relayed orders, carted around army rations and blankets, while prisoners mimed what they needed. At the boundary of the prisoners' camp, I stared up at the clock that topped the tall gatehouse. I thought about going through the gate, walking toward the SS villas. Someone would know where Karl had gone. But no matter what I wanted to believe about him, he couldn't go anywhere without a swastika branded on his lapel.

I stepped forward into the shadow of the gatehouse and nodded to the soldiers who guarded it. Above me, that warning hung like a hangman's gallows: *Jedem das Seine*. The iron words like blood on my tongue: To each what he deserves.

Behind me, prisoners crowded the muster grounds, spilled out of the blocks. There was a chance one of those weary faces belonged to Theo.

A soldier in an army helmet approached and opened the gate for me. "Are you going out?"

I scanned the road that stretched out of the camp, winding toward the officers' quarters, and then took a deep breath and glanced up at the sky, bright blue and dotted with pillowy clouds. "No," I said, "not yet."

The soldier nodded. As the gate clanged shut, I turned and started off toward the prisoners' blocks.

CHAPTER TWENTY-NINE

THE NIGHT THE GUARDS SET LASHES FREE, LUCIANO couldn't sleep. He stared at the inside of his hood until his eyes grew sore from attempting to see. At one point, he thought of the belt on his new pair of pants and snaked it from the waistband. He worked the tooth of the buckle into the rough fabric of the hood, wriggling it back and forth to create a hole a millimetre or two wide and then shifted the hood until the hole lined up right. For the first time, he saw the bare bulb that dangled high above his cell.

Next to him, Gabriel sounded restless. Luciano tried to play out the girl's journey in his head. They would have jammed her into one of the military's Ford Falcons and driven down the long road that led to the gates. He didn't know where or when they would drop her off but could hear her family's joyful tears as they flooded her with hugs and kisses. And during everything, she would have the microfilm tucked away in the hollow heel of her shoe.

Somehow, he fell asleep. The next morning, he and Gabriel quietly pushed through their work. As the day wore on, they began to relax with the realization that they would never know what she had done with those files, and Gabriel hummed a folk song Luciano remembered from childhood:

I want to get married
And don't know with whom,
With this girl yes,
With this girl no,
With this girl I'll be wed.

GABRIEL was late for dinner. His shoulders slumped as a guard brought him into the eating area, and he avoided looking at Luciano.

The guards distributed dinner, a portion of watery corn soup. The grains of corn had already been eaten, so the labourers got only the cobs. Luciano's stomach rumbled, but he snuck another peek at Gabriel, who twirled his spoon with a vacant expression.

As soon as the guard gave the order to clean up and fall back into line, Luciano found a spot behind Gabriel, but Gabriel didn't acknowledge his presence until they were back in front of the microfilmer. He went over to the files that had just come in and handed the top one to Luciano. There was Lashes' solemn face, yesterday's date and a note: *Transferred.*

"They shot her."

Luciano pressed the document to his chest and let out a long breath. "How do you know?"

"I overheard the guards talking while I was in the bathroom."

"Did they find it?"

"What do you think?"

Luciano leaned against the wall with his head in his hands. Gabriel took a seat at the microfilmer and stared at it for a long moment before switching it on. For the rest of the evening, they worked without speaking, the whirrs and clicks of the machine the only distraction from troubled thoughts. Luciano processed the files as quickly as possible, without stopping to read a single prisoner's name.

THE command came from the far corner of the photo lab. "Numbers three-four-one and five-seven-four, step forward."

In the darkroom, Luciano paused, his hands suspended over the microfilmer while the order registered. Gabriel stood beside Luciano, his pupils huge.

Shark appeared in the entrance to the darkroom. He blinked as he adjusted to the dimness, but grinned when he spotted Luciano, his teeth gleaming under the red lights. "You two are coming with me."

Before Luciano had time to comprehend what was happening, Shark threw hoods over their heads, restrained their arms, the metal digging into Luciano's wrists. Luciano's hood went on backward, the tiny peephole he'd punctured rendered useless.

Shark pushed them forward, and Luciano heard Gabriel hit a wall. Shark led them past the other workers in the photo lab and down the corridor before shoving Luciano into one of the torture chambers. The door closed behind him.

Luciano knew he wasn't alone. He bowed his head and recited verses of Neruda's poetry in whispers.

Footsteps. A set of arms grabbed him, tossing him back onto the metal bed frame. Then the nightmare unfolded once more: the cold air on his flesh as his clothes were ripped from his body, the buzz of the cattle prod, the smell of singed hair on his chest, the cries, the begging, his mind ricocheting away as the shocks grew stronger, more frequent, until his limbs screamed out and the pain consumed everything. Then it stopped. He writhed on the bed.

"What else did you do with those files?"

His throat burned, begging for water. It took three tries to form an answer. "Nothing."

"Who else has them?"

"Nobody, I swear." His voice came out in rasps.

"Who else?"

"No. Other. Copies."

Another man: "Give him the *submarino*."

Luciano heard nothing but his own heavy panting. He was yanked to his feet. His knees buckled and someone pulled him across the floor, shins scraping the tiles. His torturer propped him up against something solid. Luciano's fingers hooked around a wide metal lip, touched liquid.

"Are you going to talk?"

A hand palmed Luciano's skull, pushed him down, submerging his head. He sputtered, taking in a mouthful of water through the hood, and began to choke. He swallowed, tried to hold his breath, but a sudden kick to his groin made him cry out. His head was wrenched out again; water streamed down his face as he gargled for oxygen. Then he went back under, thrashing, bucking, battling to hold on.

CHAPTER THIRTY

KARL LEFT BUCHENWALD AT A RUN, WITHOUT ANY idea where he was headed. As soon as he neared the edge of Buchenwald's grounds, he changed into the prisoner clothing and stuffed his SS uniform into a rotten stump. His muscles soon grew sore from his bouncing rucksack, and he could manage only short bursts before slowing to a jog and gasping for air. The rough terrain made him stumble—hills pocked with crevices and thick roots that twisted from the ground— and the trees that were only beginning to bud offered little shelter. The first night, he ate a third of the food in his bag. Nuts and stale biscuits and a hunk of Gouda. He slept against a hollow log, shivering and unable to rest as he fought off apparitions of snipers creeping through the bushes.

The second day, he got lost. His attempts to navigate south using the sun and the lichen growth on trees might have worked if he hadn't needed to reroute whenever he cut too close to a village or main road. A prisoner's uniform would be a flimsy disguise for any soldiers on the lookout for Nazis. While stopping to consult the map, he heard armoured vehicles approaching. He hunched under the protection of a thicket and watched the convoy of Americans ride by. A group of them perched on top of an open jeep, a machine gun mounted between them. He flattened himself on the ground, his heart beating against a mound of soil as they passed.

Once the troops were out of earshot, he changed his trajectory to cut deeper into the hills, but the forest grew sparser and villages of half-timbered houses lined the horizon. For a few hours, he proceeded in segments, searching for cover while he scouted out the next stretch. Guilt crept in and pestered him to turn back. There was Marijke, alone in that hospital with the Americans at her side. But the thought of those soldiers knocking him to the ground with their guns kept him going, and he began to devise a plan to get to Argentina.

The rumble of artillery fire increased, a sign he'd veered too far west. It took an hour to get back on track. The water in his canteen was gone. As the sun sank over the hills, he scoured the area for a safe place to stay. When his stomach ached and his boots began to chafe his blisters, he spotted a lone farmhouse and worked his way toward it through the bushes, halting every few metres to scan his surroundings.

The house appeared empty and the front door stood open. He circled the perimeter twice before entering the building with

344

his Luger raised. A fresh loaf of bread sat on the counter with a large chunk of it missing, a pitcher of milk beside it. His mouth watered at the sight but he continued toward the back room. A noise in the bedroom stopped him. The rustling continued, the opening and closing of drawers, so he inched up to the room with his finger on the trigger.

He stepped across the threshold to find a young camp guard in uniform. Karl kept his gun aimed at him. "What are you doing?"

The pile of bread crumbs at the man's feet answered the question, and his shoulders relaxed when he saw Karl's face. "The Americans, Schutzhaftlagerführer. They've let the prisoners loose to hunt down us guards. They're beating our men to death!"

Karl lowered his gun. "Where are the owners of this place?"

"No idea, sir."

Karl left the guard and went to the kitchen to help himself to the food. Most of the shelves on the pantry had been stripped bare, but a cured sausage was hiding deep in the back of a cupboard. He unwrapped it and tore off a bite. After getting his fill of that and bread, he polished off the pitcher of milk.

The guard appeared in the doorway. "The bed is yours, sir, if you want it."

Karl contemplated the soft pillows and warm quilt before glancing out the window at the approaching nightfall. "I'm not staying."

The guard gave Karl a hopeful look, but Karl didn't invite him to tag along.

"Well," the man said, "I'll spend the night and head out at dawn."

Karl returned to the bedroom and combed through the drawers for a thin blanket, which he rolled up into his pack. As he walked out the rear door, he turned back to the guard. "Find yourself some different clothes."

A patch of forest lay two hundred metres from the house. Karl crouched low and dashed across the field toward it. By the time he reached the trees, heavy clouds shielded the dark sky. He ducked into the safety of the shadows and looked back at the farmhouse in time to see the headlights of an army jeep turn onto the driveway.

IN early 1948, three years after fleeing Buchenwald, Karl left his hiding place on an Austrian dairy farm and travelled to South Tyrol. There, he found a pocket of former SS colleagues from Berlin. They put him in touch with a bishop in the Vatican, who arranged refuge for him in a chain of monasteries in northern Italy. The immigration process dragged on, clogged by all the other high-ranked party members who hoped to slip away through the ratlines, but after several months, Karl's contacts in the Vatican had false identity papers drawn up for him. With the scratch of a new signature, Karl became Arturo Wagner: a classic German surname, which he'd requested in honour of the doctor who had helped Marijke at Buchenwald.

That same week, he picked up a German newspaper and read about Brandt's death: a heart attack in prison while awaiting execution. He brought the paper to the monastery, folded it up and hid it under his bed. The typeface of the headline felt cold, derisive: a reminder of what could have been.

When the leaves turned colour, he said goodbye to the monks and moved on to the port of Genoa. Rumour had it that the new Argentine president had made thousands of visas available to former Nazis, and within a few weeks, Karl managed to secure passage on a ship bound for South America.

On the basis of his new identity, the Red Cross issued him a passport. They didn't ask any questions, but there was always an inside man on the job, smoothing out the process. A few days later, he took an Argentine medical examination. Then, on the twenty-third of October, a sunny morning with a salt-licked wind, he boarded the *San Giorgio*. He stood on the deck as the crew raised the anchor and flipped through the pages of his new passport. The face in the photo looked tired and unfamiliar. He touched his cheeks, where his skin drooped from the weight he'd lost. For the dozenth time, he studied the identity papers. *Arturo Wagner, accountant.* A strong, admirable name. Arturo Wagner struck him as the type of man who could live a happy, quiet life. Buenos Aires was reputed to be distinguished and charming—the Paris of the South. He recalled the photographs he'd seen of wide boulevards and corner cafés and tried to picture himself lounging on one of the park benches, perusing a local Spanish newspaper with ease. Maybe one day he would find an Argentine woman to marry, one as spirited and enticing as Marijke. They would settle down together, maybe have children—a son who would carry on his German blood and bring honour to a new family name.

The ship blew its whistle and cheers broke out across the deck as they set off. The turquoise sea sparkled as the colourful houses on the hills shrank away, leaving nothing around them but water. Karl stood at the railing for some time and became aware of someone beside him, someone who was about his age, mustachioed, and reading a German copy of *Faust*. Karl recognized him as one of Himmler's top aides. The man noticed Karl staring at the spine of his book and took in his Aryan features. "German?" he asked.

Karl looked out at the horizon. The sea spread out like a safety net on all sides, ready to carry him to a strange, new world. He turned and responded in German. "No," he said, "I'm Argentinian."

CHAPTER THIRTY-ONE

Apart from the affirmation that Theo was being held in Ohrdruf, one of Buchenwald's sub-camps, I'd gone almost two years without any knowledge of him and wasn't sure what I was prepared to learn. I began my search in the blocks nearest the brothel. A large crowd of prisoners gathered outside, celebrating their newfound idleness by sitting in the sun, talking and smoking American cigarettes. A brown crust dirtied their uniforms, blue stripes faded to grey. Hollow stares greeted my approach. I recognized one man, a criminal who seemed to hold some sort of elite status among the prisoners. He had frequented the brothel, claiming feelings for Gerda, but at the sight of me, he butted out his cigarette and headed in the other direction. A tingle crept up my spine, and I wondered if it was easier to pretend I'd never seen him.

I searched the crowd around me, throwing out Theo's name in question to anyone who looked my way. At the next block, I called it out and the prisoners took it up as a chorus, relaying it through the bunks, their feeble voices like the murmur of reeds in a pond. No response.

I traipsed along, the April sun already hot on my back. Between the blocks stood five prisoners with yellow stars. Two of them women, their bare arms marked with a string of numbers. Later someone told me that they tattooed the prisoners at Auschwitz, so the women must have been transfers. If the political prisoners teetered on the brink of death, the Jews looked wasted away to the bone. At the sight of the women's shorn, scarred heads, my hand rose to touch my hair, which reached my shoulders. I thought of pillows and sweets in the brothel, of clean clothes and hot baths. As I walked past the women, I looked away.

The afternoon took me through block after block, each filthier and more depressing than the last. Most men still couldn't get out of bed. They met my inquiries for Theo with questions of their own: searching for wives, mothers, daughters. I learned the Nazis had evacuated thousands of prisoners to Dachau in the days leading up to the liberation, and worried Theo had gone with them. It was easier than considering the alternative.

Bodies scattered across the compound, piled like bales of hay, but I was too afraid to look for him among them. I encountered a prisoner who had torn off his triangle, and he guided me to the American officer in charge of the records. The officer admitted the registration ledger was in disarray. He suggested I return to find him in a few days, but pointed me toward another block, where he'd heard of some prisoners from the sub-camps.

I didn't find Theo there. By that time, I felt sick and my shoes pinched my feet. I followed a crowd carrying tin mugs and bowls to a large building with a winding line for food. My stomach grumbled. I had no mug, no spoon. A couple of prisoners had just finished their soup, and I asked to borrow a bowl. They eyed me with suspicion and shuffled away. A few more, the same response. At Ravensbrück, a bowl had been an inmate's lifeline, and it must have been the same at Buchenwald, but it was as if these people didn't realize that our imprisonment had ended. I slumped against a wall until I felt a tap on my shoulder. An adolescent boy stood before me, holding out his bowl. "You need this?" he asked in German laced with Dutch.

He joined me in line, probably to ensure that I didn't sneak off. As a Kapo dished out my portion, the boy introduced himself as Johan. His family came from Rotterdam, but his father had died of starvation, and he hadn't seen his mother or his sisters for years. I sipped at the soup, noticing that it contained a few more hints of vegetable than when the Nazis had served it, but it was still watery enough to see the bottom of the bowl. Johan asked for my story.

"I've been here almost two years," I said. "Before that, Ravensbrück."

"Why would they transfer you? I've hardly seen any women around."

"I don't know." I looked past him, out at the rows of heads bent over bowls. "I'm searching for my husband. He was transferred to Ohrdruf in the second half of '43."

"Ohrdruf? I've heard bad things. Lots of hard labour. Most men lasted only a few months there."

"Not my Theo. He's strong; he would have pulled through," I replied, but the strained optimism in my words was no match for the fluttering in my stomach.

"That's not all. The moffen evacuated Ohrdruf last week and brought those prisoners to Buchenwald."

"But that's wonderful."

He looked down. "From here, they sent those men on a death march to Dachau. We heard gunshots as they chased them down the road."

I stepped away. "No, that can't be true."

He directed me to an American soldier, who confirmed what he'd said. Several thousand men, just hours away from freedom, marched back into the bowels of the Nazi death trap.

Tears prickled at the corners of my eyes while the soldier rambled on about the absurdity of it all, the fact that they'd had no clue that something like this was going on behind enemy lines. I stopped listening, thinking only of Theo, the way he'd hunched over in concentration as he fiddled with those crystal radios, his lopsided smile when he caught me watching. Had I come so close to finding him only to lose him again?

The soldier stopped and scratched his head. "You're searching for someone? Look, those men are long gone, but we've sent a squad to clean up the road. One of the officers with them has the evacuation list, but you really ought to wait until they come back this evening. It's pretty gruesome up there."

He followed my gaze as I looked around us at the men too weak to stand, those coughing up blood. "I need to find my husband, come what may."

He took me up the hill, out of the prisoners' compound and

toward the edge of camp. For the first time in almost two years, I stepped beyond the barbed wire, but seeing a rifle bouncing against the soldier's hip I still felt as if I were being led somewhere at gunpoint. We passed the SS barracks, but I didn't allow myself to check around for Karl. Now that he'd lost possession of my body, I intended to regain control of my thoughts.

The soldier walked briskly and I matched his pace, knowing every step brought me closer to an answer. The road curved to head out of the camp, but after some fifty metres we slowed down. Bloodstains marked the pavement, while bodies lined the ditch. The soldier reached out to steady me, but I carried on. I tried to picture Theo following that road a few days earlier. As we neared the dead, I forced myself to examine them. Stone-coloured faces, many with open eyes, some bodies with flies hovering over bullet wounds in their backs. The crater in my stomach deepened.

Up ahead stood a wagon. The horses wore blinders, but they pawed their hooves as they sniffed the death-filled air. A few prisoners carried bodies to the wagon, pausing to read out the numbers on the uniforms to an American officer who was checking these off on a clipboard.

The soldier who'd brought me approached the officer, explaining my situation in English too quick for me to follow. The officer gestured for the prisoners to wait and then turned to me. "Your husband was at Ohrdruf?"

"Yes, but I don't know until when."

"What's his name?"

"De Graaf." I held my breath as he rustled through the papers. In that moment, Theo felt so close and yet so far away, like I could both stretch out to touch him and search for years but never reach him.

The officer ran his finger down the page. "Pieter or Theodoor?"

"Theodoor."

As Theo's name left my lips, the officer raised his eyes to look at me. "Mrs. De Graaf, I'm so sorry—your husband is dead."

CHAPTER THIRTY-TWO

AN INTENSE PAIN, THE WORST LUCIANO HAD EVER felt, came from his groin. He lay still until he regained some sensation in his fingertips, feeling that he was dressed and lying on a mattress. He assumed it was his bed, but couldn't remember anything.

A gash on his tongue rubbed against his gums. It felt like someone had extracted all his organs. He inched his hands down to his scrotum, which was swollen like a grapefruit. He separated his legs to ease the pain and then drifted away and back again.

Days went by, or maybe just hours, or minutes. Ragged breaths tore at his ribs. All he wanted was for the pain to end, whatever that took.

At one point, he opened his eyes to find the darkness of the hood comforting. He suddenly knew he was in his cell, and remembered the torture, being shoved under water. He couldn't recall if he'd told them anything. The Jew to his left was praying again, but there was no noise from his right. Luciano wondered if Gabriel had been tortured, how the guards had discovered the microfilm, if the girl had confessed.

The pain grew so strong that it dulled his thoughts, so he started counting again. In English this time, to help him concentrate. One, he began, two, three, four, five, six. When he got to twenty-seven, the door to his cell opened.

They took him back to the basement, near the photo lab. Other prisoners waited nearby, a large group, based on the rattle of handcuffs and ankle shackles. His legs trembled as he tried to stand still.

They were herded into a small, unfamiliar room. A guard came around to undo their binds, which fell to the floor in a cacophony of steel and iron. The prisoners filed ahead. Someone tugged Luciano's wrist, and a needle punctured his biceps with a numbing prick. They bound his wrists again, this time with rope. "Don't worry, you're being transferred." The voice sounded like it came through a soupy fog.

Transfer day. It must have been Wednesday. He was strangely unafraid. He stumbled, feeling woozy, like he'd come home from a night of beers and drag racing down Avenida 9 de Julio with Fabián's dark hair waving in the wind.

Someone around him retched. The noise brought a foul taste into his own mouth, but he swallowed and focused on staying upright. He wanted to lie down, to curl up on the basement floor and feel the cement against his cheek.

A door opened. The shock of the cold prickled his skin. A jab in the back sent him outside as the first fresh air in months hit his nostrils. He collided with a body in front of him, and someone else bumped into him from behind, but they kept moving forward until they reached a steep ramp that they had to clamber up. It led to a stuffy space where they packed together as more prisoners filed in. Luciano's arm hit a metal bar and a wall, but it wasn't until he heard the ramp drop away and the double doors close that he understood where he was. The floor began to vibrate as the truck turned on and started to move, but Luciano was too dizzy and saw no point in tracking its movements.

The others let out distorted cries and groped him as they searched for friends.

"Gabriel," he called, again and again. Nobody responded.

They arrived in a field. Luciano tumbled out onto the soft grass on all fours, pulled out a tuft and brought it to his nose. Summer afternoons in the park, passion-fruit ice cream dripping down the cone, his mother's tidy laughter. His parents dancing tango. The *bandoneon* picking up with short, rhythmic barks before the violin seized the melody. The music building up, faster and faster, Mamá circling Papá like the arms of a windmill.

Luciano was pulled up, pushed forward, the wooziness growing with each step. His feet touched pavement. Forward again, crowding up a narrow staircase, clenching the handrail to keep from tipping backward.

"Name and number?"

The prisoners in front of him answered: women, men. Cristina Almeida, Juan Carlos Fernandez, Roberto León. When he reached the top of the staircase, the question came to him.

"Luciano Wagner. Number five-seven-four."

He was calm. He stepped forward, tripping as he met a solid surface, a wall that curved inward. They crammed together, and the door shut with a heavy slam. The air inside was stale, the smell of sweat and fear and last wishes.

"Take off your clothes." The order came from somewhere in front of him. He heard belts unbuckling and shoes coming off. He struggled with his own shirt and pants, his arms still leaden, his mind clouding. Every hair on his body rose. He imagined the bare bodies around him, frozen on the spot, like a madman's sculpture garden.

Guards came around to strip those who couldn't undress themselves. Then the prisoners sat on the floor and waited in darkness. A loud rumble as the engines started up. Bodies jostling, skin slick against skin, the comfort of knowing he was not alone. The wall shook, and the noise grew to a roar, flushing out everything else. Then the ground beneath them dropped away as the plane took off.

Luciano fell back into the mass of bodies while the plane rose higher and higher. When it levelled out, he separated himself, his mind a haze. He knew they would fly over the River Plate, out to the spot where it meets the Atlantic. He tried not to think of the huge fish that circled beneath the water's dark surface.

Nobody spoke, or if they did, their voices were carried away. Fingers grazed his torso, and he grasped the hand in his, holding it tightly.

Then, an icy blast and the howling of the wind. Someone had opened the hatch. They were ordered to stand and were pushed forward from behind. Screams, swallowed by infinite blackness.

Luciano's teeth chattered, but he closed his eyes and tried to recite Neruda. A few words were all he remembered.

He took another step and saw a streak of light shifting before him, an iridescence like the inside of a moon snail. As it moved nearer, the light grew and took shape: his grandparents' ranch, an open field with a group of people. He couldn't make out their faces, but they were so close, and he knew if he could just reach them, everything would be all right.

The wind whipped at his toes and through his hood. Tears froze to his eyelashes. A pair of hands pushed him out of the plane and sent him hurtling down through the night sky. All he could hear was a thundering roar.

CHAPTER THIRTY-THREE

MARIJKE
APRIL 12, 1945
BUCHENWALD

M RS. DE GRAAF?"
The officer's mouth kept moving, but I missed whatever followed. I stood there, dumb, unable to think. All I could hear was that single word: dead. Theo, my love, dead.

"When?" I asked.

"Hard to know for sure. All it says is 'typhus,' but that was jotted down in pen. It must have been right as they were preparing the evacuation."

The officer pulled a handkerchief from his pocket and passed it to me. Only then did I realize I was crying. "I'm sorry," he repeated, before turning to the soldier at my side. "Find somewhere where she can sit down, and make sure she's taken care of." He said something more to me then, what I supposed were words of comfort, but everything hazed over as if I were anchored to the bottom of a lake, peering up at a surface far overhead.

Somehow I made my way back to the prisoners' compound. Somehow I ate soup and drank coffee and secured a place to sleep. That night I dreamed of Theo, that we were sailing together around the IJsselmeer. Lightning blazed across the sky, and we heard the rain around us but couldn't feel the drops. The baby kicked inside of me, and Theo pressed his ear to my belly to listen.

The next morning, I woke up on a bunk beside two strangers. Johan was on the bunk across from us, watching me with worry. I'd forgotten how he'd found me the night before, what I'd told him. My eyes felt puffy from weeping, but my senses had returned. I got up, nodded at him and then slipped outside. I needed to know what they'd done with Theo's body, whether I still had a chance of burying him.

A few answers from some nearby soldiers led me toward the mass grave. Dense fog cloaked the ground, and as I walked, I thought about my time in the infirmary, shaken by the understanding that Theo could have been dying in one of the blocks next to me. The idea left me hopeless, defeated, but I told myself to have courage, if only for the baby.

At the burial site, I realized that I didn't know what I'd expected to find. The Nazis had discarded the remains of the innocent just as you'd dump out an ashtray. Now we were left to bury the remaining bodies. The wagon from the day before was parked at the side of a pit, which a number of prisoners and soldiers were busy digging. The fog masked the features of the dead, so for a while I stood at a distance, watching the rote movements of the workers, the arch of their arms, the spray of earth through the murky air. The prisoners grabbed corpses by the limbs, struggling under the weight as they swung them into the grave.

The sight of the purple eyelids, the hanging jaws, the tangle of feet became too much to take. I covered my mouth and turned away. It felt impossible to go on alone.

I started back toward the blocks. Up ahead, three figures rounded a bend, pushing wheelbarrows filled with even more bodies. I averted my eyes, but as I did, something caught my attention. One of the prisoners had stopped. He stood still, beholding me, and in that moment, everything I had thought was true unravelled again.

Once, at the Theater Tuschinski in Amsterdam, I'd watched a pair of star-crossed lovers run across the screen toward each other, their faces aglow. Not us. We stared, afraid to move.

"Theo?" I took a step through the fog and then another, until I was close enough to know for certain that it was him. "You're alive," I whispered, and I began to cry.

Then he was right there in front of me. "Oh, Marijke."

I reached out and embraced him. His body felt so fragile against mine. After a long moment, he pulled away and looked down at his ragged uniform in shame. He appeared a decade older, a mere spectre of the husband I remembered. His cheeks were sunken, his glasses held together with chicken wire, his chin scabbed. "I didn't want you to ever see me like this."

"Theo—" I said, but I didn't know how to respond, how to speak to him anymore. My attention returned to the din of voices around us, the gawking soldiers. Theo studied me with a sad, broken smile.

"I always knew you'd survive." He held me again, whispering into my hair, while I started to fear the questions that would inevitably arise.

After that, I wouldn't leave his side. We held hands like newlyweds, as if any interruption to this contact might tear us apart again. He led me to the block where he'd spent the past week, presented me to the men who had helped him obtain extra rations and warmer shoes. Afterwards, we found a secluded spot to sit, and he shared stories of his friends from Ohrdruf who had been evacuated to Dachau.

"They told me you were dead," I said. "How can it be you're here?"

He replied in a hoarse voice. "I was supposed to go along with them, but I switched uniforms with a man who was dying of typhus. With all the chaos, nobody noticed."

The stench of that mass grave came back to me, the feeling of sickening devastation that had arisen with the belief that Theo lay in one of the piles of corpses. What jagged paths our lives had taken, how close I'd come to losing him forever.

"You look radiant," he added. "I knew these camps couldn't mar your beauty."

I kissed his cheek, hoping to allay his curiosity, and focused on the bony protrusion of my knees, one of the few signs of what I'd endured.

"It's such a relief to find you in decent health. And that dress—what happened to your uniform?"

"Oh, I found this when the Americans arrived. One of the nurses abandoned it."

He asked where I'd been held, in which part of the camp, to what labour force I'd been assigned. "Please tell me they didn't do anything to hurt you."

I looked away, torn between the pain of keeping secrets and the knowledge that the truth could hurt him more. I could neither answer his endless questions nor bear to tell him about the seed growing in my belly. "We're together now, darling. Let's forget about everything else."

He passed me a cup of water, watching lovingly as I sipped it, and I sensed how he longed to be able to take care of me again. I leaned back into his embrace. His eyes shone with tears. "You know," he said, "I'm only here today, alive, because of you."

"What do you mean?"

"Do you remember the time you invited me to your cousin's birthday party a few weeks after we met? I showed up in Haarlem in my Sunday best, and I couldn't figure out why you thought that was so funny until we ended up at the family farm instead of a seaside café. You see, every time things got dire here, every time I was sure I wouldn't make it, I thought back to that afternoon, you doubled over in hysterics as I learned to milk a cow, mud splattered all over my suit and hat. That devious grin of yours and your loud, goofy laughter."

How long ago that seemed, the two of us engrossed in our fledgling romance, so happy and naive. I held him closely, trying to return to that day. Then I shared my own memories, those little life rafts that had carried me through it all, and my love for him felt more certain than ever.

It didn't take long for the exhaustion to surface in his voice, so we returned to his block for some rest. The beds were all occupied, but Theo motioned to one near the entrance. The men lying on it had gone cold. We lifted them up and carried them outside. Without speaking, we climbed onto the empty bunk, and as Theo fell asleep, I pressed up against him, cherishing the sound of his breath in my ear.

THE week that followed passed like the changing of seasons as Theo and I grappled with what it meant to be together again. He'd lost the hair on his legs and a strange scar marked his back, long and curved in a wide hook. When the Americans gave him a tin of beans, he vomited. It took days to wean him off the diet of watery soup. He spoke of railway ties and tunnels and munitions factories. I said nothing in return. When he held me at night, his feeble touch reminded me of prisoners in the brothel, and when he whispered promises of our shared future, his words blurred with Karl's in my head.

We put up with constant reorganization by the Americans, who couldn't figure out what to do with the tens of thousands of people they'd stumbled across. More than once, they summoned us to stand before groups of locals they forced to tour the camp. We lined up near a display of lampshades made from tattooed skin. Women in warm jackets and felt hats came into Buchenwald smiling like they were on a nice outing, but these soon became looks of horror, and they lifted handkerchiefs to their noses as they filed past.

"I feel like an exhibit in a museum," I whispered. "They won't even look us in the eye!"

"Still," Theo said, "they claim they didn't know."

"Couldn't they see the trains coming in full and leaving empty? Or smell the burning flesh?"

Theo said nothing more until we returned to our block. "I've had two years to think about this. I don't think there's any way to move forward if we blame everything on the German people. You're right—what you said the other day—we need to try to forget all of this."

"That doesn't mean we should forgive them."

"The Allies will take care of Hitler soon enough. After that, they'll go after the top Nazis, but the bloodbath can't go on forever, can it?"

I climbed onto our bunk and placed a hand on my belly as I tried to block out the rough baritone of Karl's voice, his smell of leather and pine, the image of him shot in the head.

AFTER that, Theo stopped pushing for answers. I told him I'd cleaned one of the buildings and sewn for the officers and left it at that. He nodded, but I could see the unasked questions stacking up. Sometimes, the truth played on my lips, but I reminded myself what I stood to lose by telling him.

Several more days passed before he was strong enough to travel, but this allowed time to arrange transport. A couple of American soldiers fixed us a spot on a convoy headed west. A military truck would bring a number of other prisoners a hundred kilometres toward the border. From there, we had to find our own way.

The morning we left, Buchenwald was draped in fog. Theo and I crossed the compound hand in hand, the ground still wet from early rainfall. At the top of the slope, I turned back to the rows of blocks. Behind them and out of sight stood the brothel, but beyond that, the camp fell away into forest, the first green signs of spring. The sun sliced through the thick grey sky to brush the roofs of the buildings. For a moment, it felt like the camp was just an illusion. But then I spotted the prisoners trudging through the puddles, and again I felt their sharp shoulder bones, smelled illness on their skin.

Theo's grip tightened as we neared the iron gate. We stared up at it one last time. Somewhere, a crow cawed. Then we passed through it and we were free. He stopped to pull me in, the tears on his cheeks blending with my own. Behind him, I saw a group of camp guards and officers being herded at gunpoint toward the petrol station. A tall, hefty figure stood among them, his face battered blue. I watched while the soldiers loaded Bruno into the back of an armoured truck, his hands bound, head to the ground.

I held Theo close. "I love you."

"It's just you and me now." He kissed my hair. "We'll be home soon."

I nodded, but as he let go, the familiar queasiness returned.

We boarded our own truck with anxious relief. I sat down next to Theo, as ten others crammed on the floor beside us. The Americans left the back canvas open so we could take in the fresh air. We started down the road that led out of Buchenwald.

The truck drove by the terminus of the railway line, abandoned except for an empty railcar and a suitcase that lay open on the stones between the tracks. From there, we headed through the forest. In places, the road was still stained red, so I concentrated on the trees and inhaled the scent of moist soil, wondering if I would ever again be able to find the beauty in nature. When we passed through Weimar to stock up on supplies, I refused to look at the residents buying groceries in the streets and buried my face in Theo's chest.

Before we set out on the road again, a soldier jumped in the back to distribute a pile of clothes. I accepted a green coat without question, but when I ran my finger over the worn collar, the sweat stains under the arms, I couldn't help but feel a mix of curiosity and hatred for the woman who had worn it.

Our group included two other women, one a Jew, the other a communist. The communist had the same round features as Sophia, though in place of Sophia's thick hair, she hid her baldness beneath a kerchief. The sight of her made me sorely miss the girls. Selfish worries had preoccupied me—the baby, my future with Theo, the fear we'd run into someone who would tell him about Karl—so I'd made no effort to find out what happened to them. I promised myself that I would track down Sophia one day. I'd ask her forgiveness and show her my little one. Once life returned to normal.

After a day's travel, the soldiers left us at an emergency camp that had been set up near the border, while we awaited further transportation. Allied offensives in the Netherlands kept us there for a week. The Americans left to supervise us had a gambling habit and always invited Theo to join their card games, though he had nothing to wager. To pass the time, I offered to patch up the soldiers' uniforms. I declined the request to darn their socks.

Almost a month had passed since my hospitalization and my breasts had swollen to their pre-war size. Everything ached. Theo started to worry every time I darted off mid-sentence, hit by a new bout of nausea, but I blamed it on the fresh rations.

On a balmy evening, Theo shook me awake. "It's a warm night," he whispered, "and the stars are out."

A Frenchman snored on the cot next to me, whistling in his sleep. I pulled on my coat and let Theo lead me out of the warehouse where we slept. Outside, the sky glowed purple with stars and far-off explosions. The rumbling drone of British planes sounded overhead, bombers headed east. The smell of woodsmoke drifted from fires at the edge of the camp, where privates gathered with playing cards and mugs of beer. Their laughter reached us in shards.

"Come with me." Theo wrapped an arm around my waist and guided me toward the trees. His embrace felt stronger, a touch I recognized as his.

A soldier watched as we crossed the left boundary of the camp, where a dark hedge of trees stretched above us. I waited for him to take aim, to order us back to the warehouse, and felt a strange sense of relief when we passed out of his sight. "Where are we going?"

"I want to be alone with you."

We moved into the darkness, until we found a spot where the trees parted to offer a window to the sky.

"You're shaking," he said.

"So are you."

He kissed me. Undressed me piece by piece, like he'd never touched a woman before and never would again. He trailed kisses down my neck. When he unbuttoned his shirt, I tried not to notice the way his chest caved, the loose skin that had replaced his muscles. After spreading our clothes out on the ground, he eased me down onto the mossy forest floor. Dry pine needles crunched under our weight. As he unclasped my brassiere, I shivered and reached for him, my legs goose-pimpled.

He bent to kiss my breasts. "I've thought about this moment so many times."

I said nothing. His legs trembled as he entered me, and he clutched my back with desperate longing. But his kisses didn't stir the same current they once had, and I found myself wishing he would hurry up and get things over with. He thrust into me with what little strength he had, but my body refused to embrace his, and I bit my cheek to keep myself from wincing. I cradled his prickly scalp and looked past him, up at the bare branches that shuddered overhead.

OUR train pulled into Amsterdam a few days after the official liberation. Crowds waved handkerchiefs at the passing tanks, and couples danced in the squares while accordionists played the national anthem. Dutch flags hung from almost every gable. Canadian soldiers drank pints on the sidewalks with flirty girls who wore orange ribbons in their hair. The bridges, the cobblestone streets, the red-tile roofs—so many things were the same. But then we saw buildings with broken windowpanes, a gap of rubble where a bomb had hit. Children in patched clothing three sizes too big. The milkman's horses looked on the verge of collapse, and he had only a few litres of milk to sell. Mistrust filled the streets: it lay in the rubbish bins people set out in the darkest hour of the night; at the market, where the butcher seemed as round as before the war; in the Jewish quarter, where families returned to find their homes ransacked or occupied. We walked up to our own house without a key, unsure what to expect. When a young man opened the door, I sank into Theo, but as soon as we introduced ourselves, he beckoned us in, explaining that my parents had arranged tenants for our house following our capture. Our home was still ours. The couple returned the place to us two days later, and in some improbable twist of fate, we found it almost as we'd left it. Old dresses on the hangers, my embroidery in the drawer of the coffee table, Theo's razor under the sink. A few stools and the china cabinet were missing, along with my grandmother's silverware, all likely sold off for fuel and food, but we were lucky. It was as if the couple had lived there as guardians. But even with everything back in its place, I went to bed that first night feeling like I was in a stranger's house and knew that nothing would ever be the same.

THE countryside had been stripped of tulip bulbs during the Hunger Winter, the trees on the boulevards chopped up for firewood, but scattered roses reappeared. They clung to the tired facades that lined Noordermarkt, where we shopped for secondhand clothes. One Monday, Theo and I strolled through the market square as a few bicycles wove around us. Most of Amsterdam's bicycles had disappeared from the streets, and these ones had scraps of garden hose wrapped around the wheels for tires. An organ grinder set himself up at the base of the church with a sign asking for payment in food scraps. The stalls contained trays of costume jewellery and old porcelain, which everyone ignored as they sorted through the tables of worn coats and sweaters. Two mothers bickered over a pair of shoes, until one raised a fist and the merchant had to step in. Theo shook his head and picked out a few pairs of socks before we made our way back to the canal. A crowd had gathered at the edge of the square, the spectators hooting and jeering.

"Come on; let's keep going," Theo said, but I approached the edge of the circle to take a peek.

A young woman cowered naked on a stool, a sign around her neck. *Moffenhoer.* Traitor. Dirty, filthy, moffen whore. Two men held her wrists while a third took a pair of shears to her hair, which fell to her shoulders in dark clumps. When they raised a bucket of tar, I ran back to Theo, who took me home without a word.

THE morning Theo returned to the university, he left my old violin at the foot of our bed. He had fixed a broken string and tied a blue bow around its neck. I picked up the instrument, stroked its curves, traced a finger down its neck. Then I put it down and left the house.

It was July, and children and shopkeepers filled the streets. I kept walking toward Noordermarkt. There, I found a bench and stared at the spot where the crowd had gathered around that woman, the one they had taunted and called a whore. While I sat there, a boy ran past, chasing a rolling hoop until it came to a stop against a signpost. I moved a hand to my belly. In the past week, it had begun to swell. I'd taken to wearing loose blouses, dresses that gathered at the waist, and I changed with my back to Theo, but soon enough he would see. I tried to anticipate how he would react, given everything we'd been through. We still had to cope with ration coupons and had only just begun to buy meat again, with our list of impending expenses growing by the day. But preparations for the baby had to begin. Of course, the question that kept following me into my dreams was how Theo would respond if I told him the truth, whether it was better to be honest or to save him from that hurt.

The boy's mother caught up, calling out to him as she pushed a baby carriage across the square. That baby we'd shepherded across the city right before we were captured must have been a toddler by now. What had become of her? Theo had been unable to hide his longing to shelter her, to raise her as our own. I recalled what he'd said to the woman who'd taken her in: how happy it made him that she could care for a child who was not her own. But surely my husband was no different. He knew only generosity and love.

Along the canal, an automobile honked, startling the boy. He ran to join his mother, and I stood and continued on my way.

WHEN Theo came home that evening, his jaw formed a hard line. He went straight out back to the garden, where I found him trying to coax some life out of the tomato plants.

"What's wrong?" I asked.

"A lot has changed on campus."

"Like what?"

"So many things."

"You know you can talk to me about this."

"All right. Well, you know Cohen, the one whose wife made that chicken dish you liked at the last Christmas party? He was gassed at Auschwitz."

"Oh." I knelt to rub his back, unsure what to say. "He was such a nice man."

"Goddammit!" The garden spade flew from his hand and smacked the stone wall. He pressed a fist to his forehead and forced out a deep breath.

During dinner he said little and retreated to bed as soon as we finished the dishes. I stayed up, scrubbing every surface of the kitchen with water and vinegar until even the teapot looked brand-new again. When there was nothing left to clean, I wrung out the sponge, went into the cellar and retrieved the dust-coated bottle of genever we'd received as a gift when Theo had started teaching. For the first time in many years, I poured myself a glass, a generous one. I stood at the counter, trying to shake off the image of Karl, his hands on my shoulders, his amused smile reflected in the windowpanes of the kober-zimmer. In one sip, the drink was gone. Wincing at its piney bitterness, I wrapped my arms around myself and started up the stairs.

As I entered our bedroom, Theo flipped over. He watched as I faced him and started to undress without making any effort to conceal myself. When I turned to the side to hang my clothes on the back of the chair, he sat up. He opened his mouth to say something but paused and tilted his head, his forehead wrinkled in thought. "Come here."

I circled round the bed while he propped himself up on an elbow and reached out to feel the slight curve of my belly.

"Are you . . . ?"

I nodded.

"Already, really? I can't believe that."

At this, I started to cry.

He pulled me in, kissed my stomach and pressed his cheek to it. "What's wrong?"

I motioned for him to move over and crawled in beside him, turning my face to the wall. "It's just, with all we've been through, with everything we have to face going forward."

"Darling, shh, don't talk like that. This is the best thing I could have ever asked for."

"I just wish . . . oh, I don't know." The genever still burned my throat, bringing with it a sense of heaviness. I couldn't tell him, at least not yet, but maybe one day, when the time was right.

He rolled me over and leaned in until our lips almost touched. "Marijke," he said, "I love her already."

"Her?"

"It's a girl. I can feel it."

The affection in his voice felt promising, but nothing was certain anymore. Somehow, out of all the others, we had survived. But whenever I closed my eyes, I found myself back there, staring up at those iron gates, with the soldier asking me that question: "Are you going out?" We may have left Buchenwald that day, but would Buchenwald ever leave us?

Theo curled into me, the heat of his chest warming mine. I lay with my head on his shoulder, listening to the comforting beat of his heart until we fell asleep. And the next day, morning came to us as I hoped it would for many years to come. Bars of sunlight streaked the room, birds chirped out on the canal, and there we were, entangled in each other's arms, the two of us together as husband and wife.

EPILOGUE

DECEMBER 1, 1983
BUENOS AIRES

ARTURO WAGNER SAT AT HIS NEIGHBOURHOOD BAR, sipping a glass of Fernet. On Thursdays, Patricia marched with the other mothers in the Plaza de Mayo, grief trailing her like a stray cat, so he'd learned to come home late on those days. After another drink, he settled his bill. Arthritis slowed his pace down the darkened streets, but he whistled along the way. The night smelled of car exhaust and the remnants of grilled beef. Jacaranda blossoms formed a purple carpet across the sidewalk beneath the very same trees Luciano had climbed as a boy.

Arturo turned onto his block, unsettled by the memory. He didn't notice the man leaning against a car parked in the shadows or the figure watching from the front seat. The stranger called out. "*Herr* Müller?"

Startled, Arturo looked up. The gun had a silencer fixed to the barrel. He had nowhere left to run.

HISTORICAL NOTE

WHILE ALL OF THE CHARACTERS IN *THE DUTCH WIFE* ARE fictional, their stories are rooted in fact. In 1942, under Himmler's orders, the first prisoners' brothels opened at Mauthausen concentration camp and one of its sub-camps. Brothels were eventually established at ten of the most significant Nazi concentration camps, with the goal of increasing production efficiency among the forced labourers. In total, an estimated 190 women served in these brothels during the course of the war, yet their stories have long remained in the shadows. The bravery of these women, along with those who fought for a free and just society in Argentina, astounds me.

Among the many sources I consulted during my research, two played a vital role in shaping the novel. For Luciano's story, this was *Nunca Más* ("Never Again")—the CONADEP Report, published by the National Commission on the Disappearance of Persons. I am also greatly indebted to Dr. Robert Sommer, author of *Das KZ-Bordell*, for his counsel and extensive research on concentration camp brothels. In some instances, I have chosen to bend certain historical details or time frames for the purpose of the novel, but I've tried to be as accurate as possible in my portrayals. I hope I have done justice to the experiences of both the disappeared in Argentina and the women who were forced to work in the camp brothels.

ACKNOWLEDGEMENTS

Writing this novel became a journey that took me around the world, but it was one I could never have completed on my own. I owe enormous thanks to Rachel Letofsky at the Cooke Agency for guiding me through the publishing process and to the entire team at HarperCollins in Canada, especially Patrick Crean. Patrick, your incredible encouragement and belief in this novel kept me going, and I couldn't have asked for a better editor.

Thank you to the faculty and my fellow students in the University of British Columbia's creative writing MFA program, especially Annabel Lyon, Tariq Hussain and Nancy Lee. Nancy, you've taught me so much. Thanks for pushing me to make some difficult choices. I'm also grateful to the Canada Graduate Scholarships Program for the generous SSHRC scholarship.

Sarah, Jill, Laura, Julie—I couldn't have finished this without your feedback and enthusiasm. Special thanks to Jen and Mel for keeping the wine and laughter flowing on many a writing day. To Matt, Jason and Tom for offering advice on early drafts. Lauren, you keep me afloat from afar. Jake, thank you for sitting through

ACKNOWLEDGEMENTS

endless war movies and for your listening ear. And Hannie and Han, you're like second parents to me.

To the many others near and dear to my heart: thank you for being there for me around the world, for welcoming me into your homes when I was without one, for late-night sailboat conversations in False Creek, for salsa dances at OTR, for theatre evenings in Toronto, for sunset walks along the Seine. You bring home to me.

To my brother, Peter: your ambition inspires me. And finally, to my parents—thank you for your support while I chase this crazy dream and for setting up that old typewriter in the basement all those many years ago.